SPACEKID ILK

Invasion 101

Written and illustrated by Andrew Hammond
www.andrewhammond.co.uk

Published by Mythed Publishing
www.mythedpublishing.com

Fonts by Blambot
www.blambot.com

MYTHED

First Edition: November 2018

Text and illustrations copyright © Andrew Hammond, 2018

ISBN 978-1-9164713-0-6 (Paperback)
ISBN 978-1-9164713-1-3 (E-book)

For Mum and Dad

SPACEKID iLK

Invasion 101

by
Andrew Hammond

MYTHED

A Message from iLK

The target of Invasion 101 was a planet called "EARTH."

The invasion lasted 86 days, 7 hours and 33 seconds.

Many blame me for why it ended so abruptly.

With notes taken from my journal, here's an account of what really happened.

If you have any questions... tough!

This is a very primitive book and it doesn't answer questions, apparently.

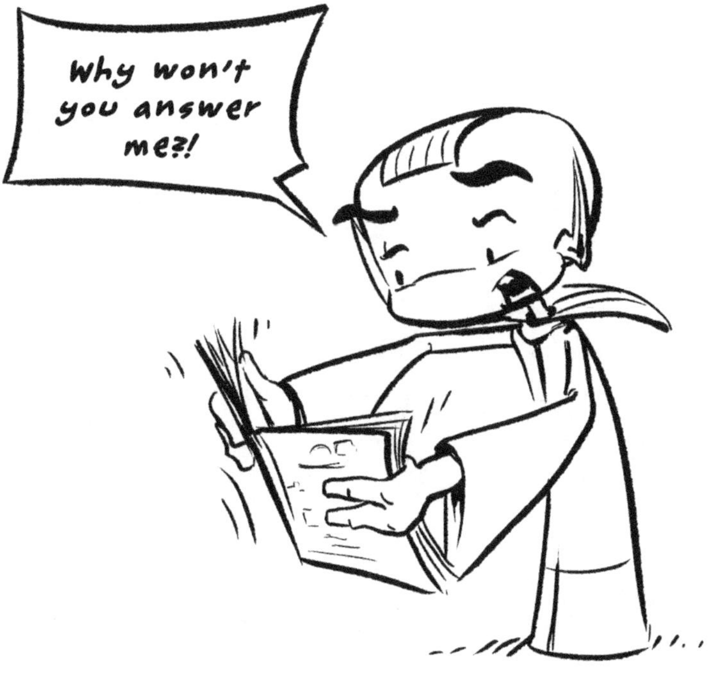
Why won't you answer me?!

Invasion 101, Day 1

OK, I guess you could say that my dad is quite a scary man.

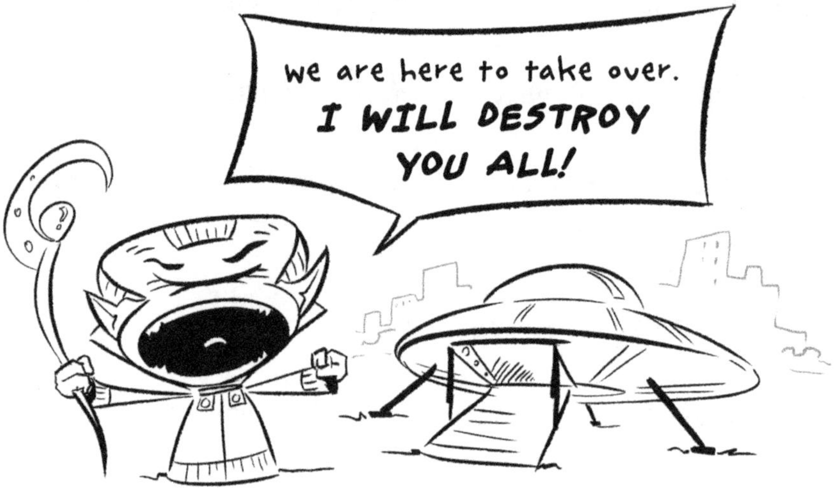
we are here to take over.
I WILL DESTROY YOU ALL!

I almost feel sorry for the people whose planets we invade. It must come as quite a shock.

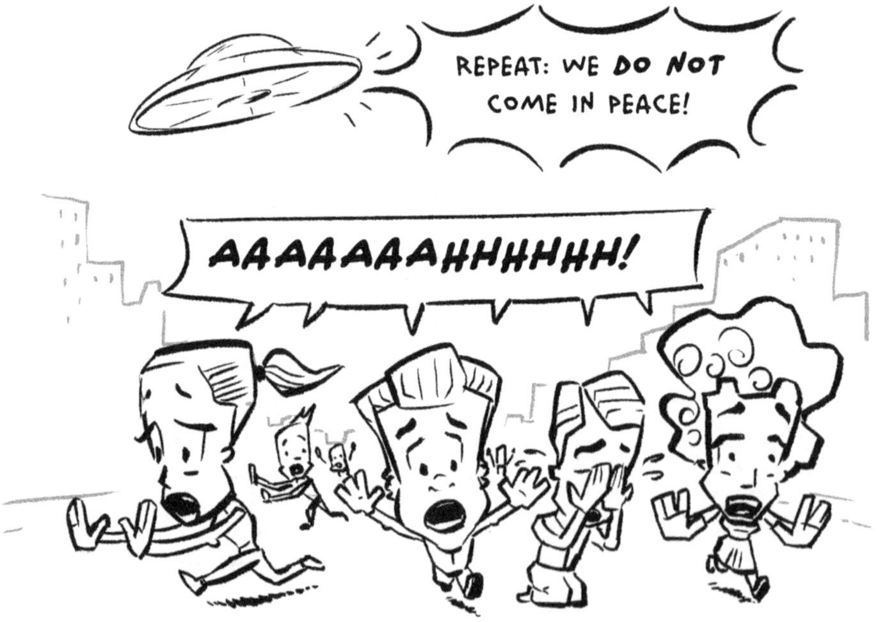
REPEAT: WE DO NOT COME IN PEACE!
AAAAAAAHHHHHH!

But at least they don't have to live with him EVERY DAY. Really, they should feel sorry for ME!

I'm the one that has to listen to him giving orders and bossing people around all the time.

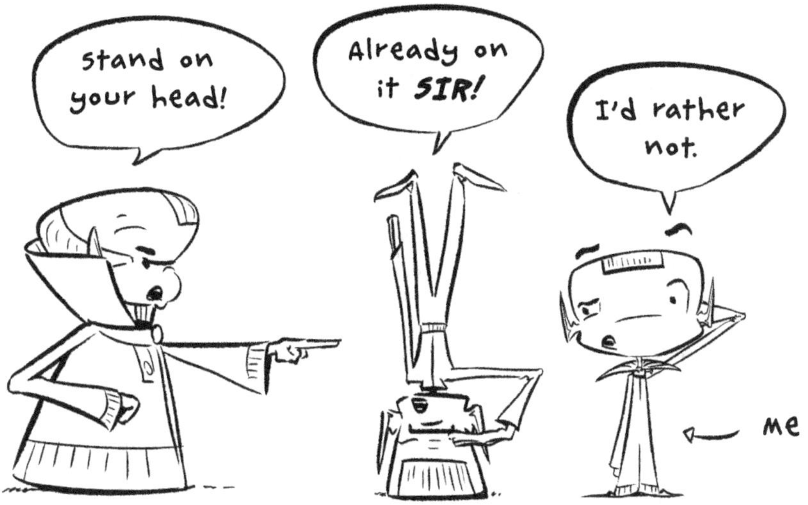
Stand on your head!
Already on it SIR!
I'd rather not.
me

Everyone else on the ship does exactly as they're told. I'm not sure why.

Every time we invade a new planet, they all rush around, make lots of noise and get really stressed.

Meanwhile, I hide in my room and tend to my plants.

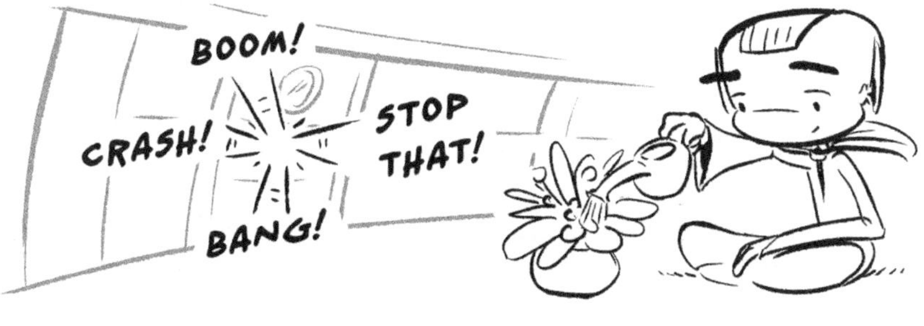
BOOM!
CRASH!
STOP THAT!
BANG!

That is until someone drags me out of my room, like today.

Dad told me that I needed to grow up and start learning the family trade. So he sent me down to Earth to help with the invasion.

That's where I first met "HUMANS."

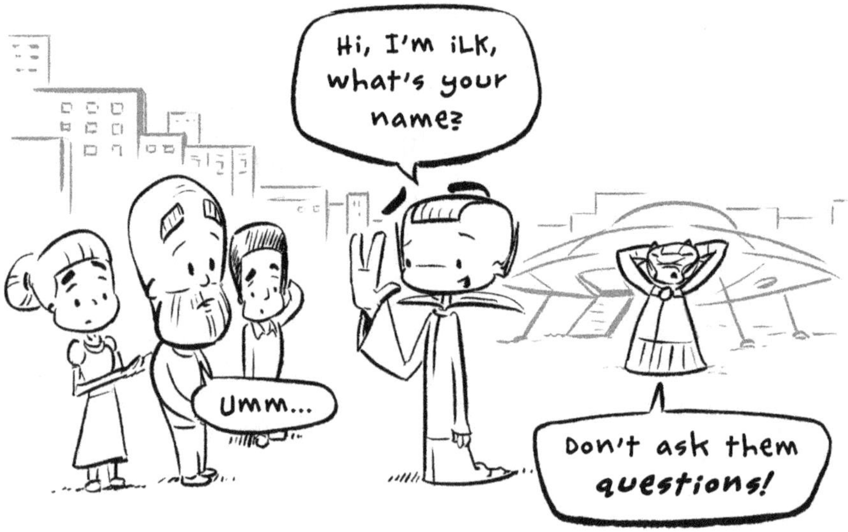
Hi, I'm iLK, what's your name?
Umm...
Don't ask them *questions!*

We all agreed that I didn't do a very good job, so now my job is to "stay out of the way."

I'm very good at that.

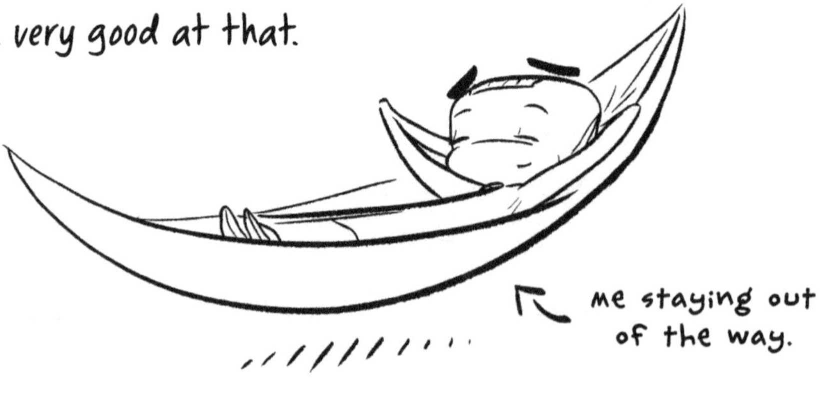
me staying out of the way.

Invasion 101, Day 2

I haven't left my room now for a whole day and I must admit, I've found it very productive.

I've been able to think, gather my thoughts and plan for the week ahead.

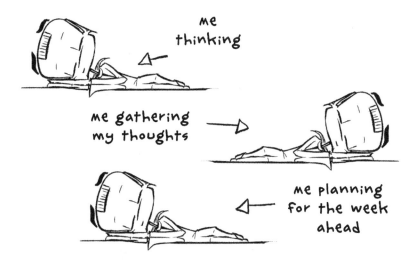

me thinking

me gathering my thoughts

me planning for the week ahead

Sadly, however, following Dad's orders has harvested its first casualty.

This is Pancita:

Or at least that is what she looked like when I first found her. I picked her up on the second moon of Joomper and brought her back to my room. This is what she looks like now:

I'm no expert, but I think she might have died.

She was so young! I had so much of the Universe left to show her!

How am I supposed to take care of her if every time I step outside my door something like THIS happens:

What are you doing out here!? I have an entire **world** to conquer! I can't be worrying about something something while *blah blah* something *etc!*

Dad doesn't appreciate that I have my own problems. I have 113 lives to care for!

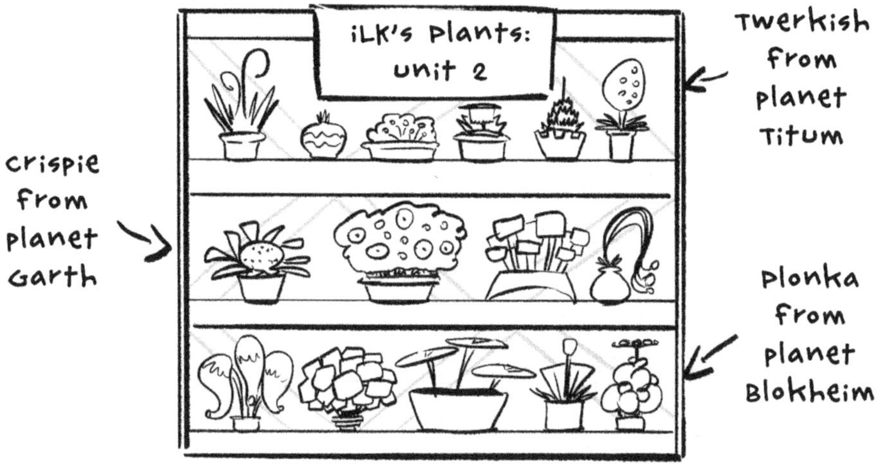
iLK's Plants:
unit 2
Twerkish from planet Titum
Crispie from planet Garth
Plonka from planet Blokheim

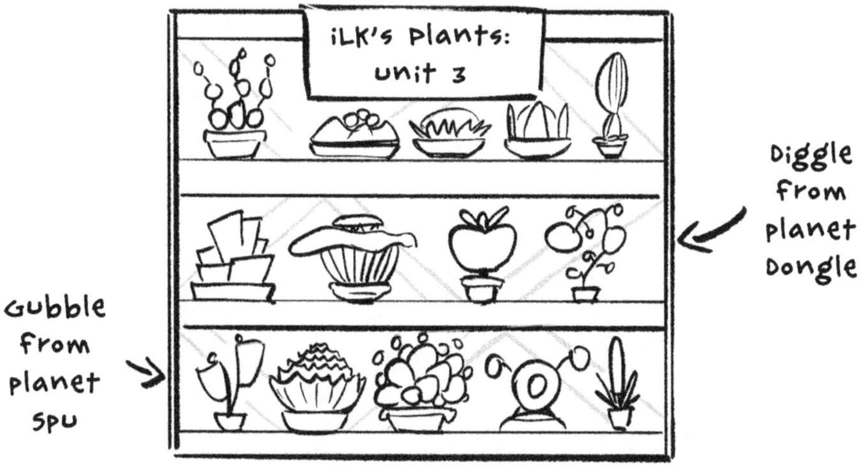
iLK's Plants:
unit 3
Diggle from planet Dongle
Gubble from planet Spu

These are just a handful of the plants that I keep in my room.

And then there's all of the new technologies that I've been working with, some of which are incredibly irritating!

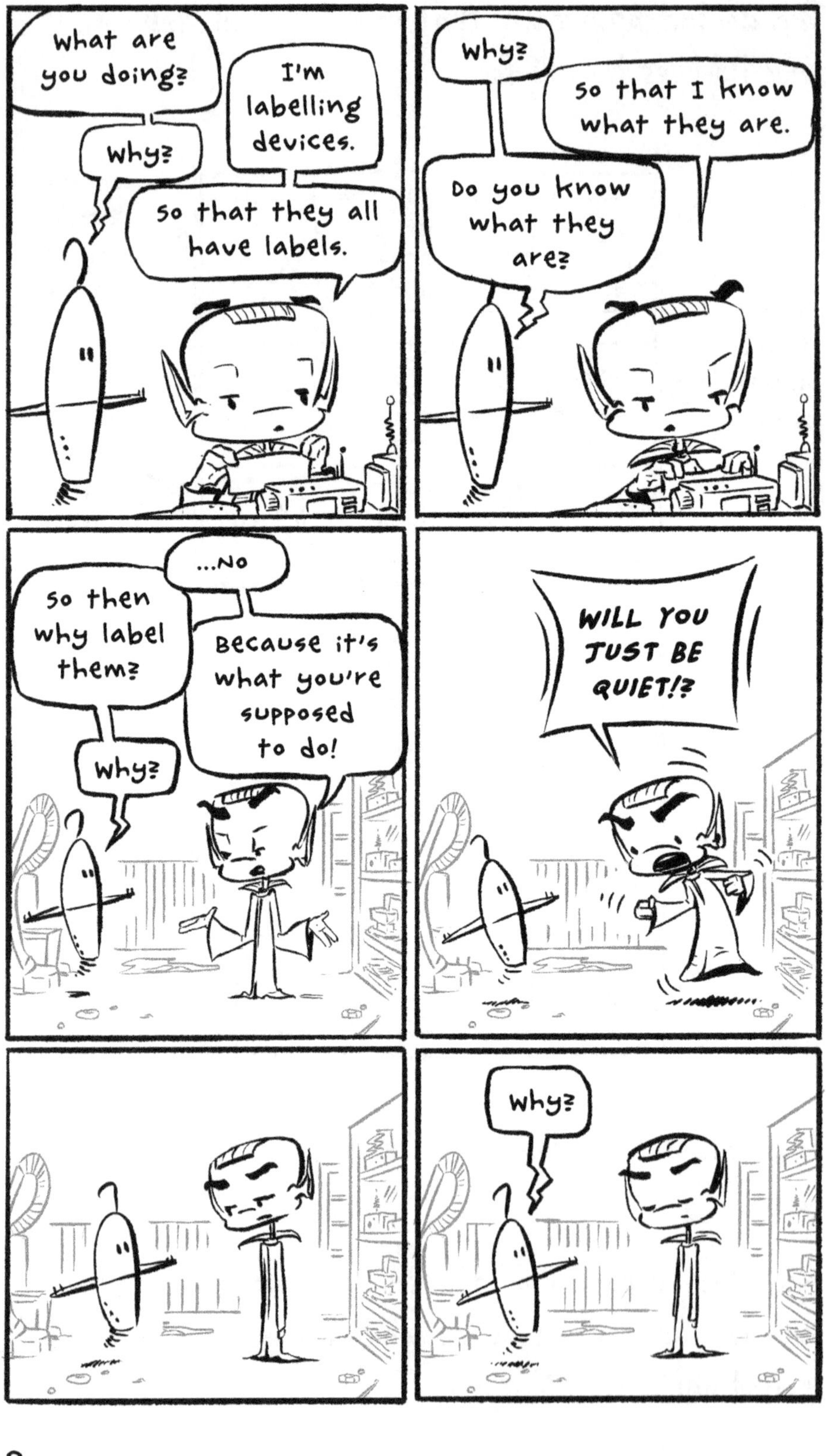
What are you doing?
I'm labelling devices.
Why?
So that they all have labels.
Why?
So that I know what they are.
Do you know what they are?
...No
So then why label them?
Because it's what you're supposed to do!
Why?
WILL YOU JUST BE QUIET!?
Why?

Y-bot is an analysis robot. He was designed to ask questions and assess a situation, but I think his real purpose is to annoy me.

Here is his analysis of the labelling incident:

Labels are used to label things that need labelling.

Y-bot printout

Aside from my desire to find some respite from this annoying little robot, I keep a lot of important discoveries in my room and it's my DUTY to look after them.

To do that, I HAVE TO leave my room.

It may mean sacrificing myself, but I've told these plants that I'd take care of them and take care of them I WILL!

Even after they might have already died.

If only my dad could understand the kind of daily trials I have to contend with.

Invasion 101, Day 3

Today's task was to find a way to save my plants, while also staying out of the way.

It started off well. By not going to class I made sure that I didn't disturb Professor LuCH.

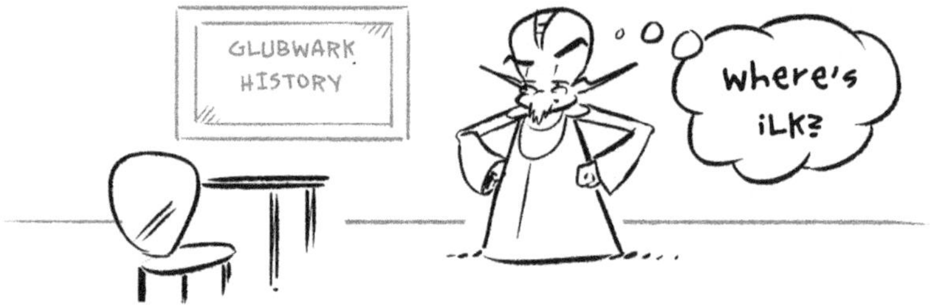
GLUBWARK HISTORY
where's iLK?

But, when I tried sneaking out to get what I needed from the Botanic Lab, Dad stopped me. He then had the gall to tell me off for not going to class.

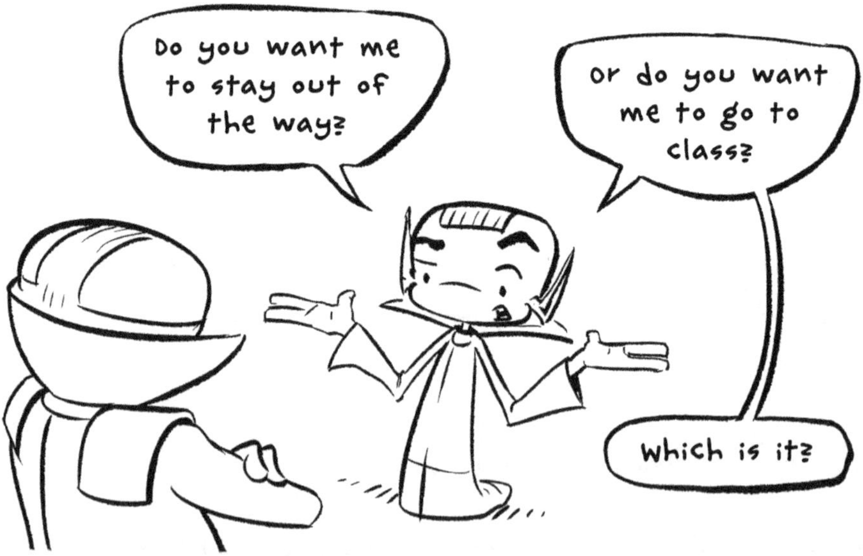
Do you want me to stay out of the way?
Or do you want me to go to class?
Which is it?

I wish he'd make up his mind.

Invasion 101, Day 4

I left my room again today and, summoning all of my courage, stepped right into the DANGER ZONE!

The DANGER ZONE is the area just outside Dad's office. If I'm going to get caught being "in the way," it's there.

But today I was feeling brave! Also, I thought Dad would be on Earth looking for more people to boss around.

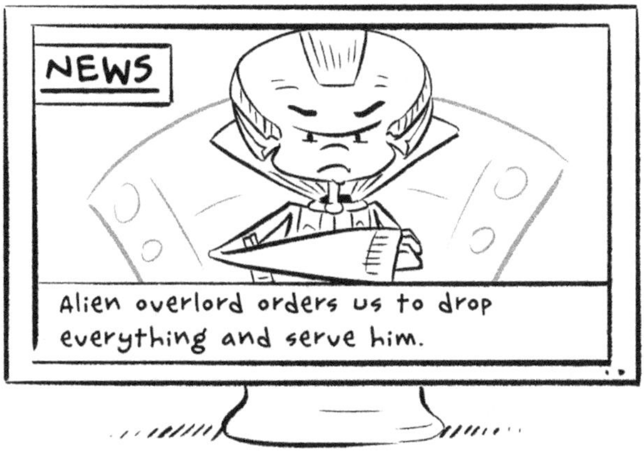
NEWS
Alien overlord orders us to drop everything and serve him.

I crept past Dad's door and that's when I heard it!

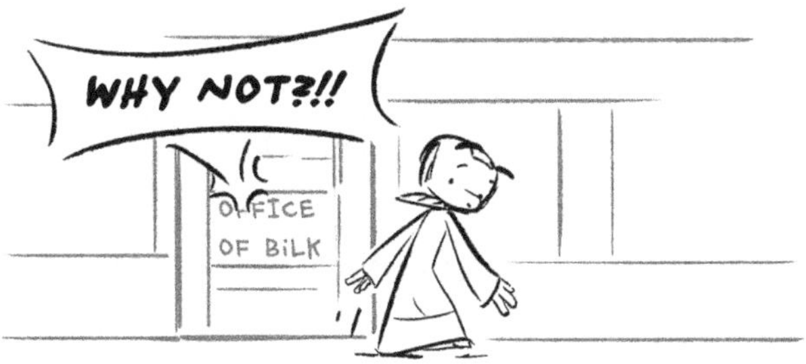
WHY NOT?!!
OFFICE OF BILK

Someone was shouting inside of Dad's office! No one is allowed to shout in Dad's office... except for Dad.

I pressed my ear up to the door to investigate. The loud one was DEFINITELY Dad and it sounded like someone was trying to boss HIM around!

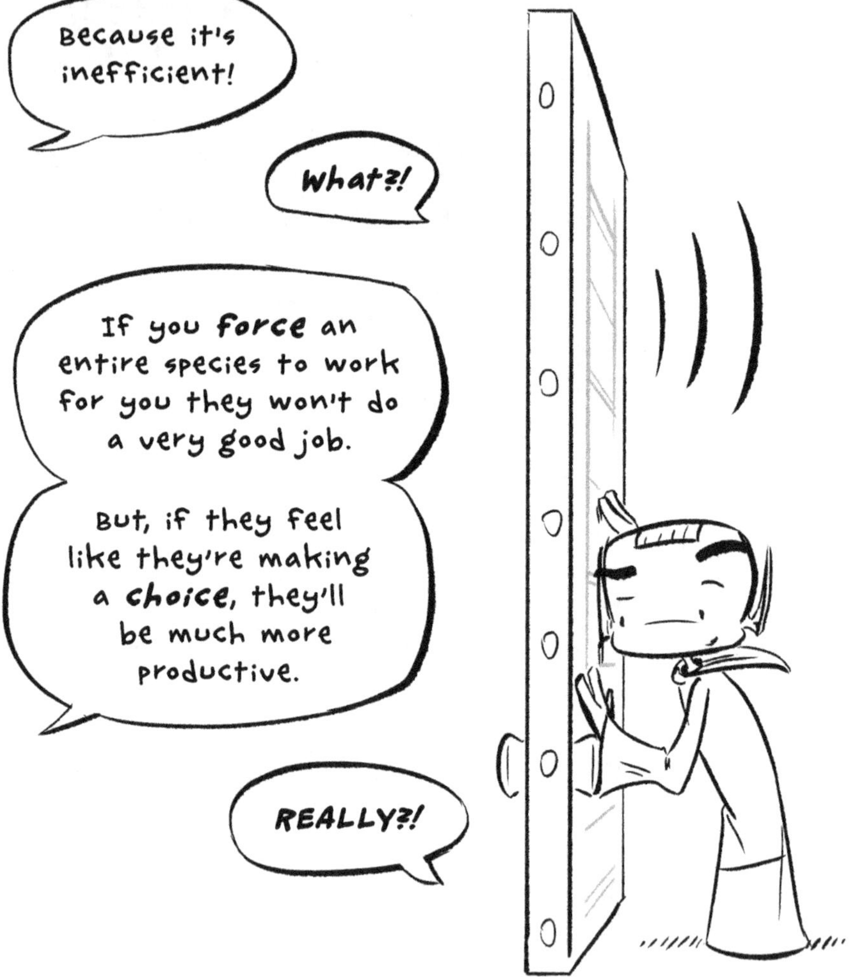
Because it's inefficient!
What?!
If you **force** an entire species to work for you they won't do a very good job.
But, if they feel like they're making a **choice**, they'll be much more productive.
REALLY?!

The other voice was quite muffled due to the fact there was a door in the way.

But there aren't many people it could be. In fact, I can only think of two potential candidates.

Option one: Dad vs Dad

Talking to himself

This seems unlikely. Dad isn't much of a talker. He'd probably agree with himself and then never speak again.

Having said that, it's difficult to imagine who else would be allowed to tell him what to do. The only other option could be...

Option two: Dad vs Mum

The only one Dad listens to

Option two makes more sense than option one. I've never actually SEEN my parents arguing, but sometimes Dad changes his mind for no reason.

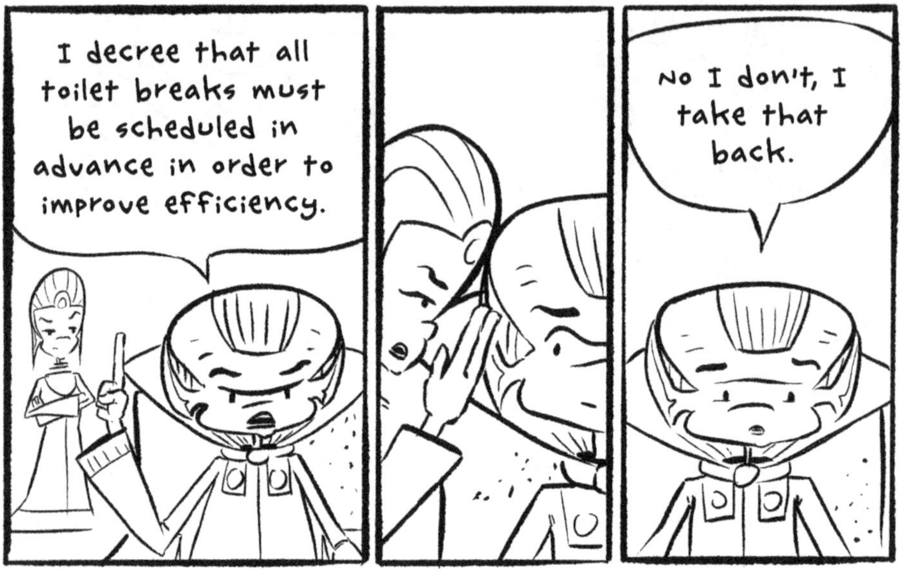
I decree that all toilet breaks must be scheduled in advance in order to improve efficiency.
No I don't, I take that back.

Either way, this was great to hear. If someone else can disagree with Dad and get away with it, then maybe one day I can do the same.

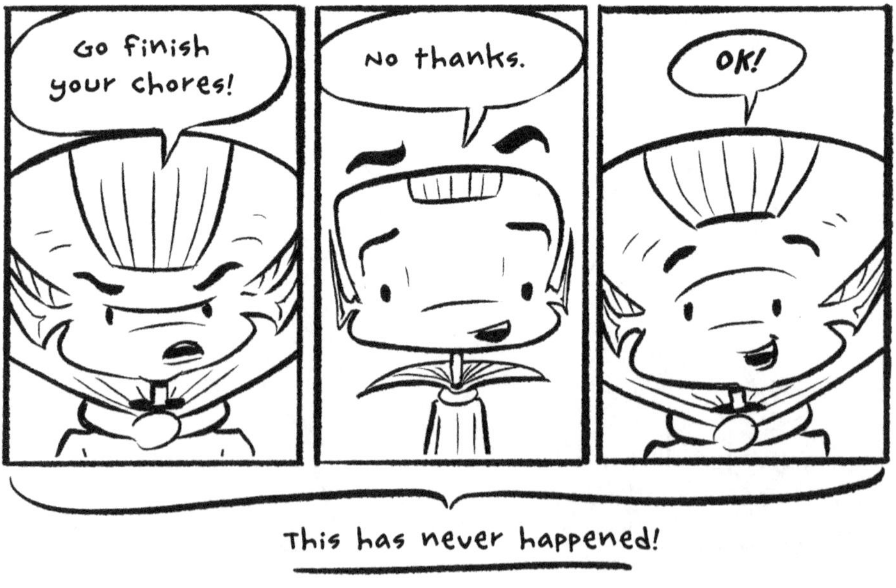
Go finish your chores!
No thanks.
OK!

This has never happened!

It's time to get serious!

I need to come up with a strategy. My plants are fading fast and Y-bot is getting more annoying by the second.

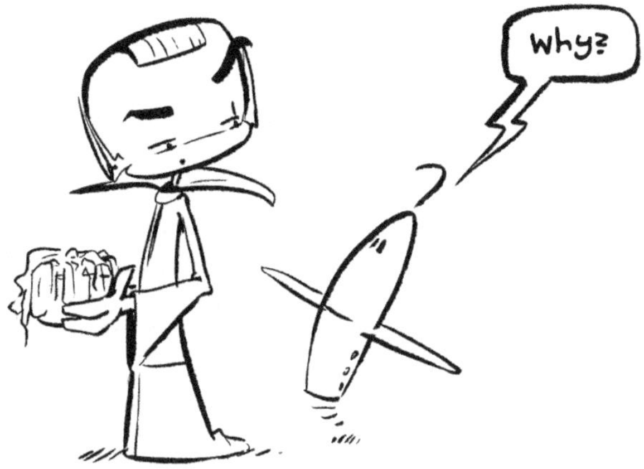
Why?

With just a little planning, I can avoid being caught and retrieve what I need from the Botanics Lab.

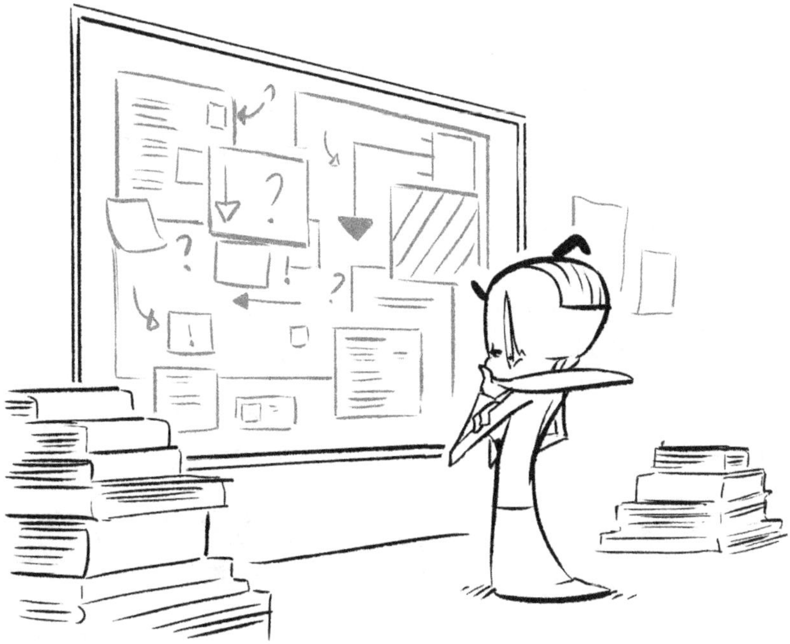

Meanwhile, on Earth...

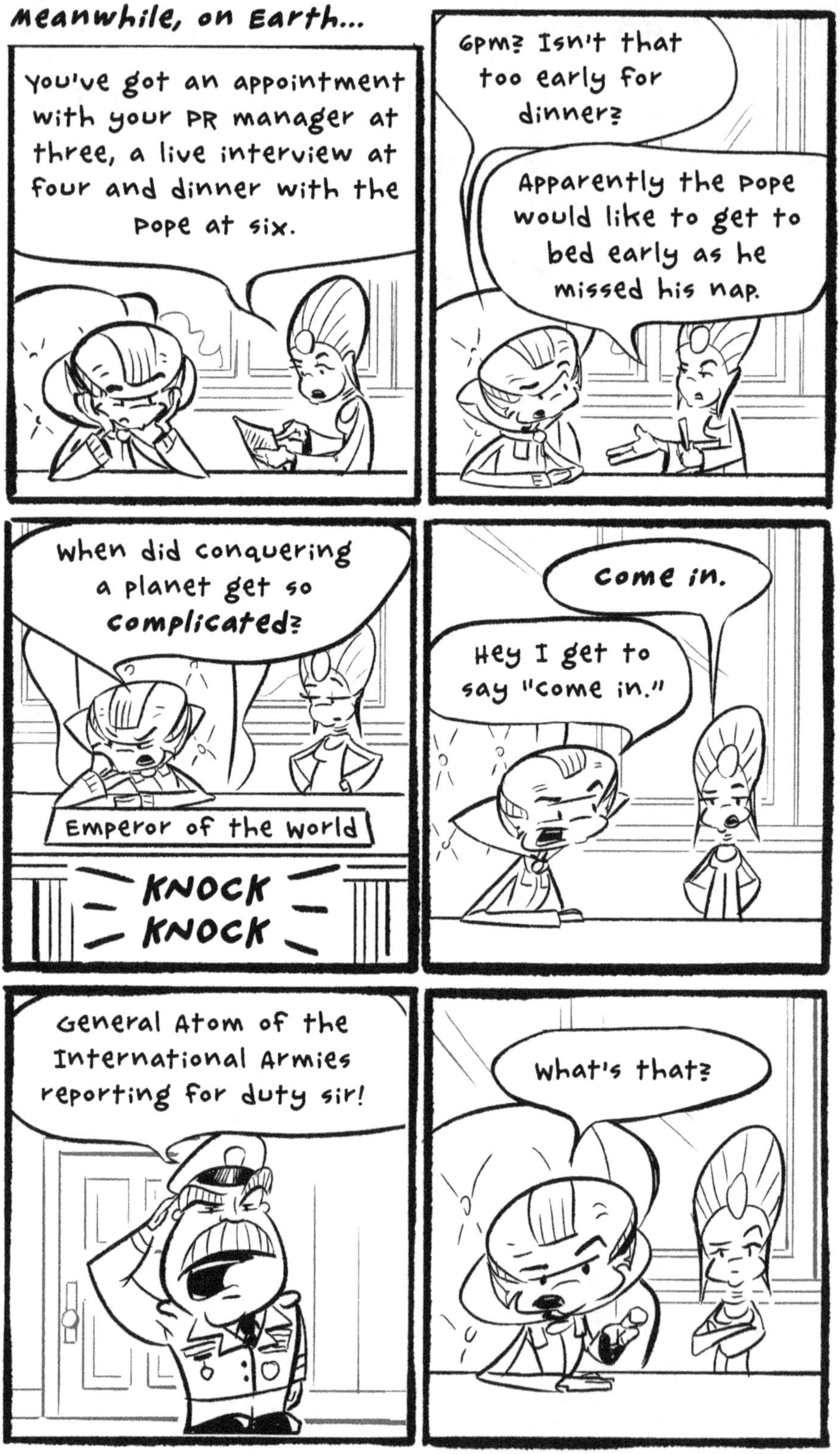
You've got an appointment with your PR manager at three, a live interview at four and dinner with the Pope at six.
6pm? Isn't that too early for dinner?
Apparently the Pope would like to get to bed early as he missed his nap.
When did conquering a planet get so **complicated**?
Emperor of the World
KNOCK KNOCK
Come in.
Hey I get to say "come in."
General Atom of the International Armies reporting for duty sir!
What's that?

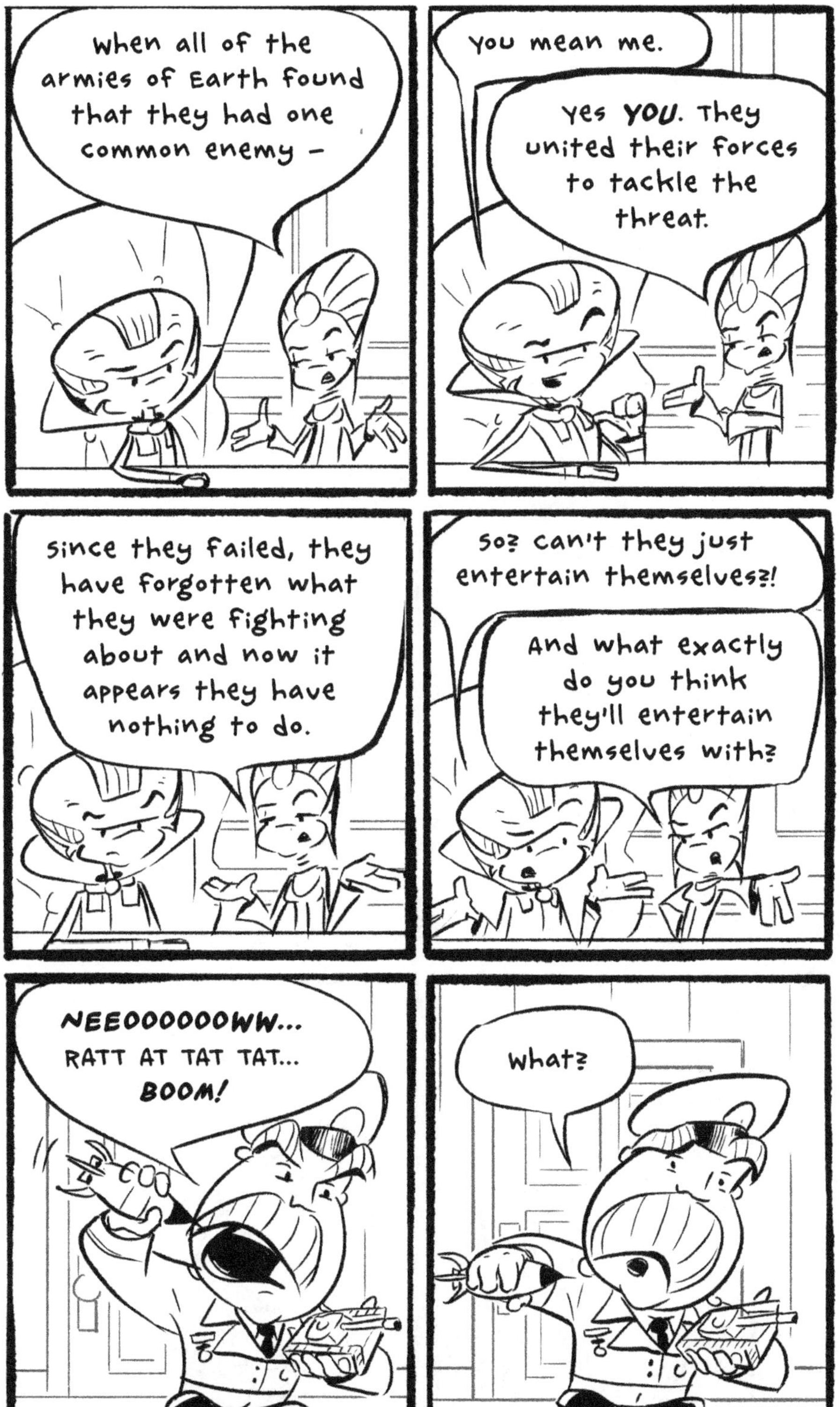
When all of the armies of Earth found that they had one common enemy –
You mean me.
Yes YOU. They united their forces to tackle the threat.
Since they failed, they have forgotten what they were fighting about and now it appears they have nothing to do.
So? Can't they just entertain themselves?!
And what exactly do you think they'll entertain themselves with?
NEEOOOOOOWW... RATT AT TAT TAT... BOOM!
What?

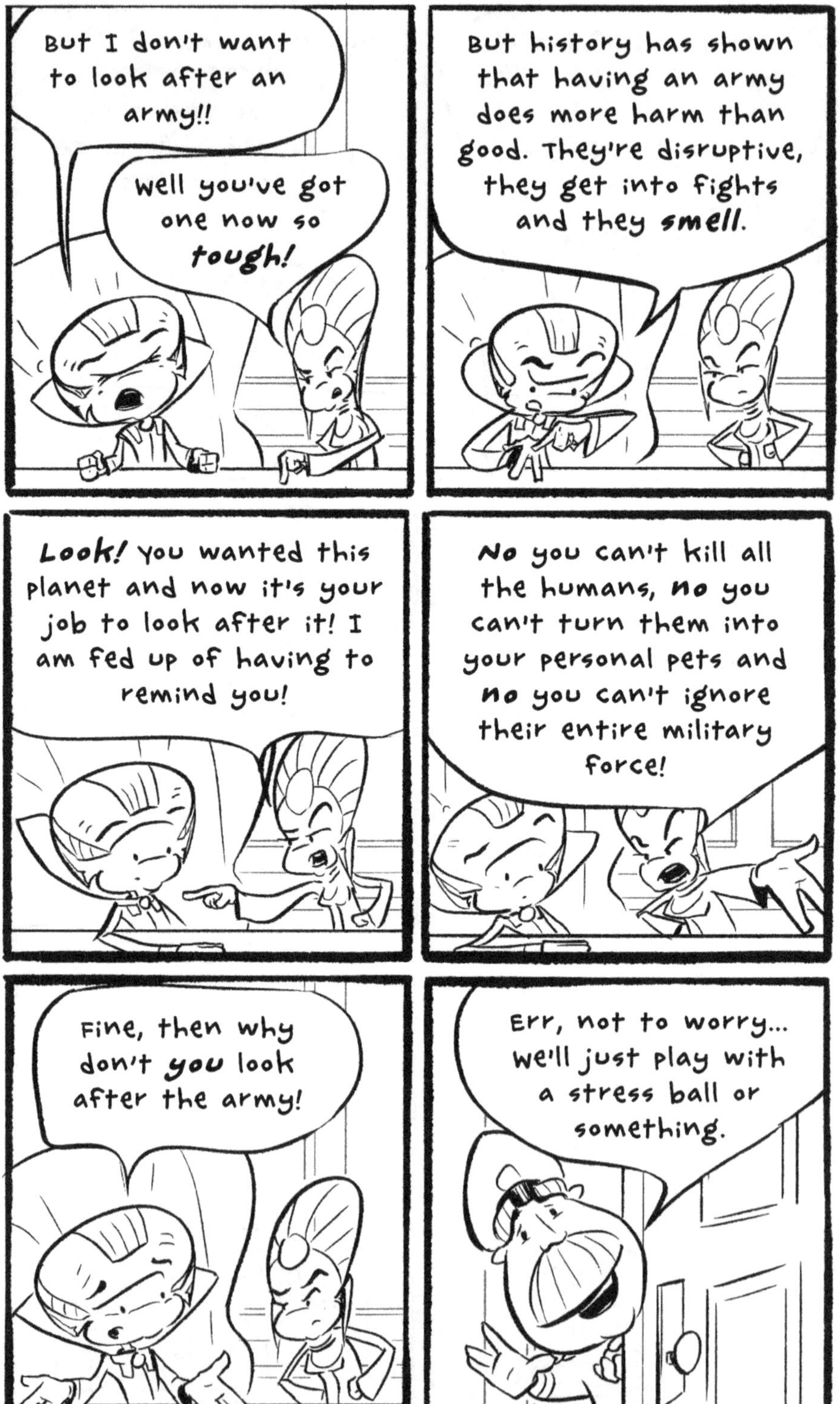

But I don't want to look after an army!!
Well you've got one now so tough!
But history has shown that having an army does more harm than good. They're disruptive, they get into fights and they smell.
Look! You wanted this planet and now it's your job to look after it! I am fed up of having to remind you!
No you can't kill all the humans, no you can't turn them into your personal pets and no you can't ignore their entire military force!
Fine, then why don't you look after the army!
Err, not to worry... We'll just play with a stress ball or something.

Invasion 101, Day 6

My first attempt to become a Stealth Ninja involved a lot of guesswork. All I had to inform my approach was this report taken from the planet OrrSumm.

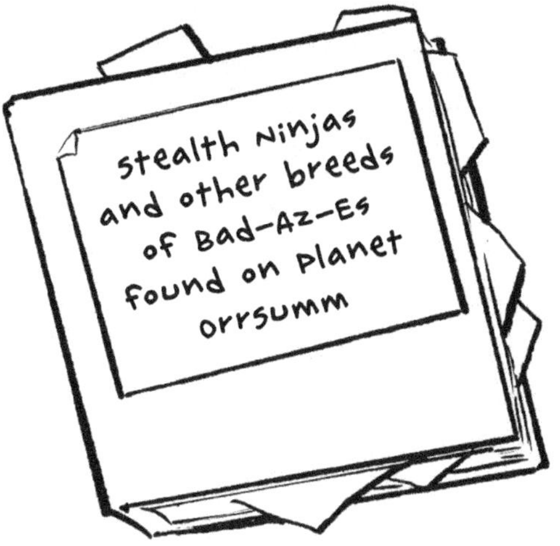
stealth Ninjas
and other breeds
of Bad-Az-Es
found on Planet
orrsumm

Fortunately it included an illustration of one of these OrrSumm creatures.

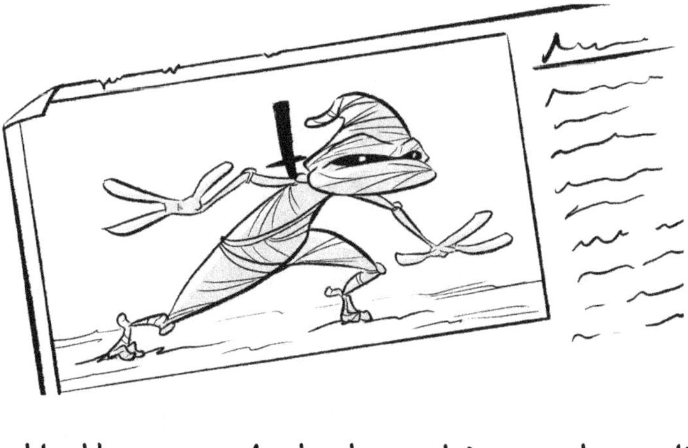

Apparently they are adept at sneaking past any living thing, which was exactly what I needed if I wanted to leave my room without being noticed.

By paying close attention to their strategies and techniques, I prepared myself for the task ahead.

A great man once said, "If something is worth doing, then it's worth... um... something."

The point being that it has fallen upon me to save the lives of these now 111 plants (one died and one fell behind the shelf - presumed dead).

They need medicine and supplies and they can't get them themselves.

It would require sacrifice, but I needed to stand up and accept my fate with a brave face, hidden behind a mask.

Having said that, what was ahead was fairly huge.

This is TalC.

He's the beast that was posted outside my door by my dad to keep me "safe."

The truth is that he's like a silent ogre, watching my every move, waiting to report to my dad about everything I'm doing wrong. He's a cruel and merciless creature.

Oh hi iLK! What are you doing up so late?

My first instinct was to respond with a simple non-truth. I chose something believable so as not to raise suspicion.

"Just going to the toilet," I said.

The toilet? OK, um, is that a plant on your back? Is it OK? It looks sick.

It sounded like he was threatening my plant so I asserted my strength and made sure he knew that I would carry out this mission whether he liked it or not.

"I've got a job to do, touch me and I'll run."

Sounds important can I help? It looks like you're carrying a lot of stuff.

He was right, I was carrying a lot of stuff, containers to hold medicine, a few samples for testing and a couple of the plants in most urgent need of care.

It was a good thing he offered to help.

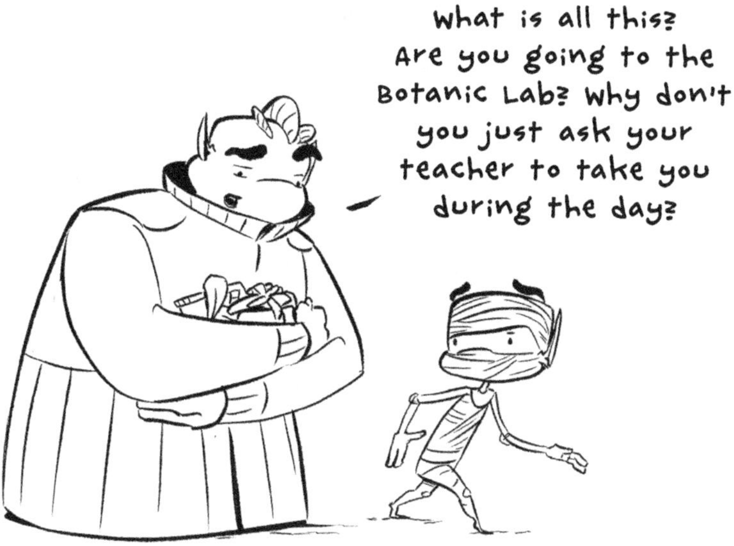
What is all this? Are you going to the Botanic Lab? Why don't you just ask your teacher to take you during the day?

And there it was. Having seen his intimidation techniques fail miserably he was trying to manipulate me with rational thought. Fortunately I'm impervious to such things.

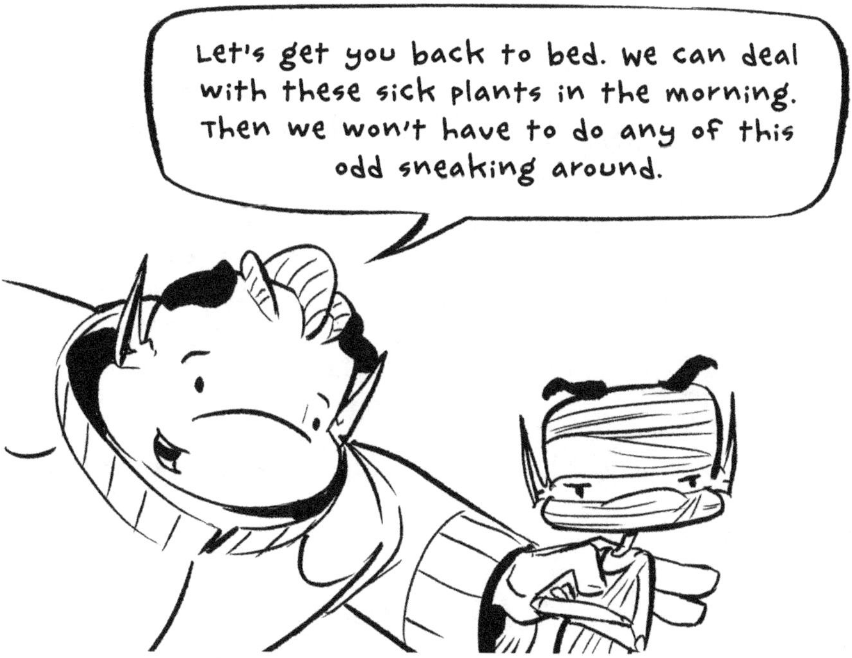
Let's get you back to bed. We can deal with these sick plants in the morning. Then we won't have to do any of this odd sneaking around.

That's when he turned around and started heading back to my bedroom with all my stuff. The sneaky devil had tricked me. I wasn't going to let him get away with this.

calm down little guy, I'm on your side.

Sadly there wasn't much I could do, he clearly had the physical advantage.

Let me go TaLC, if I don't get the supplies I need there's a lot of lives at risk.
But then why don't you just tell your dad that you need these things for your plants, we can –

Suddenly we were startled by a loud noise coming from behind TaLC.

THADDUNK!

I froze. Even my Stealth Ninja suit couldn't help me now.

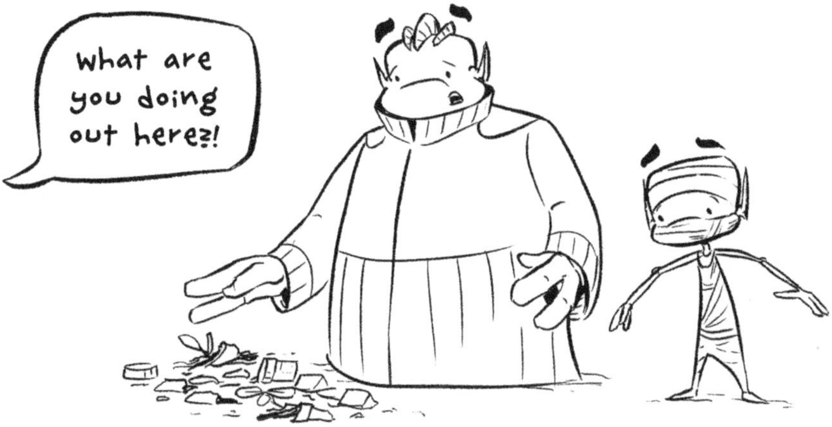
What are you doing out here?!

Needless to say, Dad didn't look happy. Some things in life are predictable. Like his response to this situation. It's as if he has a wheel of preprepared comments and he simply spins it to pick what he'll say.

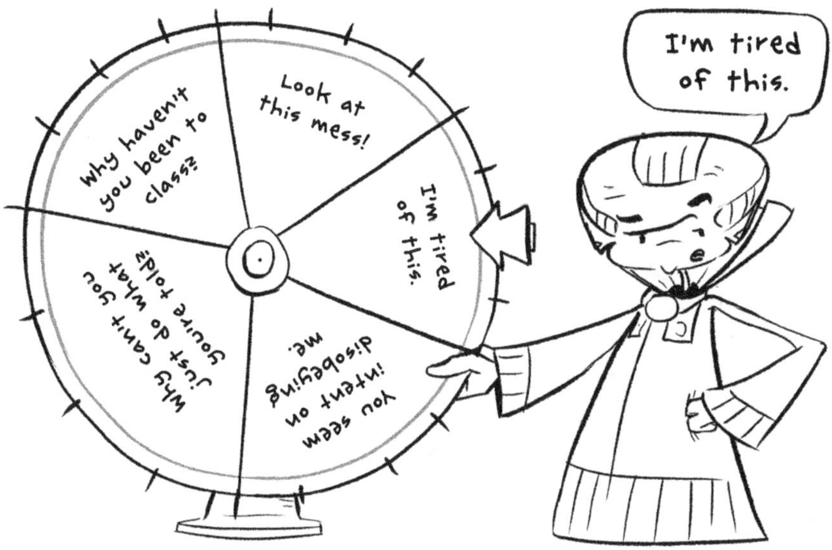
Look at this mess!
I'm tired of this.
You seem intent on disobeying me.
Why can't you just do what you're told?!
Why haven't you been to class?
I'm tired of this.

But what happened next put a fortunate new twist on the same old story.

All of a sudden it was like he was reading my mind.

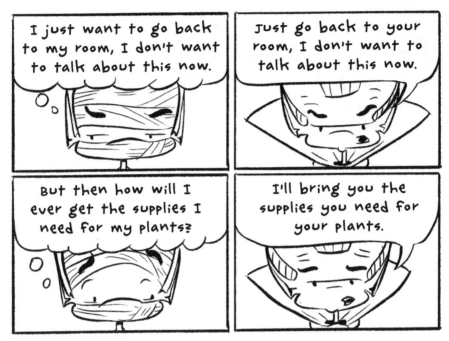

I just want to go back to my room, I don't want to talk about this now.

Just go back to your room, I don't want to talk about this now.

But then how will I ever get the supplies I need for my plants?

I'll bring you the supplies you need for your plants.

I found this very strange. First, only Vulchars can read minds and I'm pretty sure my dad's not a Vulchar because he has eyes, ears and a mouth. Vulchars are basically just blobs that live on rocks on the planet Splunge.

I can read your mind, but I can't do anything about it.

Second, he didn't even punish me! Well, apart from the fact that he told TalC that I wasn't allowed to leave my room at all from now on. Not even for class! This sounds like the best punishment ever!

The next 4 days on Earth:

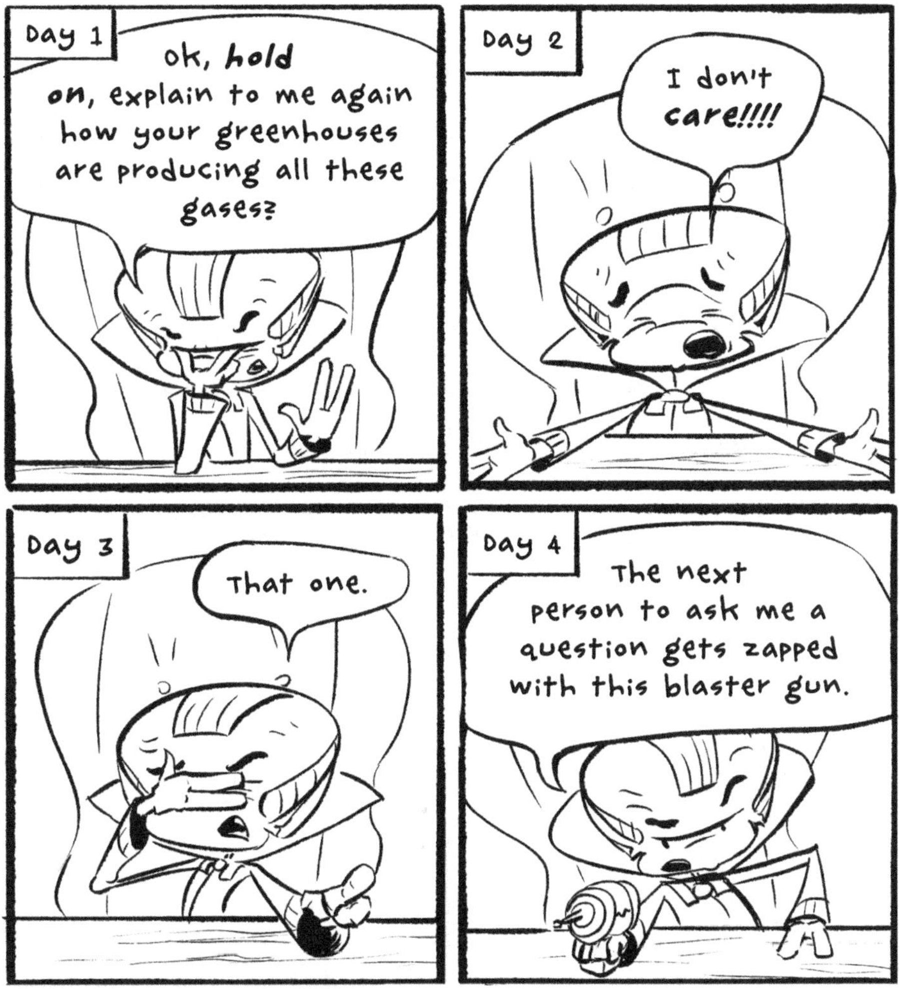

Day 1
ok, hold on, explain to me again how your greenhouses are producing all these gases?
Day 2
I don't care!!!!
Day 3
That one.
Day 4
The next person to ask me a question gets zapped with this blaster gun.

Meanwhile, in my room:

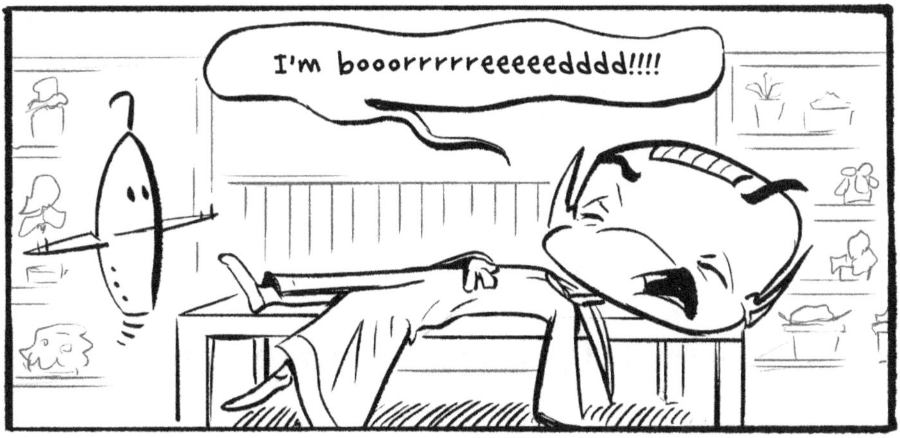

I'm booorrrrreeeeedddd!!!!

Invasion 101, Day 10

It turns out my room sucks. I would have written in this journal more over the last few days, but aside from the great hunt for the missing toenail clipping (location still unknown) there hasn't been a lot to tell.

I usually love staying in my room and when I'm not in my room all I can think about is being back there, but now it's like everything has switched around.

All I can think about is getting out of here! I'd even go to class if I could.

No!

That's EXACTLY what Dad wanted!

He's an evil genius!

MWAH HAHA HAHA!

I'm not even sure what has changed.

Maybe, when my dad put me in my room, he also trapped a really specific kind of monster in there with me.

The Boredom Monster!

It stalks you for hours like you're its prey, until eventually it catches you. When it does, it doesn't eat you. It's much more cruel.

Instead it just sits next to you poking you in the arm reminding you how bored you are.

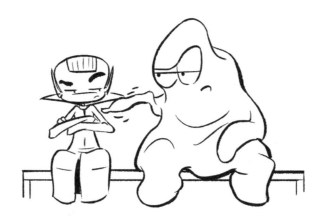

It can stay like that for days, maybe even decades!

The only way to get rid of it, IS TO GET OUT OF MY ROOM!

Then suddenly I noticed it, staring right at me. Mocking me.

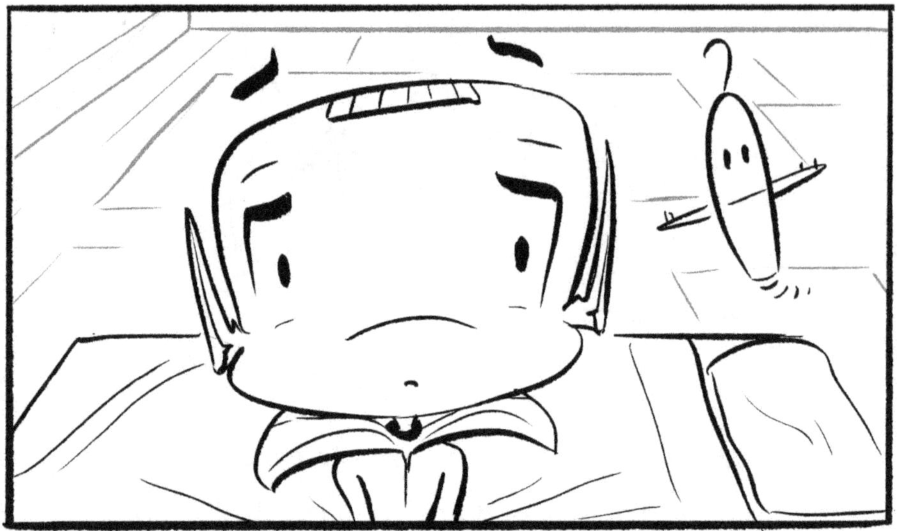

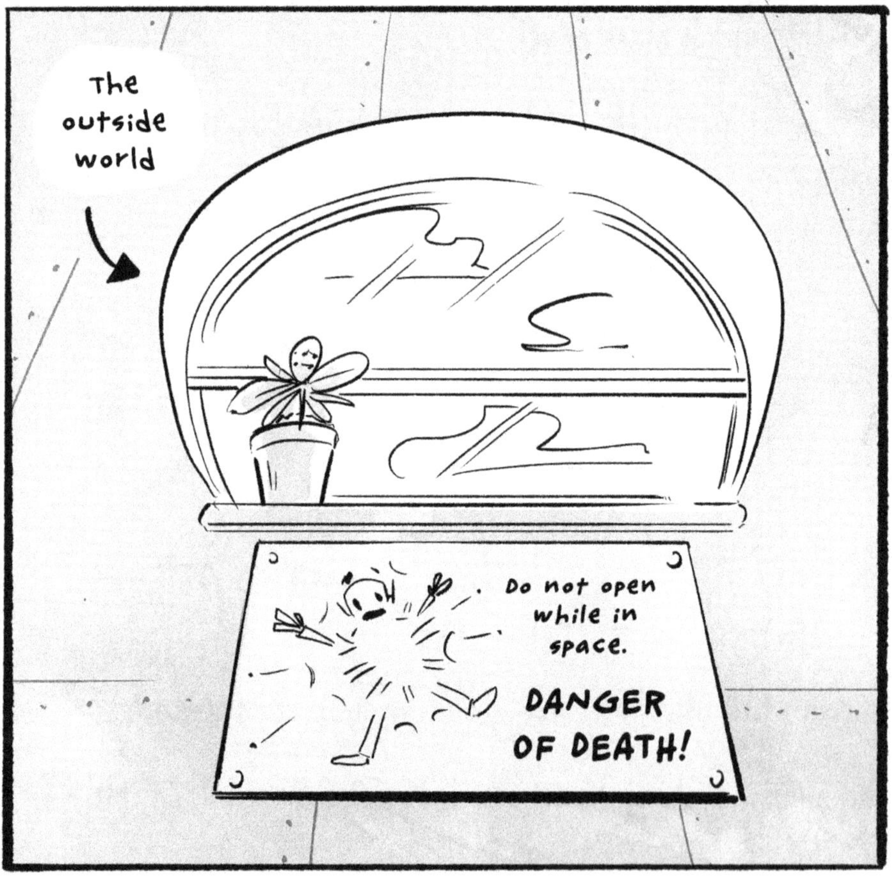
The outside world
Do not open while in space.
DANGER OF DEATH!

Invasion 101, Day 11

After an embarrassingly long time staring at the "Danger of Death!" sign, it struck me. We were no longer IN space! We've been parked over Earth for a while now.

Space
Us
Them

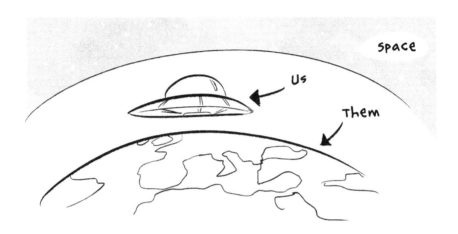

Faced with this opportunity all I needed was a plan and I could be a part of the outside world again.

My room (Just me)
outside world (Everything else)

My plan was to first construct something that would allow me to reach the annoyingly high window.

Annoyingly high window.

And then all I needed to do was to wait until night time so that no one would see me outside of the ship.

Night time.

construction.

Success!

But I was shocked by what I discovered outside my window.

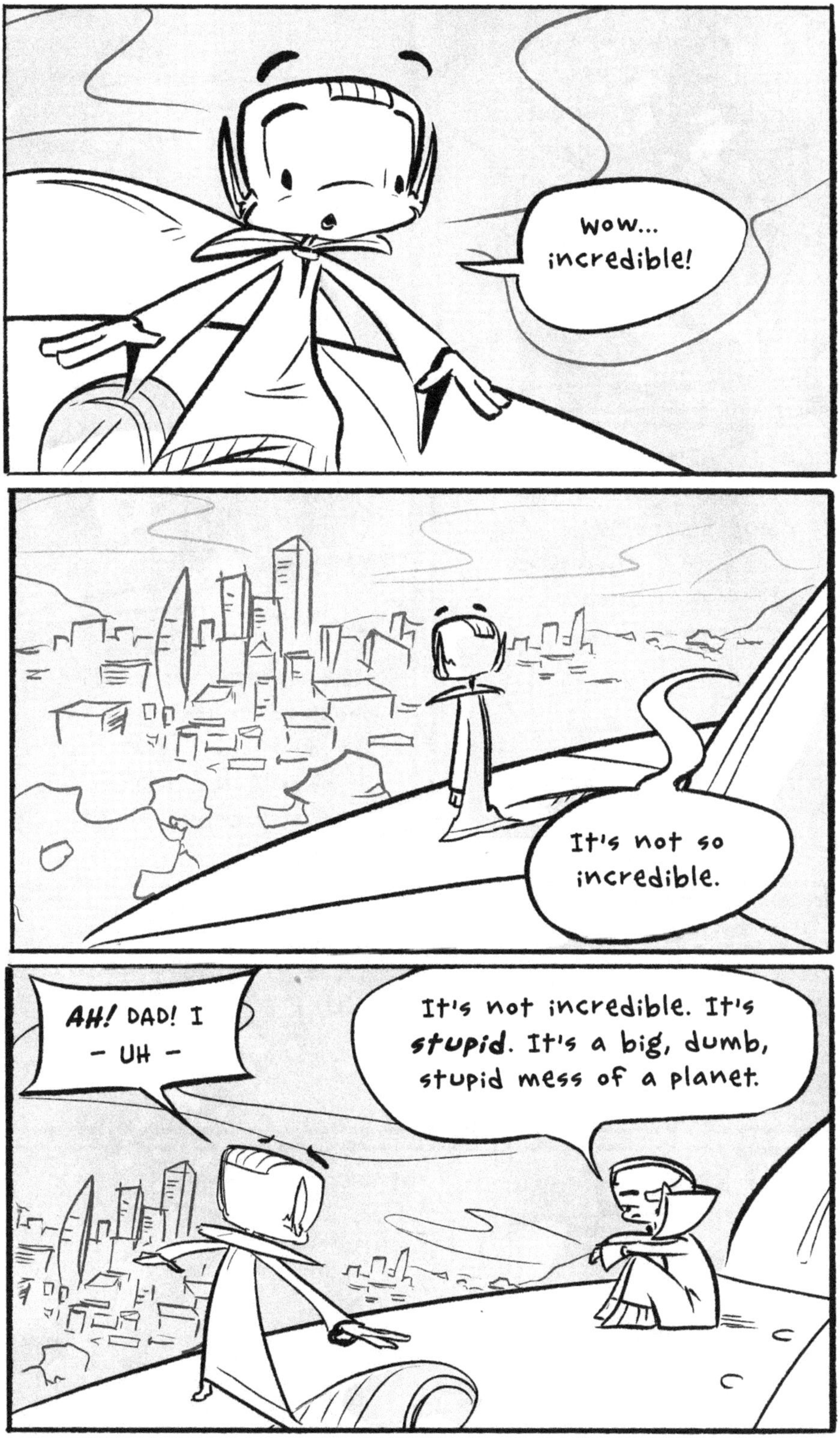
wow... incredible!
It's not so incredible.
AH! DAD! I - UH -
It's not incredible. It's **stupid**. It's a big, dumb, stupid mess of a planet.

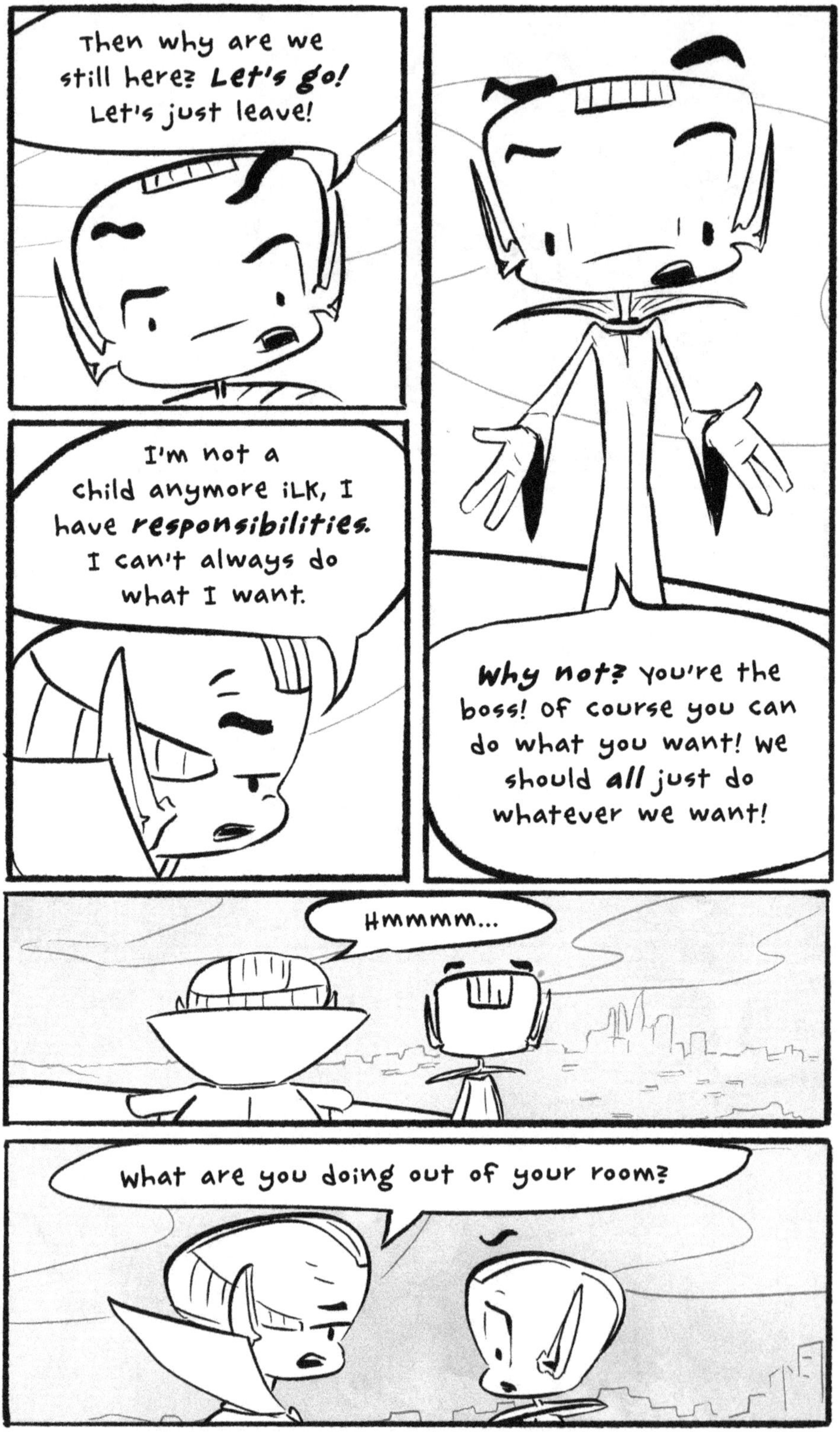
Then why are we still here? Let's go! Let's just leave!
I'm not a child anymore iLK, I have responsibilities. I can't always do what I want.
Why not? You're the boss! Of course you can do what you want! We should all just do whatever we want!
Hmmmm...
What are you doing out of your room?

I know I probably shouldn't have, but I did, right there and then, without deciding to, I told him the truth. I said that I was so bored staying in my room that I'd even go back to class if I had to.

Even the plants have started talking to me... I mean... the ones that aren't supposed to. I know it's what I wanted but it's just not anymore.

I expected my confession to be immediately followed by this...

HAHA! *I WIN!* I KNEW IT! I'M SO MUCH OLDER AND SMARTER THAN YOU. NAH NAH N-NAH NAH!

Instead what happened was much more surprising.

Don't worry son. I understand.

And from that moment I knew that everything was going to get better.

Invasion 101, Day 12

AAAAAAAAAAAAAAAAAAAAAAAAAAAAAAAAAAAAAAAAAAAAAAA AAAAAAAAAAAAAAAAAAAAAAAAAAAAAAAAAAAAAAAAAAAAAAA AAAAAAAAAAAAAAAAAAAAAAAAAAAAAAAAAAAAAAAAAAAAAAA AAAAAAAAAAAAAAAAAAAAAAAAAAAAAAAAAAAAAAAAAAAAAAA AAAAAAAAAAAAAAAAAAAAAAAAAAAAAAAAHHHHHHHHHHHHHH HHHHHHHHHHHHHHHH!!!!!!

No, no, no, no, no, no, no, no, no, NO!

I can't tell you what just happened, not yet. I think I'm going to need a few days to let it sink in first. I need to wait for my face to stop looking like this...

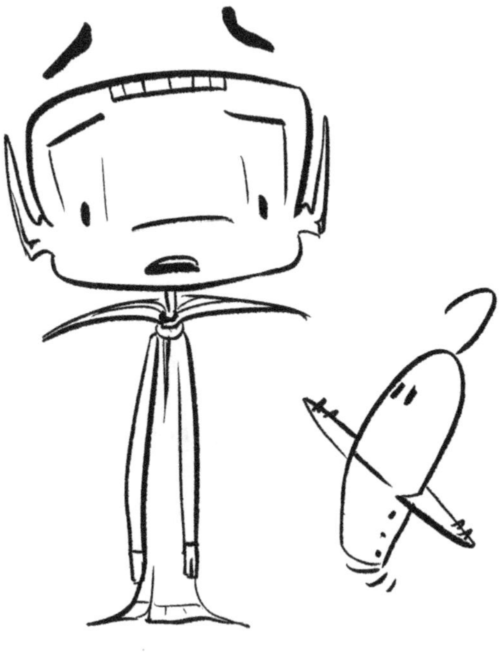

Invasion 101, Day 13

I've had some time to process what has happened. There are only two ways of seeing it.

The real way... and the way my dad wants me to see it.

I feel pretty stupid now for what I had been thinking just before I entered the council hall. I'd assumed that being summoned to the most important room on the ship was a good thing. What a fool I was.

As I strolled through the corridor, so young and naive, I imagined what the future might hold.

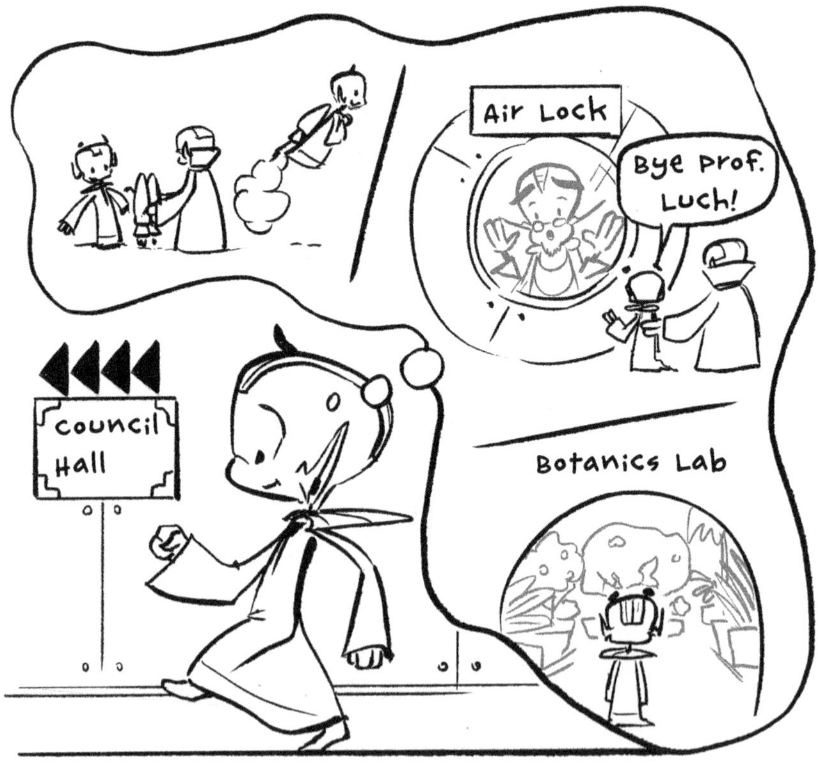

Air Lock
Bye Prof. Luch!
Council Hall
Botanics Lab

Maybe school would be cancelled for good or maybe I'd finally be allowed into the Botanics Lab without supervision!

It wouldn't be THAT surprising would it? Not after seeing Dad on the hull of the ship! Maybe he wanted to help me because he could finally understand what it was like to BE me.

Ever since that night I thought that he had actually grasped how difficult my life was.

You are an incredible Glubwark. The most impressive Glubwark I have ever met.

What I thought Dad meant when he said he *"understood."*

Maybe I would receive my first letter!

When the Council decides that you've become a proper adult you're given free roam of the ship and to mark this moment everyone has a naming ceremony.

A bunch of stuff happens at this that I don't really care about, the big thing though is that you receive your first letter!

I don't have my
first letter yet.

BiLK
SiLK
TALC
iLK

With that there are no longer any boundaries. You can go wherever and do whatever you want. It's the answer to all my problems.

The annoying thing is you have to wait for ages to get your first letter. Sometimes I feel like it's never going to happen.

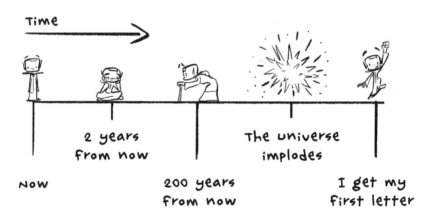

Time

Now

2 years
from now

200 years
from now

The universe
implodes

I get my
first letter

With my first letter, no one could tell me what to do.

But sadly, none of that happened.

I was wrong about everything.

I entered the council hall.

Some other important council men said some things, but I wasn't really listening. (I tend to tune out when I hear boring things.)

Then I noticed that dad was no longer wearing his shoulder things.

Why aren't you wearing your shoulder things Dad?

They're called 'The Leader's Epaulettes' and they're yours now iLK.

If you're going to rule Earth you really need to start paying attention.

Those words took a moment to sink in.

...

Longer than that.

...

Dad wanted me to RULE EARTH!! For a teeny, tiny millisecond I thought to myself, "Cool! My own planet!" but then the reality kicked in. This was not a good thing. This was a punishment.

Dad wasn't just going to put me in my room and lock me away from the rest of the ship, he wanted to put me on EARTH and lock me away from the ENTIRE ship!

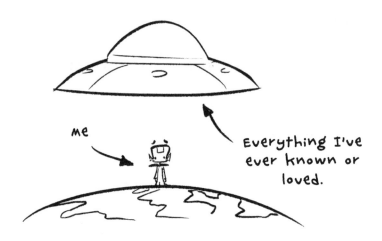

me

Everything I've ever known or loved.

This was a DISASTER! On top of that, he wanted to put me IN CHARGE down there!

I failed my last history test and my parents made me clean the sludge slide in the smelliest part of the ship. What will happen when I fail an entire planet?!

I broke it.

Finally, let's not forget the actual, real, physical danger I'll be in.

We've just invaded this planet, what if there are people there that aren't happy about that? Sure, I have a giant spaceship to back me up, but I'm not sure that'll be enough.

Unless of course they really are as simple as everyone says they are.

Either way, I was wrong, this was not a gift, or a special treat, this was the worst punishment imaginable and it was totally unfair.

Dad, however, did not agree.

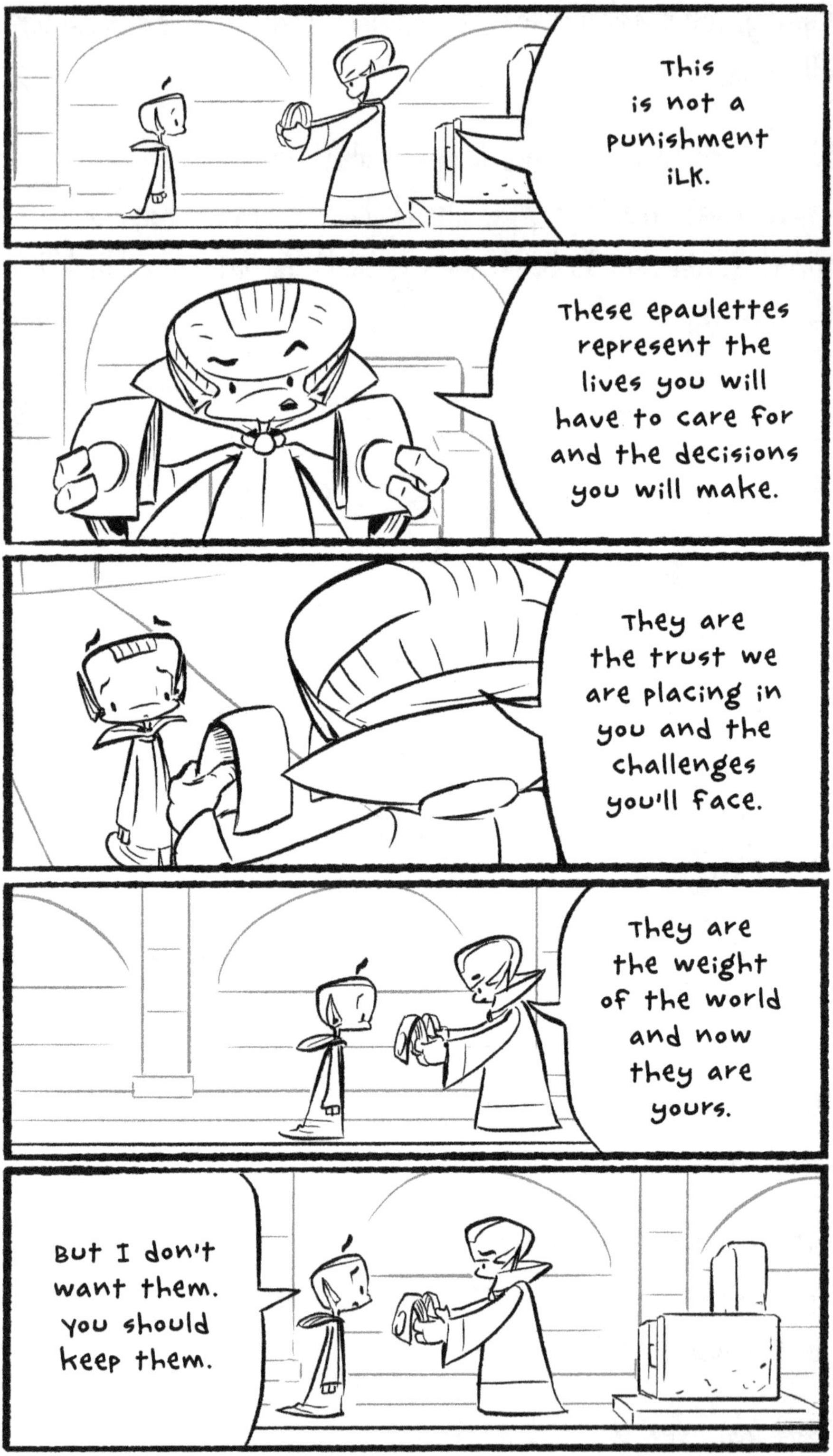
This is not a punishment iLK.
These epaulettes represent the lives you will have to care for and the decisions you will make.
They are the trust we are placing in you and the challenges you'll face.
They are the weight of the world and now they are yours.
But I don't want them. You should keep them.

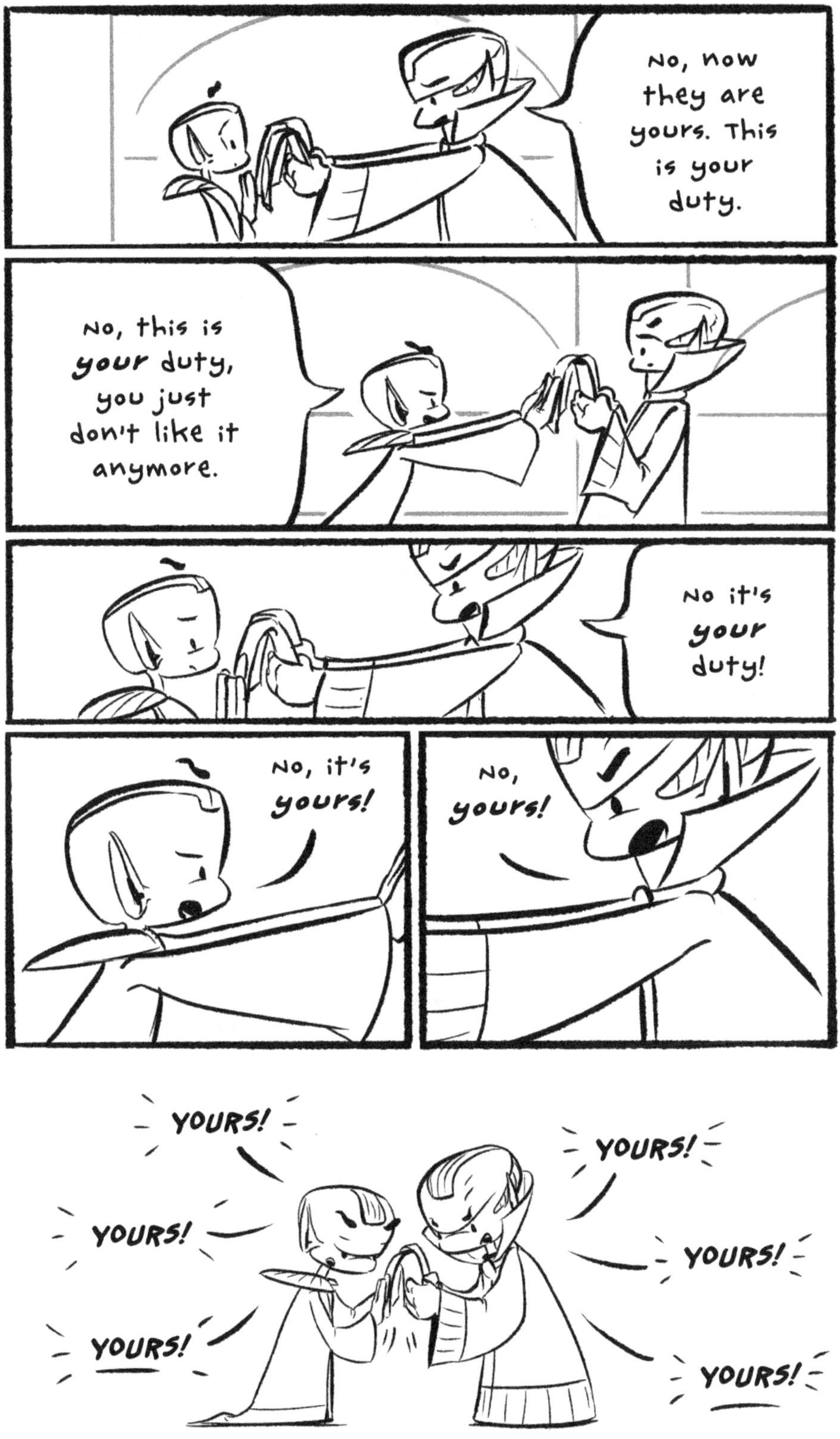
No, now they are yours. This is your duty.
No, this is *your* duty, you just don't like it anymore.
No it's *your* duty!
No, it's *yours!*
No, *yours!*
YOURS!
YOURS!
YOURS!
YOURS!
YOURS!
YOURS!

In conclusion, Dad is behaving like a child so I am going to wait here in this fort I've built until he calms down.

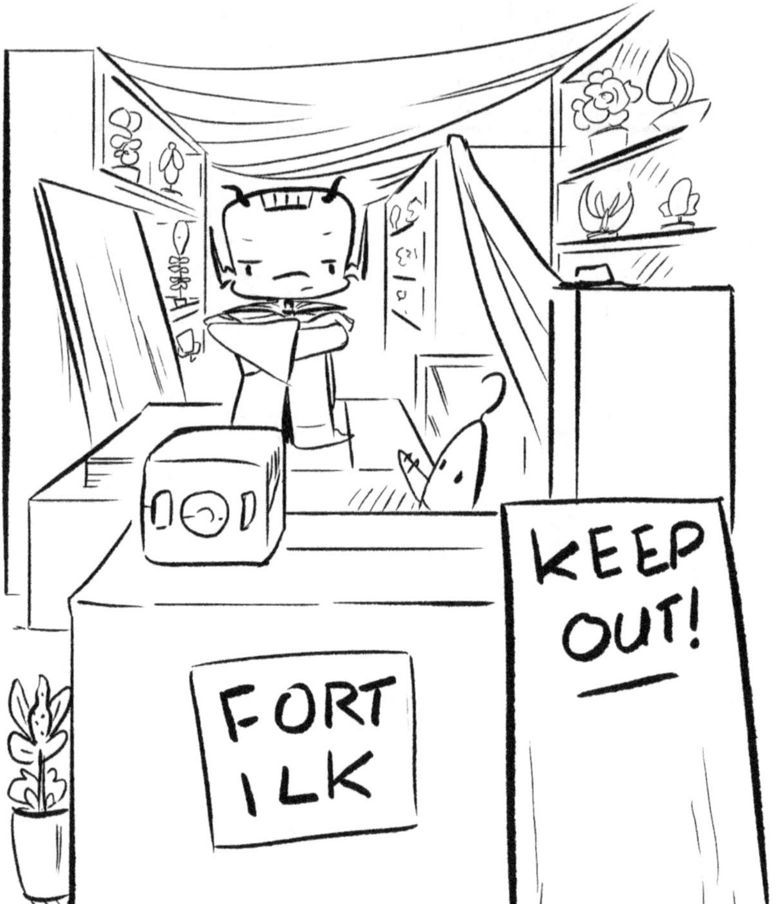
KEEP OUT!
FORT ILK

Invasion 101, Day 15

What you see here is Fort iLK version 6.0

This in fact only represents the east wing. It stretches across my entire bedroom and it's littered with traps and tricks that only I know how to get around.

I've become an excellent fort builder for my relatively young age. Some of the mechanisms are really quite sophisticated.

Check out this raised platform for example.

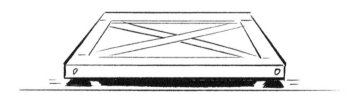

Some may think they'd know how to avoid this one. They'd be wrong.

1.

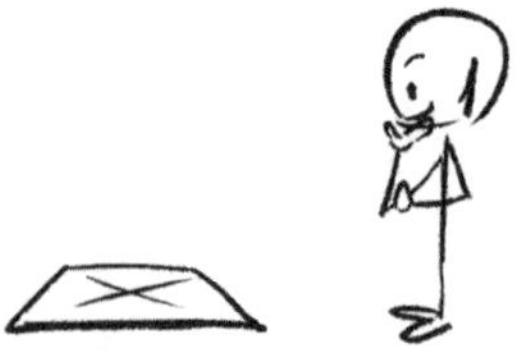

As you approach the target, you're immediately wary.

2.

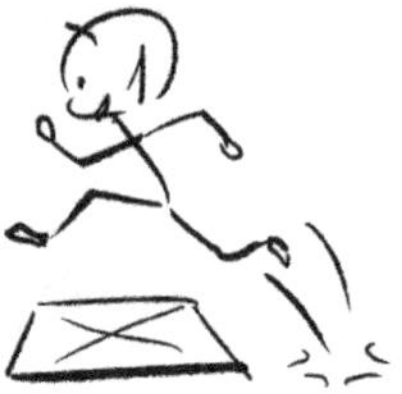

So you hop over it, thinking you're safe...

3.

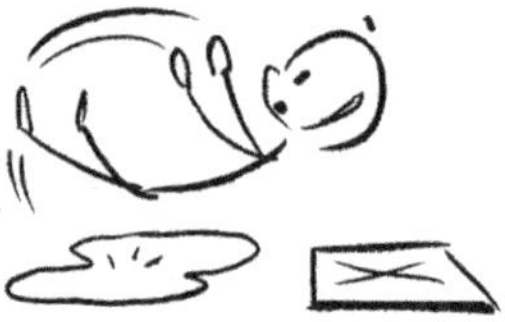

But then you trip on the aqua gel I've smeared on the floor!

4.

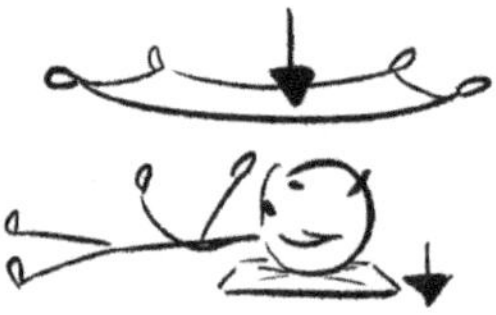

You fall backwards landing on the raised pad and down drops the weighted bedsheet!

OK, the sheet might not be a permanent impediment. Nevertheless, I'm sure it would confuse a person enough to make them question whether they wanted to continue.

Most can't even make it that far.

After being in my room for a few days, surviving on the delicious insta-pot meals Y-bot fetched for me, Dad sent TaLC in to get me. He fell at the first hurdle.

My micro-species moat.

Poor TaLC, he hates bugs and those ones will follow him around for days thanks to the plant extracts I put in that water. Sometimes I scare myself with my own genius.

With all of this in mind, with all of this progress I'd made, imagine my disappointment when, today, Fort iLK v6.0 met the same fate as versions 1.0, 2.0, 4.0 and 5.0. In fact, all previous versions except 3.0.

Version 3.0 I had to destroy myself because I built myself into it, but I forgot to build myself a way out.

Fort iLK v3.0

Every other previous build however, was brought to its knees by...

The Fort conquerer!

(AKA MUM)

We cannot blame the forts, nor their maker, for failing to stand up to this juggernaut. She appears to have some kind of superpowers.

Just watch what she did when faced with my aqua gel trap...

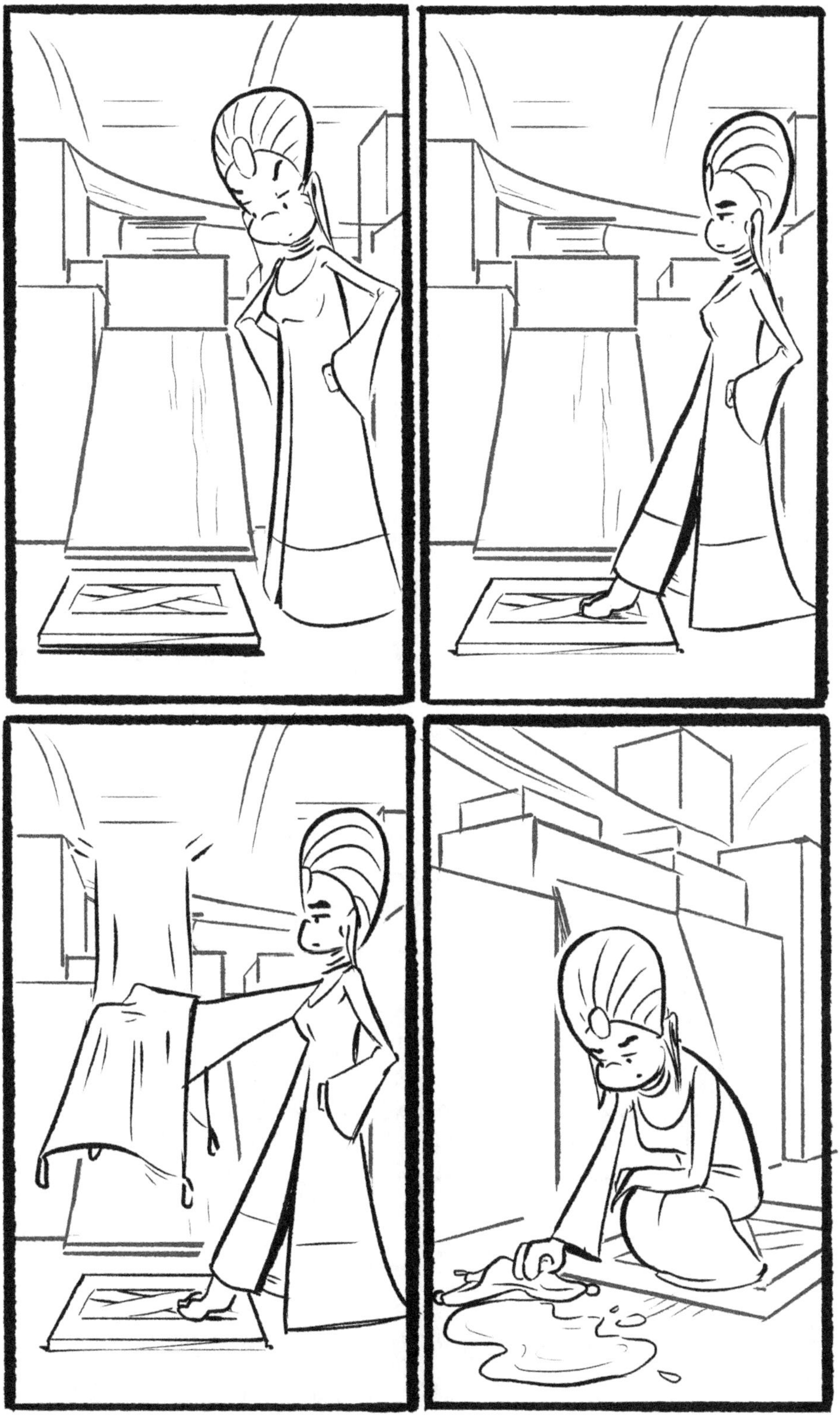

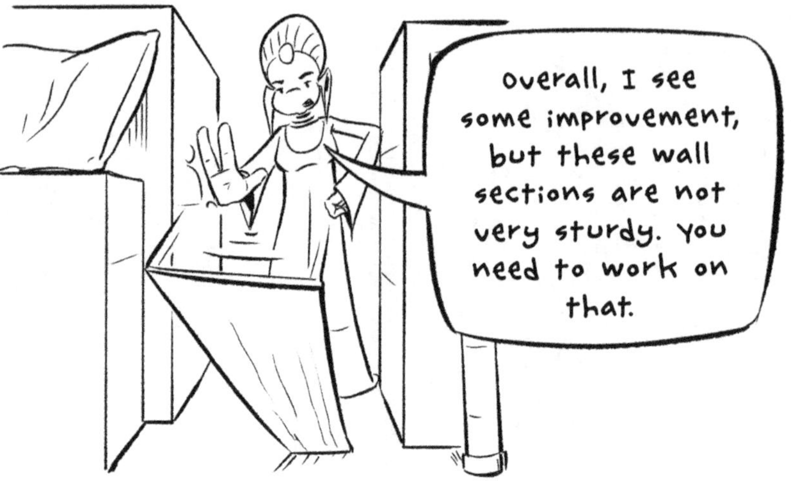
overall, I see some improvement, but these wall sections are not very sturdy. You need to work on that.

Mum has always been my harshest critic, but I don't mind so much when it comes from her.

I explained to her how Dad had gone crazy and he wanted me to rule Earth. Apparently she already knew.

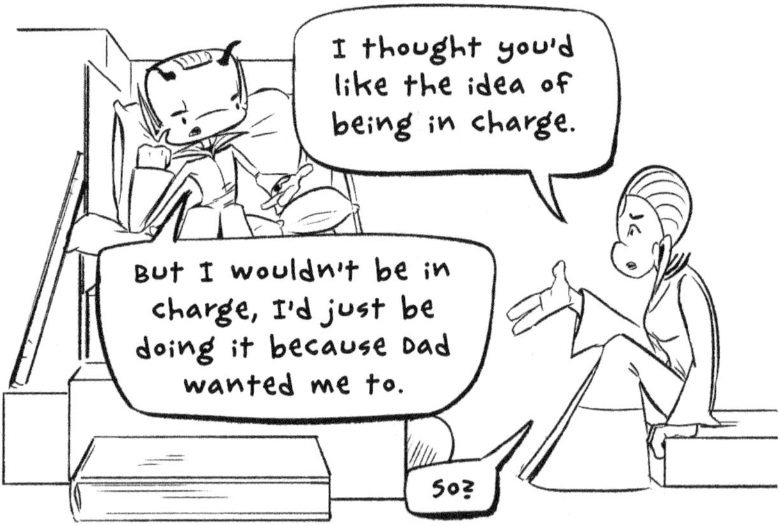
I thought you'd like the idea of being in charge.
But I wouldn't be in charge, I'd just be doing it because Dad wanted me to.
So?

Mum has a way of saying very simple, annoying things, that also make a lot of sense. It can be very confusing.

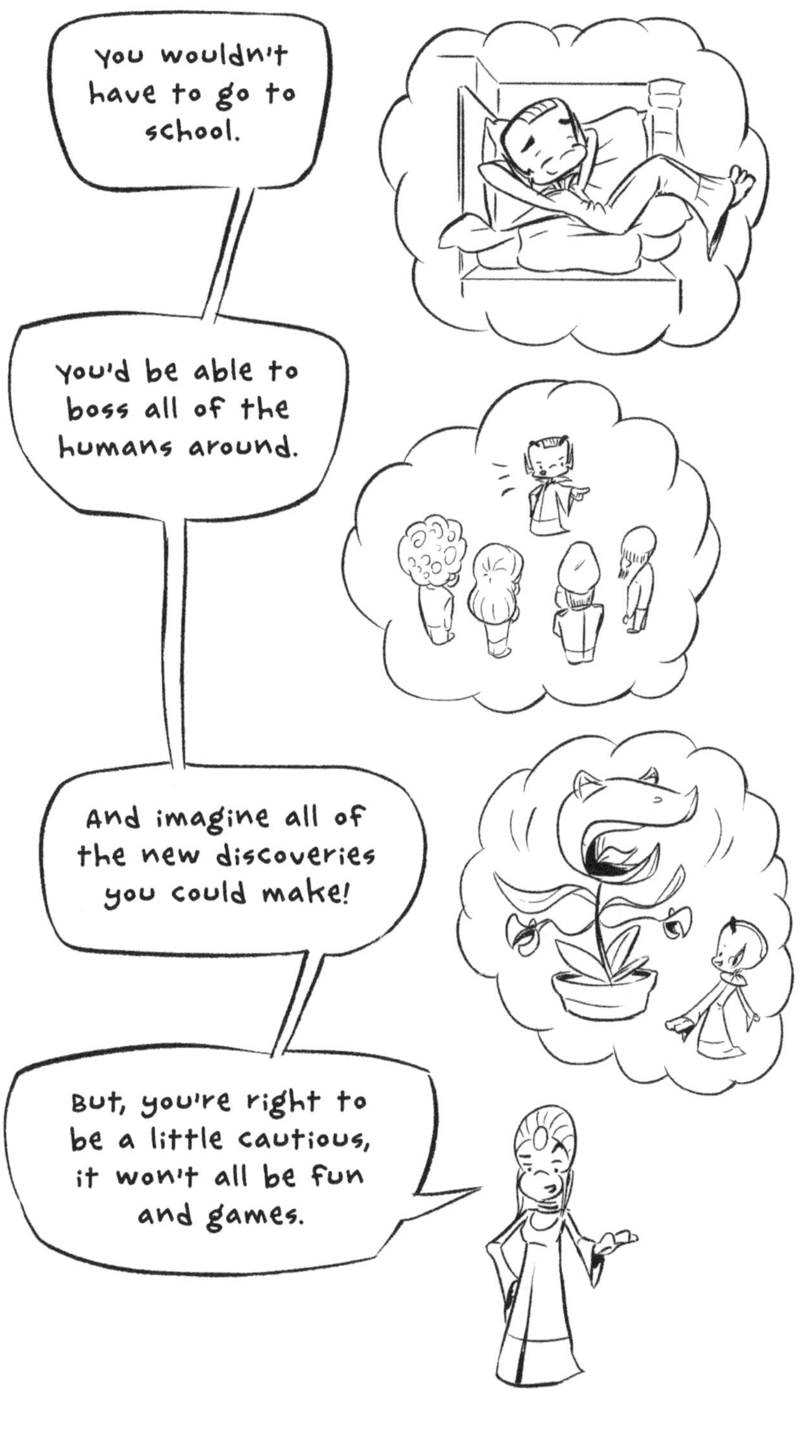
You wouldn't have to go to school.
You'd be able to boss all of the humans around.
And imagine all of the new discoveries you could make!
But, you're right to be a little cautious, it won't all be fun and games.

Mum never lets me hear the good without the bad.

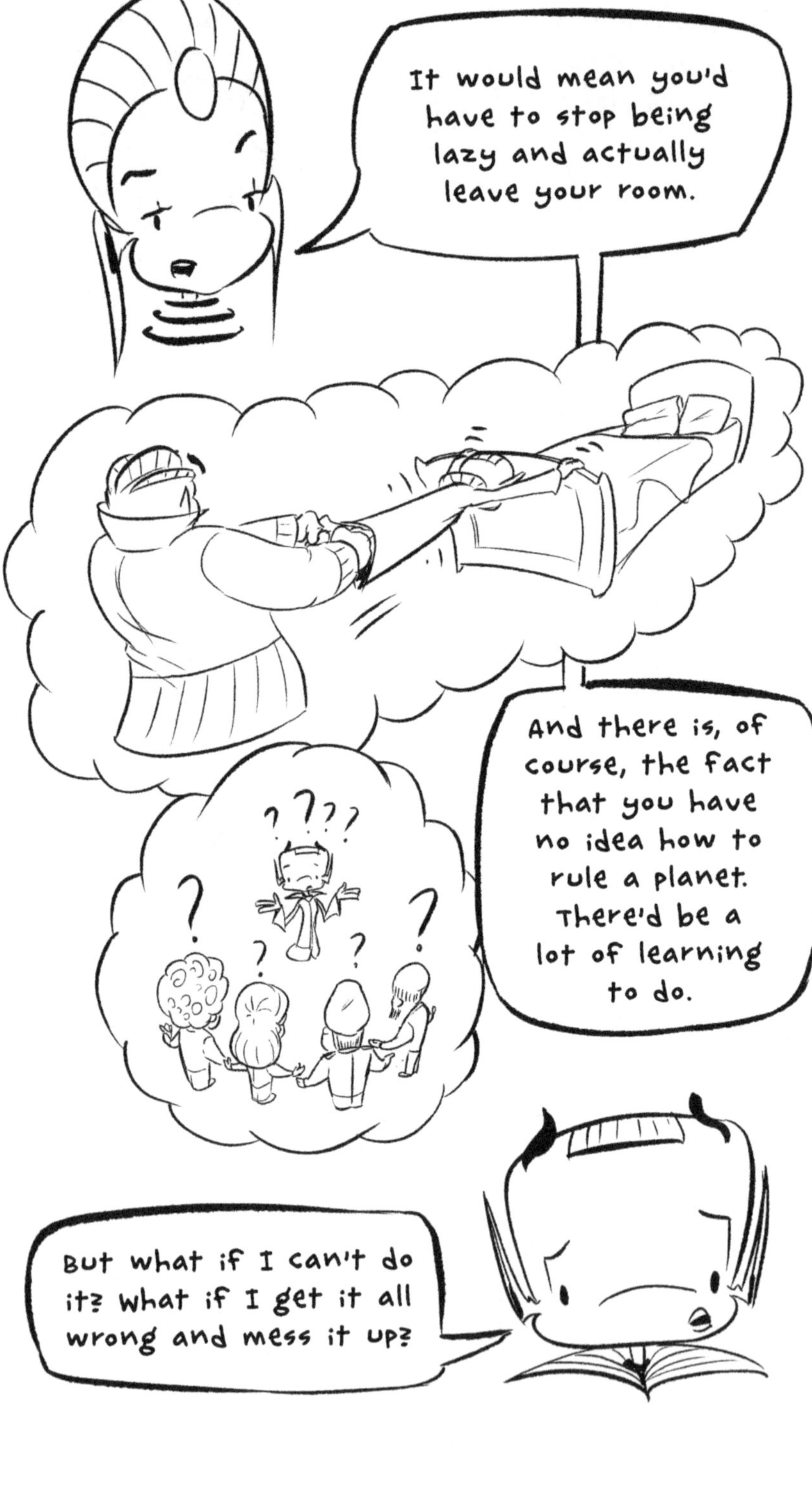
It would mean you'd have to stop being lazy and actually leave your room.
And there is, of course, the fact that you have no idea how to rule a planet. There'd be a lot of learning to do.
But what if I can't do it? What if I get it all wrong and mess it up?

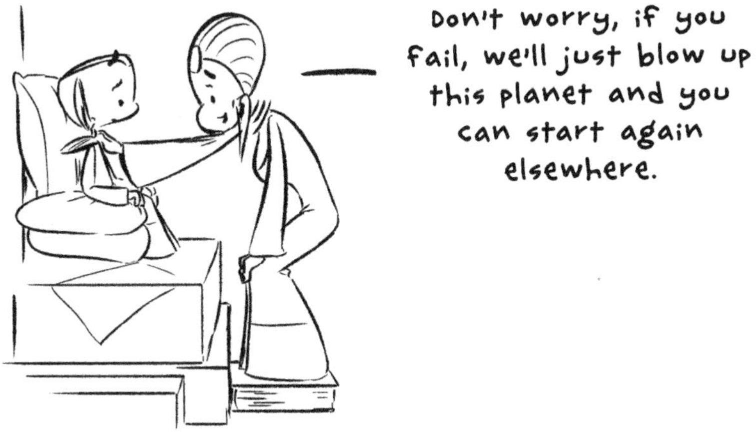
Don't worry, if you fail, we'll just blow up this planet and you can start again elsewhere.

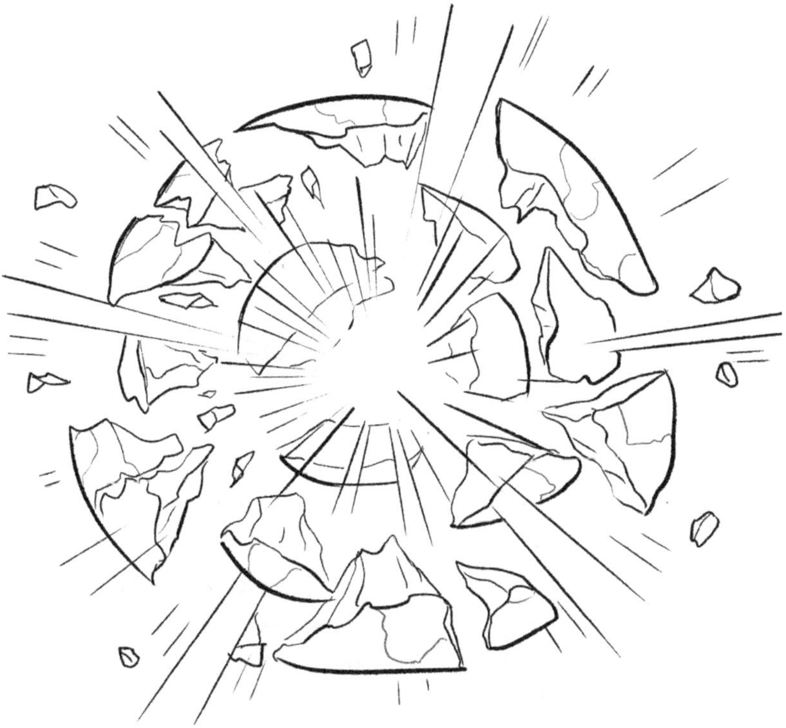

That did make me feel a little bit better.

But no one seems to understand that Dad is only doing this because he can't be bothered anymore!

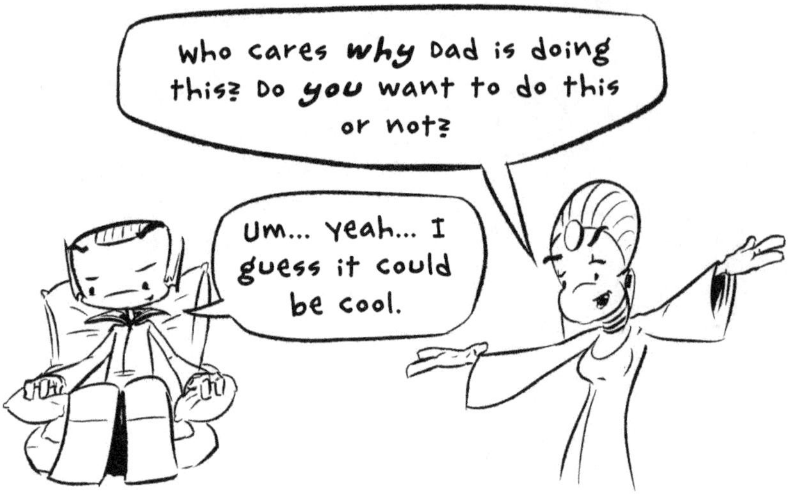
Who cares **why** Dad is doing this? Do **you** want to do this or not?
Um... yeah... I guess it could be cool.

I was nearly convinced, but before I could 100% agree to becoming the supreme ruler of Earth, I had one more request.

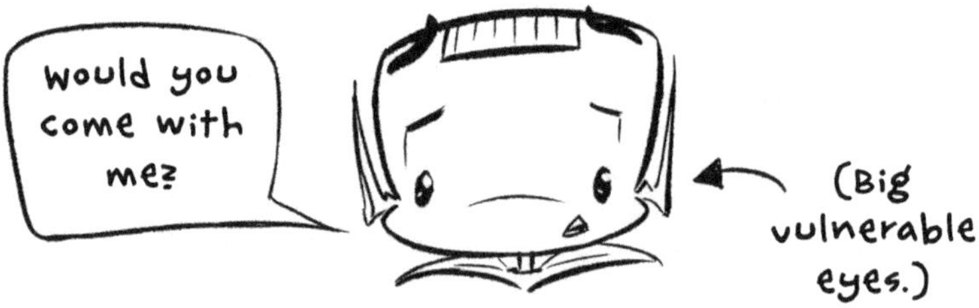
Would you come with me?
(Big vulnerable eyes.)

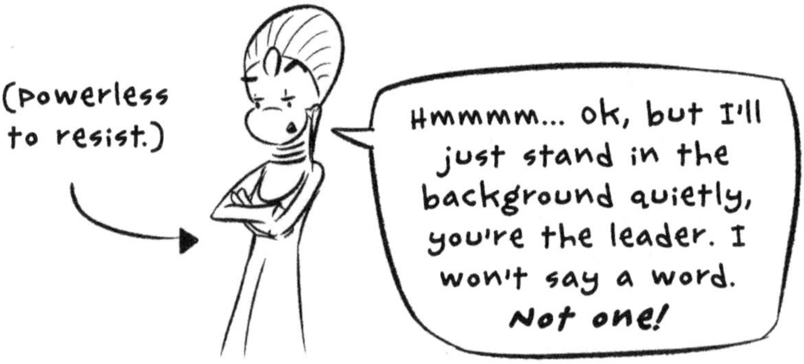
(Powerless to resist.)
Hmmmm... ok, but I'll just stand in the background quietly, you're the leader. I won't say a word. **Not one!**

Ha! No way that'll happen! I can let Mum handle the difficult stuff while I have all the fun. This might just work out. 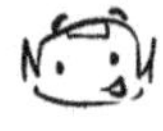

Invasion 101, Day 17

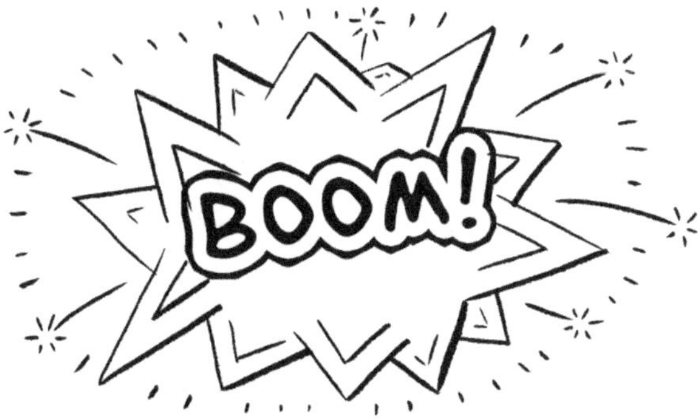
BOOM!

That, apparently, is a "Firework."

However, it wouldn't surprise me if you mistook it for the work of a Mildred Missile.

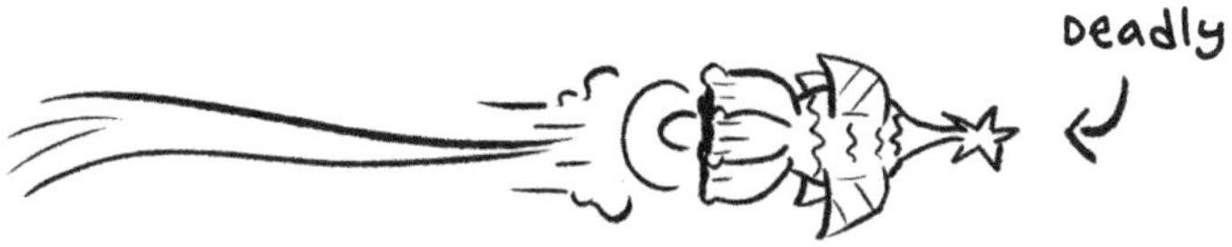
Deadly

...Which I did.

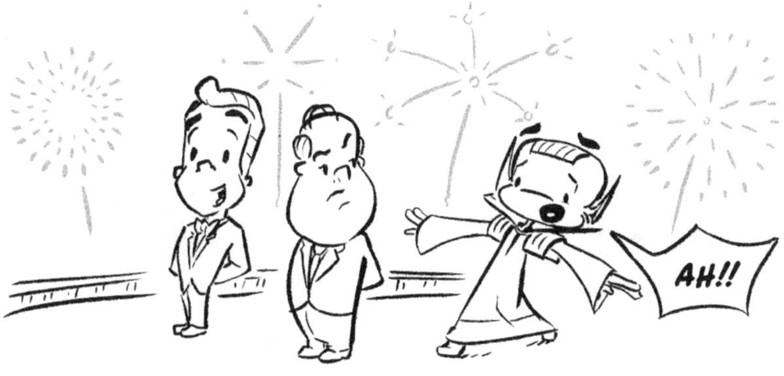
AH!!

Apparently humans like to blow up portions of their sky on special occasions. It turns out, meeting the new Emperor of the World is just such an occasion.

As their new leader, this was not the first impression I wanted to give...

Fortunately I was watching from my own private area and there weren't many people around to see me cower so feebly.

Dad had sent me straight down to Earth when I accepted the position and Mum was getting her ears curled so was going to join me later.

In the end the "Public Relations" team my Dad had assembled made sure the first images anyone saw of me were much more impressive.

THE CLOCK MAG

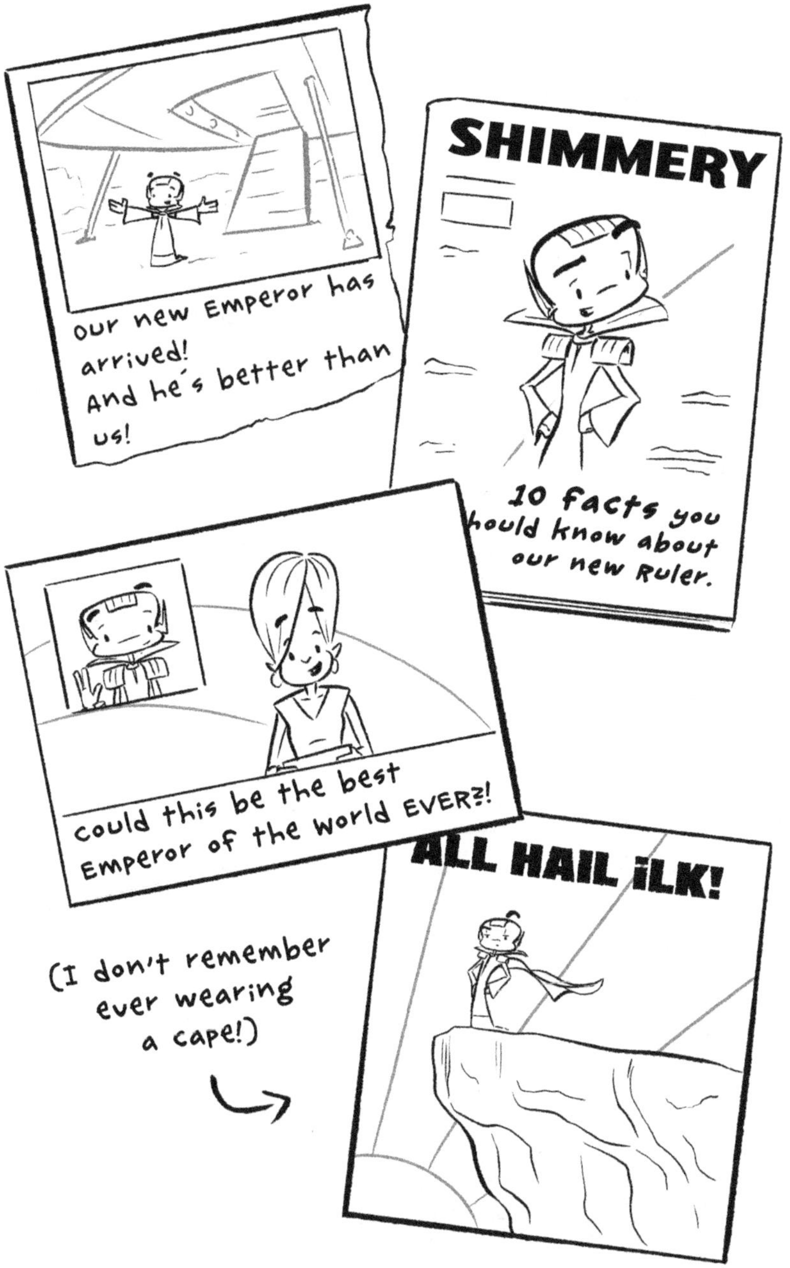
our new Emperor has arrived!
And he's better than us!
SHIMMERY
10 facts you should know about our new Ruler.
could this be the best Emperor of the world EVER?!
ALL HAIL iLK!
(I don't remember ever wearing a cape!)

I appreciated the help, but I'd only been on Earth a few hours when I realised that I'd already made my first big mistake...

...Bringing Y-bot!

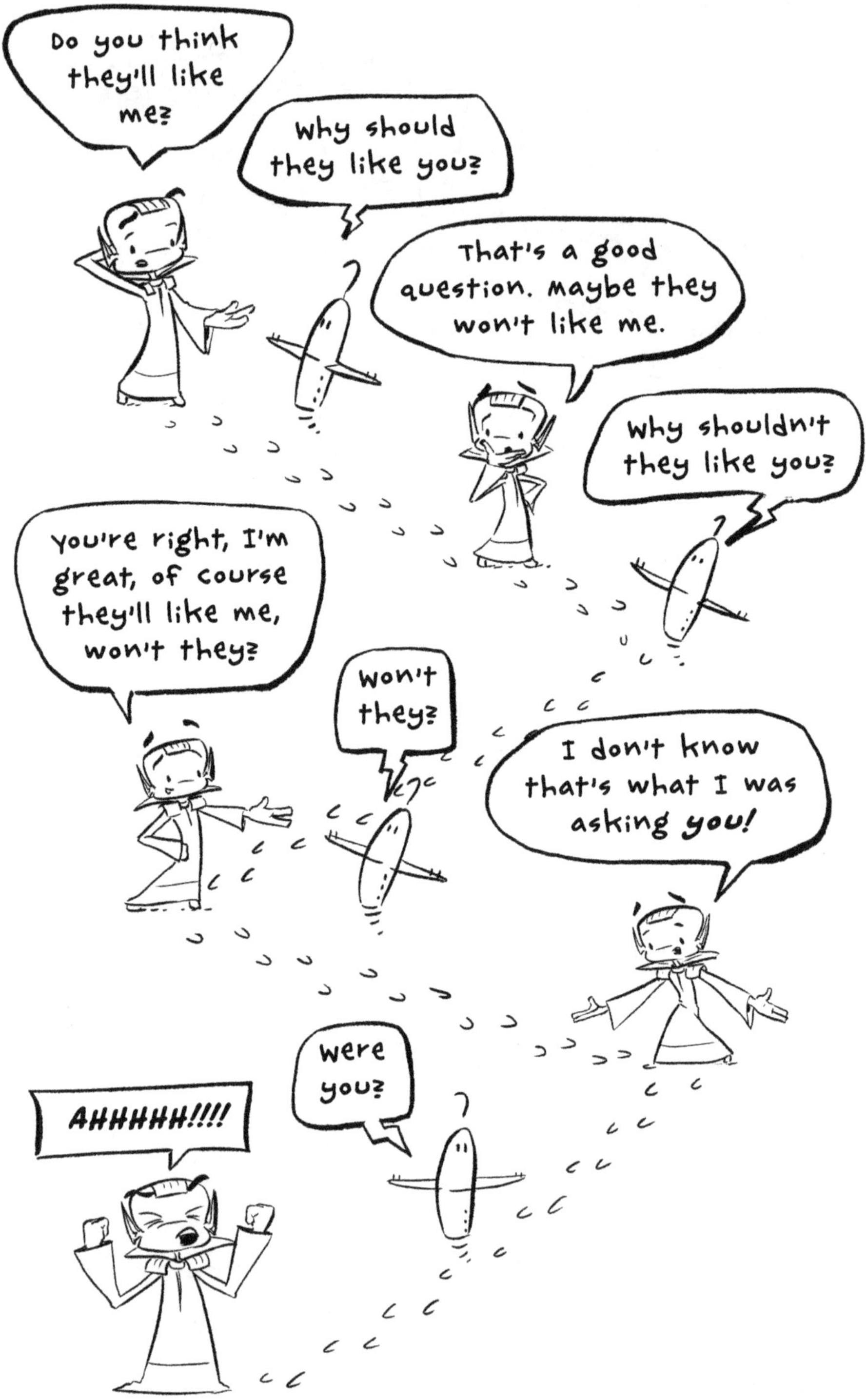

Do you think they'll like me?
Why should they like you?
That's a good question. maybe they won't like me.
Why shouldn't they like you?
You're right, I'm great, of course they'll like me, won't they?
Won't they?
I don't know that's what I was asking *you!*
AHHHHH!!!!
Were you?

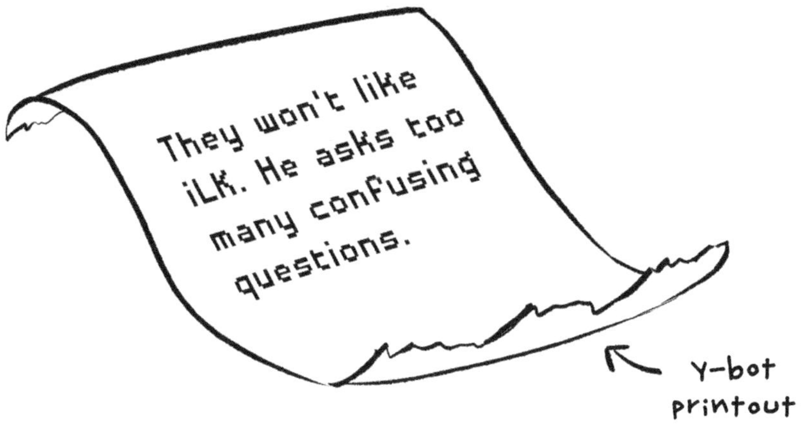
They won't like iLK. He asks too many confusing questions.
Y-bot printout

It's a good thing Mum turned up when she did.

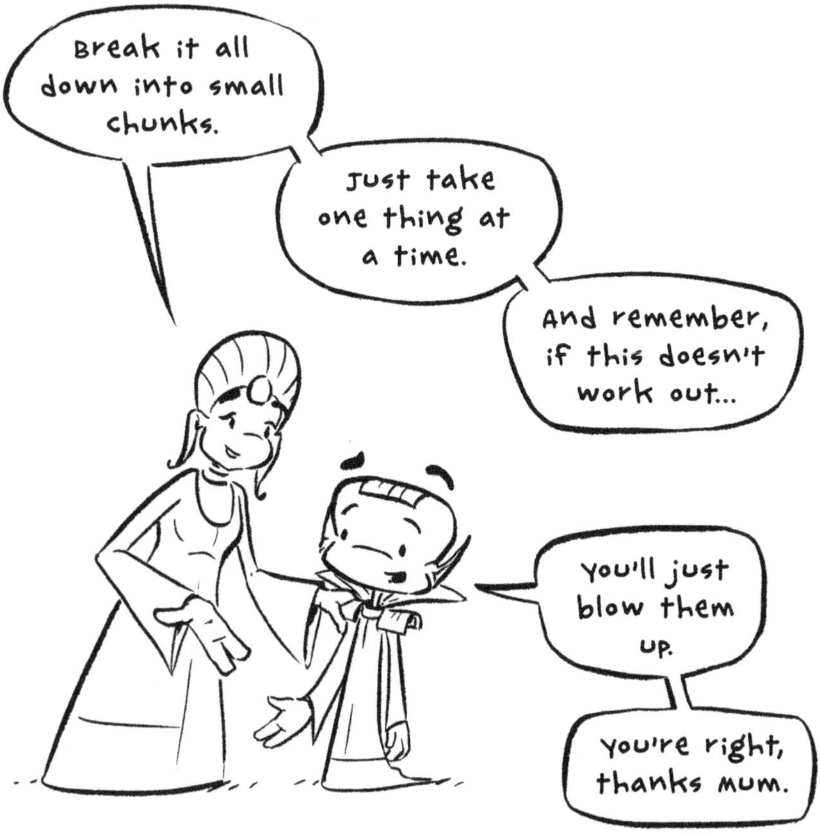
Break it all down into small chunks.
Just take one thing at a time.
And remember, if this doesn't work out...
You'll just blow them up.
You're right, thanks mum.

Invasion 101, Day 18

It occurs to me as I write this that it's very lucky that we speak the same language. I could understand everything the humans were saying.

It's a shame that none of it was very interesting.

This is the one that seemed to like talking the most.

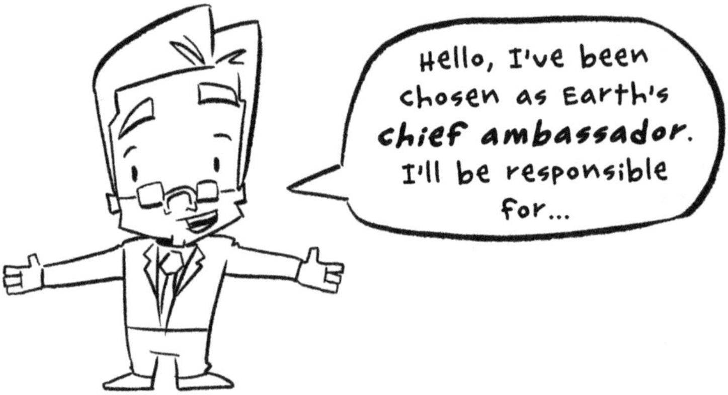
Hello, I've been chosen as Earth's **chief ambassador**. I'll be responsible for...

He spoke so much, he started to sound like a Dullrat yipping.

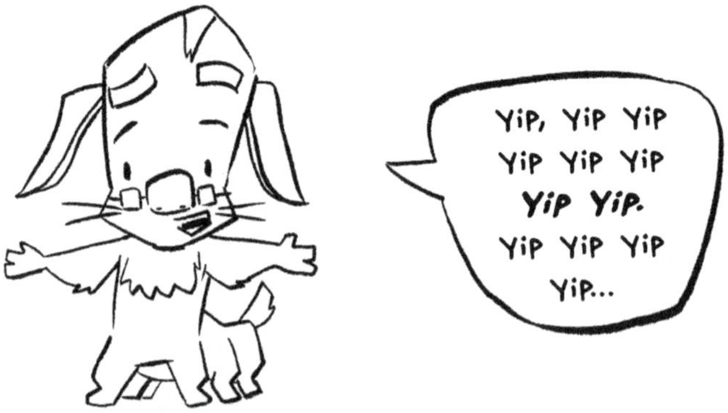
Yip, Yip Yip Yip Yip Yip **Yip Yip.** Yip Yip Yip Yip...

Dullrats are my favourite kind of animal on Glub.

They crave attention and never stop yipping, but we keep them around anyway. A bit like humans. Except dullrats are smarter.

When the human stopped yipping, he pointed to a long line of other humans all waiting to meet me.

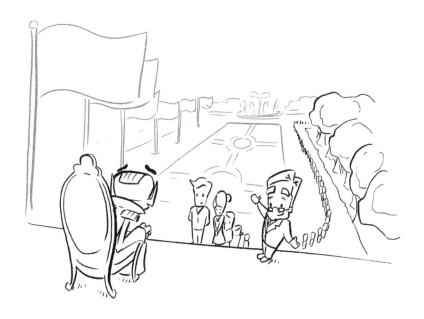

After "Shaking Hands," with around four or five of them I fell asleep. It was simply too dull.

WEIRD CUSTOM #106
shaking hands

STEP 1: Hold

STEP 2: wobble
(just the hand)

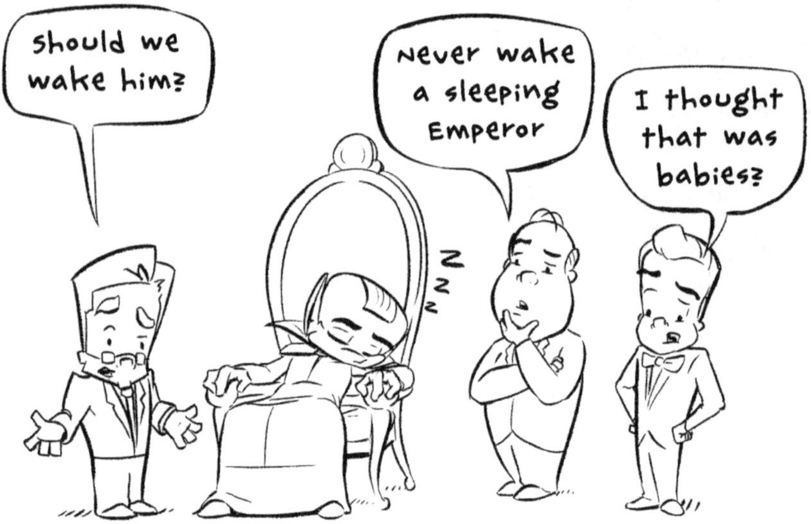
Should we wake him?
Never wake a sleeping Emperor
I thought that was babies?

I woke up to discover...

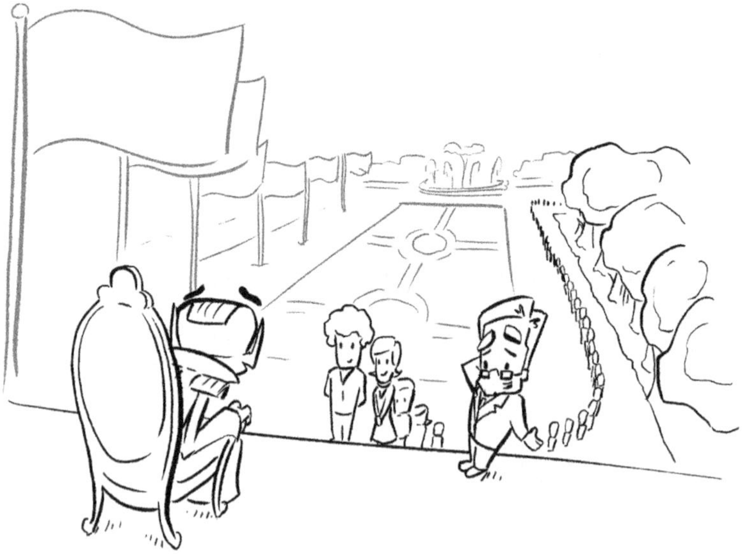

...nothing had changed.

So I decided to put a stop to this boring farce straight away.

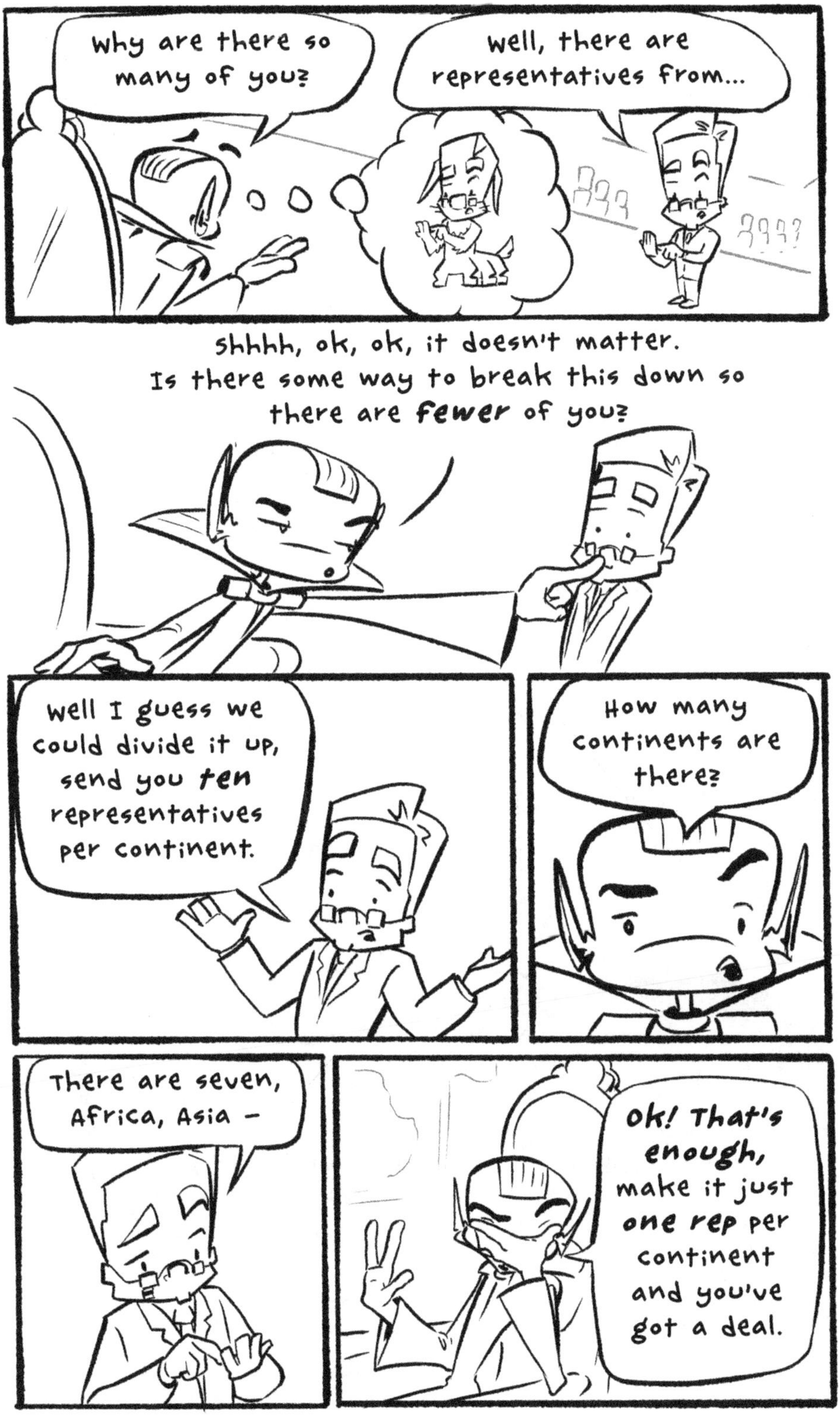
Why are there so many of you?
Well, there are representatives from...
???
????
Shhhh, ok, ok, it doesn't matter. Is there some way to break this down so there are *fewer* of you?
Well I guess we could divide it up, send you *ten* representatives per continent.
How many continents are there?
There are seven, Africa, Asia –
Ok! That's enough, make it just **one rep** per continent and you've got a deal.

Invasion 101, Day 22

While they went off and chose their representatives, I had to take lessons in how to rule the world. As expected, this has all been a sneaky plan to make me learn things.

How To Rule World: Lesson 1
Objectives:
1. Learn about Earth
2. Prevent the humans from doing anything too dumb.

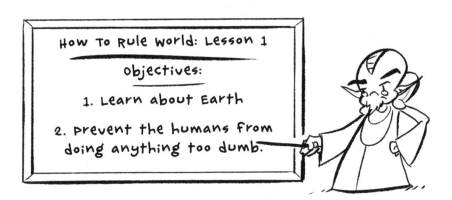

The problem came when all that learning started to make me think. I knew going to class was a bad idea.

Suddenly my head became filled with all these THOUGHTS that weren't there before.

How will I manage to do all this?
What if everyone else knows more than me?
What if they realise that I have no idea what I'm doing?

So by the time it came to actually starting to "rule" and to meet the people I'd have to "rule over," I was nervous. Really, REALLY nervous.

why are you hiding in me?

Unfortunately, the one thing my teacher didn't teach me, was that Y-bot was the worst hiding place I could have chosen.

So I started to write a to-do list for myself.

EMPEROR OF THE WORLD TO-DO LIST

~~#1 Build a good hiding place into headquarters~~

#1 Build a Headquarters

#2 Build a good hiding place into headquarters.

It's a good thing then, that when I finally met the seven representatives I'd be working with, they looked more scared than I did!

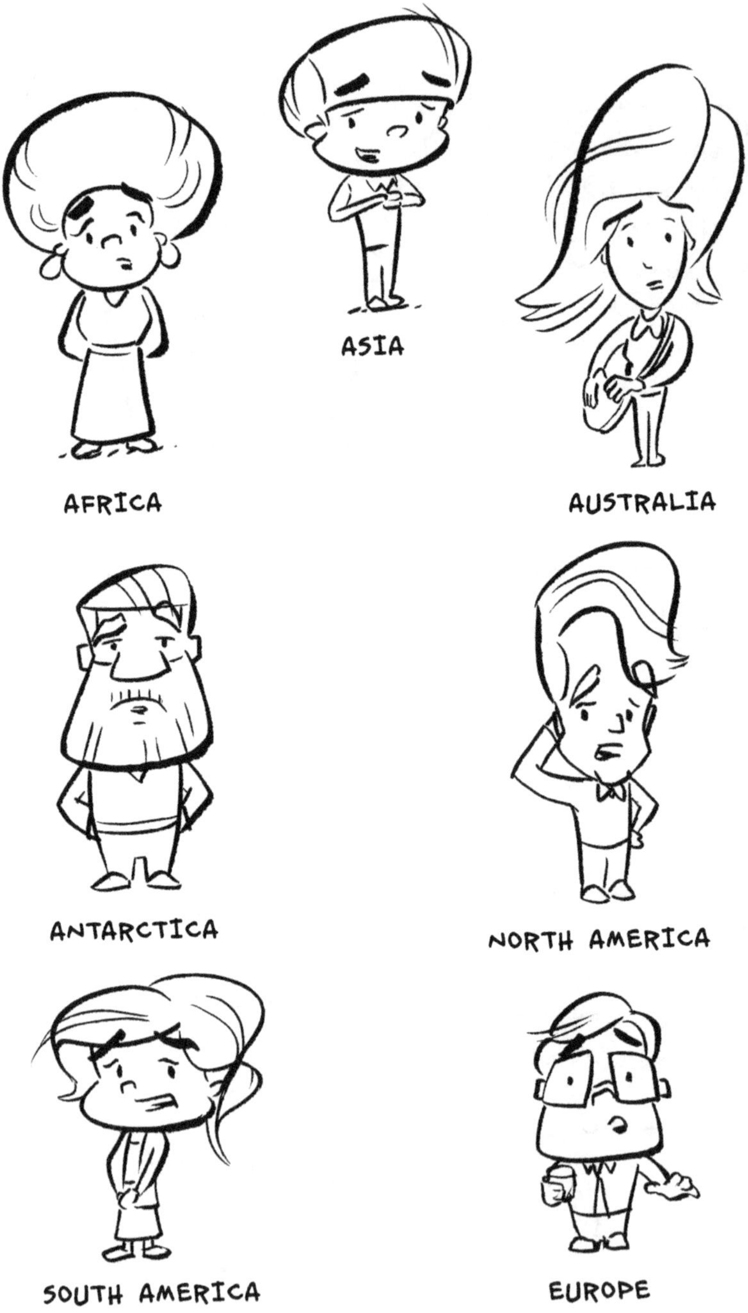
ASIA
AFRICA
AUSTRALIA
ANTARCTICA
NORTH AMERICA
SOUTH AMERICA
EUROPE

After we were all introduced, the Chief Ambassador (his real name is Steve, but to me he'll always be a dullrat) started to explain how each continent chose its representative.

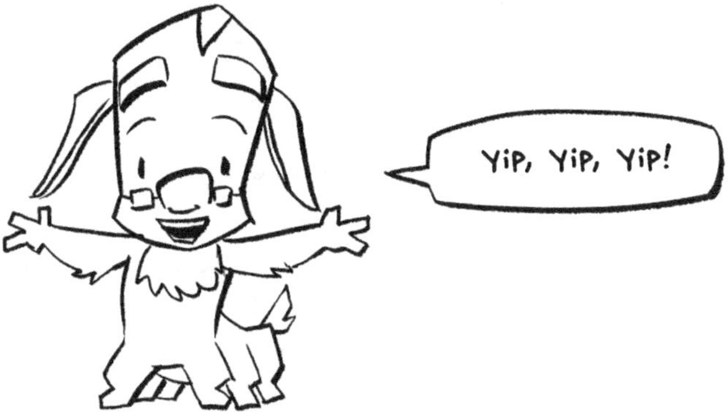
YIP, YIP, YIP!

When he was done, the Australian lady piped up.

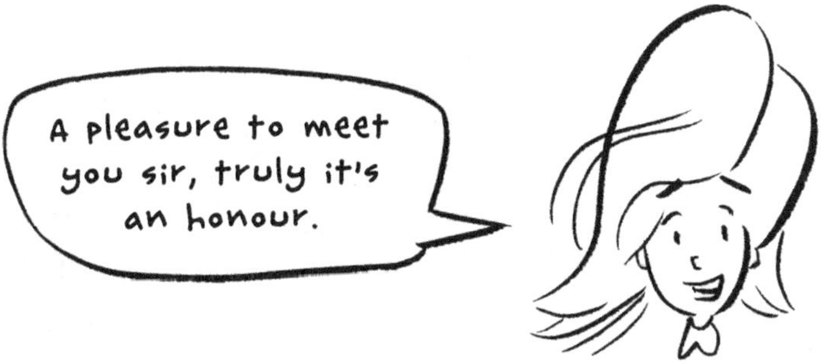
A pleasure to meet you sir, truly it's an honour.

To which the representative from Antarctica replied.

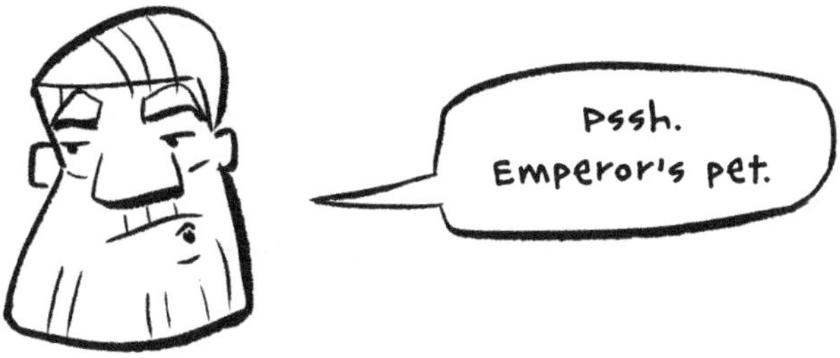
Pssh.
Emperor's pet.

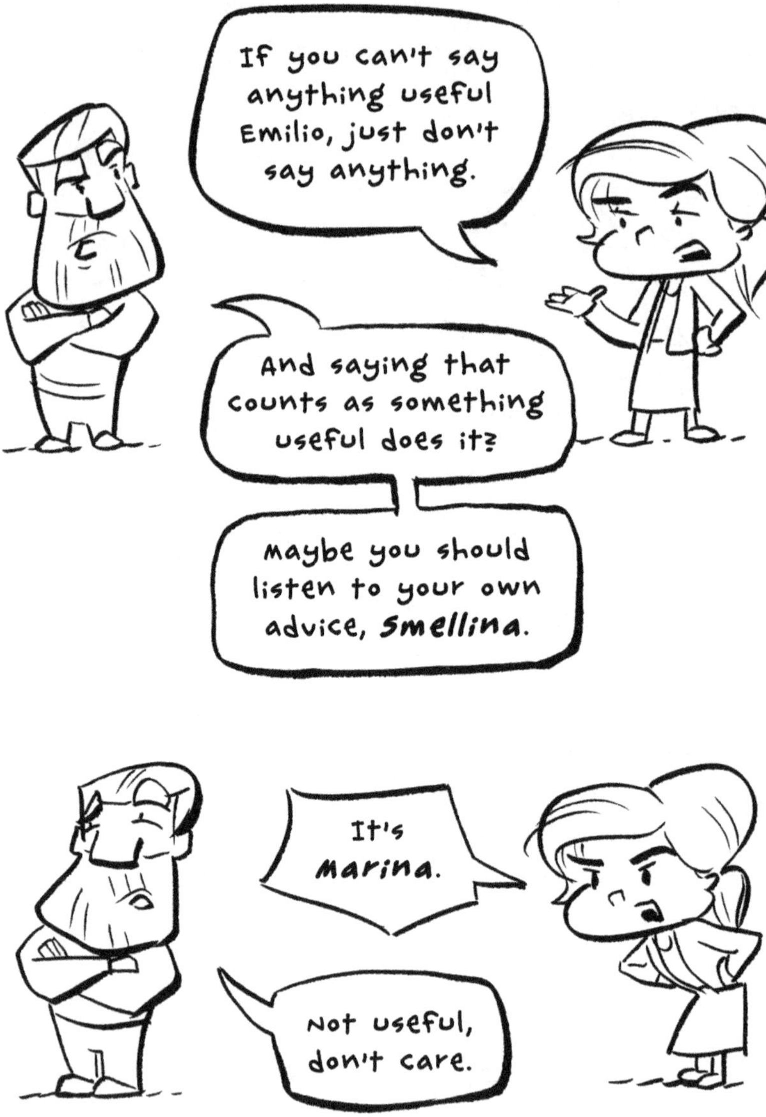
If you can't say anything useful Emilio, just don't say anything.
And saying that counts as something useful does it?
Maybe you should listen to your own advice, Smellina.
It's Marina.
Not useful, don't care.

The others didn't really say much after that.

In fact, everyone was quiet for a really long time...

Myself included.

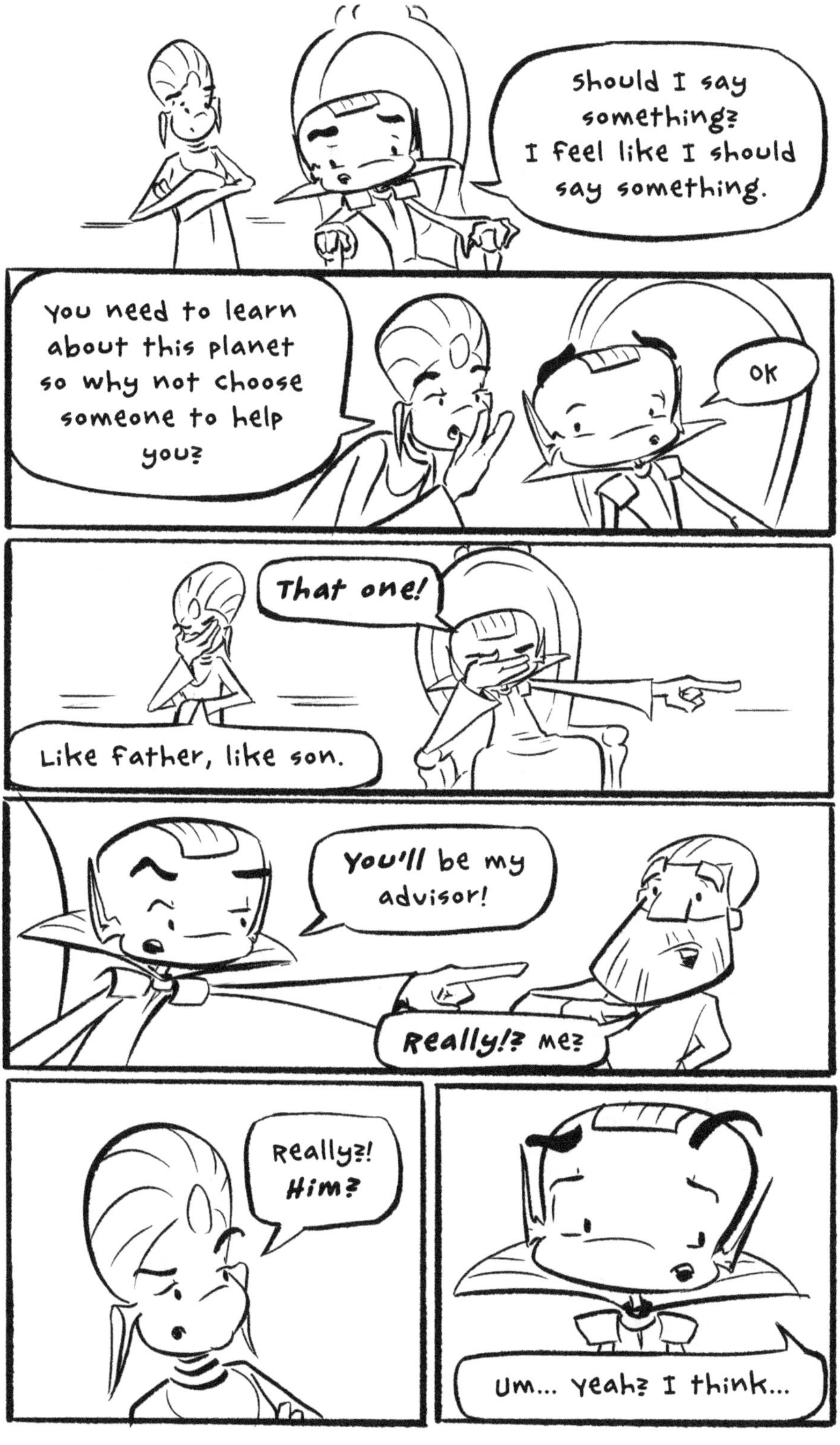
Should I say something? I feel like I should say something.
You need to learn about this planet so why not choose someone to help you?
OK
That one!
Like father, like son.
You'll be my advisor!
Really!? Me?
Really?! Him?
Um... yeah? I think...

Invasion 101, Day 24

This is my Emperor's chamber, which is basically my bed-room on Earth. Unfortunately it's much worse than my bedroom on the ship.

Huge windows, too lazy to build walls?

Shelf with door which blocks the light. Useless for plants.

Why is the bed so big? Do humans fall out of smaller beds?

Note to self: must find new Headquarters soon!

And THIS chair is where I sit and ponder my biggest problem on Earth so far...

Mum.

I'm not sure Mum knows what her role on Earth is supposed to be. She refuses to do my job for me, but then she keeps making comments about the way I do it.

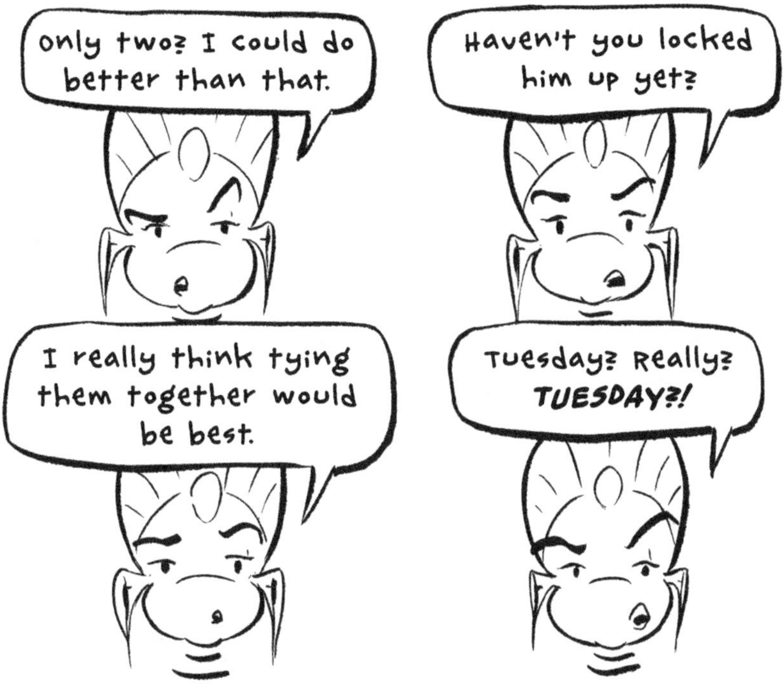
only two? I could do better than that.
Haven't you locked him up yet?
I really think tying them together would be best.
Tuesday? Really? TUESDAY?!

So when Emilio came to my chamber, I listened to what he had to say, mostly because Mum wasn't there to tell me not to.

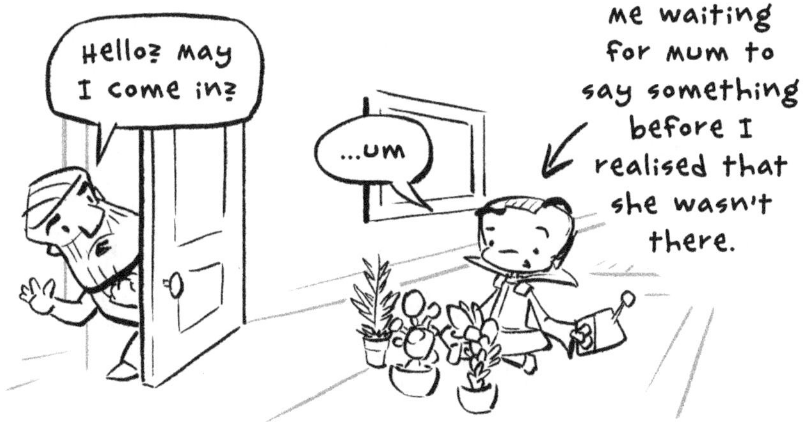
Hello? May I come in?
...um
me waiting for mum to say something before I realised that she wasn't there.

Fortunately for Emilio I had just been spending time with Finnifir, Brickly and Wacksy.

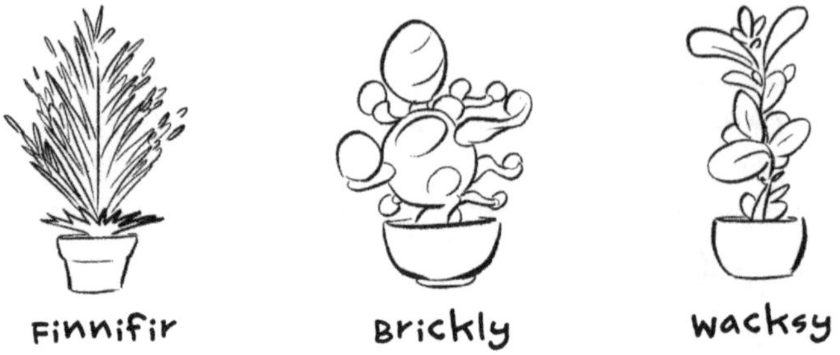
Finnifir
Brickly
wacksy

I tend to these guys whenever I get a chance. They've actually been thriving since I brought them down to Earth. Brickly has even glowed a few times, which is, well, awesome!

Shoop didn't do well though. Shoop exploded.

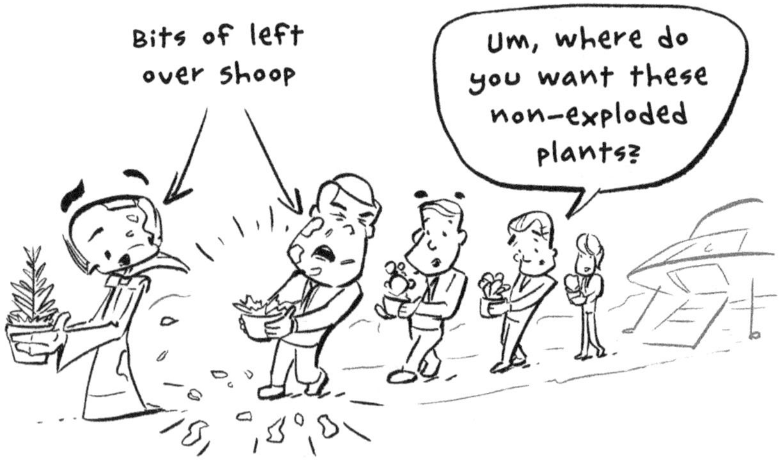
Bits of left over shoop
Um, where do you want these non-exploded plants?

I've learned to accept the losses. However, it is much better when they don't explode and instead they glow, which is why I was in such a good mood when Emilio knocked.

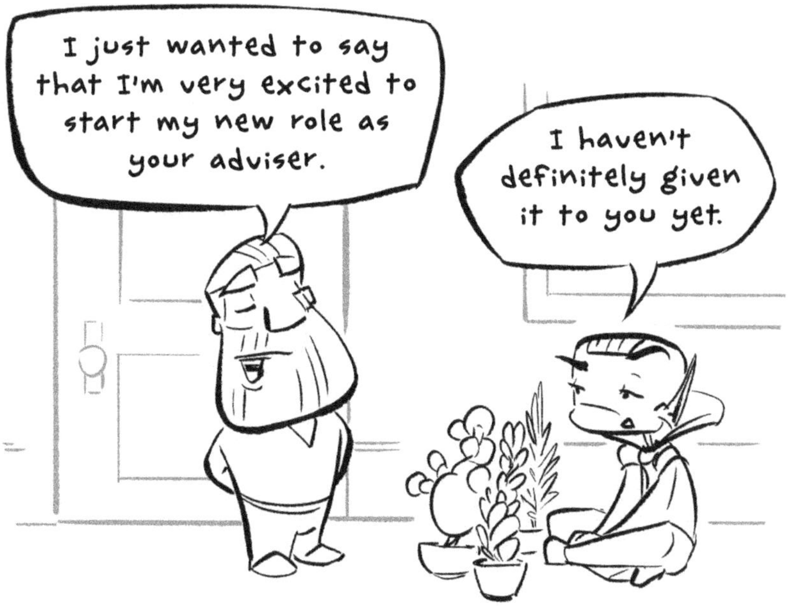
I just wanted to say that I'm very excited to start my new role as your adviser.
I haven't definitely given it to you yet.

I may have been in a good mood, but I wasn't going to let Emilio boss me around like Mum does.

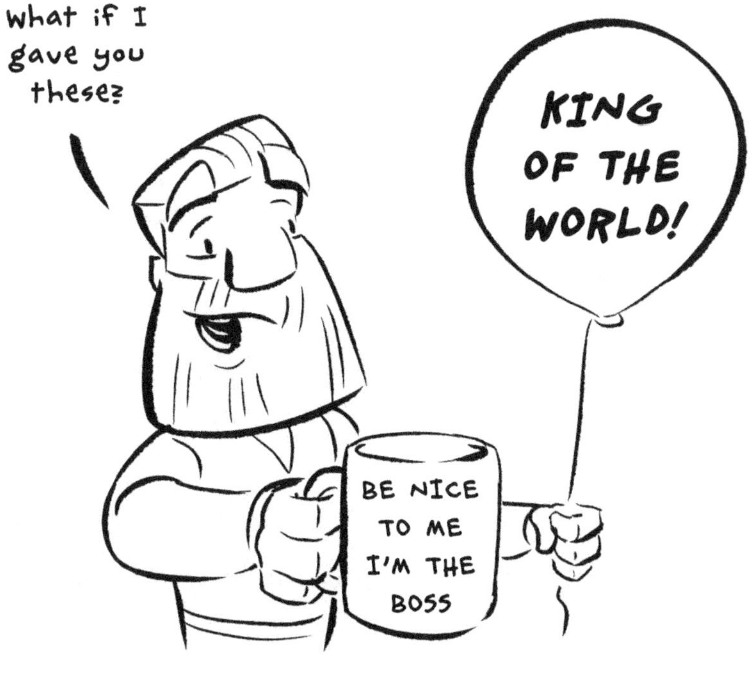
What if I gave you these?
KING OF THE WORLD!
BE NICE TO ME I'M THE BOSS

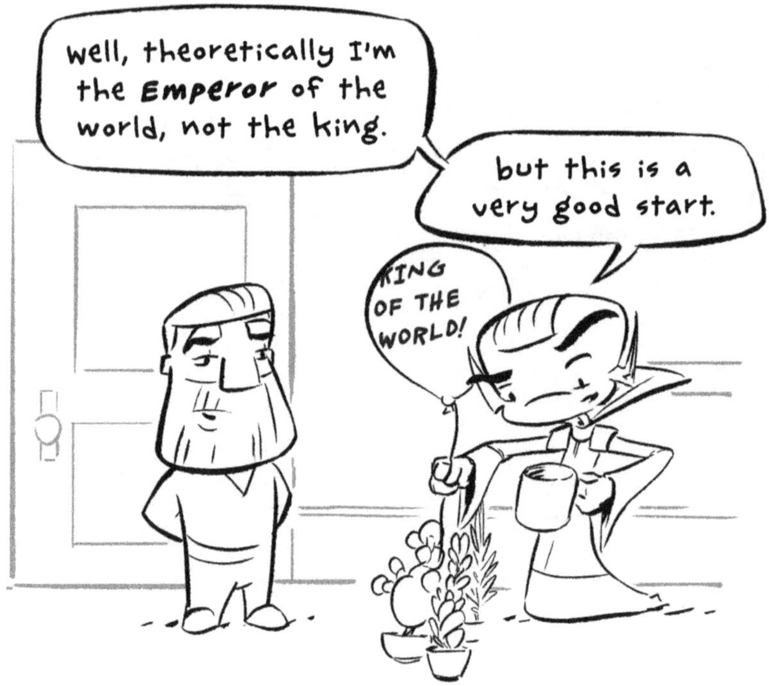
well, theoretically I'm the **Emperor** of the world, not the king.
but this is a very good start.
KING OF THE WORLD!

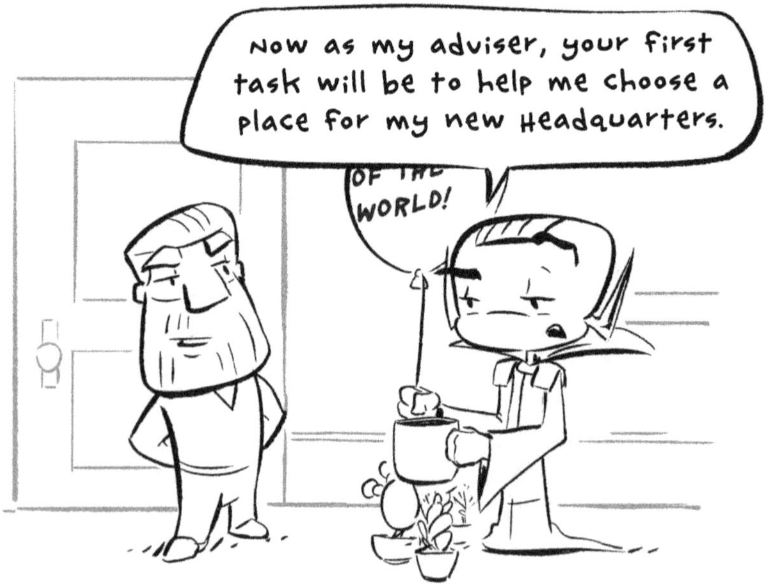
Now as my adviser, your first task will be to help me choose a place for my new Headquarters.
WORLD!

It's very possible that I'm the greatest Emperor this world has ever seen! Why else would he get me all that stuff?

The next day, on the ship...

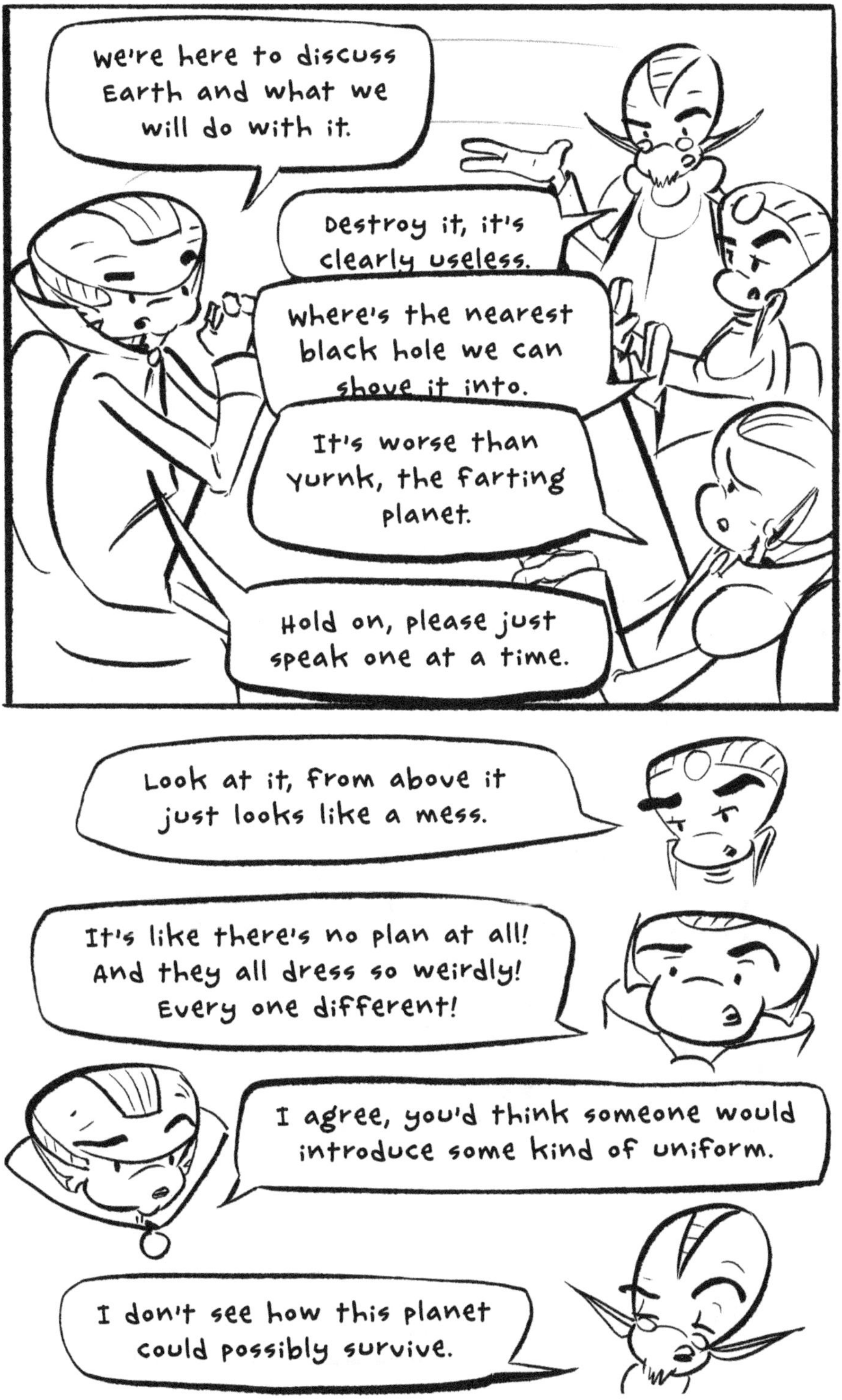
We're here to discuss Earth and what we will do with it.
Destroy it, it's clearly useless.
Where's the nearest black hole we can shove it into.
It's worse than Yurnk, the farting planet.
Hold on, please just speak one at a time.
Look at it, from above it just looks like a mess.
It's like there's no plan at all! And they all dress so weirdly! Every one different!
I agree, you'd think someone would introduce some kind of uniform.
I don't see how this planet could possibly survive.

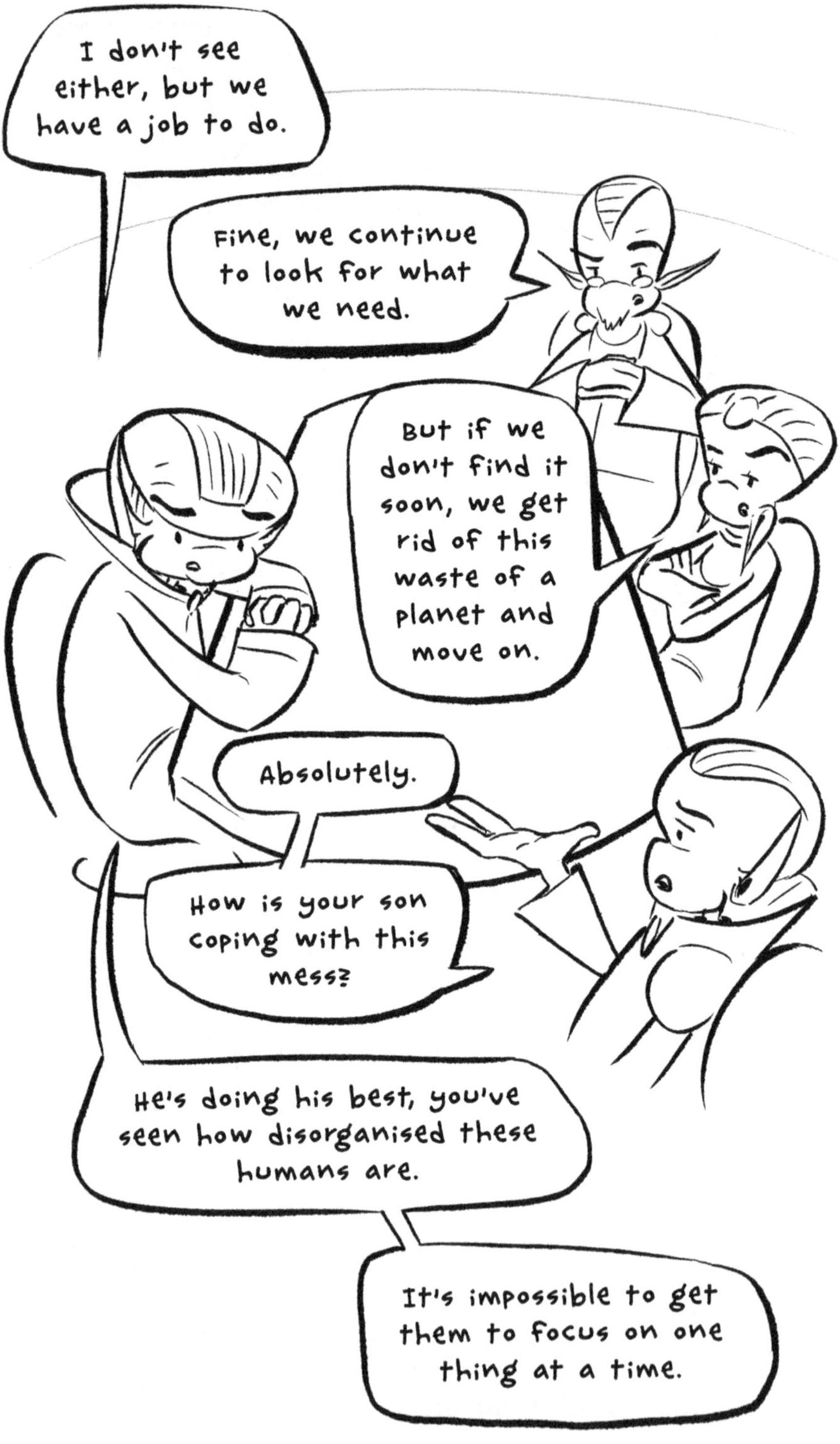
I don't see either, but we have a job to do.
Fine, we continue to look for what we need.
But if we don't find it soon, we get rid of this waste of a planet and move on.
Absolutely.
How is your son coping with this mess?
He's doing his best, you've seen how disorganised these humans are.
It's impossible to get them to focus on one thing at a time.

Meanwhile on Earth...

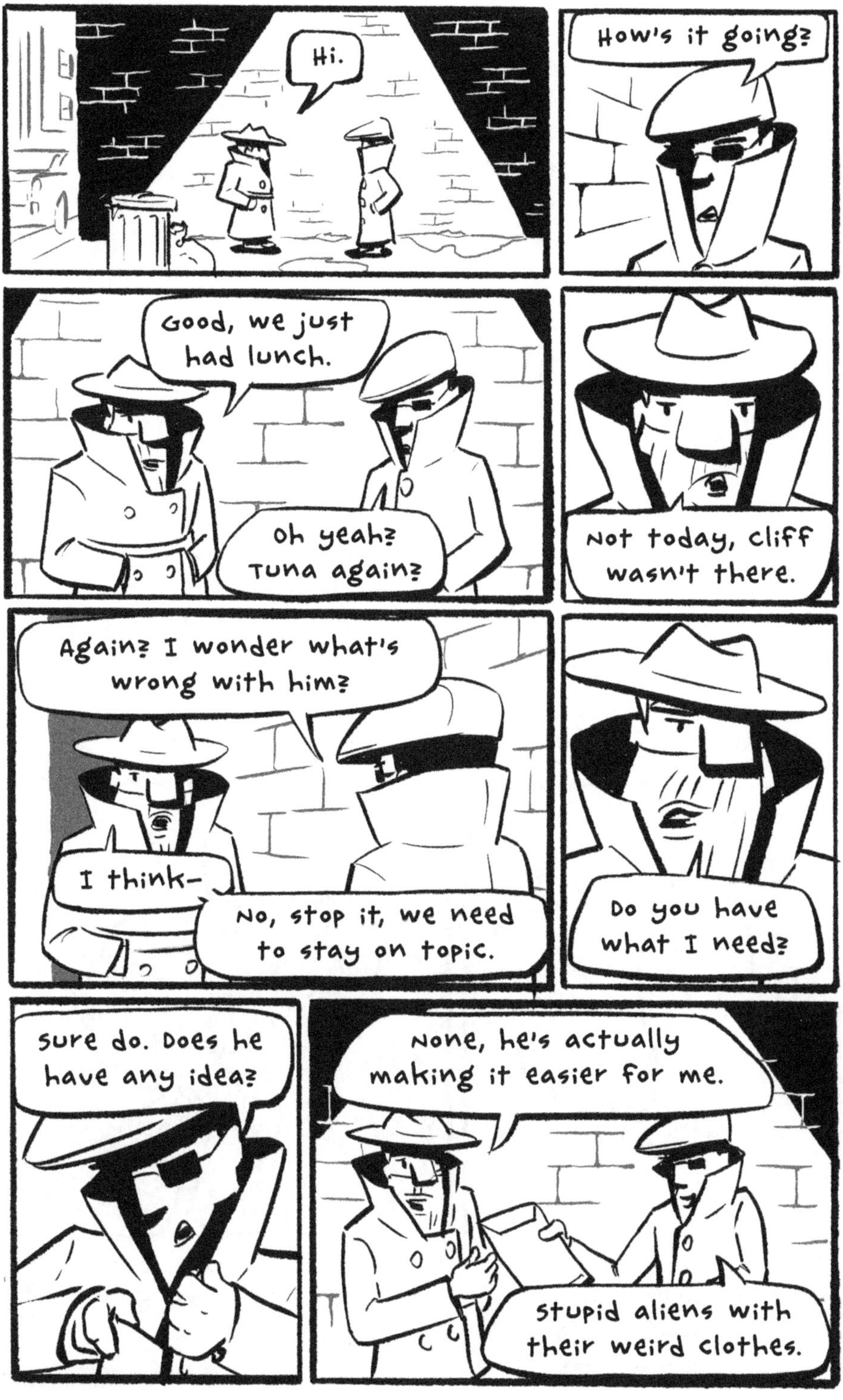

Hi.
How's it going?
Good, we just had lunch.
Oh yeah? Tuna again?
Not today, Cliff wasn't there.
Again? I wonder what's wrong with him?
I think–
No, stop it, we need to stay on topic.
Do you have what I need?
Sure do. Does he have any idea?
None, he's actually making it easier for me.
Stupid aliens with their weird clothes.

Invasion 101, Day 29

Here it is, my new headquarters, Fort iLK version 7.0

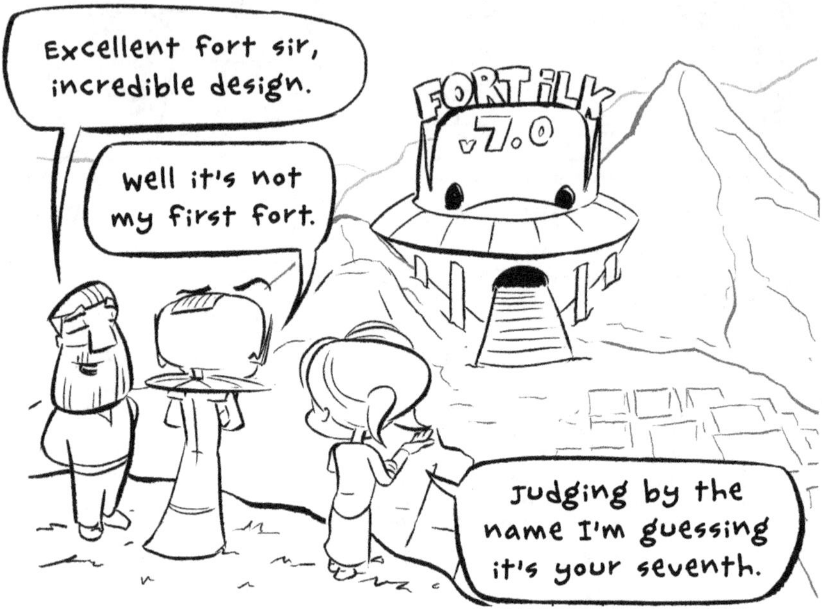
Excellent fort sir, incredible design.
FORT iLK v7.0
Well it's not my first fort.
Judging by the name I'm guessing it's your seventh.

Even Mum was proud when she saw it.

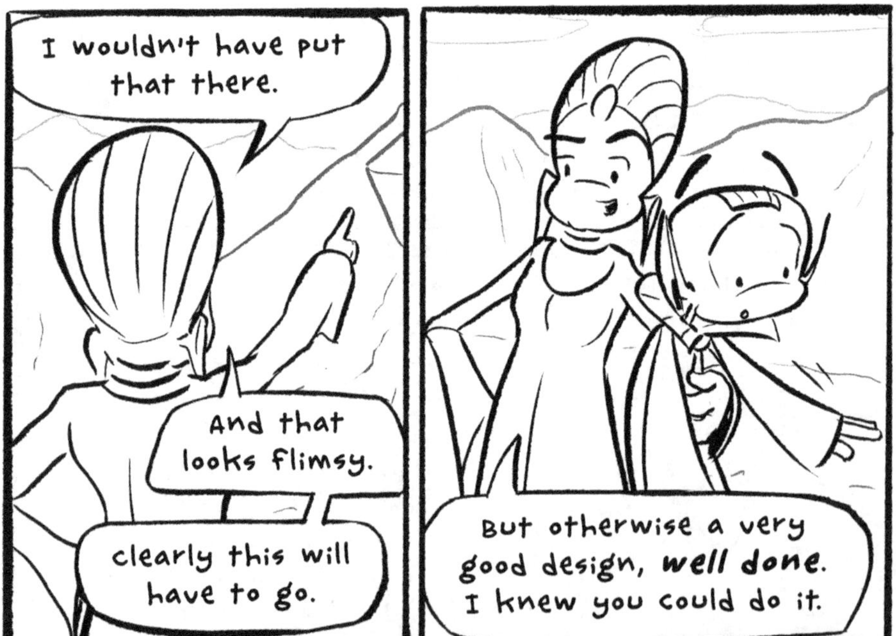
I wouldn't have put that there.
And that looks flimsy.
Clearly this will have to go.
But otherwise a very good design, **well done**. I knew you could do it.

It didn't take long to build, I just came up with the design and then we used our Constructa-laser to print it right here. It probably took just over a day.

Constructa-laser

Can you believe that they wanted to build it by hand? Brick by brick! These humans are so odd.

That would have taken at least a few more days.

I was BORED just trying to IMAGINE what that would be like.

I chose this location thanks to my adviser, Emilio. It's called Machu Picchu and apparently some other Emperor used to live here. Therefore I assumed that it must be of a suitable Emperor-like standard.

Inca Emperor Pachacuti, previous owner?

Having said that it doesn't look like he took very good care of this place because the buildings are all broken.

So, um, this human wasn't very good at building roofs I take it?

Another bonus is that it's close to the largest collection of living plants and animal species on Earth. It's known as the "Amazon Rainforest."

I'll find out when it's open and go visit it one afternoon.

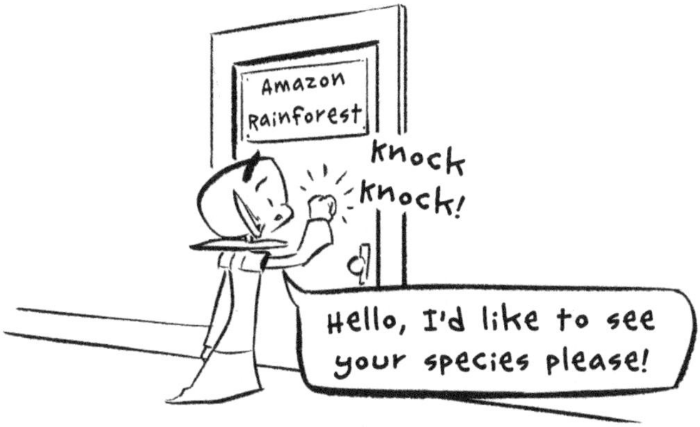
Amazon Rainforest
knock knock!
Hello, I'd like to see your species please!

As well as Emilio, I've also been spending a lot of time with Marina, as this mountain is on her continent, South America.

She's very nice and tries to help where possible.

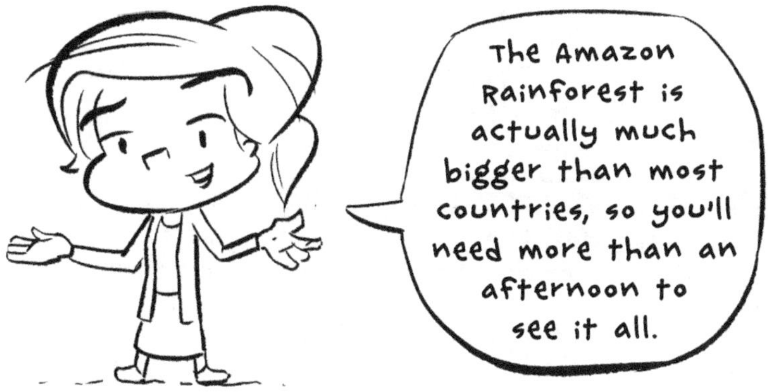
The Amazon Rainforest is actually much bigger than most countries, so you'll need more than an afternoon to see it all.

She may know a lot for a human, but she still has much to learn about how much smarter we are than them.

Invasion 101, Day 31

I'm feeling very settled already in my new base. I've managed to make it feel as luxurious as possible. Inside it's been designed perfectly with low ceilings and small windows, just like on the ship.

Plus, now I have somewhere to put all my plants!

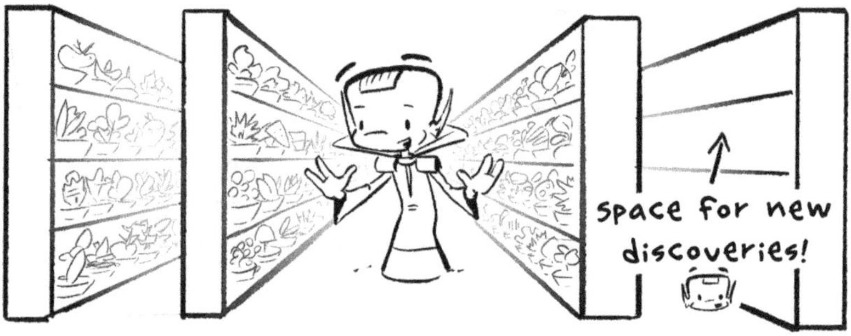
space for new discoveries!

The one downside is people keep coming to me with all these questions, asking me to do things...

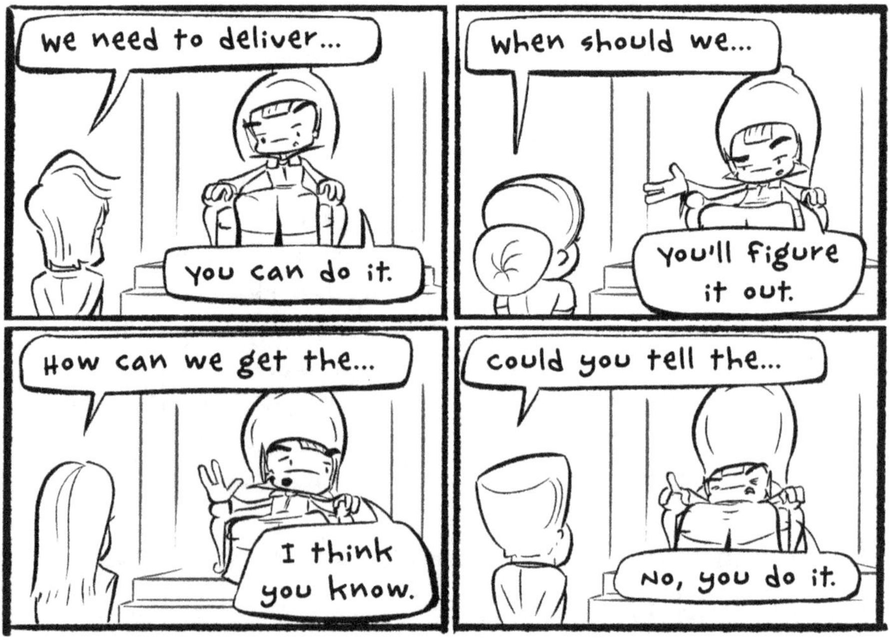
we need to deliver...
you can do it.
when should we...
you'll figure it out.
How can we get the...
I think you know.
could you tell the...
No, you do it.

While my initial management style seemed effective, I couldn't shake the feeling that it wasn't as efficient as it could be. So I developed a new method.

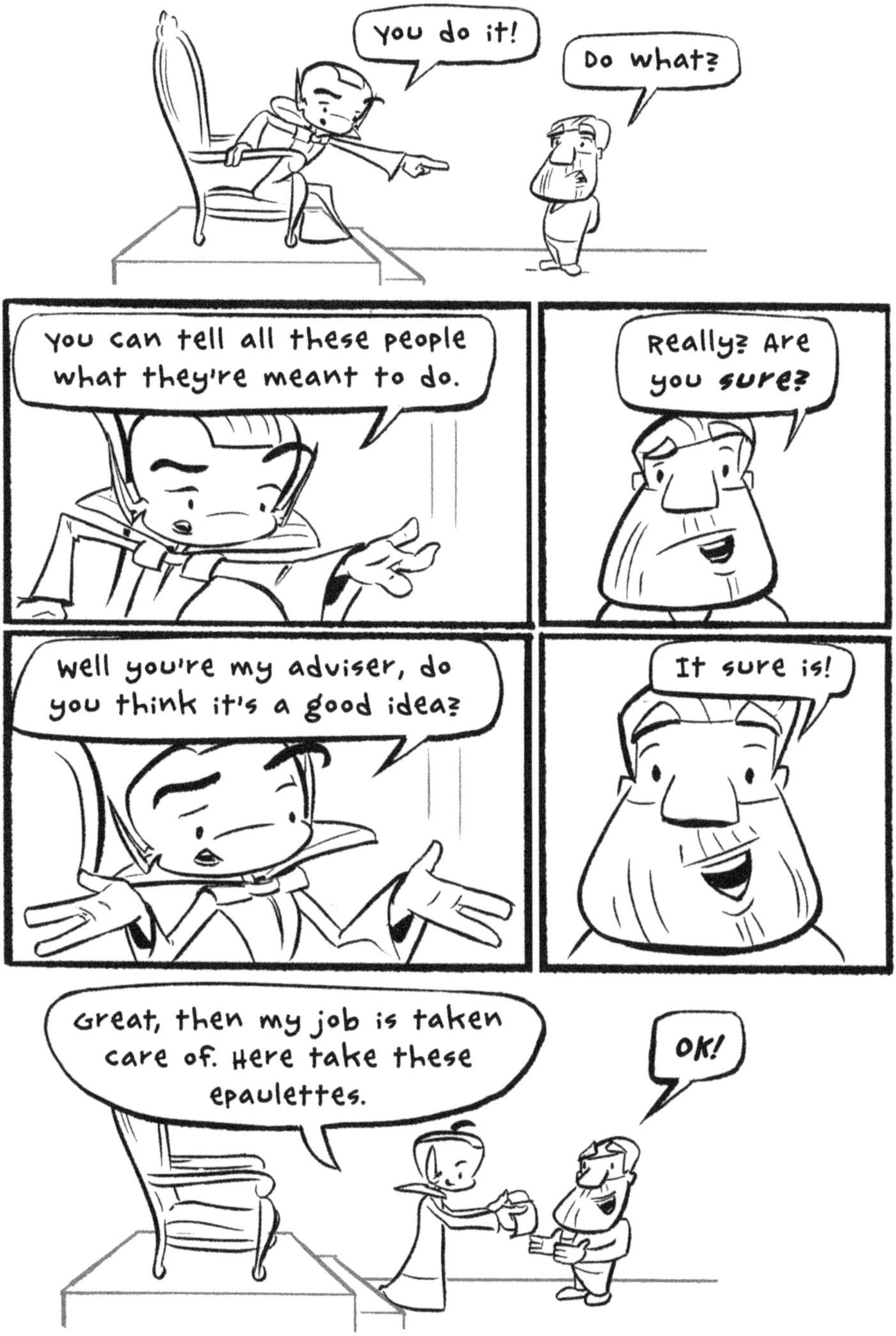
You do it!
Do what?
You can tell all these people what they're meant to do.
Really? Are you *sure*?
Well you're my adviser, do you think it's a good idea?
It sure is!
Great, then my job is taken care of. Here take these epaulettes.
OK!

Now that I've solved that problem what am I to do with all this free time?

Maybe I'll start a new hobby or do a spot of tourism. I've heard the Sahara Desert is really big and hot this time of year, maybe I'll go check that out.

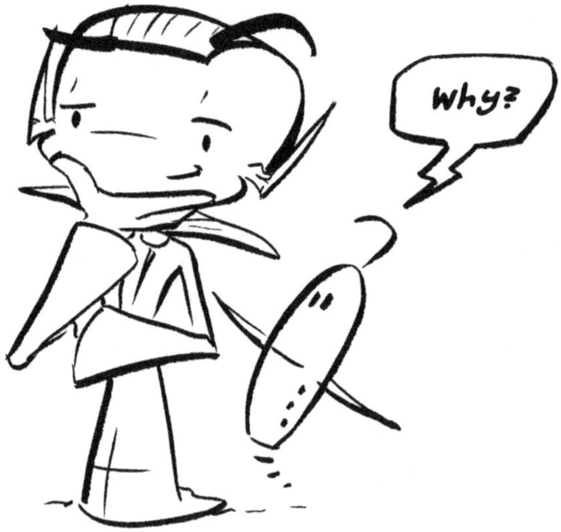
Why?

Invasion 101, Day 34

I was just starting to wrap Brickly in toilet paper when Marina entered.

Uh...
Um...
you have been in here a few days, I just came to check that you were ok...

I thought it was pretty clear that I was mid-experiment and needed to focus. I didn't have time for chit-chat. Yet still she insisted on asking questions.

"What's all that stuff on the floor?"

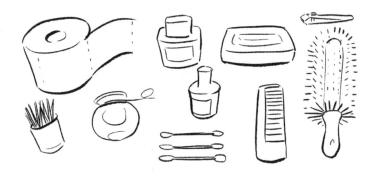

"I'm doing research," I told her.

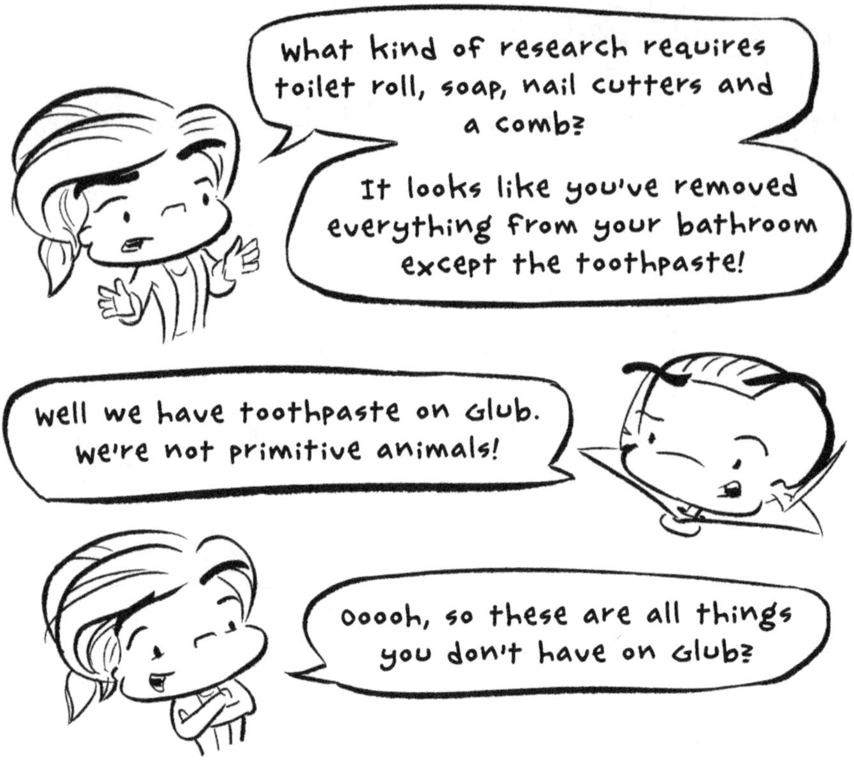
What kind of research requires toilet roll, soap, nail cutters and a comb?
It looks like you've removed everything from your bathroom except the toothpaste!
Well we have toothpaste on Glub. We're not primitive animals!
Ooooh, so these are all things you don't have on Glub?

Finally she'd figured it out, which I assumed meant she could now leave. However, much like Y-bot, it appears Marina likes asking questions.

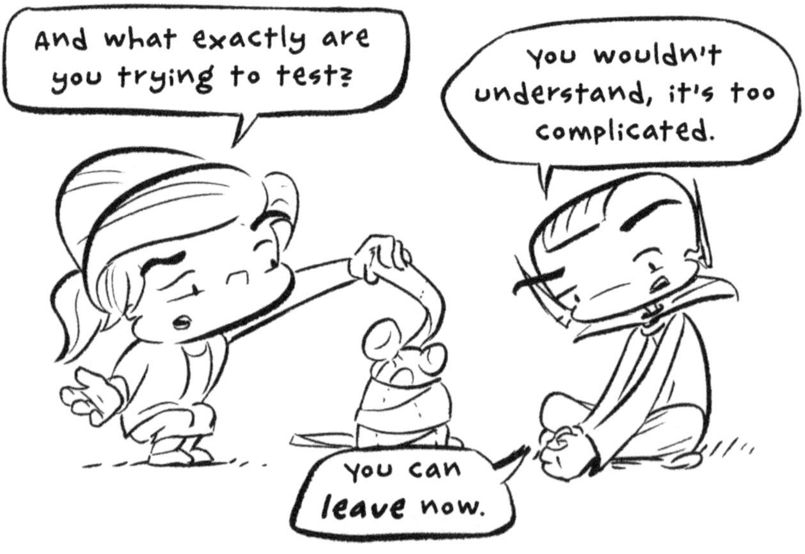
And what exactly are you trying to test?
You wouldn't understand, it's too complicated.
You can leave now.

No, **please** tell me, I'm interested. This is the most active I've seen you since you got here.

I explained to her how Brickly had started glowing when I brought him down to Earth and so I was testing him against various objects you couldn't find on the spaceship or on Glub to see what was making it glow.

It had recently stopped glowing entirely, so the main objective of this test was to make it glow again. Partly because it looked cool, but also when it glowed it functioned as a handy night-light.

This seemed to make her very excited.

oh my god, **really?!** Then maybe you can help us?

She showed me a photo of this large seed like plant. I couldn't remember what it was called, but I was sure I'd seen it before somewhere.

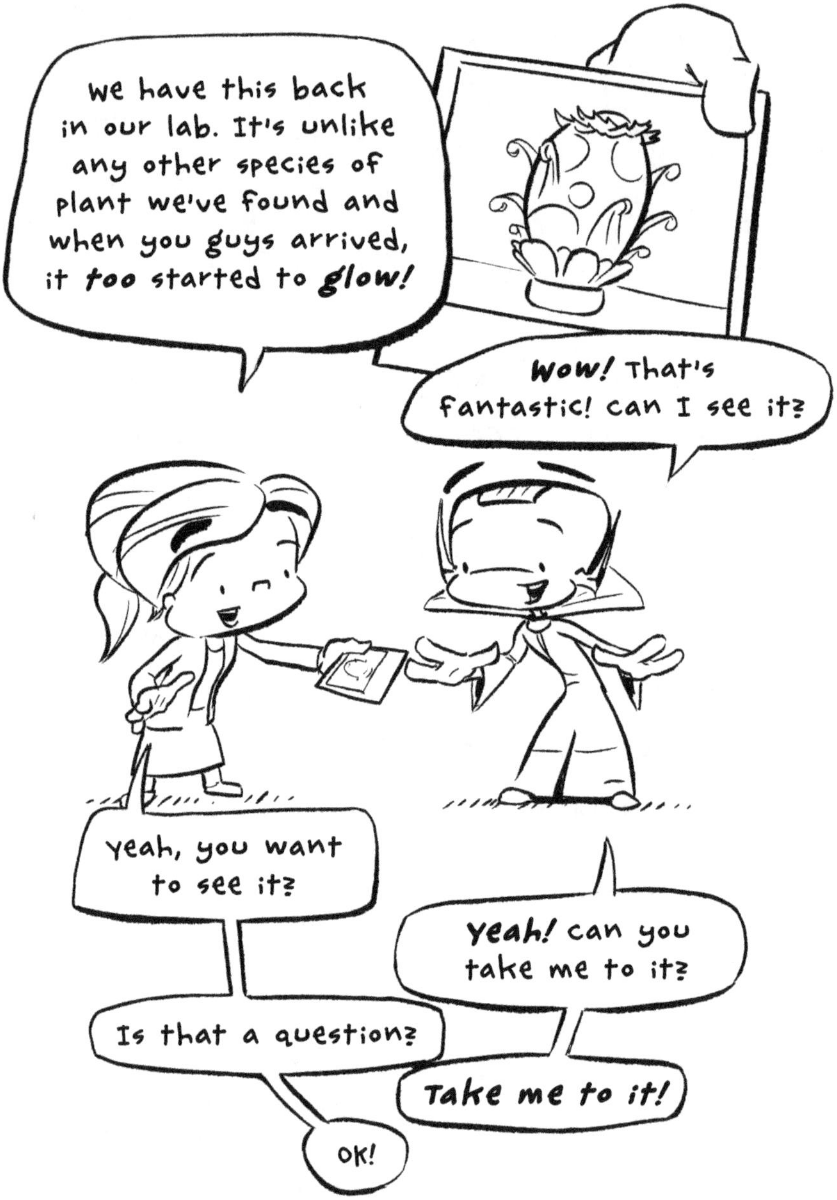
we have this back in our lab. It's unlike any other species of plant we've found and when you guys arrived, it *too* started to *glow!*
Wow! That's fantastic! can I see it?
Yeah, you want to see it?
Yeah! can you take me to it?
Is that a question?
Take me to it!
OK!

I'm getting really good at giving people orders. I was made for this job.

Invasion 101, Day 36

Humans... It's possible I may have underestimated them.

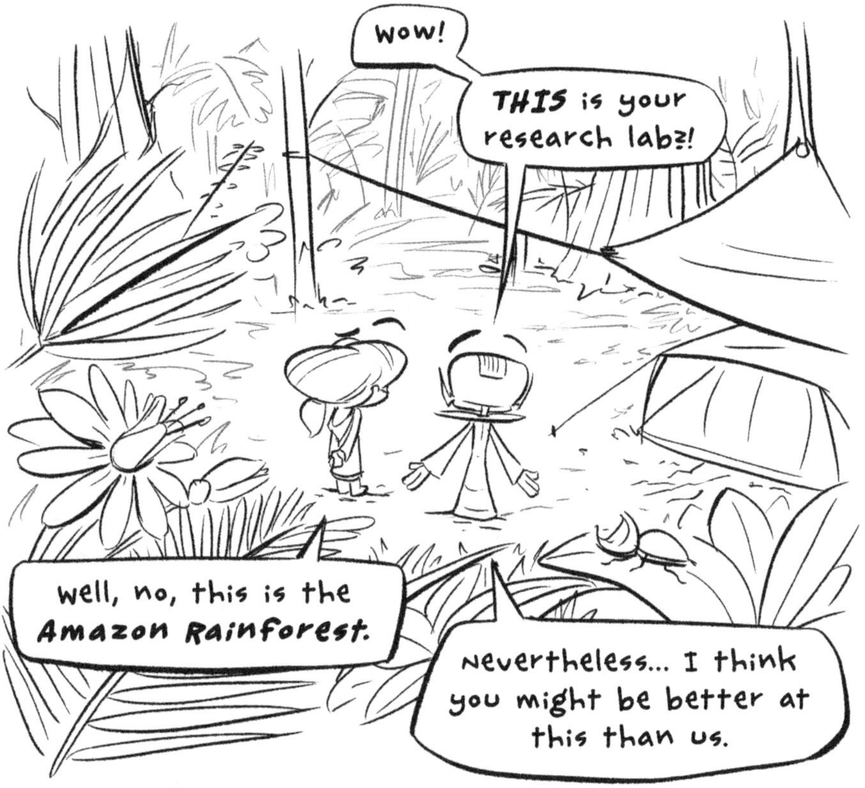

WOW!
THIS is your research lab?!
Well, no, this is the Amazon Rainforest.
Nevertheless... I think you might be better at this than us.

I had never seen anything so impressive. Apparently 10% of the all of the world's species live there. It's quite the collection.

How did they manage to get all those plants and animals in one place?

Marina took me to the laboratory where they look after some of the rarer species to see this odd, glowing plant they had found.

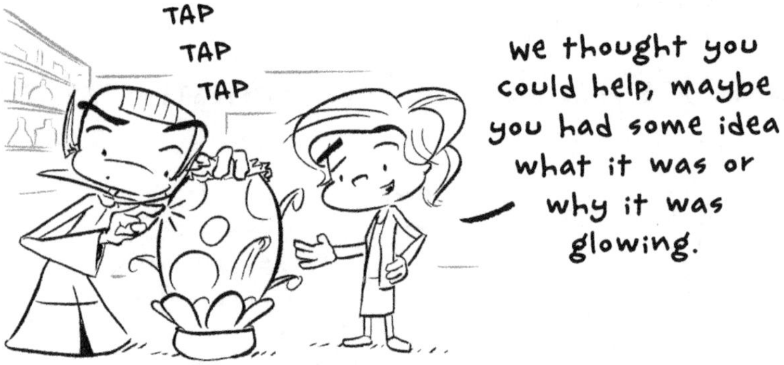
TAP
TAP
TAP
we thought you could help, maybe you had some idea what it was or why it was glowing.

I didn't know how to say that the only idea I had was to try tapping it.

Nothing happened... I was out of ideas.

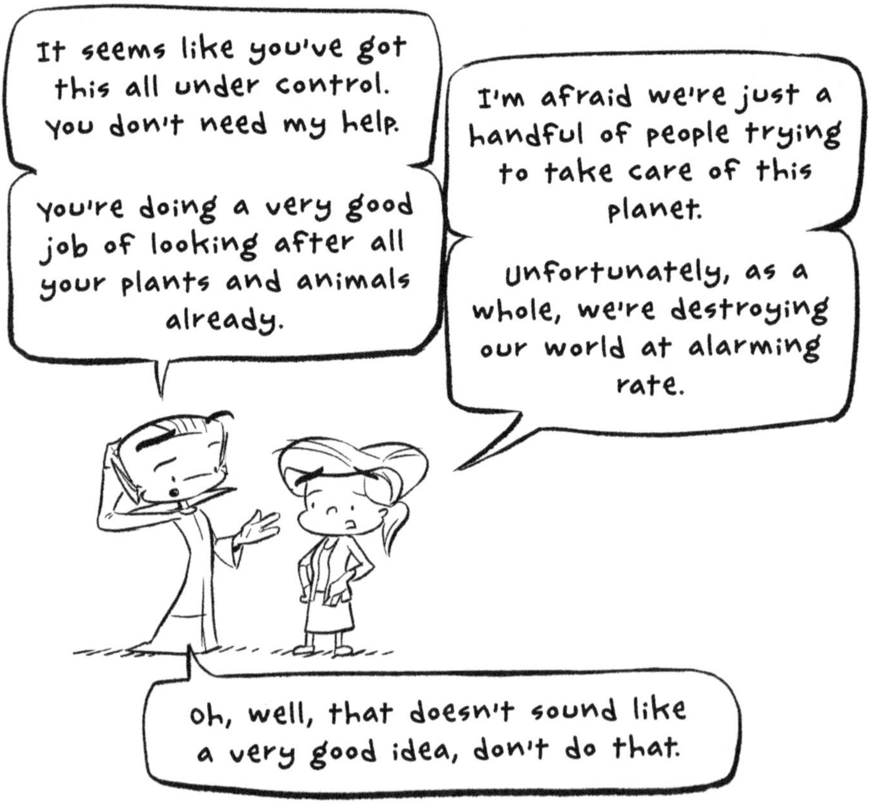
It seems like you've got this all under control. You don't need my help.
You're doing a very good job of looking after all your plants and animals already.
I'm afraid we're just a handful of people trying to take care of this planet.
Unfortunately, as a whole, we're destroying our world at alarming rate.
Oh, well, that doesn't sound like a very good idea, don't do that.

I felt proud to share my wisdom.

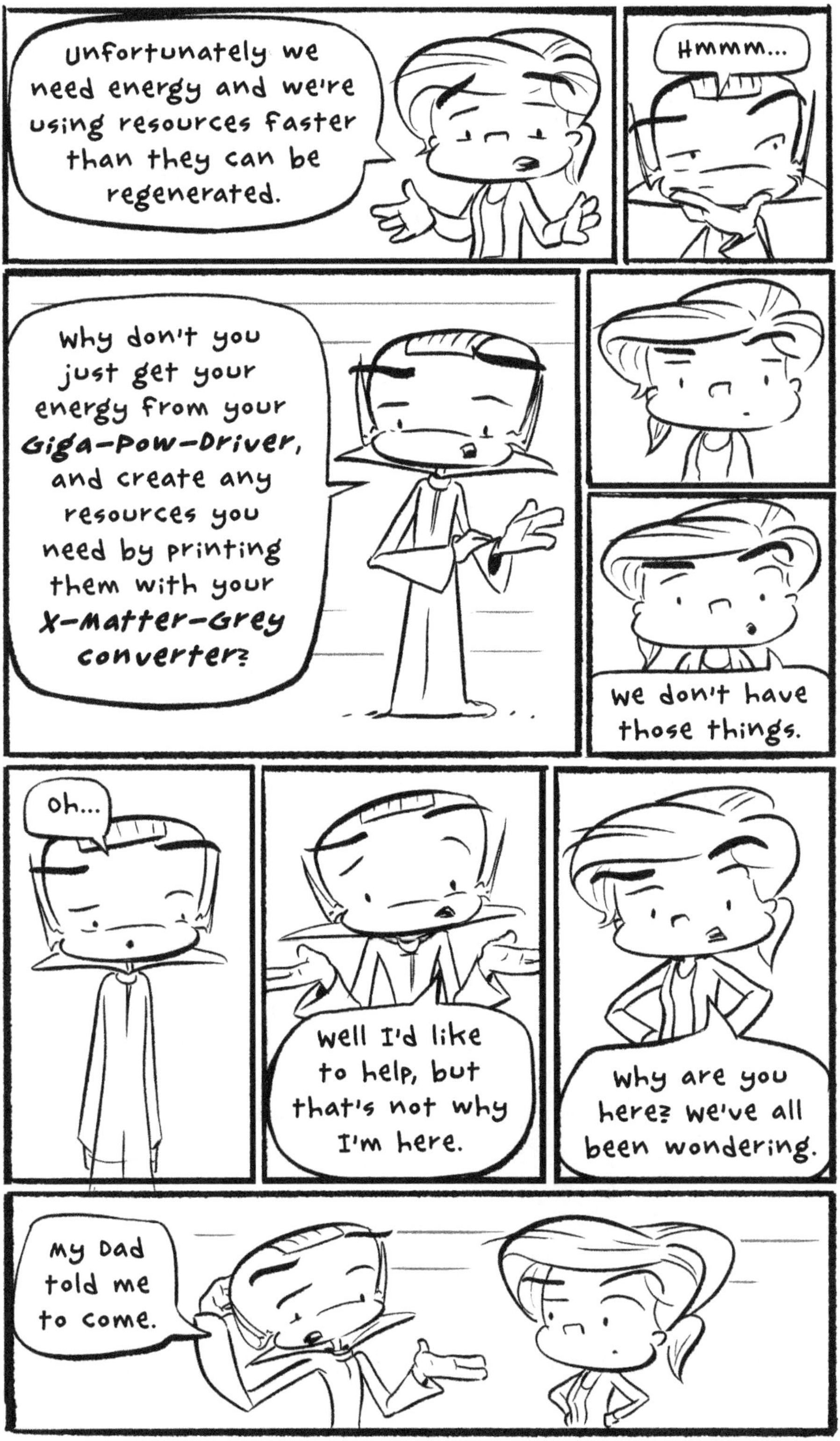
Unfortunately we need energy and we're using resources faster than they can be regenerated.
Hmmm...
Why don't you just get your energy from your **Giga-Pow-Driver**, and create any resources you need by printing them with your **X-Matter-Grey converter**?
We don't have those things.
Oh...
Well I'd like to help, but that's not why I'm here.
Why are you here? We've all been wondering.
My Dad told me to come.

Invasion 101, Day 40

Something has been on my mind recently. How do you fire your own mother? Or at least give her a different job so she's less... nearby, all the time.

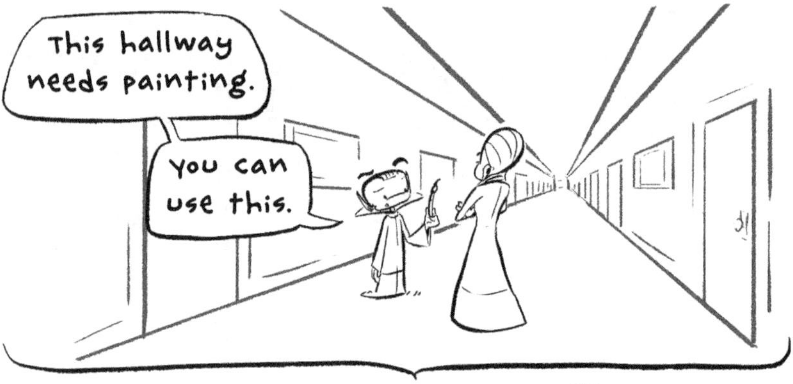
This hallway needs painting.
You can use this.

This wouldn't work.

I need to think of something for her to do because I can't have her hanging around me all the time. She's making everything worse.

Although I'm not sure how exactly.

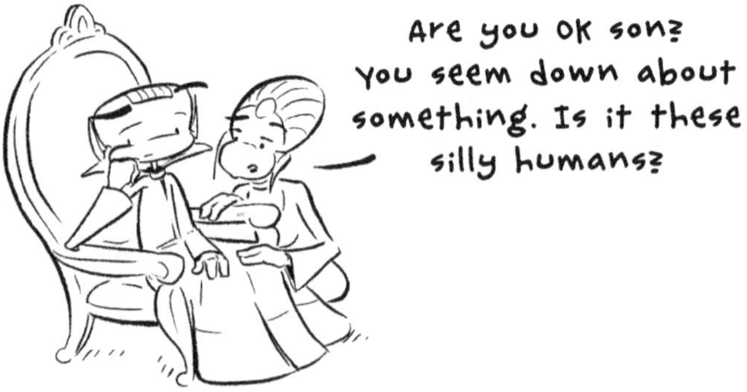
Are you OK son? You seem down about something. Is it these silly humans?

The truth is though, I've actually been enjoying myself recently.

I have been visiting the Amazon a lot and have seen some really dangerous things.

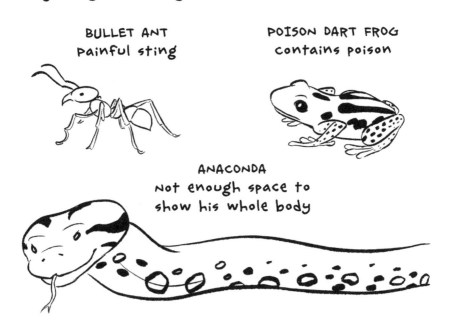

BULLET ANT
painful sting

POISON DART FROG
contains poison

ANACONDA
Not enough space to
show his whole body

The Amazon is great!

I've also met some nice people at the research centre that like teaching me things.

Some teach me about plants...

The corpse flower is the biggest flower in the world and it smells really bad.

Others have taught me about humans...

All humans will find ways to get along with others, but they'll also try to get ahead of them.

While some just like telling me about their lunch...

The filling has to be thicker than one of the slices of bread.

I've become very fond of sandwiches and have found their construction to be a fine art.

So when Mum tried to help me in her usual way, I found that, well, it didn't help at all.

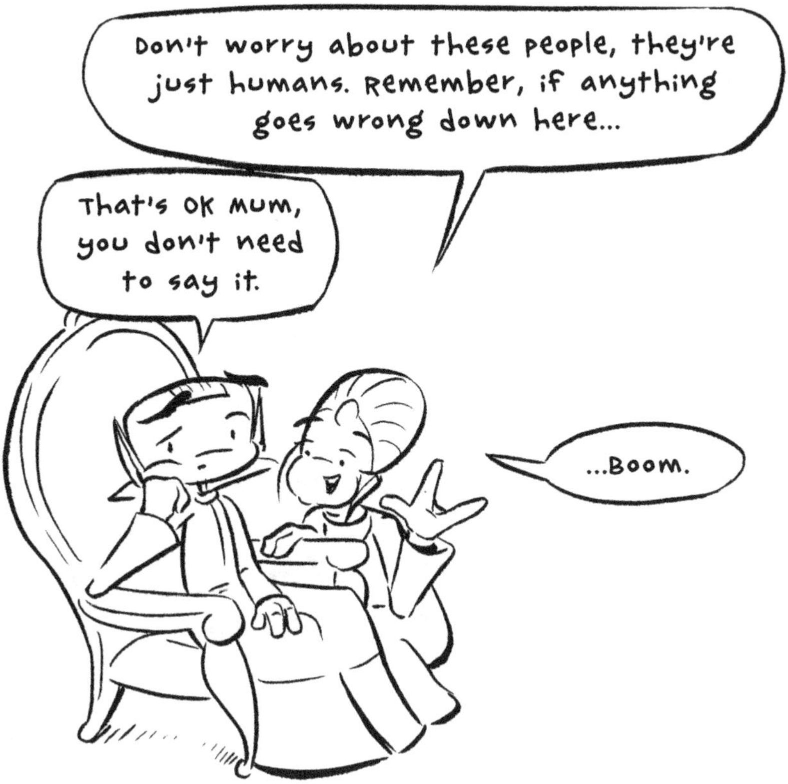
Don't worry about these people, they're just humans. Remember, if anything goes wrong down here...
That's OK Mum, you don't need to say it.
...Boom.

That wasn't what I wanted to hear.

Hmm, maybe I do want this planet to survive.

No it's not that.

I just don't like the idea of it NOT surviving.

Invasion 101, Day 42

I assume they composed this to be some kind of test.

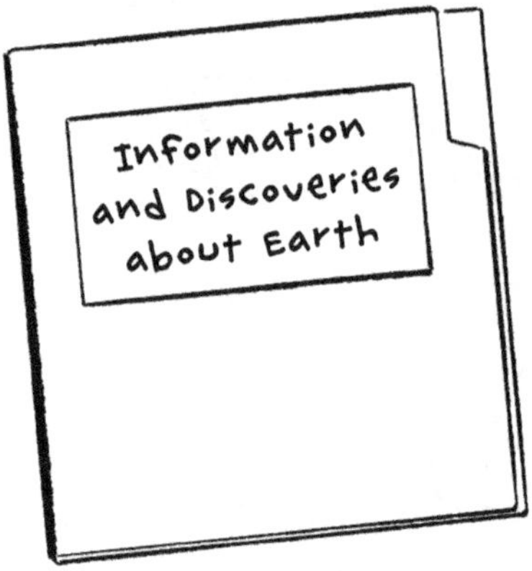
Information
and Discoveries
about Earth

There was no way I could fit all of the information and discoveries I'd collected on Earth into this one tiny folder.

Looking at what I'd gathered to take to my meeting with Dad it was very clear that I'd need another solution.

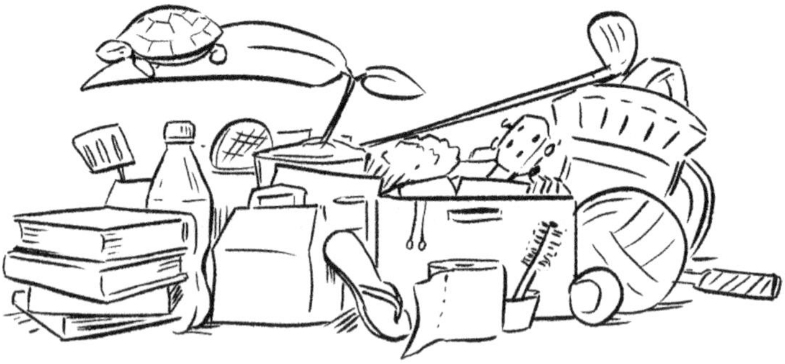

A flimsy paper folder would definitely not suffice.

I can't wait to see their faces when I drag all this up there. They're going to be so impressed!

Take this for example!

You're either meant to sit on it, stroke it or use it as some kind of instrument. The truth is I'm not sure what you're meant to do with it, but it looks so cool!

And wait until they find out what this is for!

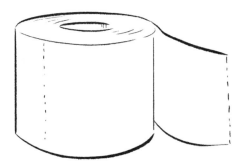

The whole council will be on the floor with laughter when I tell them.

Humans have also shown evidence that, while primitive, they do have the potential to be, well, less stupid, sometimes.

When they showed me the following example, I couldn't help but think, "Wow you guys are slow, but at least you're making some progress."

solar panel

They've just started producing energy from the Sun using these solar panels, which means they are way behind, but at least they're making some cool stuff in the meantime, like that wooden stool/instrument thing!

I think, with my help, Earth could actually become quite good.

Maybe even better than good. By combining some of their less useless ideas with everything I know about the Universe, Earth could even be incredible. It definitely has the potential!

BEST WORLD IN THE UNIVERSE

AWARDED TO
EARTH, 4024

And I would be it's champion!

Just imagine it, all of the humans would love me for all of the success I'd brought them.

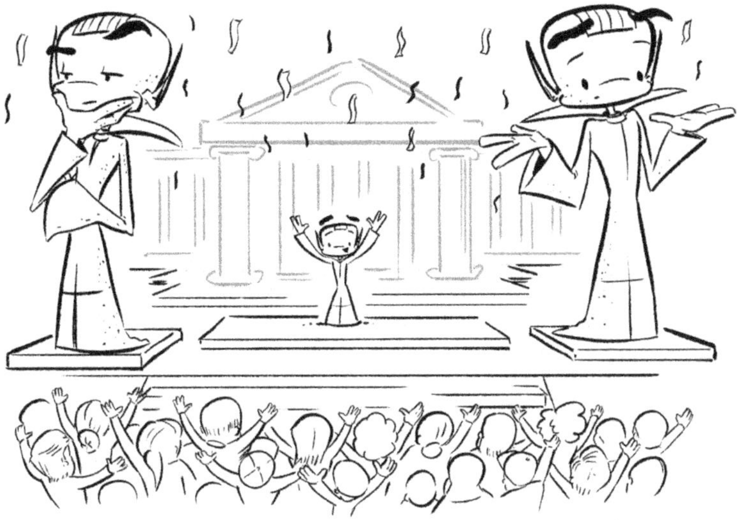

From there it would be just one short step to Earth becoming the Central Hub for the whole Universe Community.

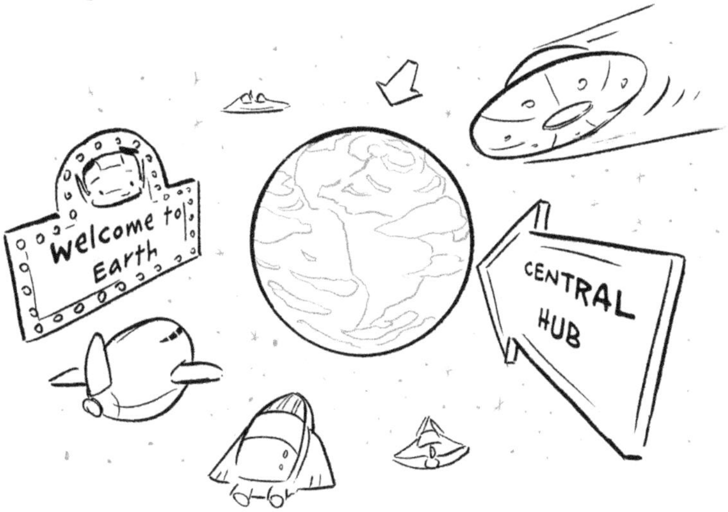
Welcome to Earth
CENTRAL HUB

...And I would be at the centre of it all! The centre of the Universe!! I hope my head doesn't get too big.

Maybe this is what Dad wanted me to figure out all along? I just had to discover all of these things and decide for myself what to do with Earth.

If this was a test, I will have exceeded all expectations. Especially when they see my folder of discoveries!

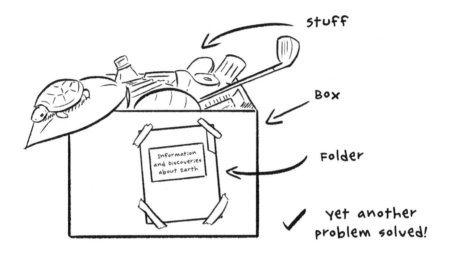

stuff
Box
Information and Discoveries about Earth
Folder
yet another problem solved!

I did have to leave a few things behind because they wouldn't fit. Only one of them complained about it.

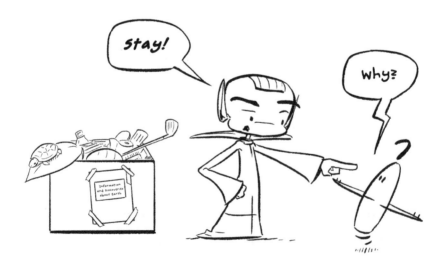

Stay!
Why?

Invasion 101, Day 44

With a little help I was able to drag my box of discoveries to the transport. Then, once on the ship, I carried it all the way to the council hall.

I only stopped 27 times to rest.

I arrived sweating, but at least finally I could stand in front of my Dad, proud of what I had achieved.

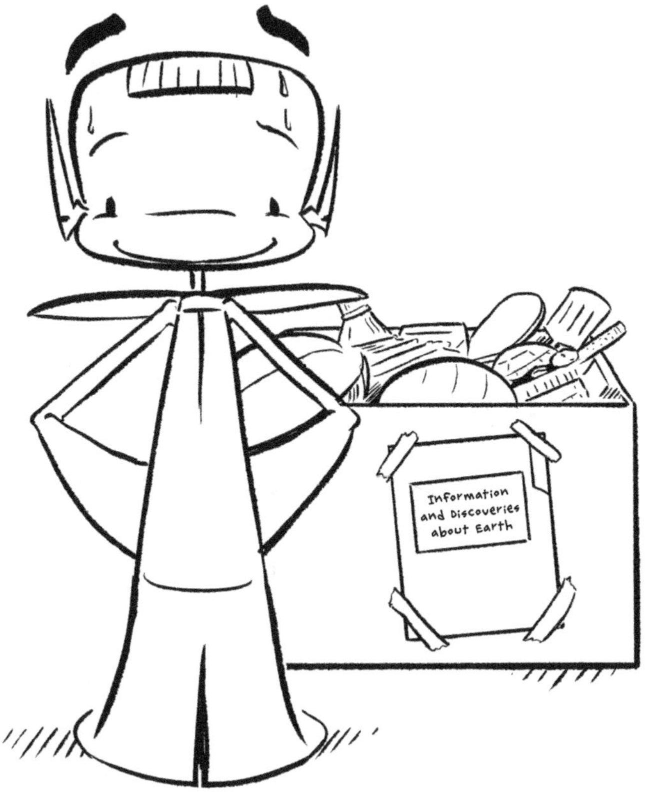
Information and Discoveries about Earth

I stood like that for a while.

I wasn't sure who was meant to speak first.

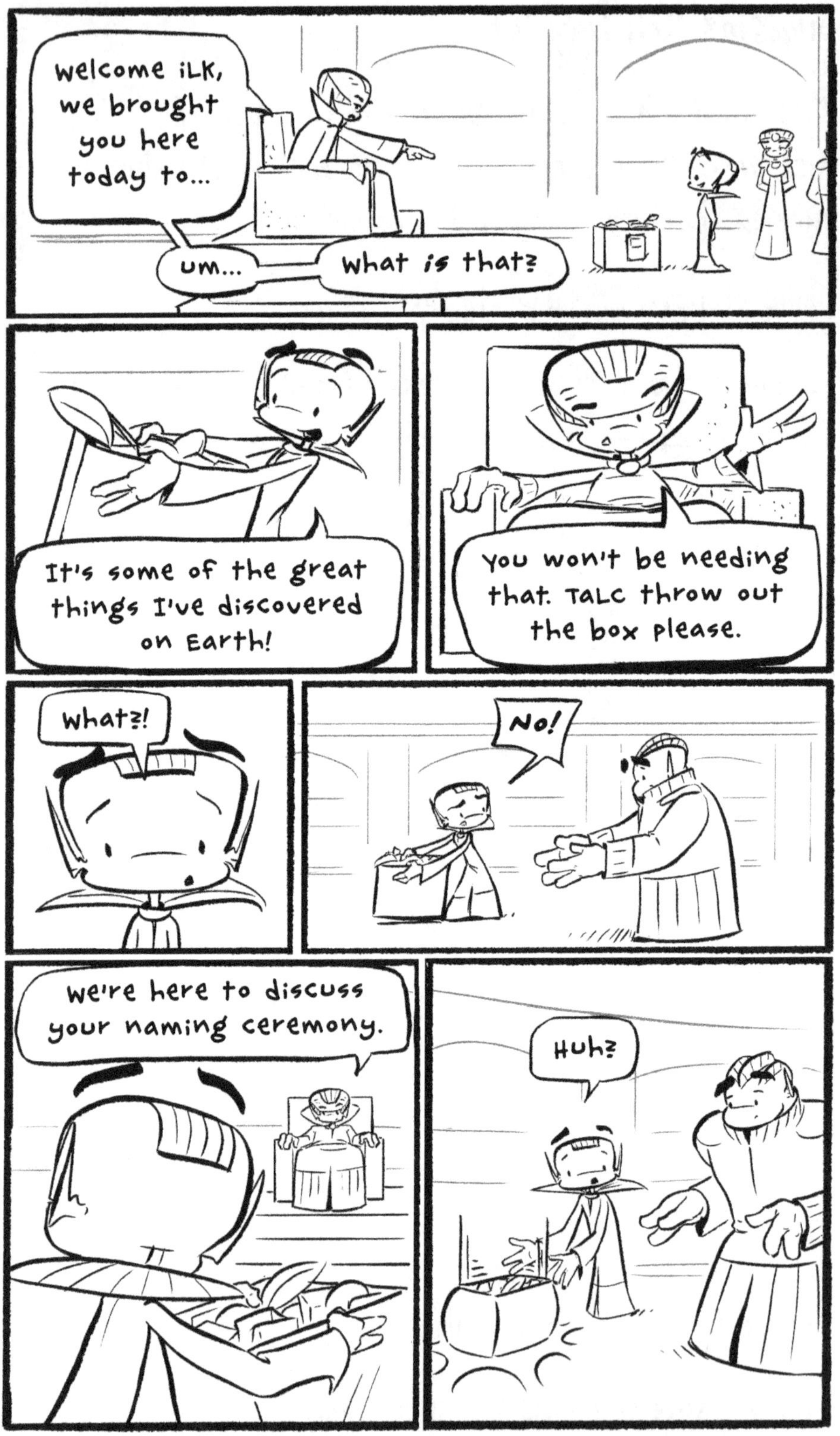
welcome iLK, we brought you here today to...
um...
what is that?
It's some of the great things I've discovered on Earth!
You won't be needing that. TALC throw out the box please.
What?!
No!
we're here to discuss your naming ceremony.
Huh?

It should be years until my naming ceremony!

If they'd decided to bring it forward I'd be given free roam of the ENTIRE SHIP and NO ONE could tell me what to do.

Then again, Dad tells TalC what to do all the time and he has his first letter.

I guess that's because TalC ALLOWS Dad to tell him what to do. I wonder what would happen if he didn't.

The strange thing is, at that moment in front of my Dad, I didn't really think about all that. The fact he mentioned my naming ceremony was a surprise, but all I could think of was what was in my box.

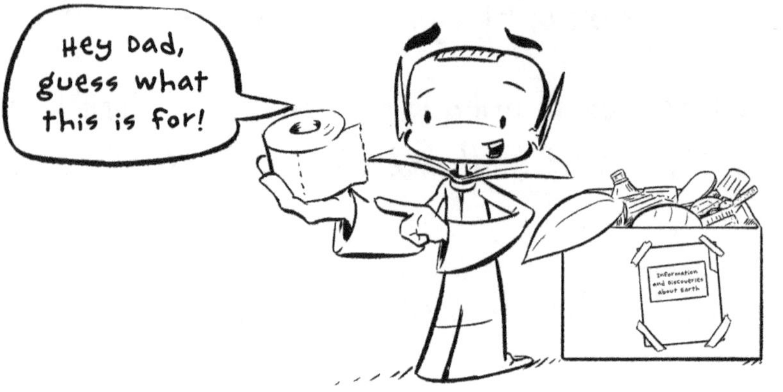
Hey Dad, guess what this is for!
Information and Discoveries about Earth

He didn't care. "Put that down, I know where it's been," he replied.

Apparently our purpose here isn't to serve Earth. We're not meant to be looking after it or caring about it. Our role is to serve The Universe Community. We have a job to do.

"But what about this! You're meant to hit it or sit on it or something!" I said.

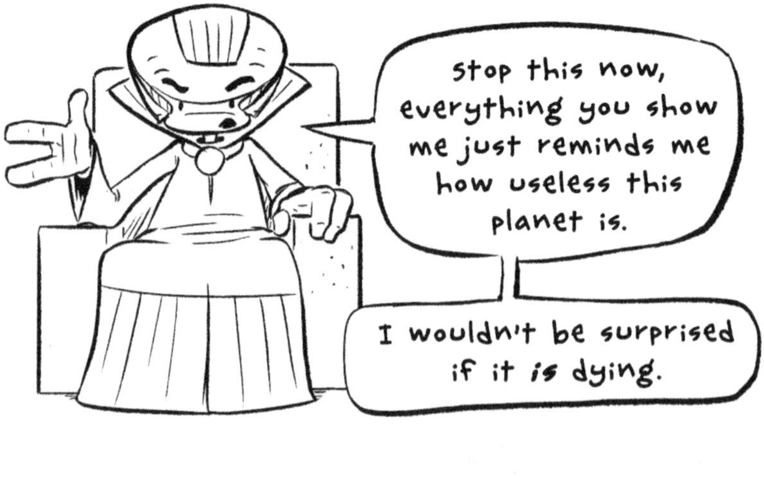
Stop this now, everything you show me just reminds me how useless this planet is.
I wouldn't be surprised if it *is* dying.

Dad then explained what we're REALLY doing here.

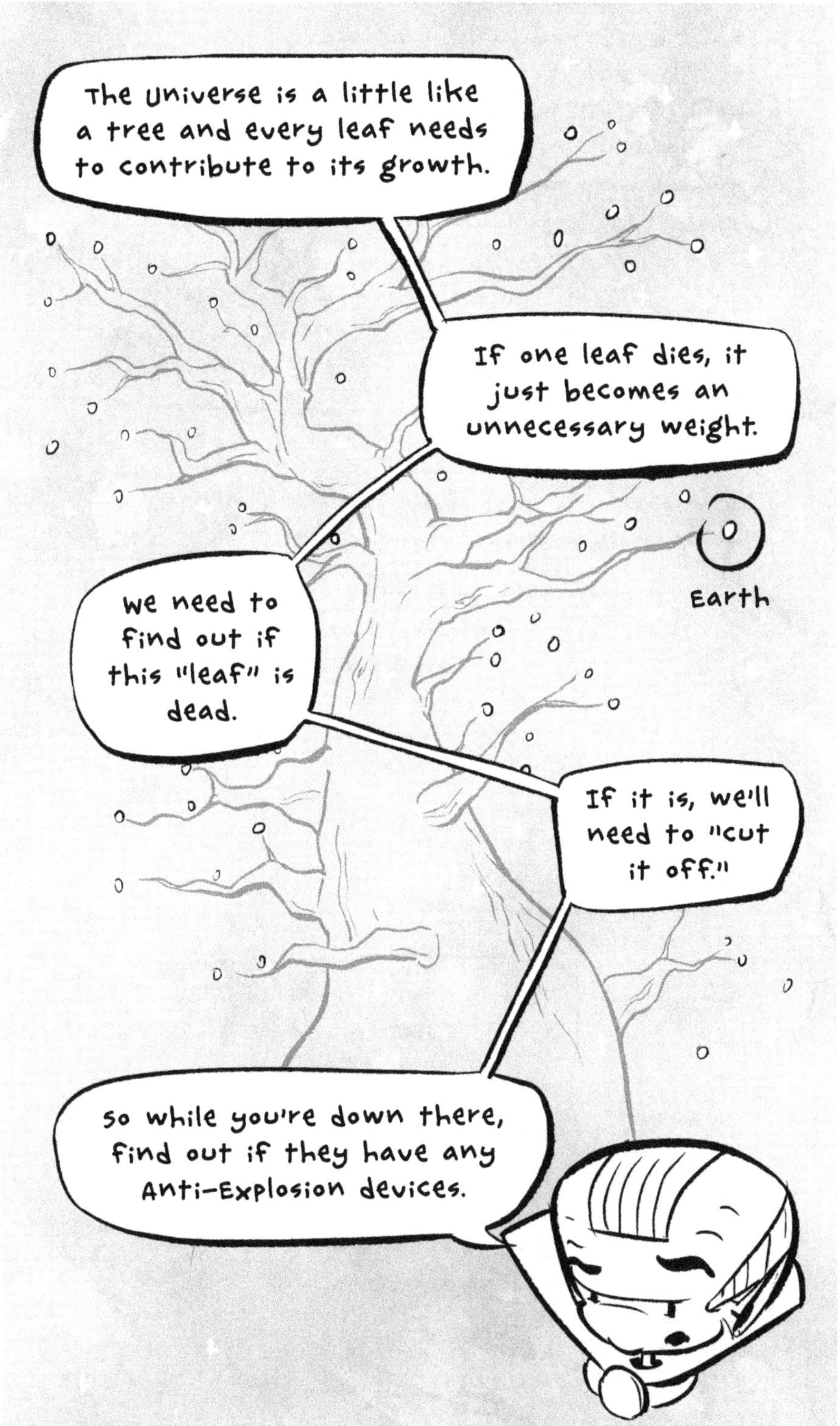

The Universe is a little like a tree and every leaf needs to contribute to its growth.
If one leaf dies, it just becomes an unnecessary weight.
Earth
We need to find out if this "leaf" is dead.
If it is, we'll need to "cut it off."
So while you're down there, find out if they have any Anti-Explosion devices.

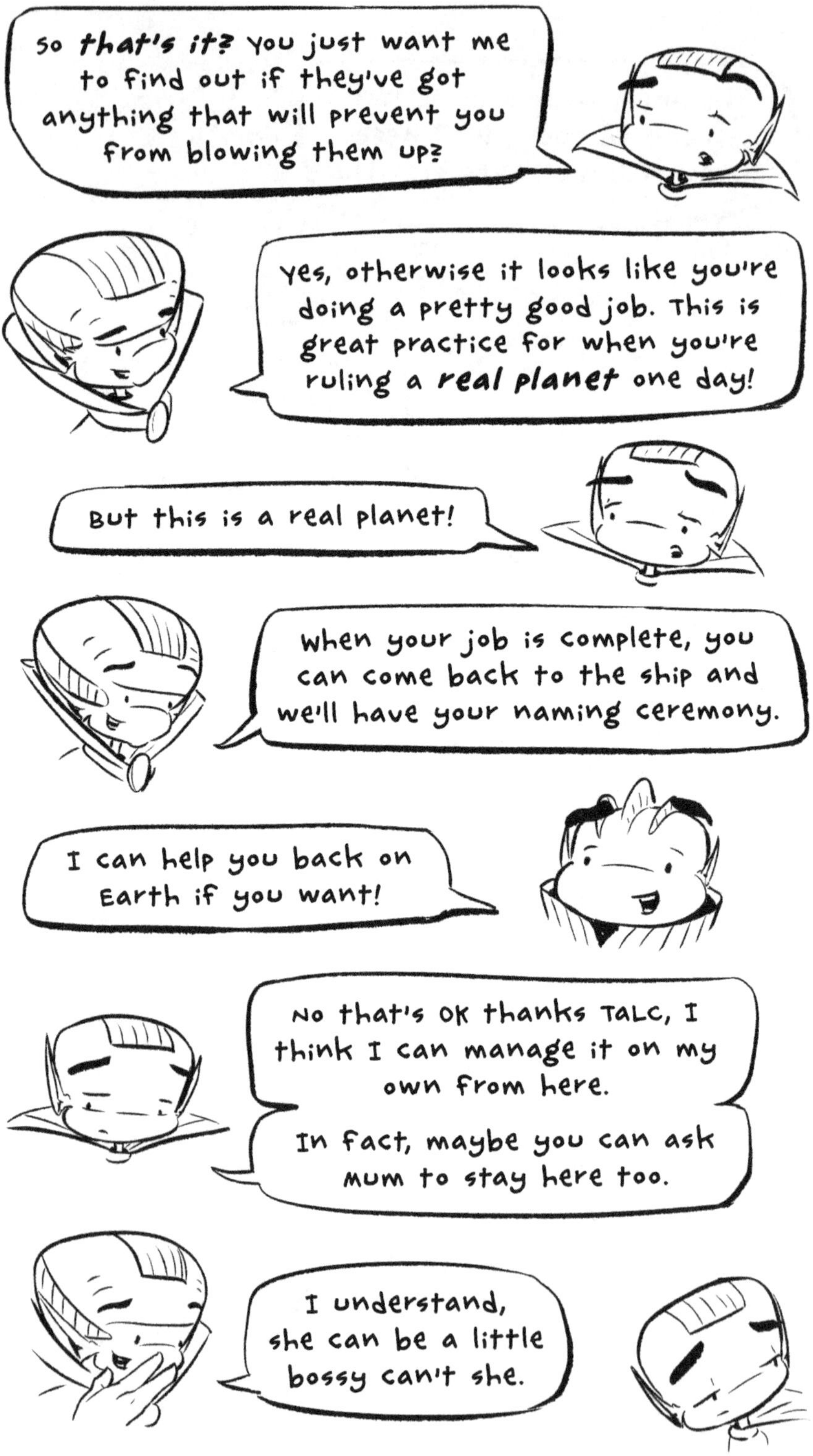
So that's it? You just want me to find out if they've got anything that will prevent you from blowing them up?
Yes, otherwise it looks like you're doing a pretty good job. This is great practice for when you're ruling a real planet one day!
But this is a real planet!
When your job is complete, you can come back to the ship and we'll have your naming ceremony.
I can help you back on Earth if you want!
No that's OK thanks TALC, I think I can manage it on my own from here.
In fact, maybe you can ask Mum to stay here too.
I understand, she can be a little bossy can't she.

Invasion 101, Day 45

While I was back on the ship, I went to visit my room to see if anything had changed.

It HAD changed! A LOT! It was CLEAN and it was TIDY!

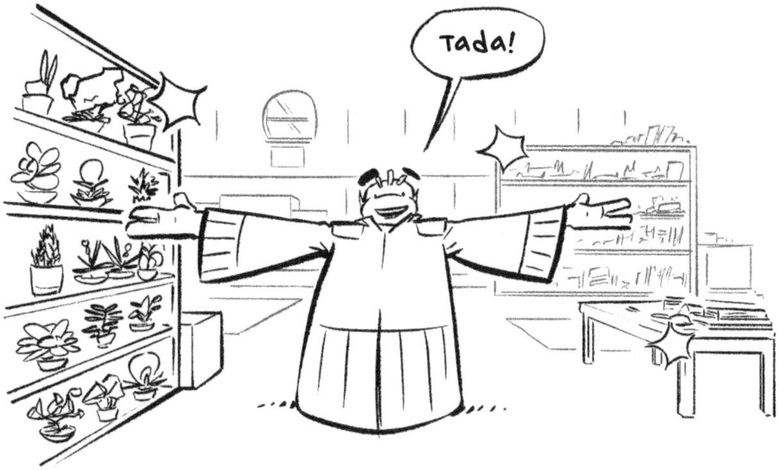
Tada!

Apparently TaLC has been looking after it for me while I was away.

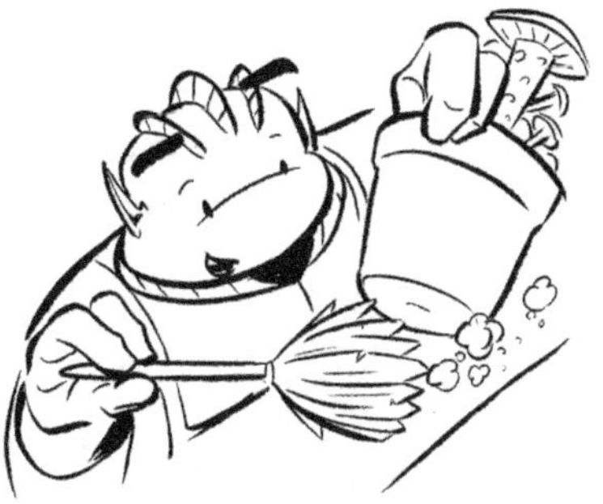

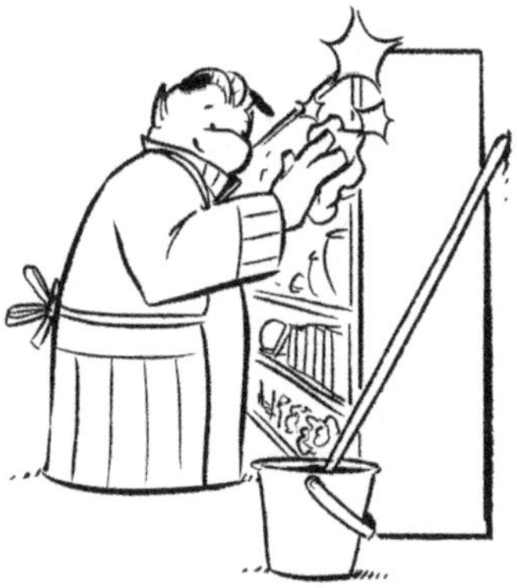

He had even pinned a photo of me on the wall opposite the plants so they didn't feel like I had abandoned them.

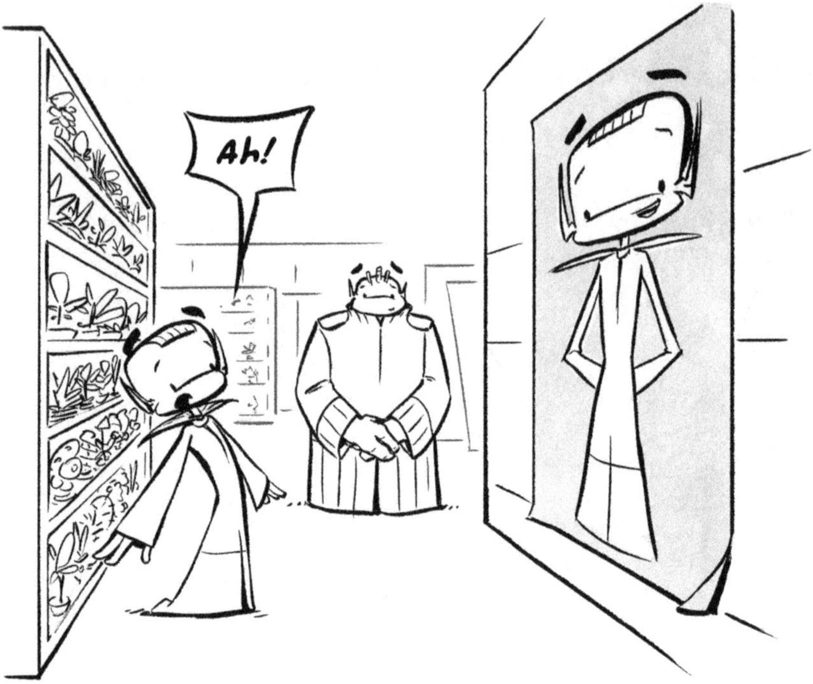
Ah!

It was a nice thought, albeit a little scary to be confronted with such a large image of myself.

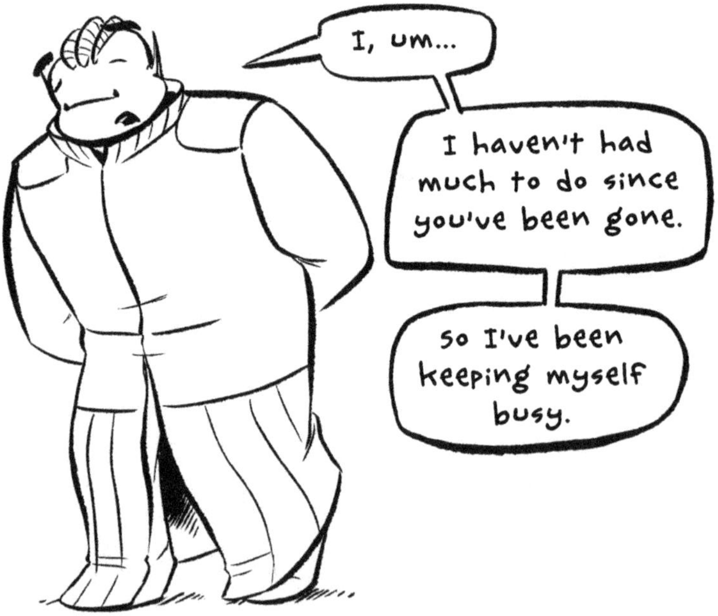
I, um...
I haven't had much to do since you've been gone.
So I've been keeping myself busy.

He lead me over to a table to show me a little collection he had put together.

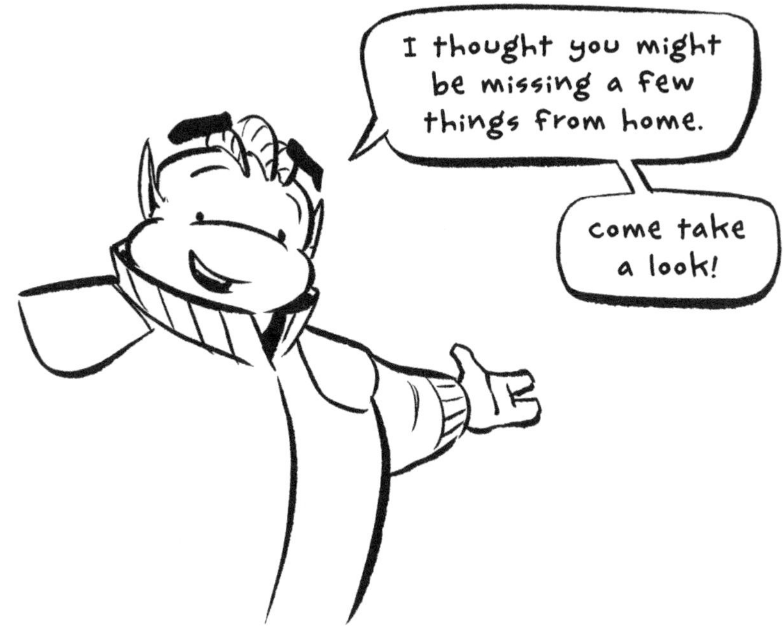
I thought you might be missing a few things from home.
come take a look!

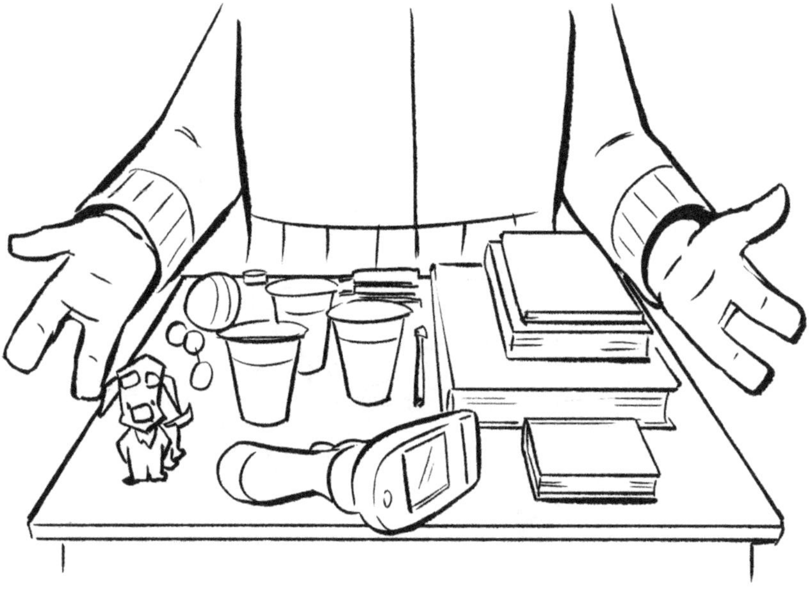

He went through them one by one.

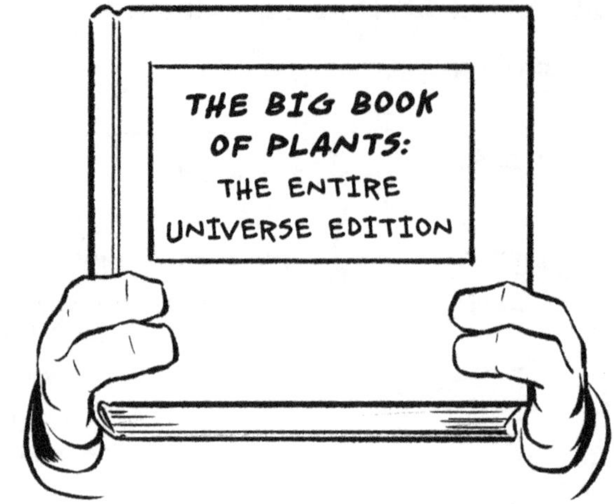
THE BIG BOOK
OF PLANTS:
THE ENTIRE
UNIVERSE EDITION

"You used to love reading this book at night."

It's true, that book was a classic. It's incredible how much they were able to fit in it. The writing was tiny and the pages were thin like the wings of a fly.

He had also collected a variety of insta-pot meals for me.

My favourite was "Wretch Skin Flavour."

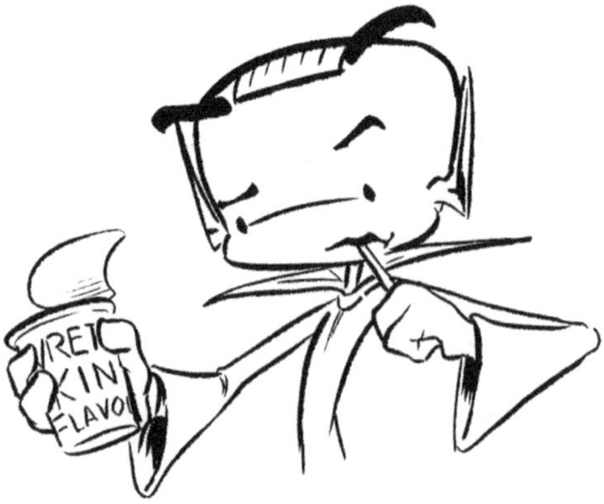

Unfortunately, this time when I tried it, all I could think was how much I wanted a sandwich.

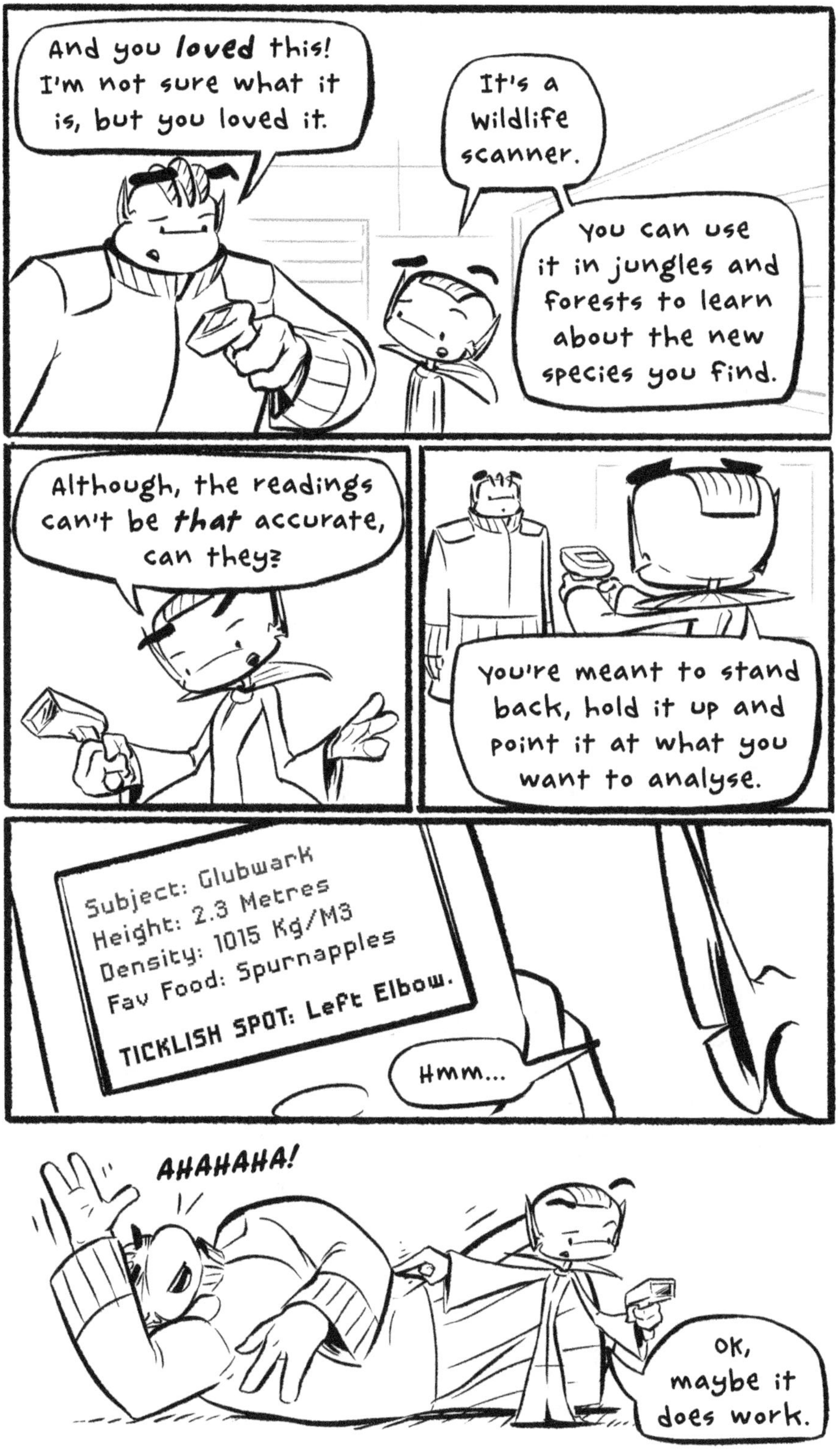
And you *loved* this! I'm not sure what it is, but you loved it.
It's a wildlife scanner.
You can use it in jungles and forests to learn about the new species you find.
Although, the readings can't be *that* accurate, can they?
You're meant to stand back, hold it up and point it at what you want to analyse.
Subject: Glubwark
Height: 2.3 Metres
Density: 1015 Kg/M3
Fav Food: Spurnapples
TICKLISH SPOT: Left Elbow.
Hmm...
AHAHAHA!
OK, maybe it does work.

I guess the scanner thing is OK and maybe my dad is right.

Maybe the way humans do things is "slow," "inefficient" and "a colossal waste of time," but at least they don't hide in their ship and let SOMEONE ELSE do the work!

Humans actually go deep INTO the Amazon and get up CLOSE to what they're studying to do research.

They SEE the bugs with their EYES,

FEEL the leaves with their HANDS,

SMELL the faeces with their NOSES.

sniff
sniff

How will my *Dad* know if this planet has died? What if he misses something because he won't come down from his ship?

I asked TaLC if he knew how my Dad planned to find out if this planet was alive or dead.

I received this thoroughly annoying reply.

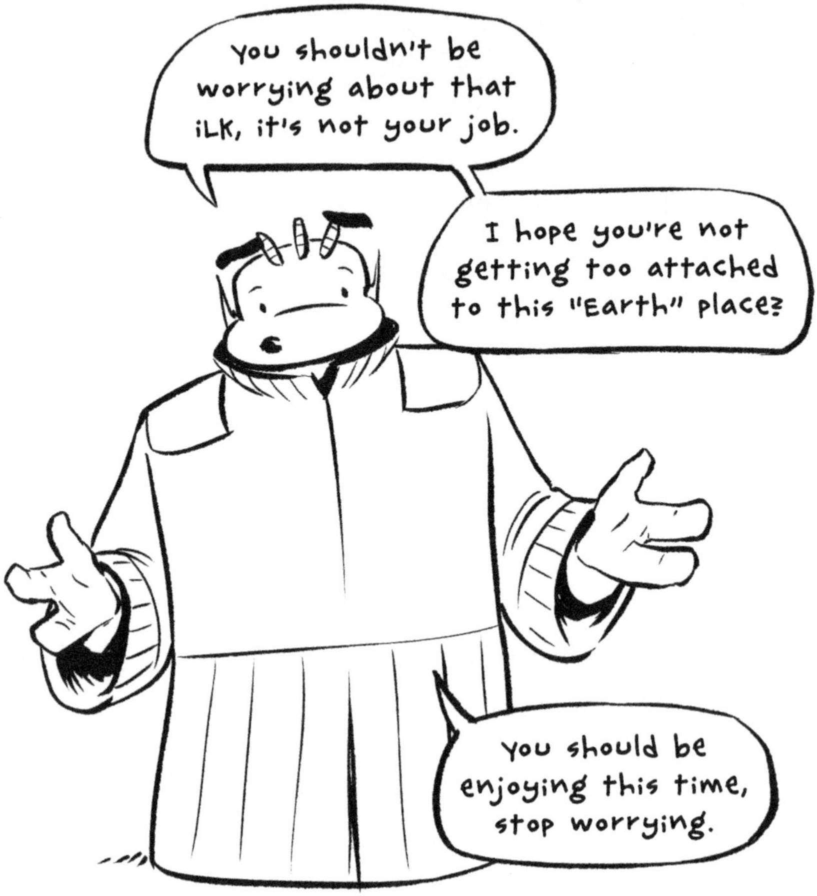
you shouldn't be worrying about that iLK, it's not your job.
I hope you're not getting too attached to this "Earth" place?
you should be enjoying this time, stop worrying.

So I ignored him and repeated my question, at which point he caved in and told me everything.

I'm a master of interrogation.

He lifted up my BIG BOOK OF PLANTS: THE ENTIRE UNIVERSE EDITION and opened it to a specific page.

Pointing at this image he said,

"If they find this plant and it's ALIVE, then so is this planet."

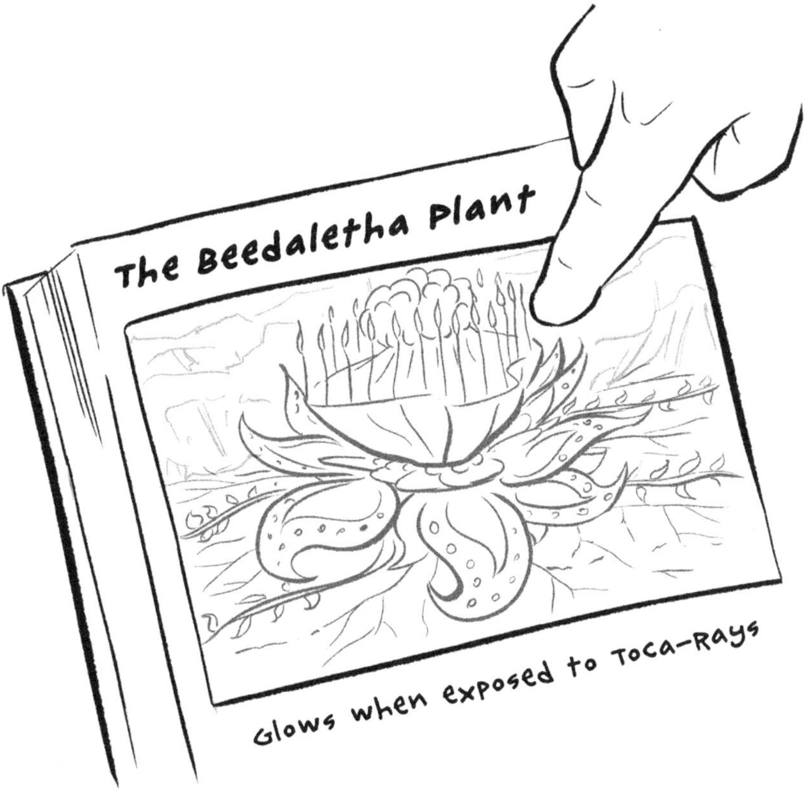
The Beedaletha Plant
Glows when exposed to Toca-Rays

"Unfortunately, if it's DEAD or if it's already disappeared, then there's no hope for this place."

So, apparently, the BEEDALETHA plant is really quite important.

How did I not know about it before today?

Adults keep way too many secrets.

Invasion 101, Day 47

I was sitting in my most important-looking chair at my headquarters when I finally had a chance to study the page that TalC had shown me.

From the **BIG BOOK OF PLANTS:** THE ENTIRE UNIVERSE EDITION

(Torn out because the book itself was to big to bring.)

Prior to this I hadn't had a moment to spare.

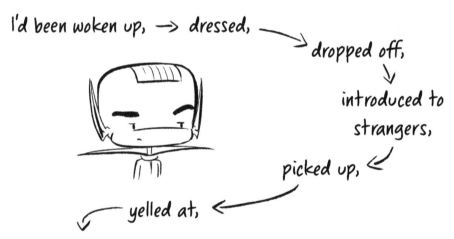

I'd been woken up, → dressed, → dropped off,
↓
introduced to strangers,
picked up, ↙
— yelled at, ←
↓

and asked way too many questions.

For being the one in charge there seems to be an awful lot of things that I have no choice in.

There are moments when I understand why Dad left.

But in this rare moment of peace, surrounded only by silence, I could suddenly see the importance of something that I'd previously paid no attention to.

Glows when exposed to Toca-Rays

The Beedaletha plant glows just like Brickly and that weird, egg-plant-thing that Marina found!

Maybe they're related?!

Family photo?

If they are connected genetically, they could grow in the same places!

I had to go back to where they found the egg plant to see if I could discover any clues to Beedaletha's whereabouts.

I jumped out of my chair and headed towards Las Piedras to find Marina and tell her about Beedaletha.

But I made it about five metres before being stopped by the Dullrat.

Yip, yip, yip!

I needed to get past him as quickly as possible, but he wasn't listening and he wasn't moving!

What?!
What is it you want? Do you have more papers for me to sign? More pointless meetings for me to go to?

After muttering something too quietly for me to hear, he held out his hand...

In his hand was a sandwich.

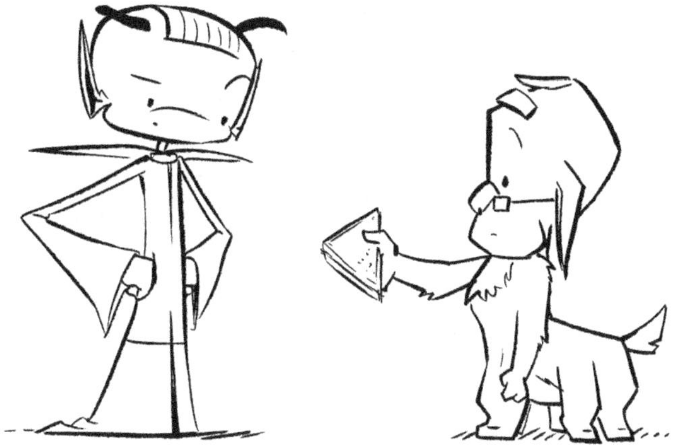

It was a ham sandwich.

I didn't understand the significance.

We had already had lunch.

Then he showed me the front page of today's newspaper.

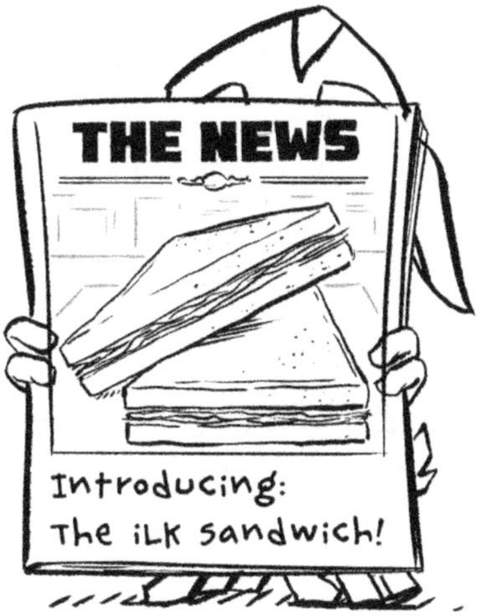
THE NEWS
Introducing:
The iLK sandwich!

As a sign of their respect and gratitude, they had decided to name something important after me.

Given how much I like sandwiches, they thought the most appropriate thing would be to rename the classic ham sandwich, "The iLK."

I'll have one croque monsieur, one club sandwich and one iLK please.

Apparently they think that I've been doing quite a good job; not great, not amazing, but good enough.

Well, nothing's perfect and if I've done well enough to have had a sandwich named after me then that was something to feel proud about.

I couldn't help but say the first words that came to mind.

Thank you. Now get out of my way.

It had just become more important than ever to find that damn plant.

Invasion 101, Day 48

Marina thought she had something important to tell me.

I thought I had something important to tell her.

The truth is we had both greatly underestimated how important our news was to the other.

In hindsight we probably could have handled this situation better.

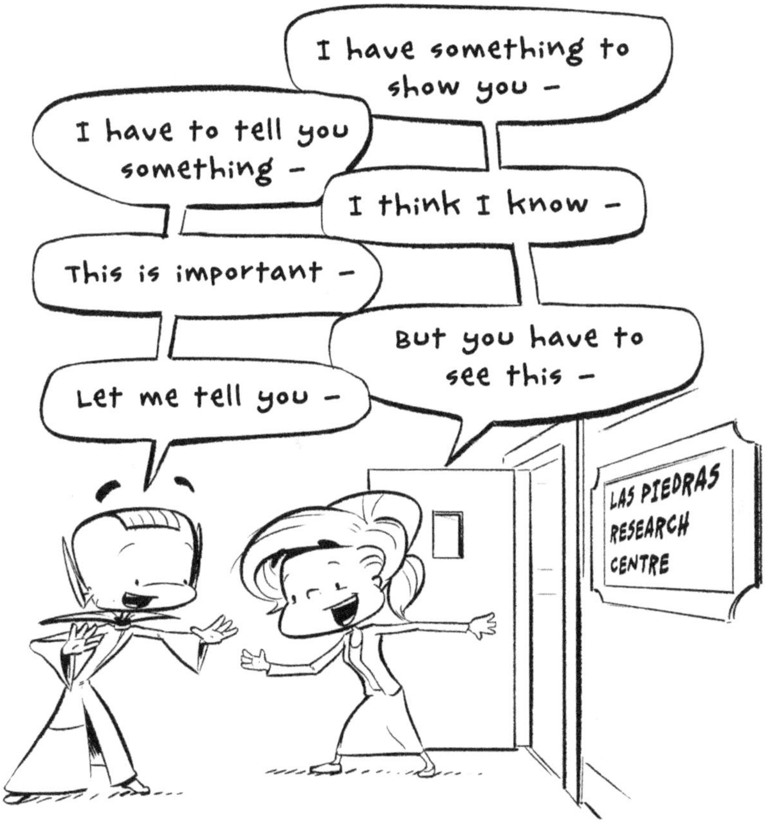
I have something to show you –
I have to tell you something –
I think I know –
This is important –
But you have to see this –
Let me tell you –
LAS PIEDRAS RESEARCH CENTRE

It seems that being the Emperor of the World counts for nothing when faced with a determined biologist.

I've heard about your sandwich, this is much more important than that. Now listen.
No this isn't about that!
I've found out what my Dad is looking for.
ok well you can tell me while we walk. I have something to show you.

She told me that they thought they'd discovered ANOTHER new species of plant and, more importantly, it glowed!

Dead-looking-leaf-thing.
Not glowing.

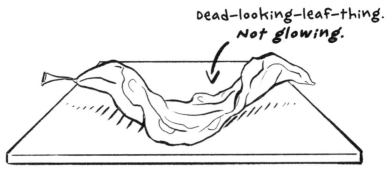

Sadly, it had since shrivelled up and died.

Apparently, all of the plants that glowed before had started glowing again, but then when this leaf-thing died, they all stopped.

we think this is what has been making the other plants glow!

or at least a part of it.

When she held it up like that I recognised it!

I told her to keep it held up and I brought out my paper to compare.

The Beedaletha Plant

...ws when exposed to Toca-Rays

That was it! It was a petal from the Beedaletha plant! Only, much bigger and more dead looking than how it appeared in the book.

Look!

That's it!

I explained to her what this plant was and that if it was dead, then so was her planet.

This seemed to dampen her excitement.

It's a good thing I didn't mention anything about Dad wanting to destroy them all.

But if this is dead then there is no hope left for our planet.

But she was wrong! There was hope!

This was only a petal, but it means that the plant still exists here on Earth! If we can find it it might still be alive, then my Dad won't need to destroy the planet!

I'm sure a lot of people would be glad about that. Apart from maybe my dad.

It says here that it reacts to these Toca-Rays.

So it wasn't this plant that was making the other plants glow.

maybe they were all just reacting to these rays?

She then said something very clever that I hadn't thought of.

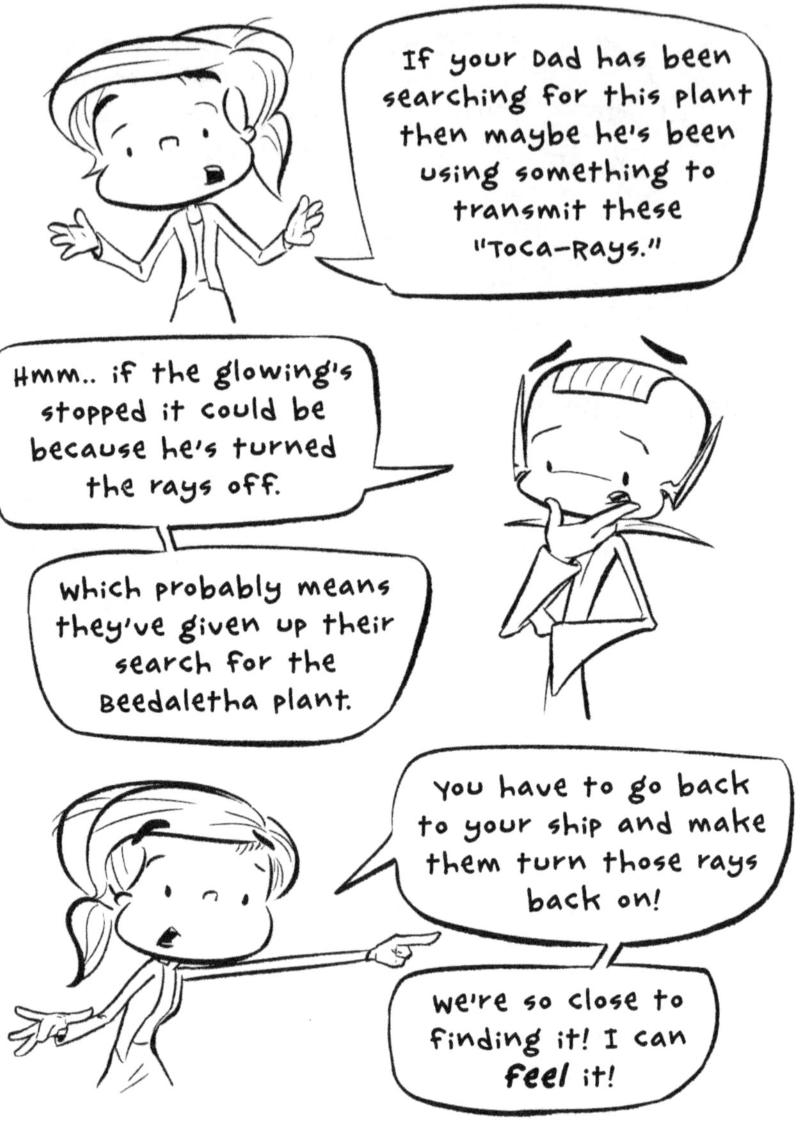
If your Dad has been searching for this plant then maybe he's been using something to transmit these "Toca-Rays."
Hmm.. if the glowing's stopped it could be because he's turned the rays off.
Which probably means they've given up their search for the Beedaletha plant.
You have to go back to your ship and make them turn those rays back on!
We're so close to finding it! I can *feel* it!

If Dad has stopped looking for the plant, then he's already preparing to destroy this planet.

But if Marina was right, I could turn those rays back on and we could make the Beedaletha plant glow again! Then, with the help of Marina and her team, we can still find it and prove to Dad that this planet is still alive!

Invasion 101, Day 50

I thought it would be obvious. That there'd be a switch or something and I'd know when I found it.

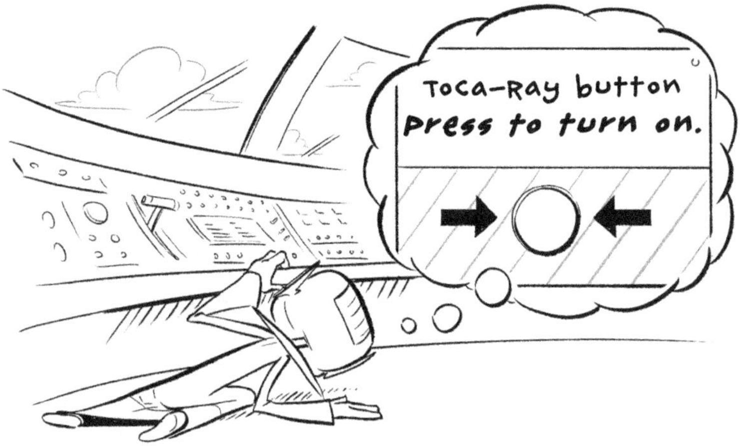

Toca-Ray button
press to turn on.

This wasn't the first location I searched on the ship. Before this I went to the starboard storage unit. They weren't very helpful there.

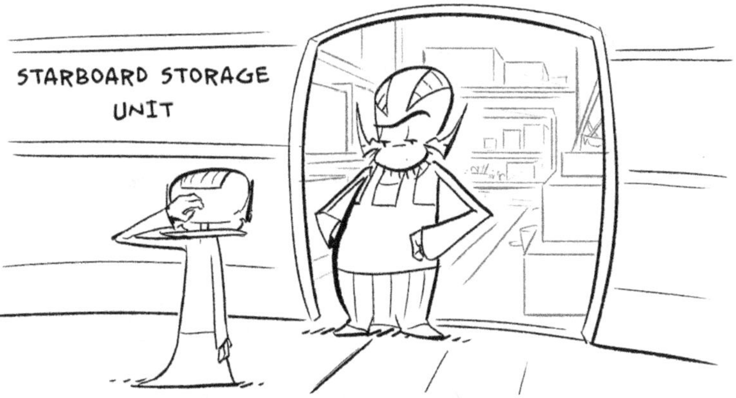

STARBOARD STORAGE UNIT

Apparently, if I was looking to CONTROL any kind of device via some kind of CONTROL panel I was better off looking in one of the CONTROL rooms.

He was right of course. That did make much more sense. It's just the control room was much more difficult to get to.

So I enlisted the assistance of TalC. He was more or less willing to help given he was so bored and I think he likes me more than Dad.

control
Room 2B

me hiding under
TALC's cloak.

It's a good thing I already had so much experience as a Stealth Ninja.

I suppose I could have just asked Dad politely to turn the Toca-Ray transmitter on so the plants would glow again, but that seemed excessively complicated.

I had concluded instead that it was better to avoid Dad by any means necessary.

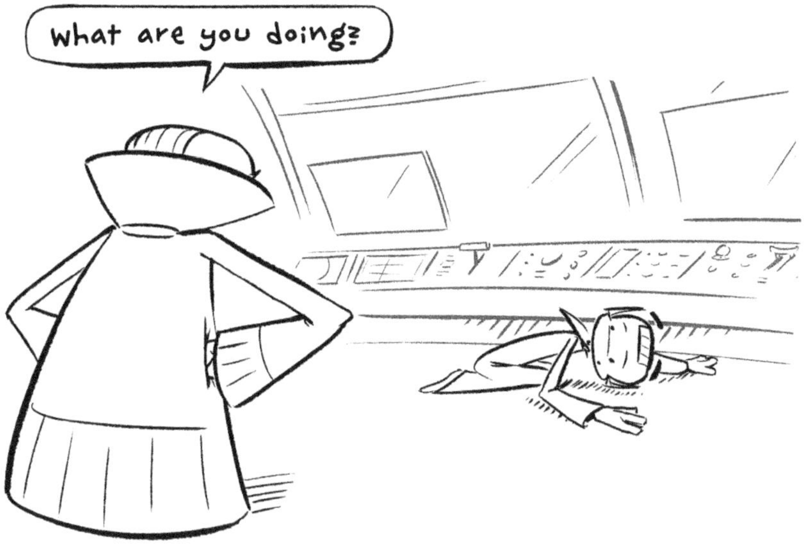
What are you doing?

That was of course until he found me. At which point I concluded that I needed a change of tack. I decided to subtly tease the location of the button out of him using the power of words.

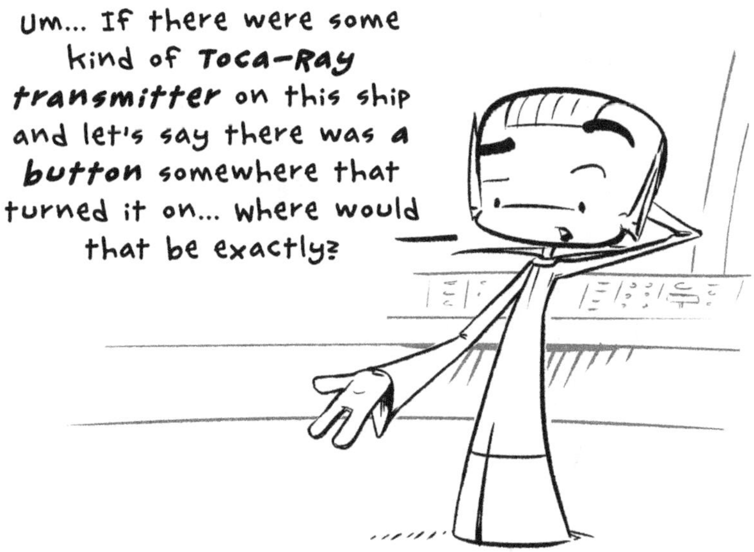
Um... If there were some kind of **Toca-Ray transmitter** on this ship and let's say there was a **button** somewhere that turned it on... where would that be exactly?

I probably could have been more subtle than that.

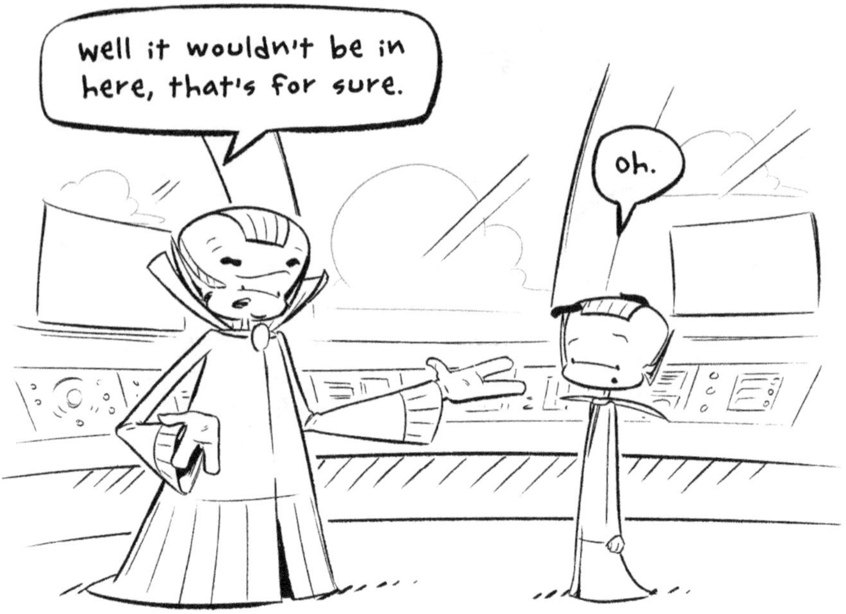
Well it wouldn't be in here, that's for sure.
Oh.

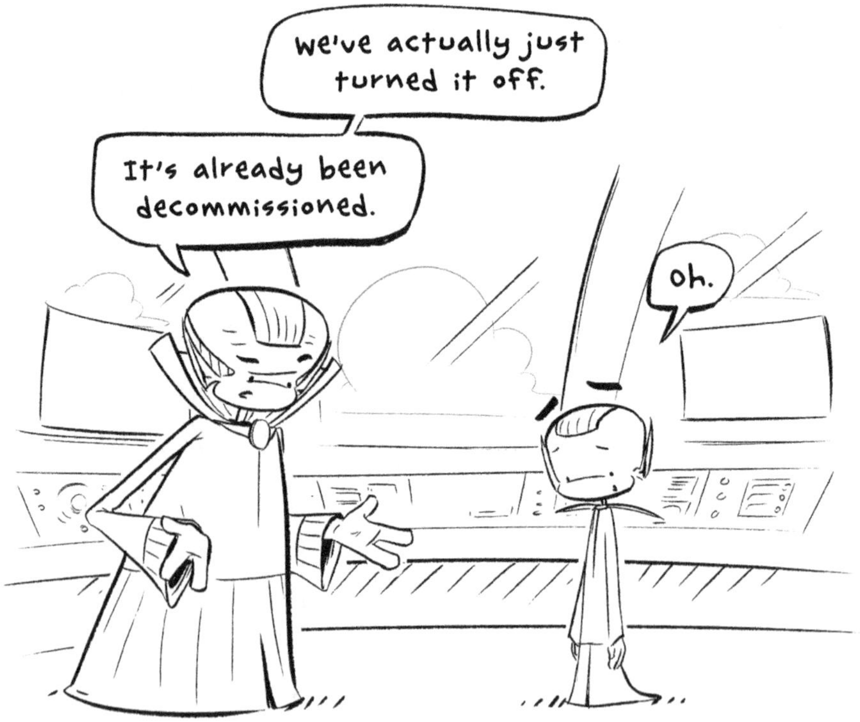
We've actually just turned it off.
It's already been decommissioned.
Oh.

Clearly Dad thought I knew what "decommissioned" meant. I did not, but it didn't sound good.

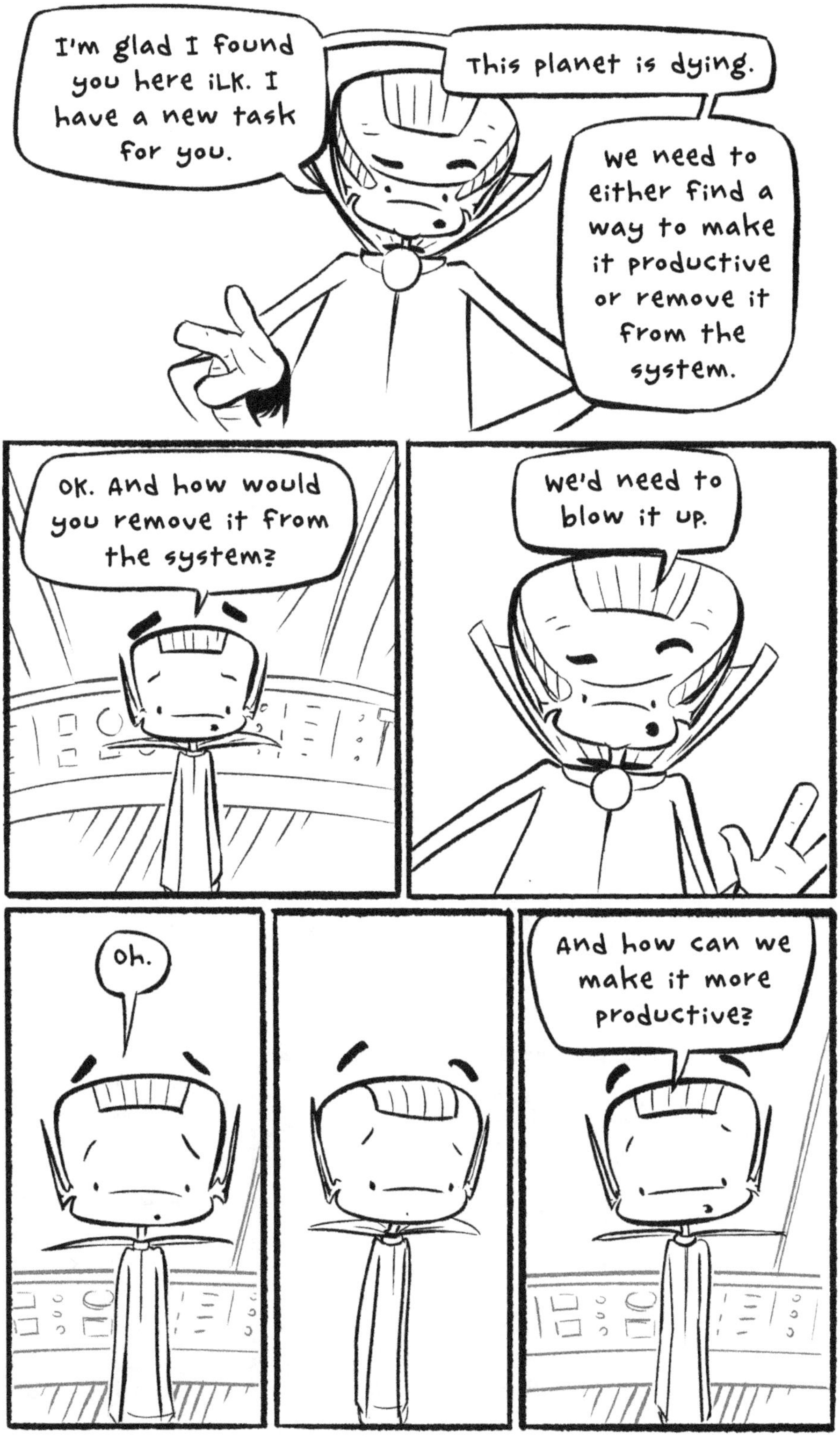
I'm glad I found you here iLK. I have a new task for you.
This planet is dying.
We need to either find a way to make it productive or remove it from the system.
OK. And how would you remove it from the system?
We'd need to blow it up.
Oh.
And how can we make it more productive?

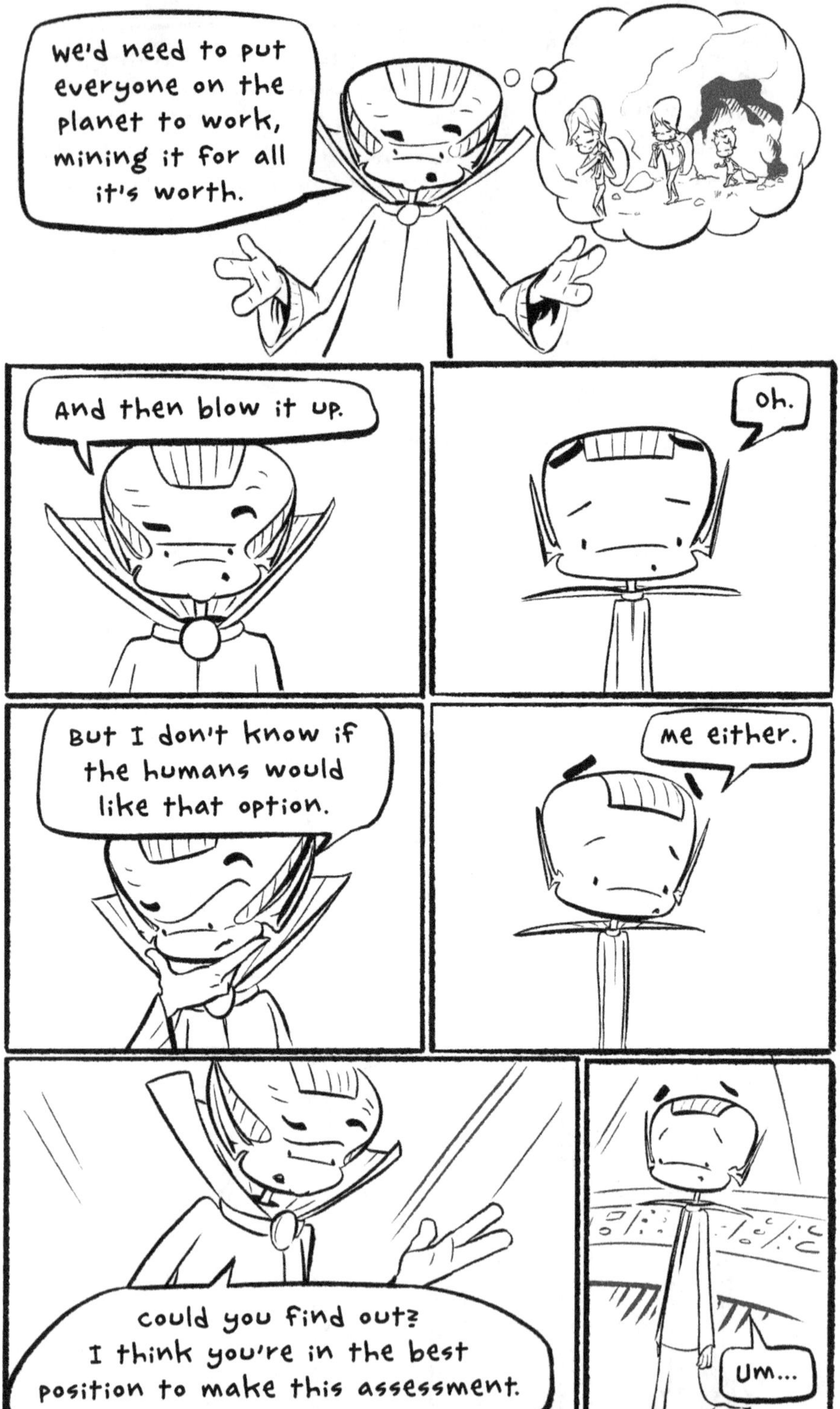
We'd need to put everyone on the planet to work, mining it for all it's worth.
And then blow it up.
Oh.
But I don't know if the humans would like that option.
Me either.
Could you find out?
I think you're in the best position to make this assessment.
Um...

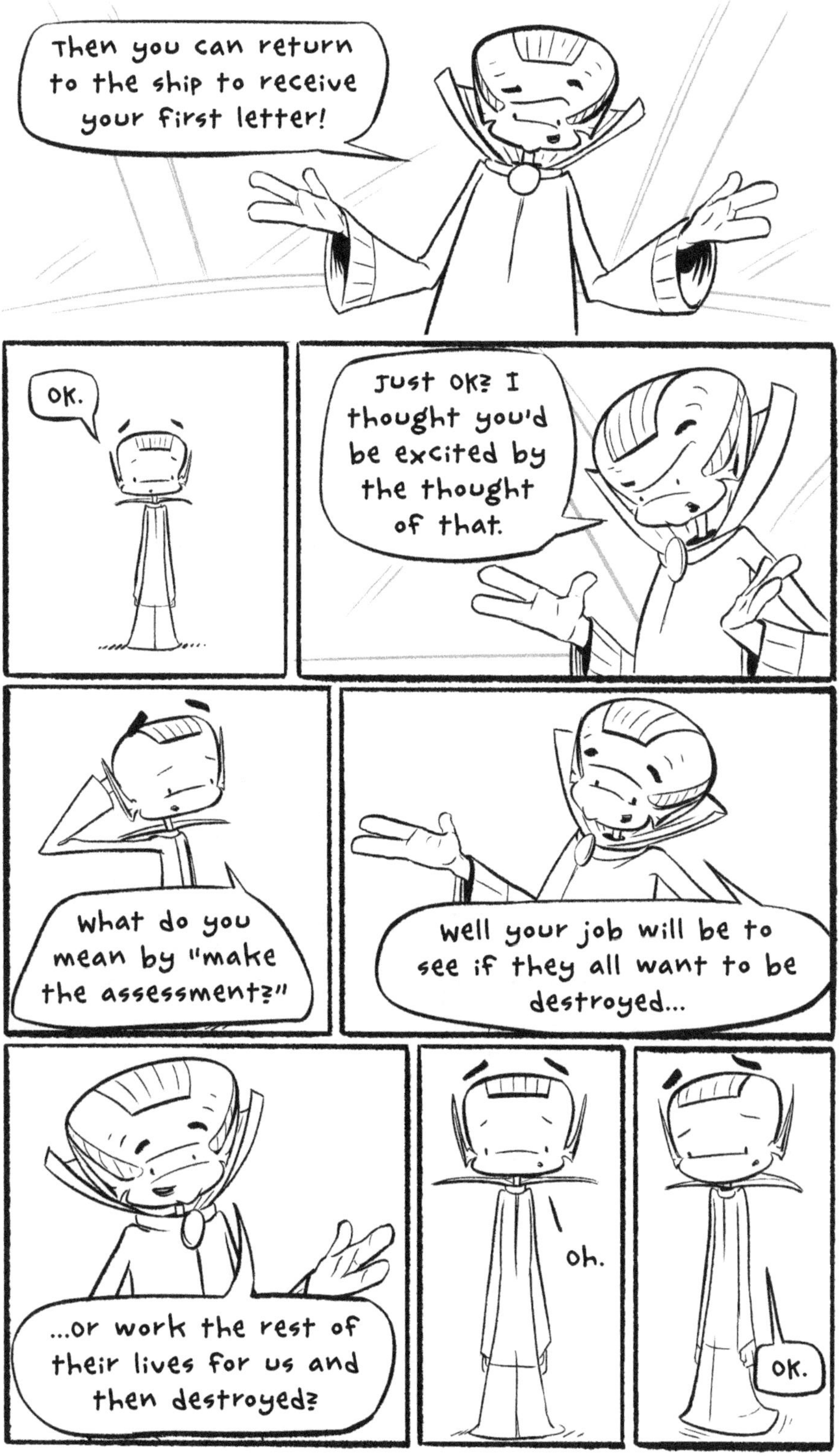
Then you can return to the ship to receive your first letter!
OK.
Just OK? I thought you'd be excited by the thought of that.
What do you mean by "make the assessment?"
Well your job will be to see if they all want to be destroyed...
...or work the rest of their lives for us and then destroyed?
Oh.
OK.

Invasion 101, Day 51

I should have yelled!

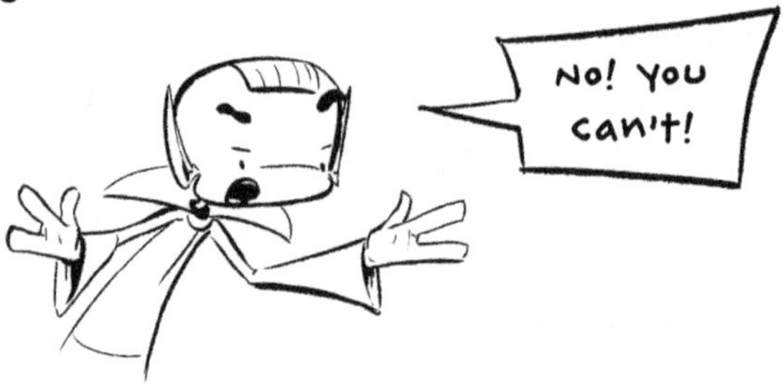
No! You can't!

Or argued!

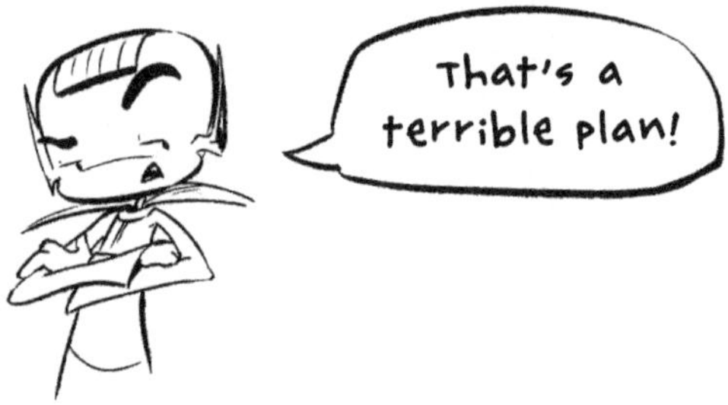
That's a terrible plan!

Or locked him in a cupboard!

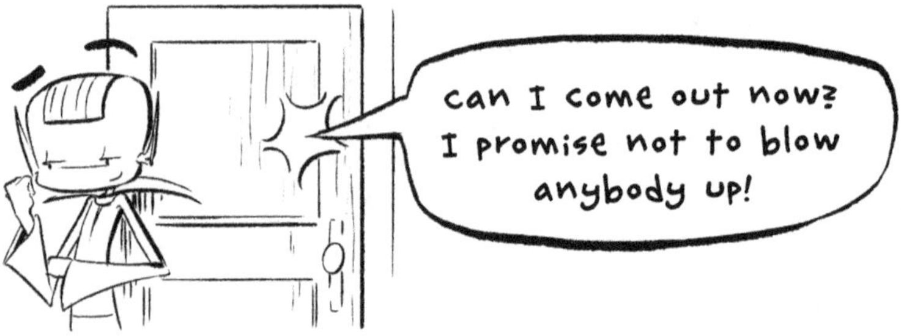
can I come out now? I promise not to blow anybody up!

Anything but...

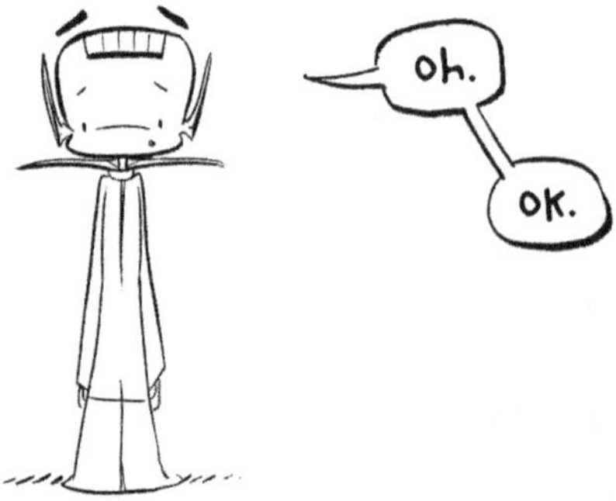
Oh.
OK.

Recently I haven't been given a choice in anything.

I've been made to stay in my room.

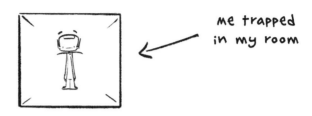

me trapped in my room

Then I've been made to stay on Earth.

me stuck on Earth

But now they're making me decide THIS and I DON'T WANT TO!

It feels like I'm being tossed around like some kind of dummy.

Why does everyone else get to do what they want, but I can't?!

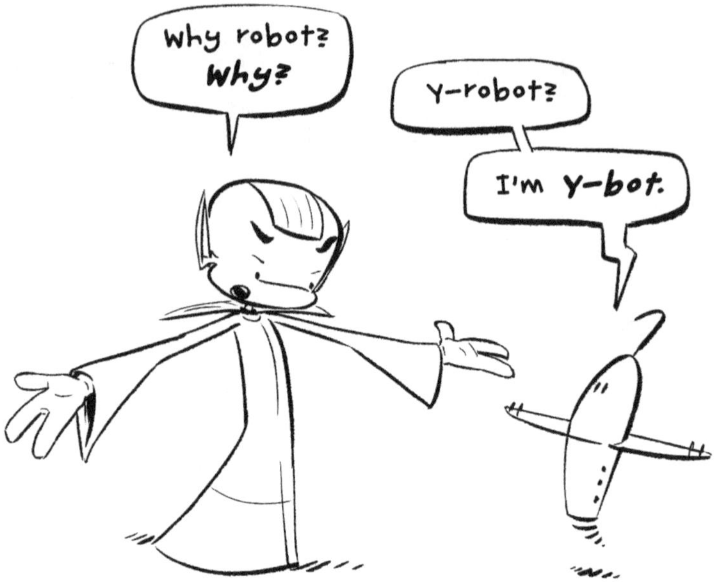
why robot? why?
Y-robot?
I'm Y-bot.

Why did I just accept it? What about WHAT I WANT? Shouldn't someone listen to THAT?!

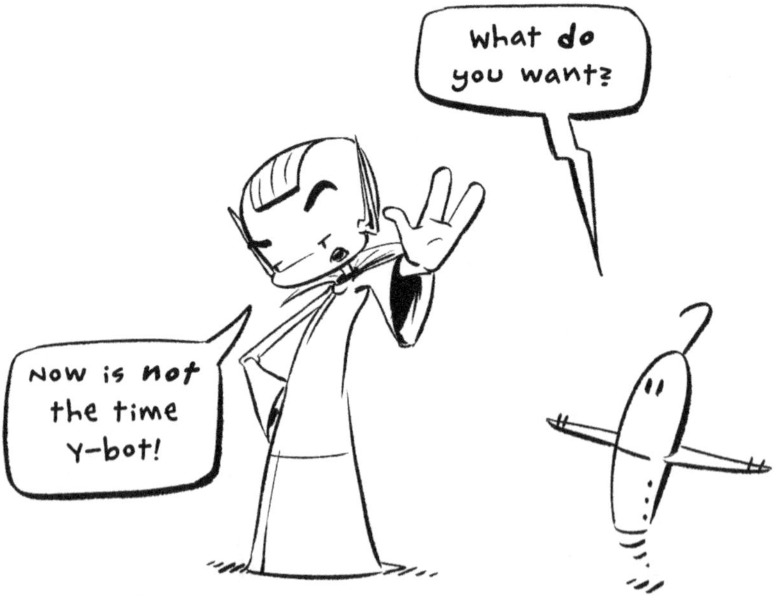
what do you want?
Now is not the time Y-bot!

I just stood there while he told me they were going to destroy Earth. I didn't say a thing. Why did I do that?

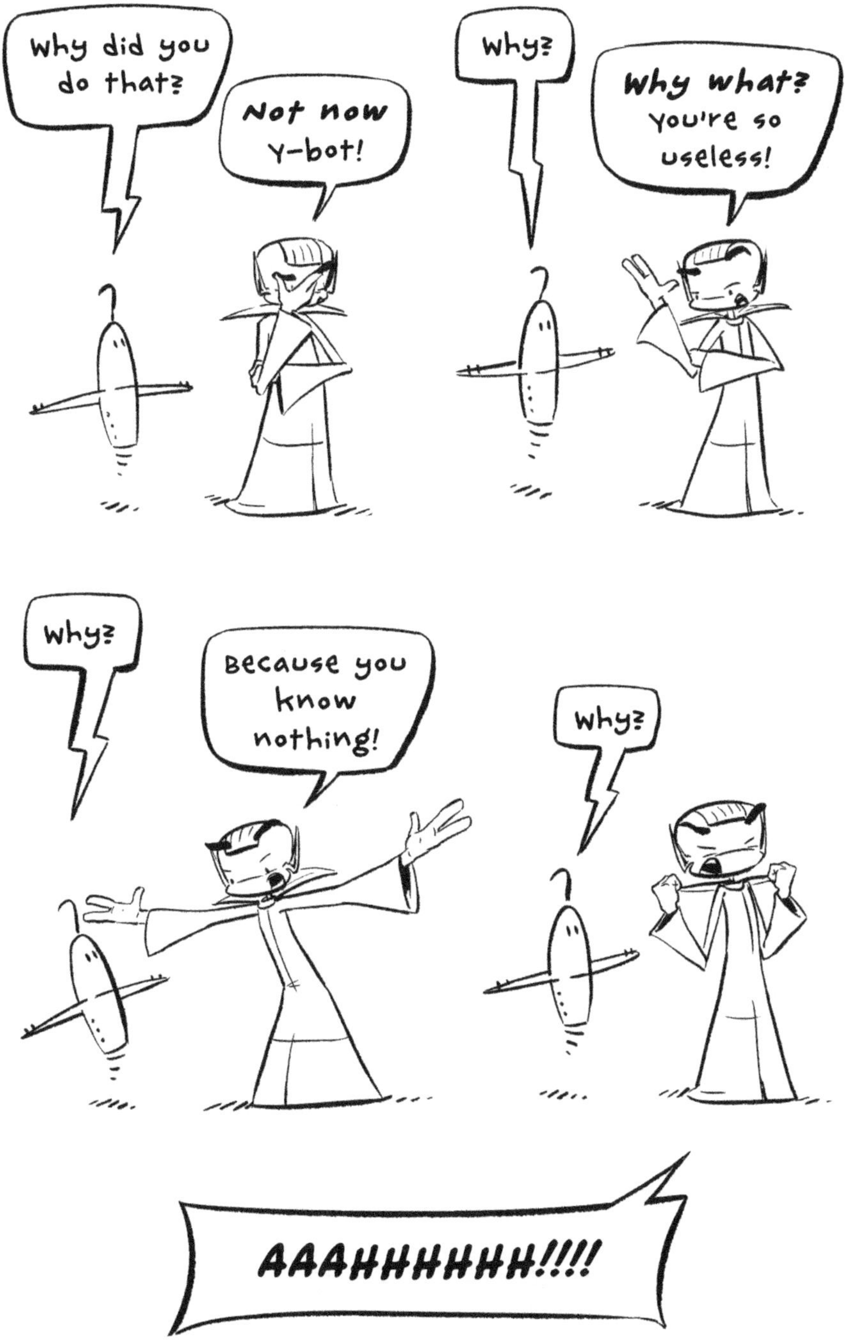

Why did you do that?
Not now Y-bot!
Why?
Why what? You're so useless!
Why?
Because you know nothing!
Why?
AAAHHHHHHH!!!!

THWACK!

...In conclusion, I think I might have broken Y-bot.

I'm dfeinltely
brpken.
Y-bot printout.

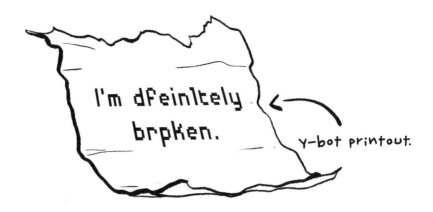

Invasion 101, Day 52

I probably shouldn't have taken out my frustration on Y-bot. Particularly as now I'll need to find a way to fix him.

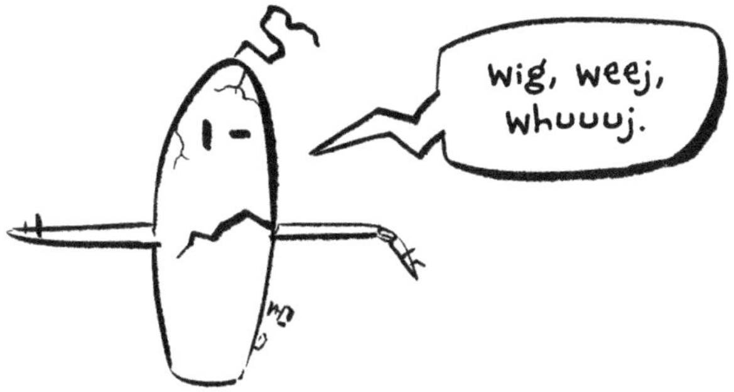
wig, weej, whuuuj.

Poor Y-bot, I just needed some space. As a result I haven't left the bedroom in my headquarters for a few days.

It's given me the time I needed to think.

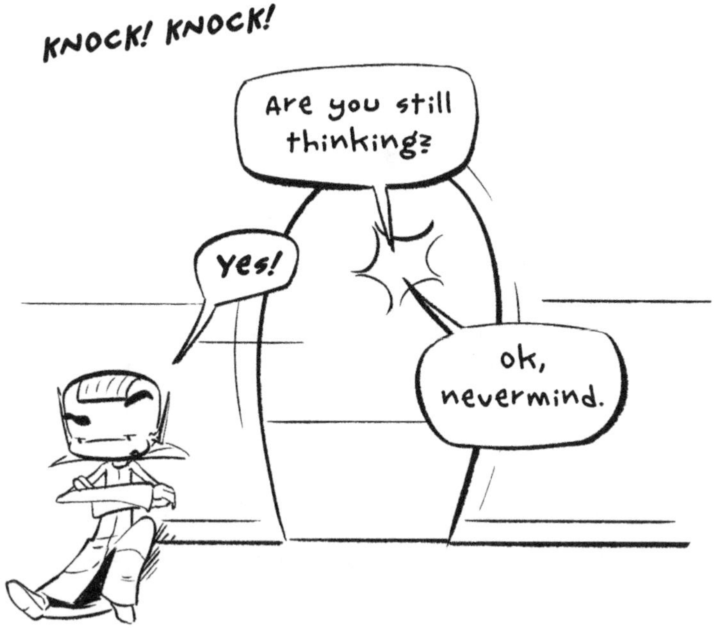
KNOCK! KNOCK!
Are you still thinking?
Yes!
ok, nevermind.

I think I was still in shock when Dad first told me, but now I've realised that I have a responsibility to this planet and its people.

I must decide whether they should be destroyed now...

OR...

...eventually.

To help me make this decision I have acquired this coin.

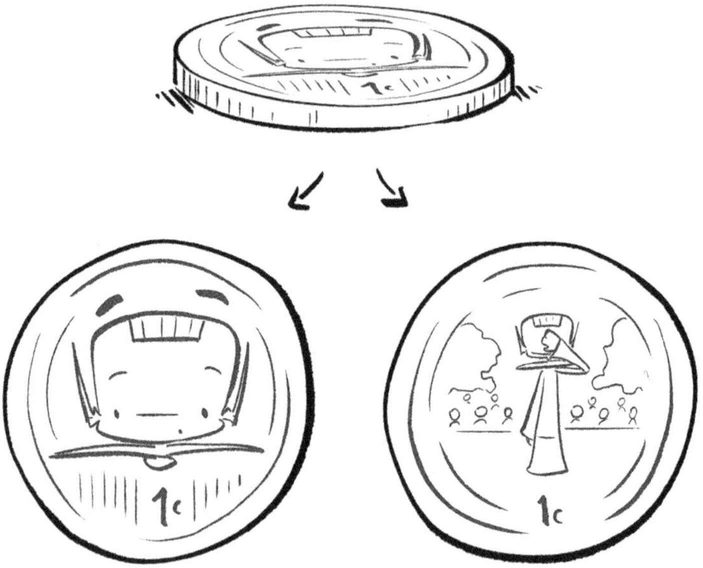
1c
1c
1c

Heads = Destroy planet now.

Tails = Destroy planet after forcing humans to work for us.

Flipping a coin in order to make a decision is a custom I have learned here on Earth and now it will decide their fate.

Unfortunately, no one warned me how difficult it was to catch these things after you'd flipped them.

Maybe that's why it's good to have more than three fingers.

Here goes attempt number 63...

Invasion 101, Day 54

After 147 flips of the coin I had slightly improved my technique, but I still didn't like any of the choices it made.

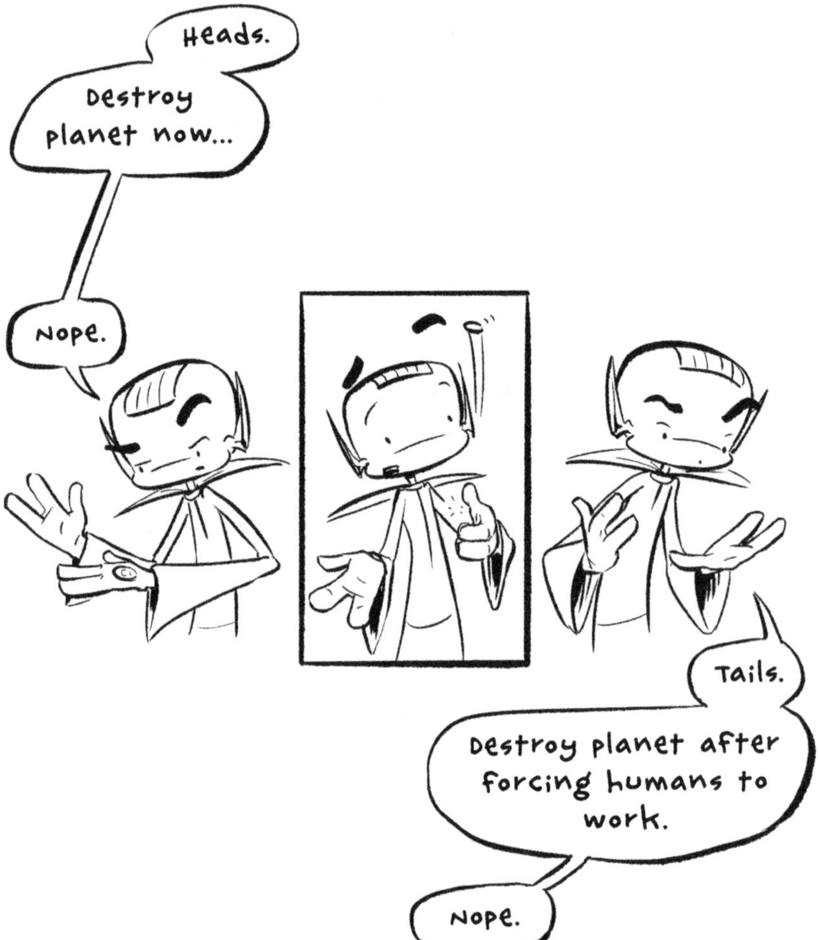
Heads.
Destroy planet now...
Nope.
Tails.
Destroy planet after forcing humans to work.
Nope.

With Mum back on the ship, Y-bot broken and my adviser Emilio keeping the world running smoothly I had no one else to talk to, so I went to visit Marina at Las Piedras to get her thoughts on my dilemma.

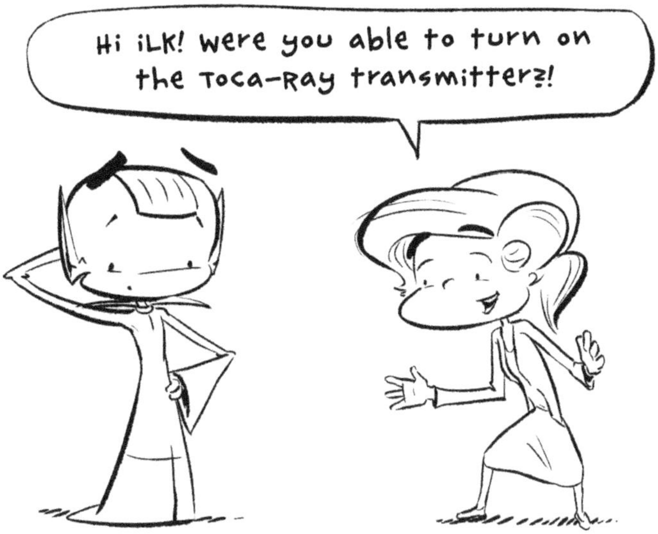
Hi iLK! were you able to turn on the Toca-Ray transmitter?!

I had completely forgotten about the Toca-Ray Transmitter.

It appears Marina and her team had not forgotten about the Beedaletha plant, like I had, and they'd been searching for it all this time.

I decided it would be a good idea to give her something else to focus on for a while.

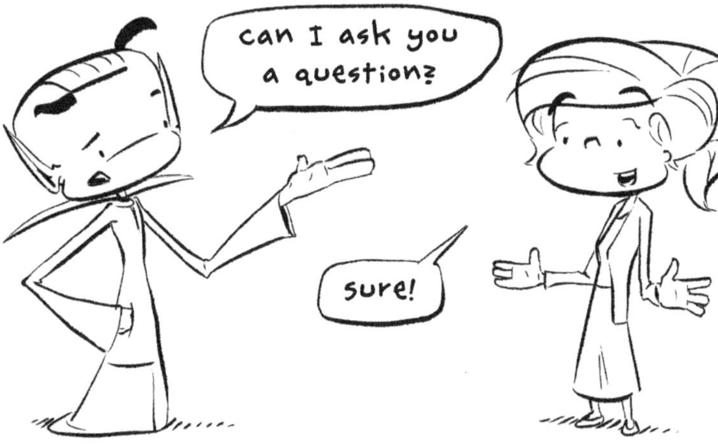
can I ask you a question?
sure!

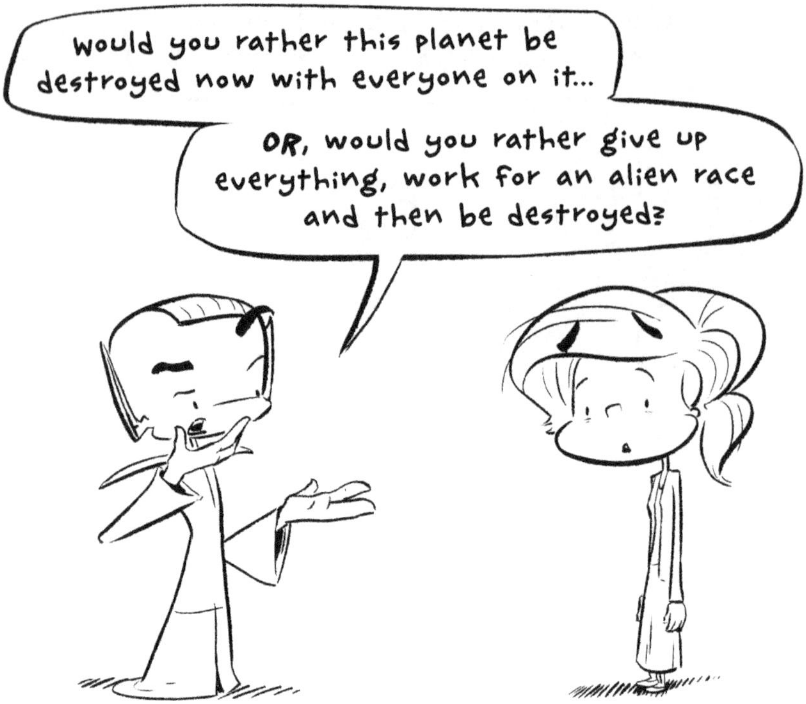
would you rather this planet be destroyed now with everyone on it...
OR, would you rather give up everything, work for an alien race and then be destroyed?

Her face didn't stay that way for long.

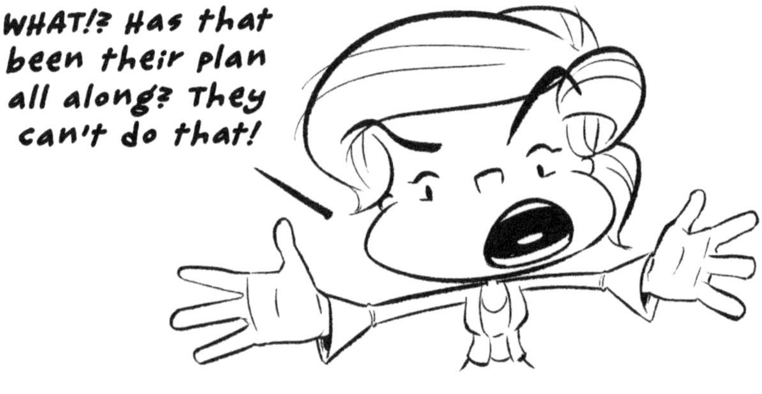
WHAT!? Has that been their plan all along? They can't do that!

I might have said too much.

Fortunately, I knew that I could fix this with just one magic word.

I explained to her that this scenario was entirely "hypothetical," and that this wasn't actually going to happen.

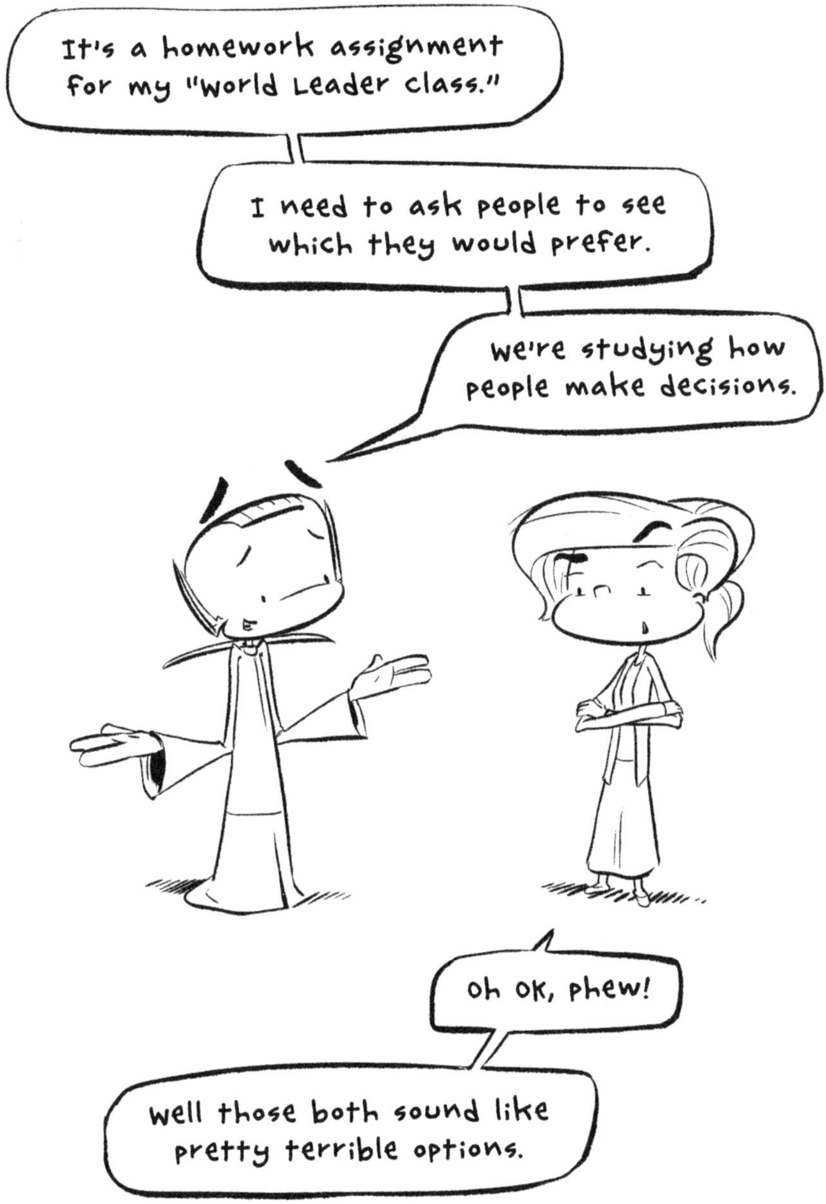
It's a homework assignment for my "World Leader class."
I need to ask people to see which they would prefer.
We're studying how people make decisions.
Oh OK, phew!
Well those both sound like pretty terrible options.

She made a good point.

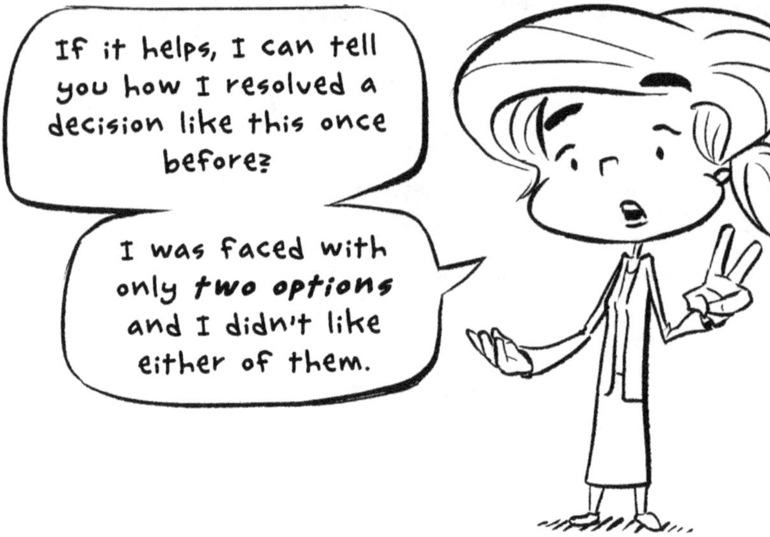
If it helps, I can tell you how I resolved a decision like this once before?
I was faced with only *two options* and I didn't like either of them.

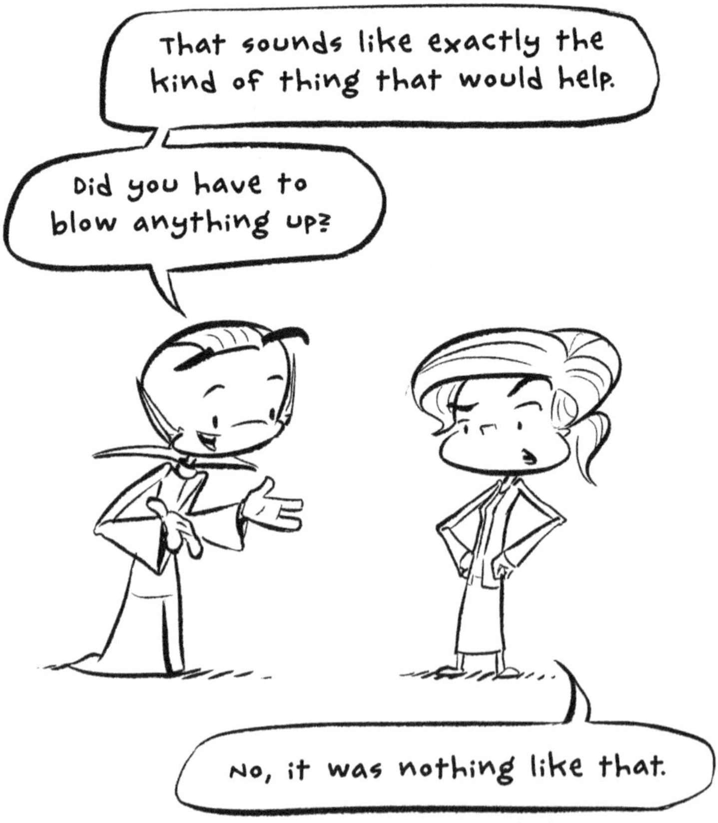
That sounds like exactly the kind of thing that would help.
Did you have to blow anything up?
No, it was nothing like that.

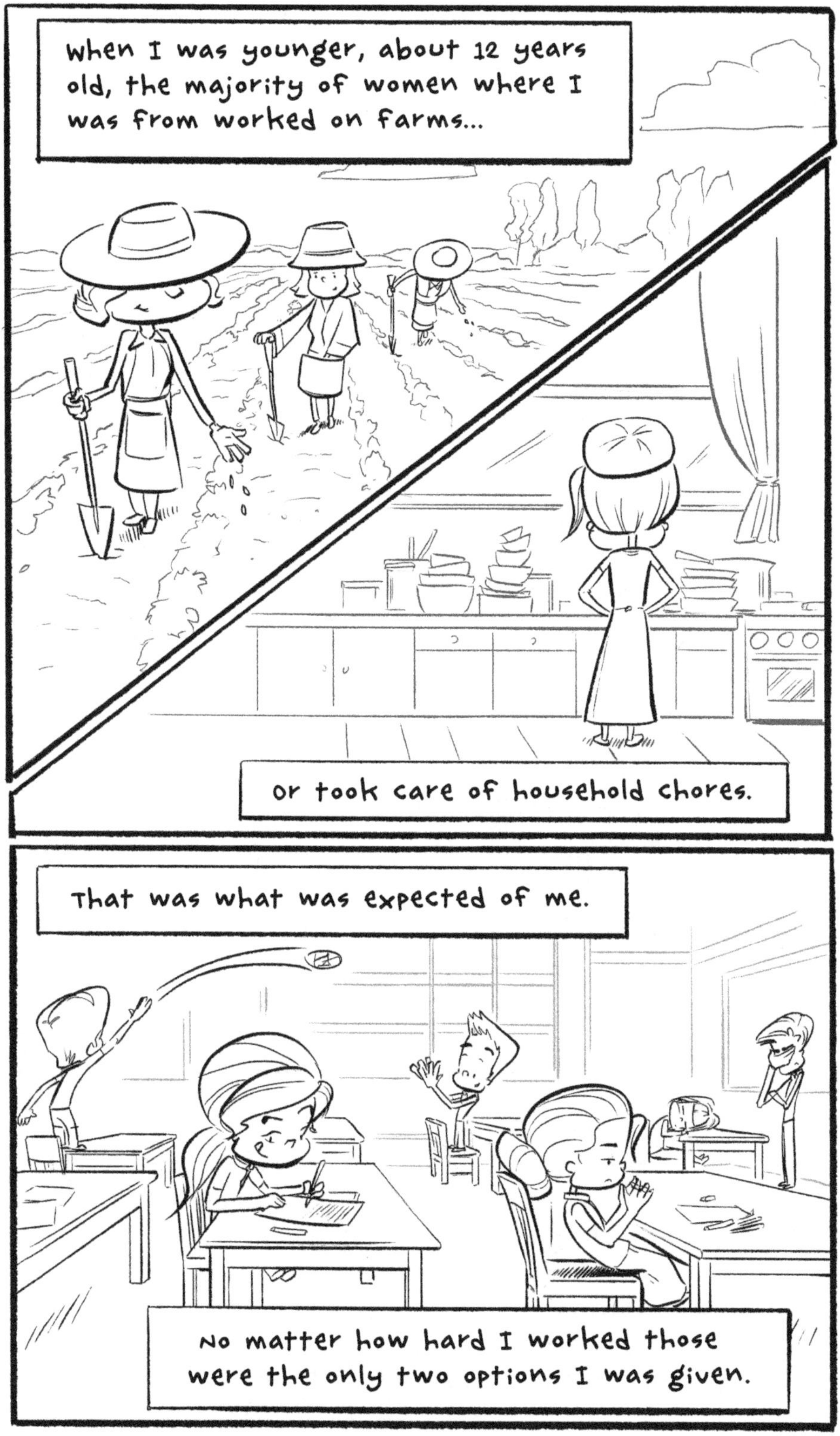
When I was younger, about 12 years old, the majority of women where I was from worked on farms...
or took care of household chores.
That was what was expected of me.
No matter how hard I worked those were the only two options I was given.

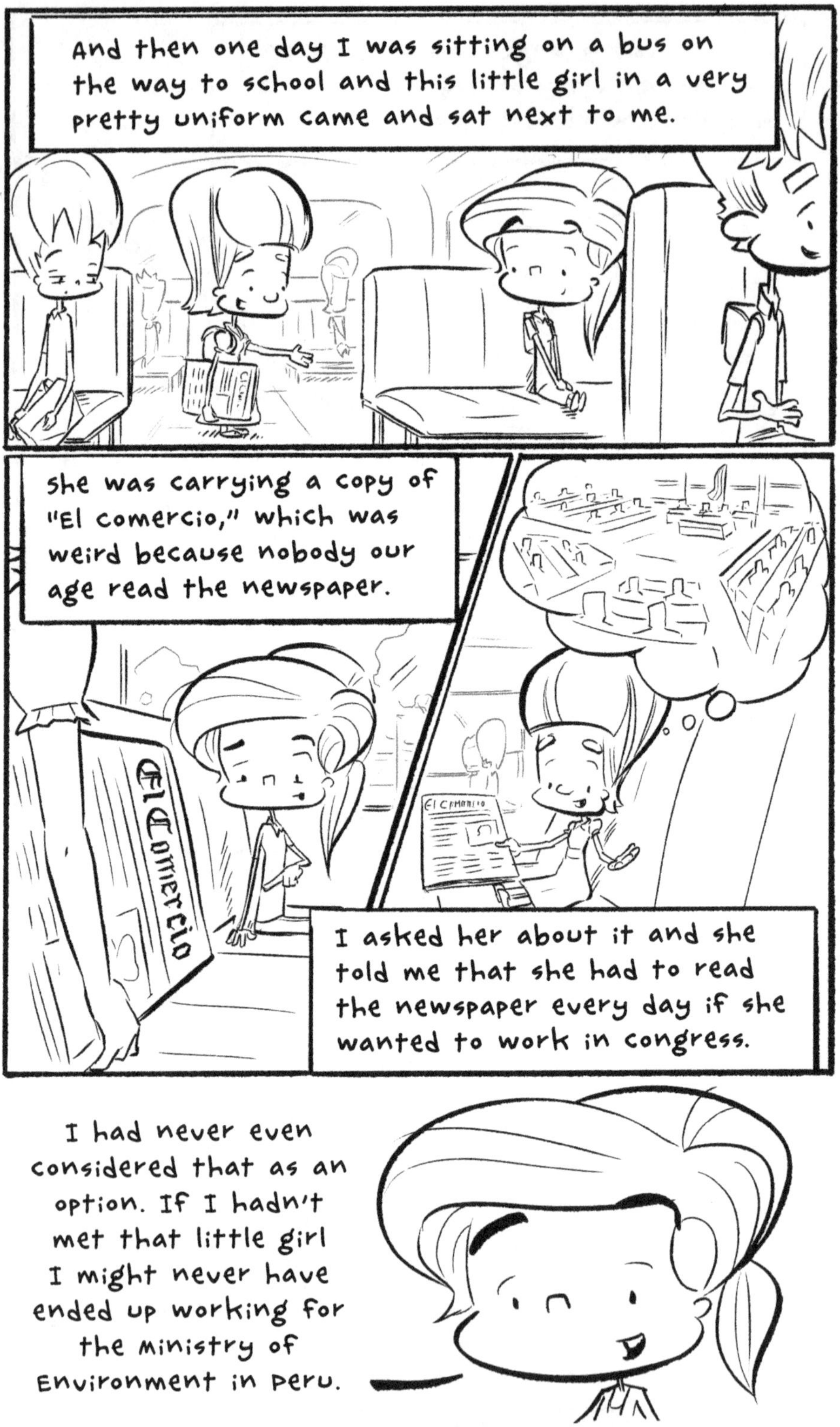
And then one day I was sitting on a bus on the way to school and this little girl in a very pretty uniform came and sat next to me.
She was carrying a copy of "El Comercio," which was weird because nobody our age read the newspaper.
El Comercio
I asked her about it and she told me that she had to read the newspaper every day if she wanted to work in congress.
I had never even considered that as an option. If I hadn't met that little girl I might never have ended up working for the ministry of Environment in Peru.

And then I wouldn't be right here now talking with you.

Do you see what I'm saying?

Sometimes, if you don't like the options you're given, you can try making up new ones.

Um...

I had no idea what she was talking about. She was clearly off on some kind of tangent, but she seemed to enjoy telling her little story.

Unfortunately it brought me no closer to solving my problem.

I needed to carry on with my research and survey the rest of the people that worked at Las Piedras to see what they would choose...

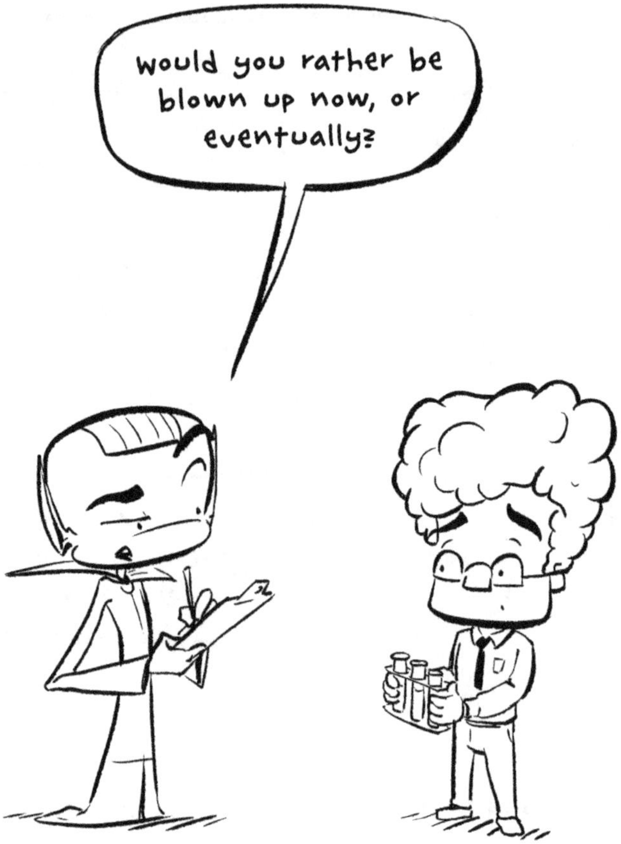
would you rather be blown up now, or eventually?

Invasion 101, Day 56

This doesn't look like the workshop of an engineer who is capable of doing incredible, unique, mind-bending things, but I've been reassured that it is.

I'm here because the research I was doing to aid me in my decision about the fate of Earth had revealed... well... nothing useful.

Names	Blown up now	Blown up eventually	Neither
Jo-something			✓
Glasses			✓
Funny voice			✓
sweaty hands			✓
Tim			✓

So I had decided to distract myself. I asked around to see if anyone knew where I could get Y-bot fixed.

It's a hard thing to find the kind of genius mind required to fix a mechanical marvel like Y-bot.

His technology is so sophisticated that together, the ship's engineer, biochemist, physicist and electrical technician couldn't even figure out how to open his battery pack.

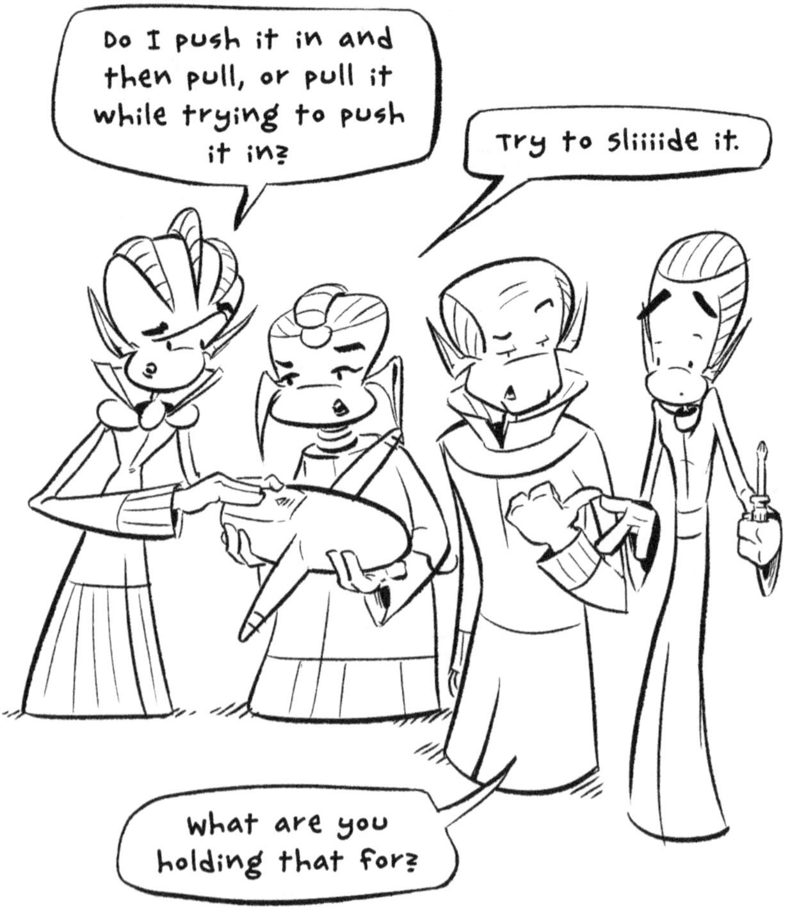
Do I push it in and then pull, or pull it while trying to push it in?
Try to sliiiide it.
What are you holding that for?

It seemed even less likely that a human would be able to help, but when everyone I spoke to recommended one man for the job, I decided I had to pay him a visit.

When I arrived at his location, you couldn't blame me for thinking it looked more like a junk yard than somewhere I'd find a gifted mind.

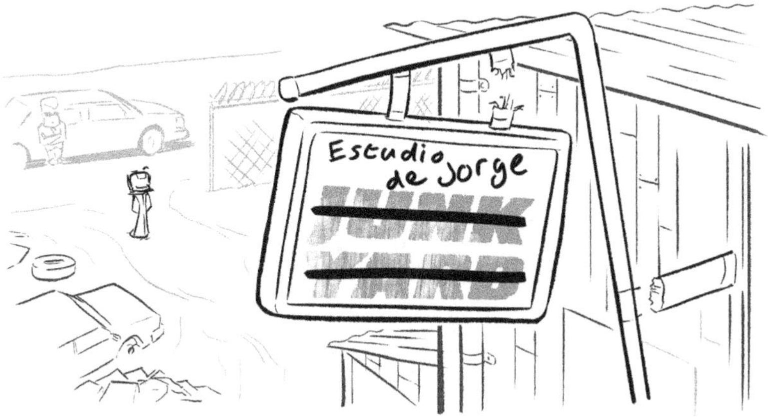
Estudio de Jorge
~~JUNK~~
~~YARD~~

Upon meeting Jorge, I was eager to get straight down to business.

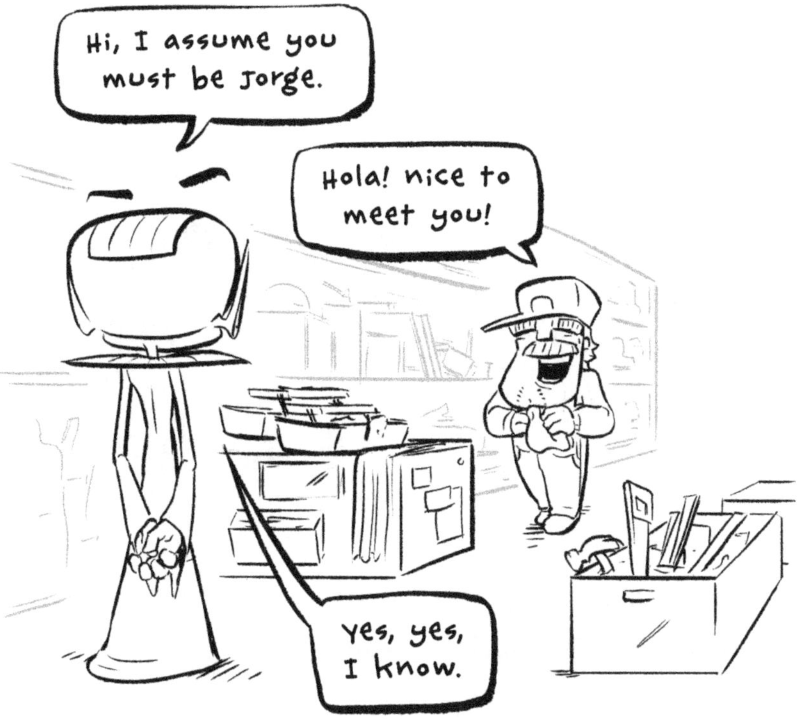
Hi, I assume you must be Jorge.
Hola! nice to meet you!
Yes, yes, I know.

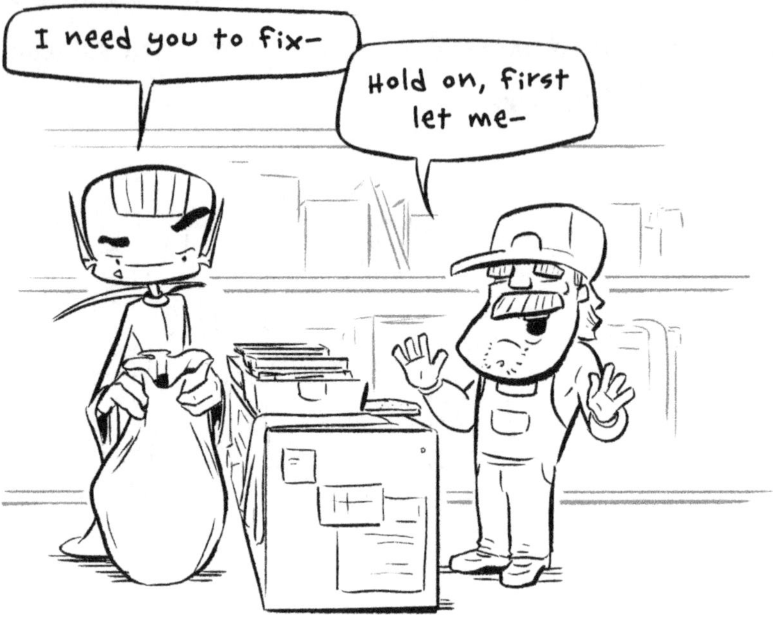
I need you to fix-
Hold on, first let me-

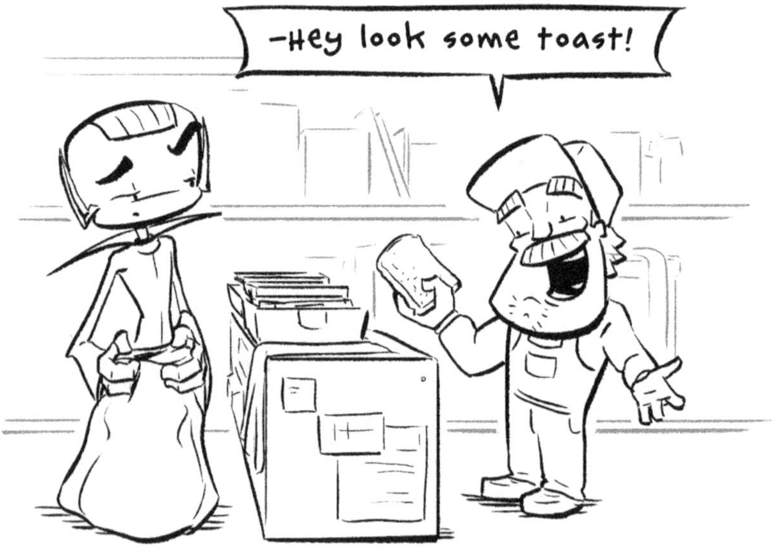
-Hey look some toast!

He seemed very easily distracted. This didn't exactly fill me with confidence, but I've been warned to expect this from a "creative" mind.

However, I was extremely pressed for time. Deciding the fate of the world was still at the top of my to-do list.

Finding someone to fix Y-bot was meant to be just a temporary distraction. I needed to get this issue resolved as quickly as possible.

So things like this didn't really help.

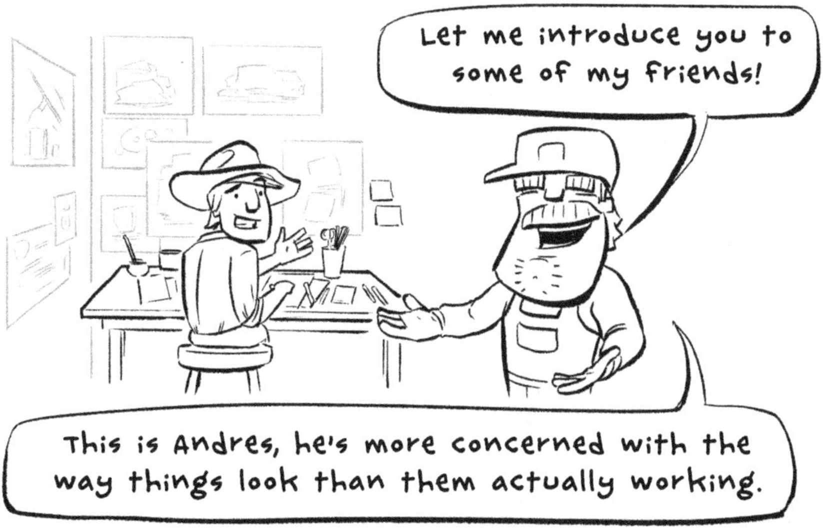
Let me introduce you to some of my friends!
This is Andres, he's more concerned with the way things look than them actually working.

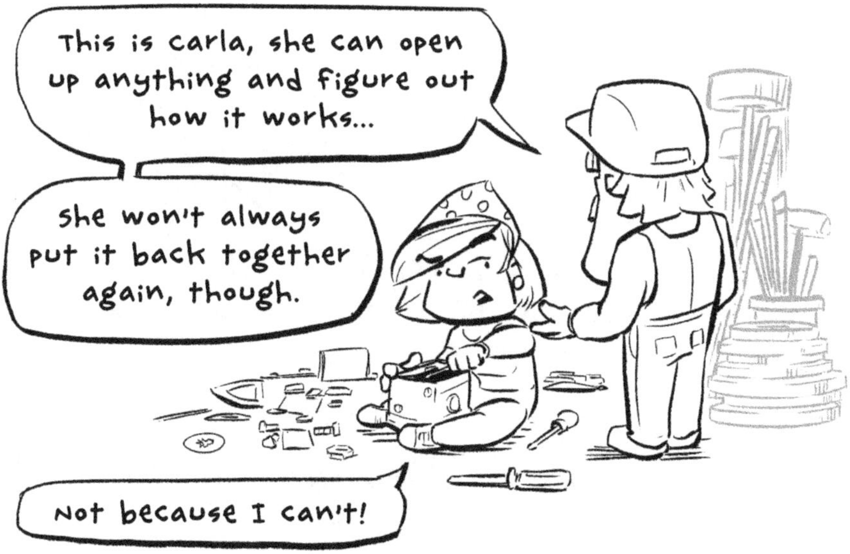
This is carla, she can open up anything and figure out how it works...
she won't always put it back together again, though.
Not because I can't!

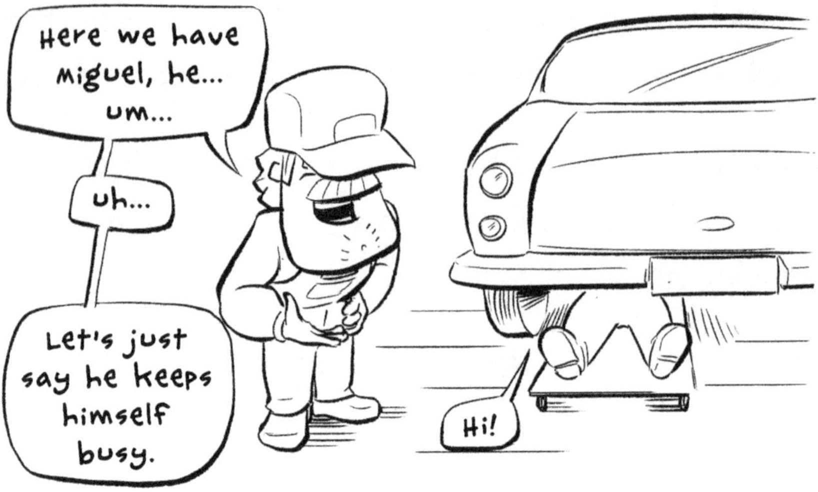
Here we have miguel, he... um...
uh...
Let's just say he keeps himself busy.
Hi!

The more I saw of this place, the less I trusted that they could fix Y-bot.

On Glub we assign one person to each industry and that person is the best for the job.

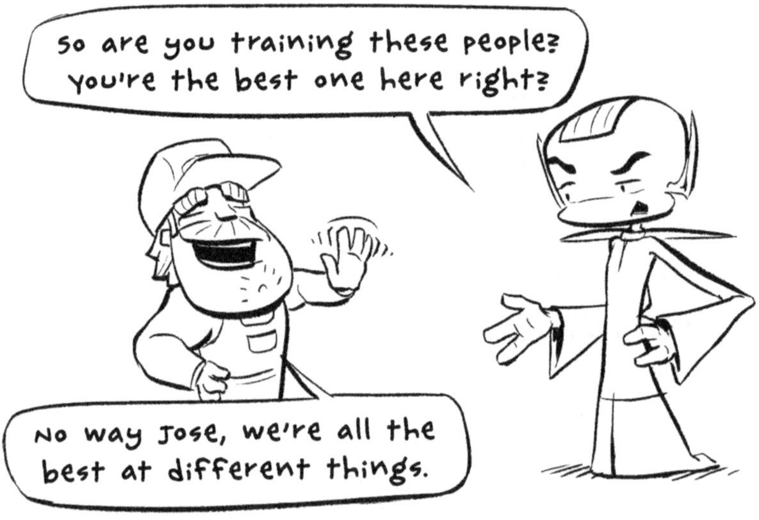
So are you training these people? You're the best one here right?
No way Jose, we're all the best at different things.

That didn't make any sense. How could any of them be "the best" if they all needed help from the others? And who was Jose? This didn't bode well.

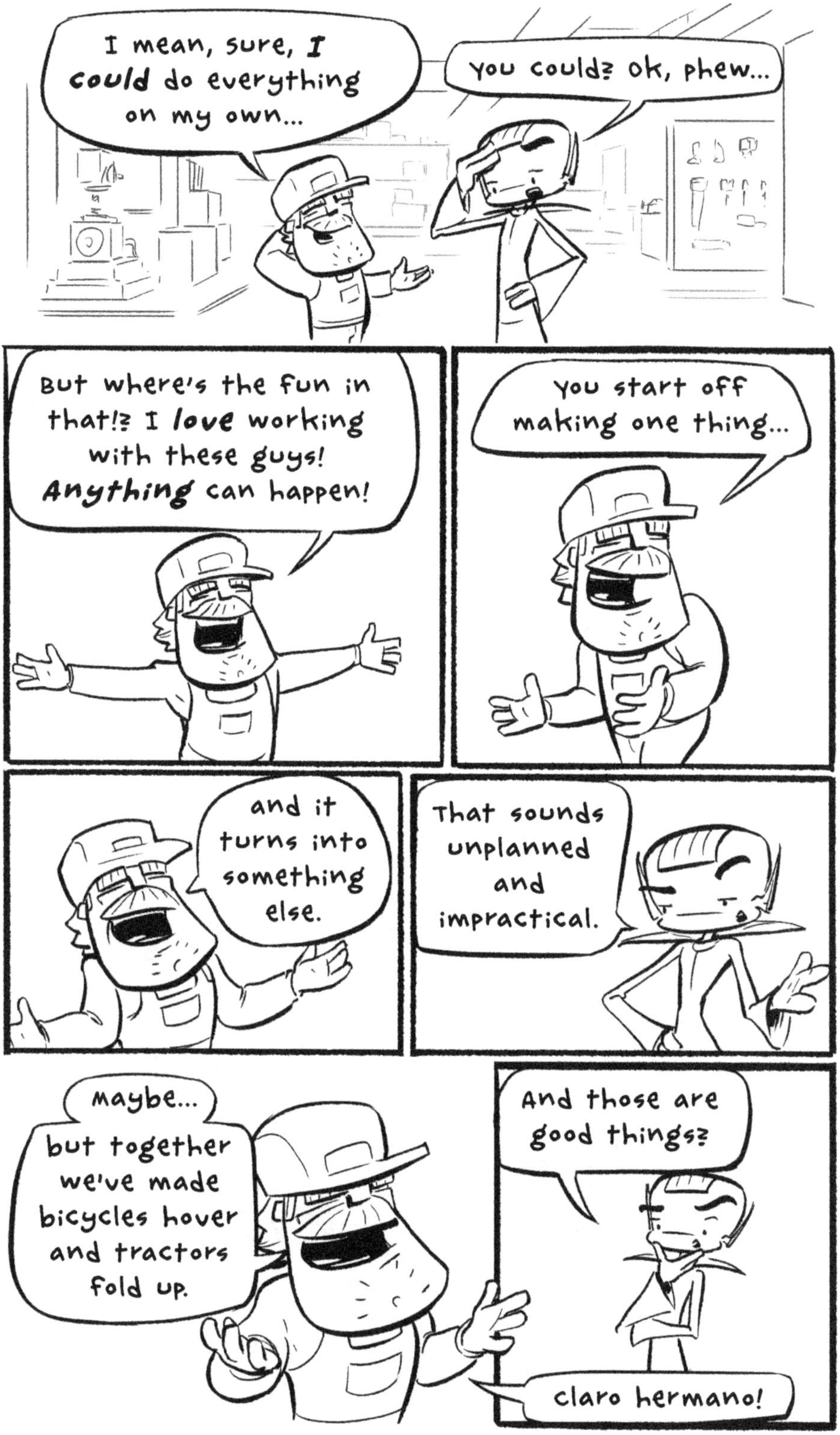
I mean, sure, I could do everything on my own...
you could? ok, phew...
But where's the fun in that!? I love working with these guys! Anything can happen!
You start off making one thing...
and it turns into something else.
That sounds unplanned and impractical.
maybe...
but together we've made bicycles hover and tractors fold up.
And those are good things?
claro hermano!

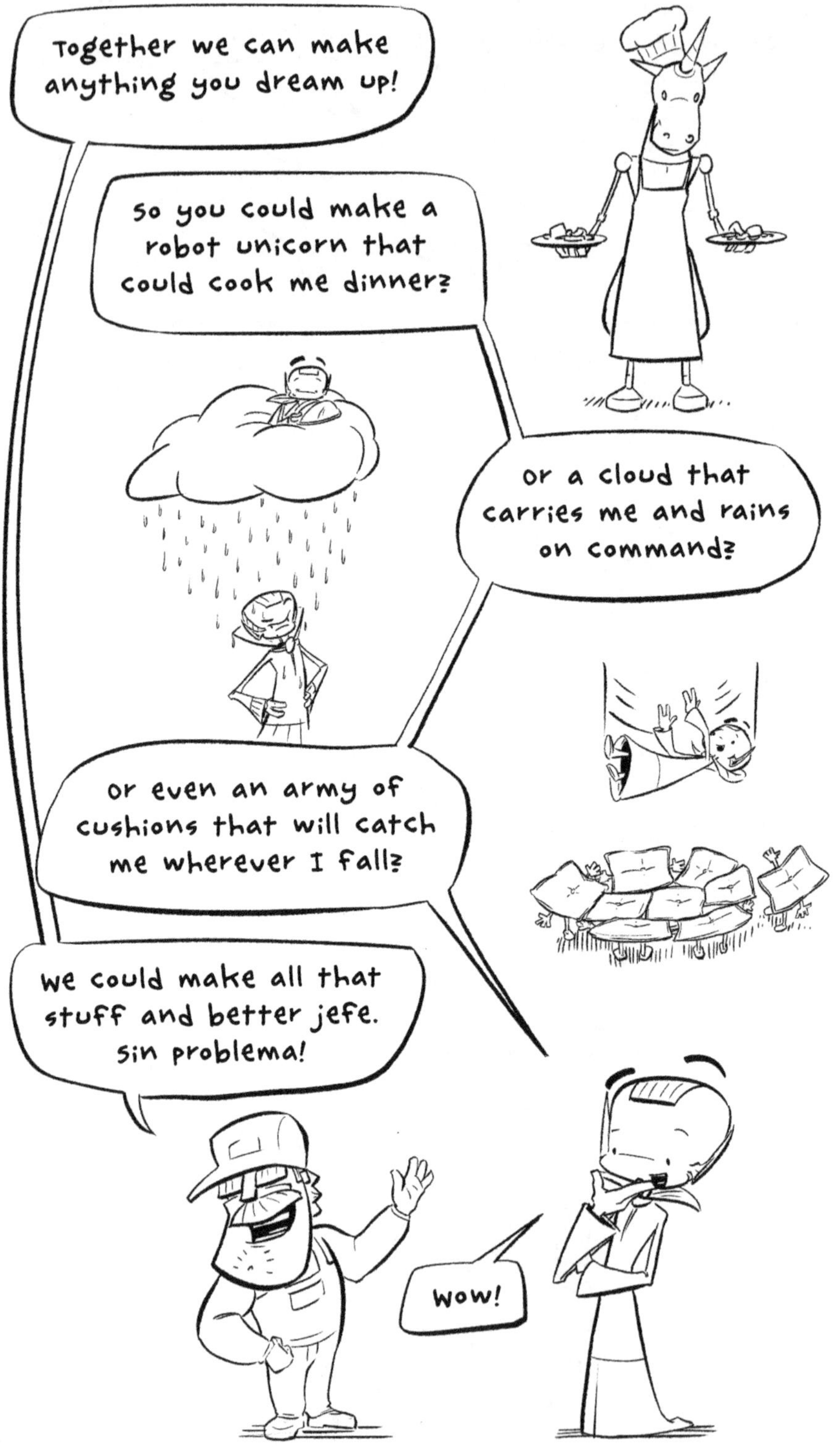
Together we can make anything you dream up!
So you could make a robot unicorn that could cook me dinner?
Or a cloud that carries me and rains on command?
Or even an army of cushions that will catch me wherever I fall?
We could make all that stuff and better jefe. Sin problema!
Wow!

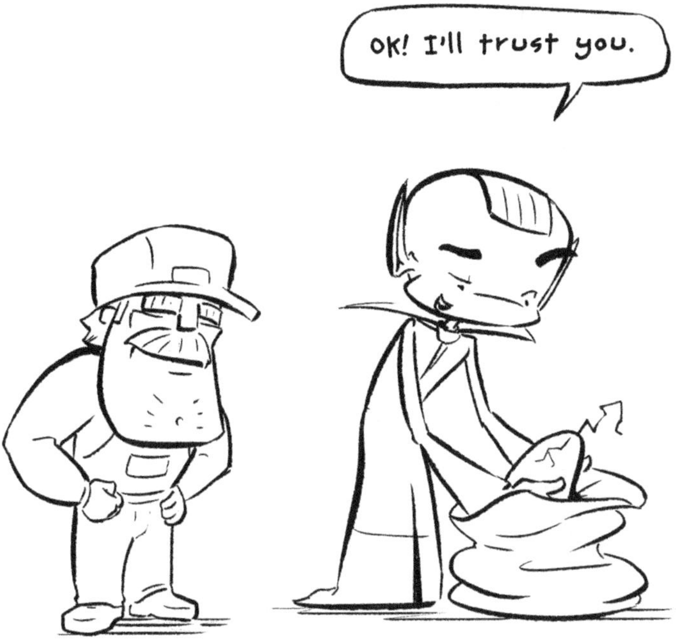
OK! I'll trust you.

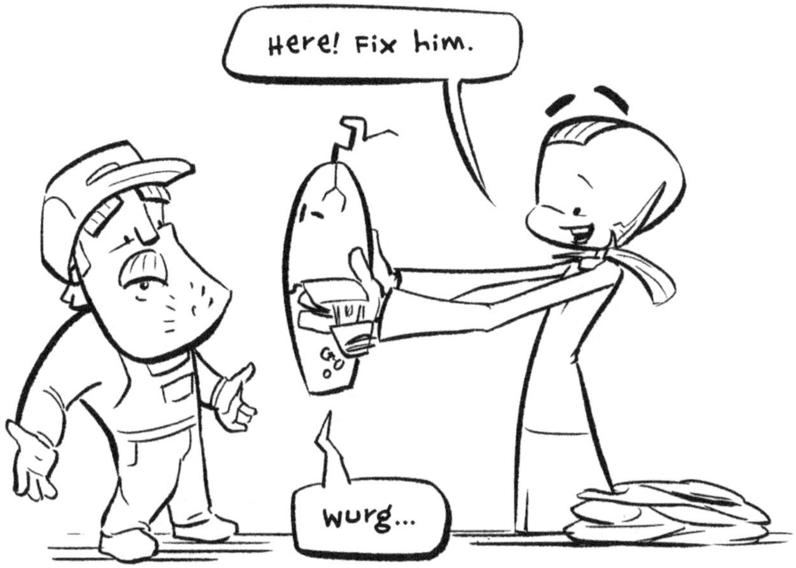
Here! Fix him.
wurg...

If what he says is true, Y-bot is going to be awesome when these people have finished with him!

I can't wait to see what they come up with!

Invasion 101, Day 66

I was feeling a little bit better about the important decision that still lay before me. Mostly because I had completely ignored it for over a week.

Thanks to my need to avoid "The Impossible Choice," I had become much more productive elsewhere. I realised that there were a lot of people who needed my help.

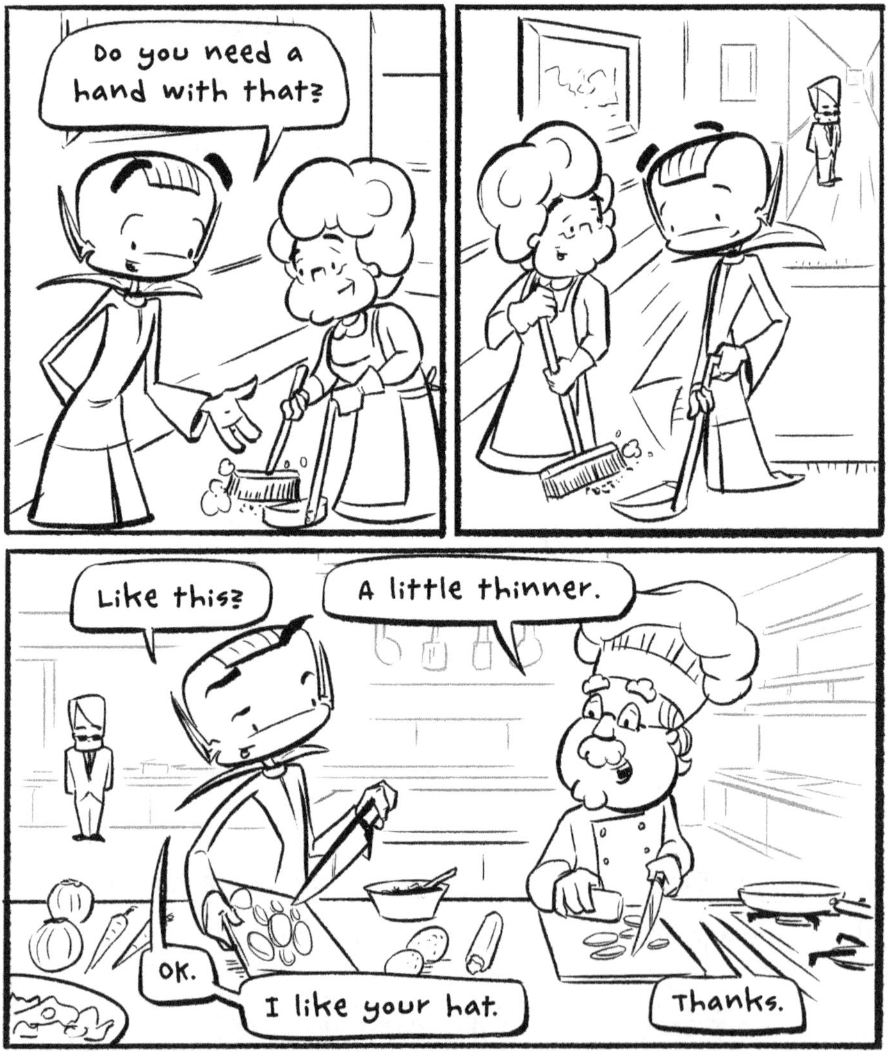

Do you need a hand with that?
Like this?
A little thinner.
OK.
I like your hat.
Thanks.

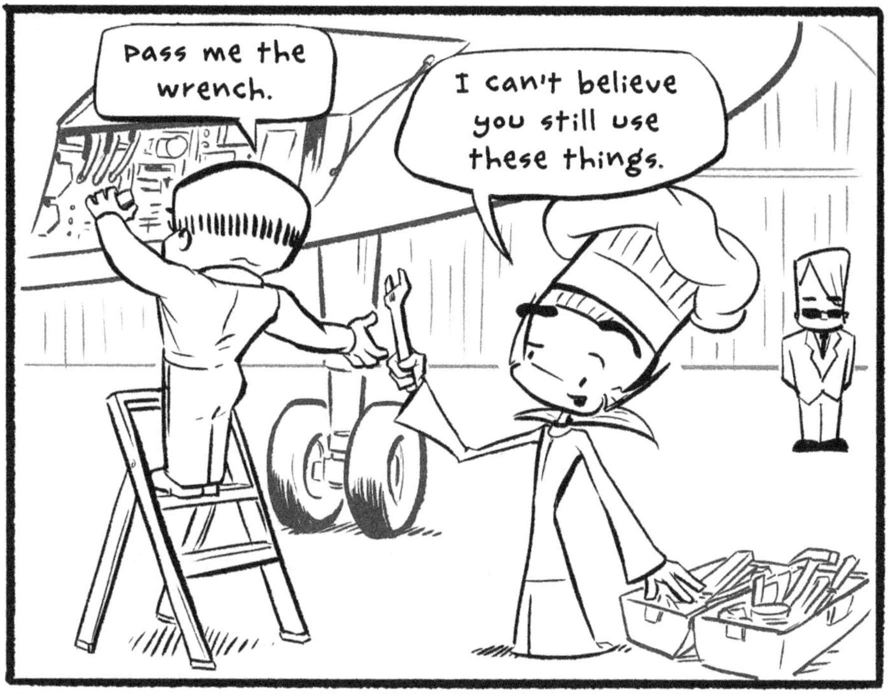
Pass me the wrench.
I can't believe you still use these things.

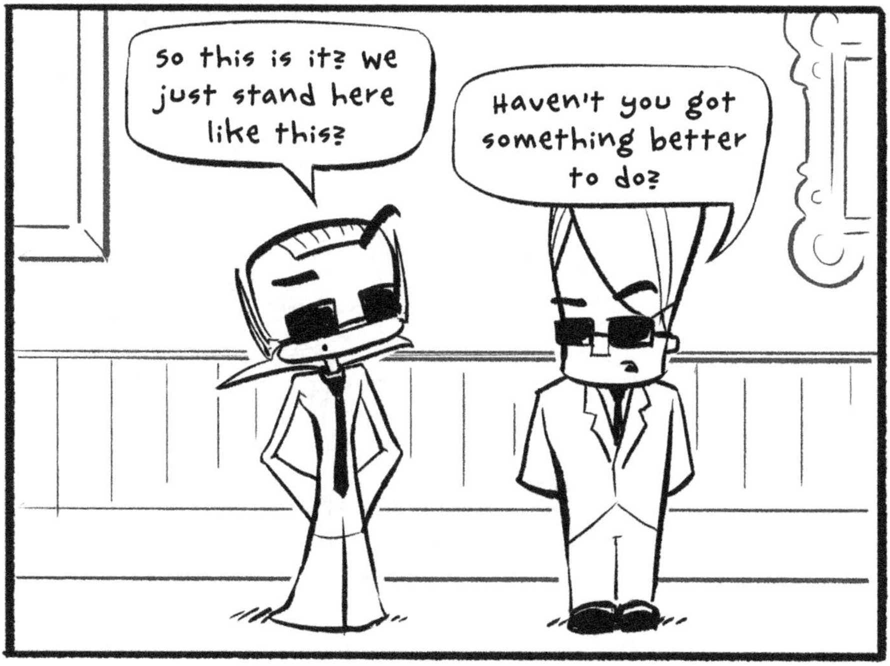
So this is it? We just stand here like this?
Haven't you got something better to do?

I even felt inspired to check in on Emilio. I wanted to see how he was managing the simple task of running the planet.

As the representative from Antarctica he has decided to set his base up at the South Pole.

I would have chosen somewhere warmer.

I found him in his control room in front of a wall of screens. He says he's been able to manage everything from here and I trust him. Apparently working "remotely" is very popular these days.

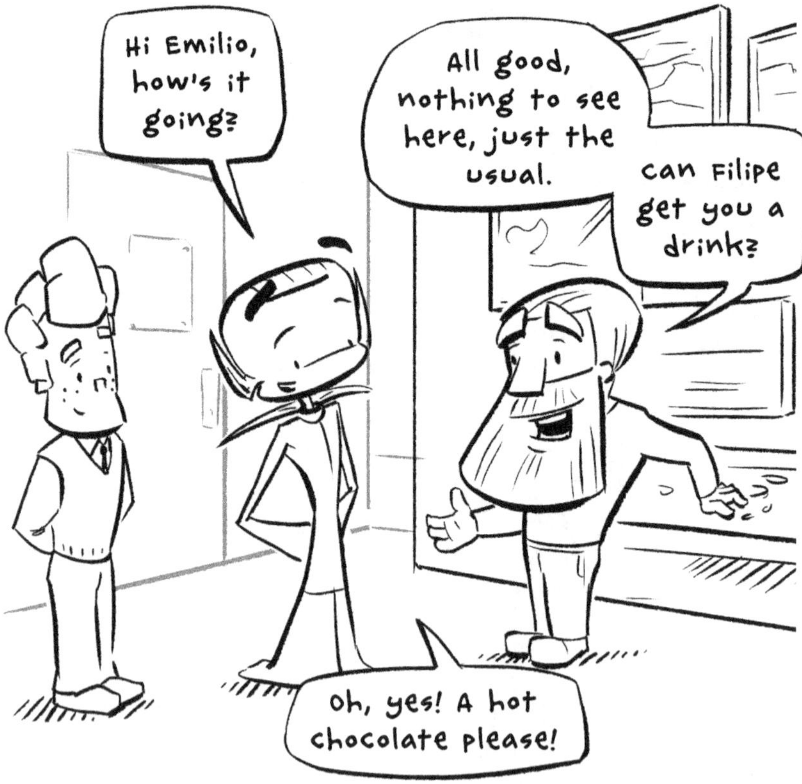
Hi Emilio, how's it going?
All good, nothing to see here, just the usual.
Can Filipe get you a drink?
Oh, yes! A hot chocolate please!

They have nothing quite like drinkable hot chocolate on the ship, or on Glub, or on any other planet I've been to for that matter. I must remember to take some with me before I leave and we destroy everything.

While waiting for my drink, I had a moment to practise another thing I've learned on Earth.

It's called "small talk" and, interestingly, it's the only size talk seems to come in on Earth. I've yet to hear of anyone engaging in "large talk" or "medium-sized talk."

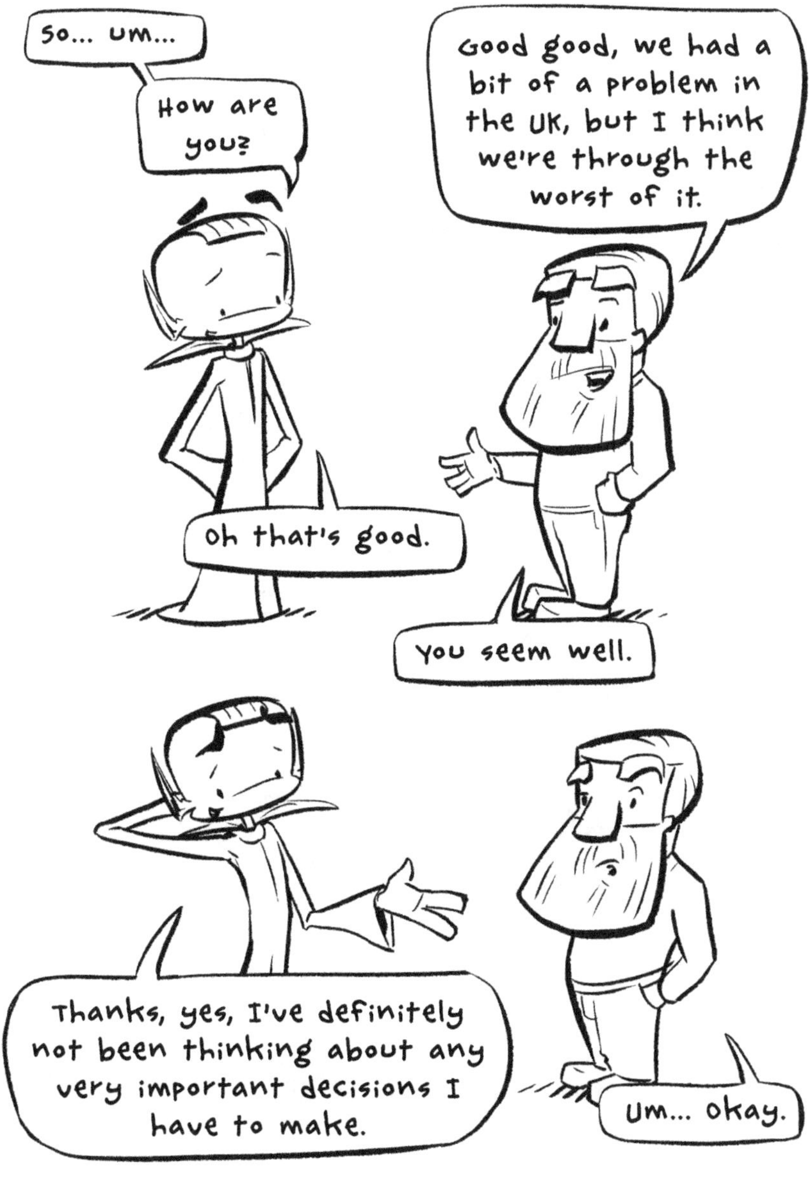
So... um...
How are you?
Good good, we had a bit of a problem in the UK, but I think we're through the worst of it.
Oh that's good.
You seem well.
Thanks, yes, I've definitely not been thinking about any very important decisions I have to make.
Um... okay.

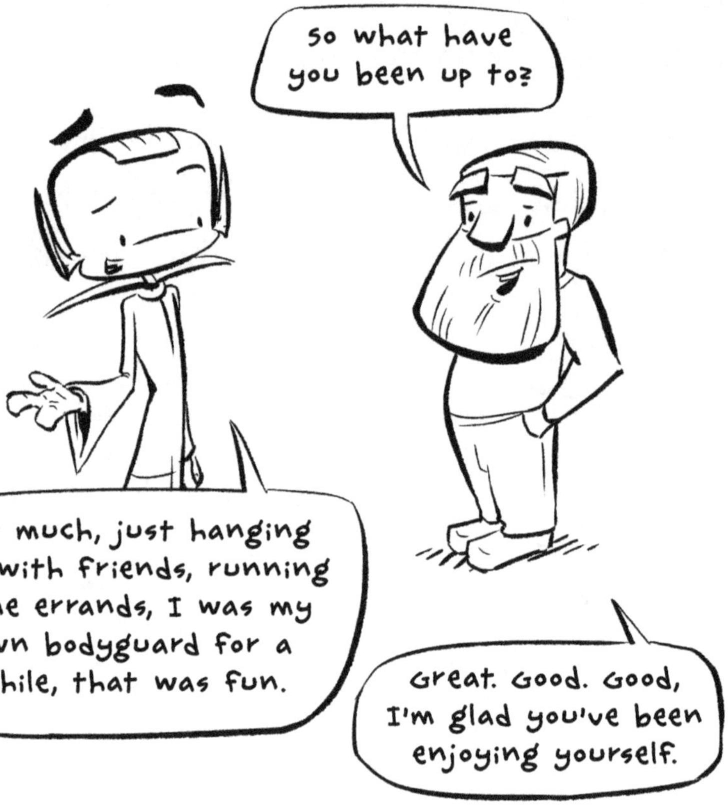
So what have you been up to?
Not much, just hanging out with friends, running some errands, I was my own bodyguard for a while, that was fun.
Great. Good. Good, I'm glad you've been enjoying yourself.

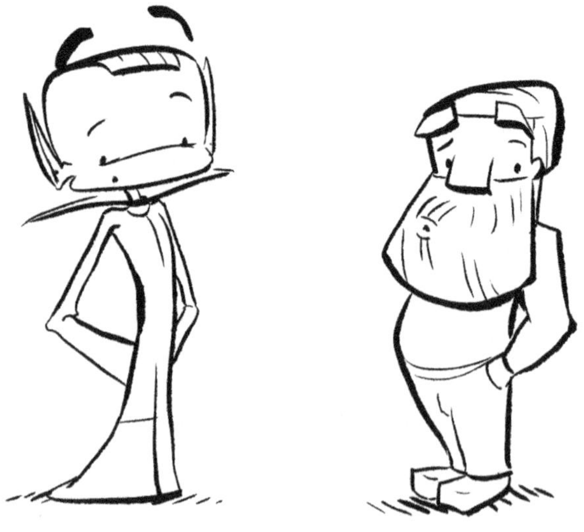

For something they describe as "small" it seemed to last an unnecessarily long time.

We had just started talking about the weather when another one of Emilio's assistants entered the room.

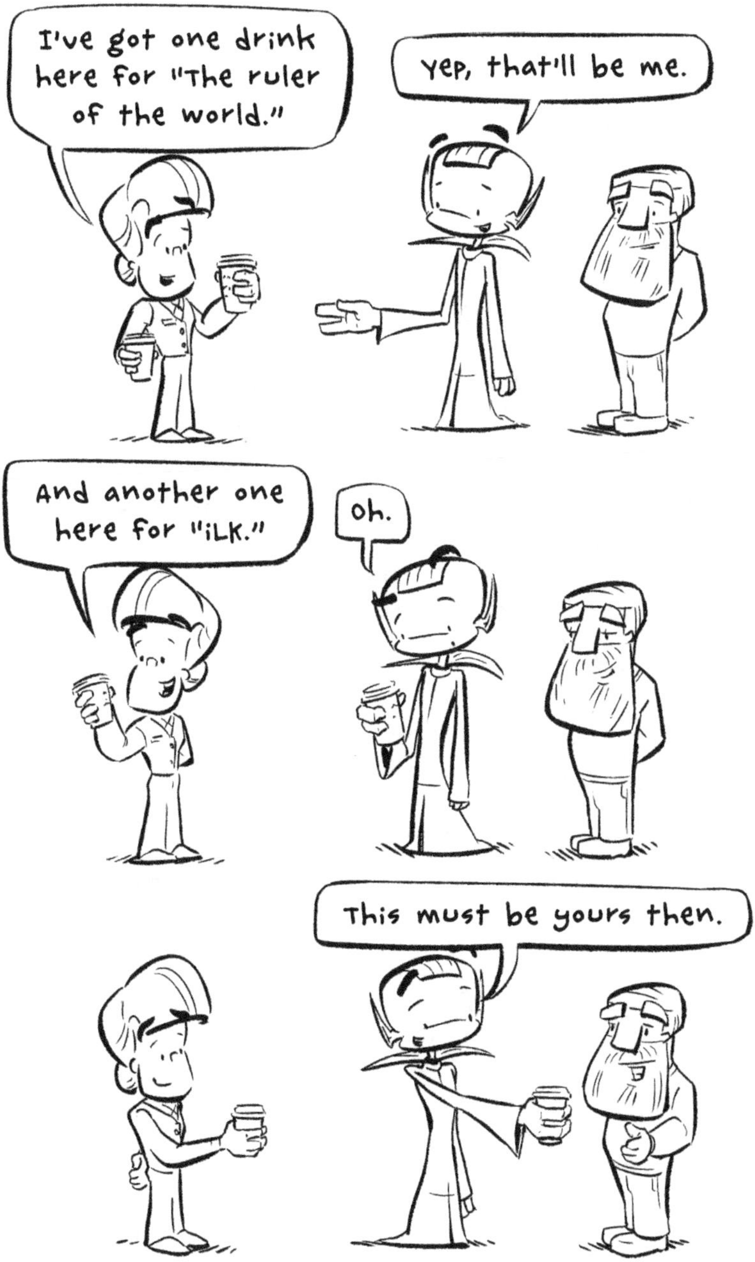
I've got one drink here for "The ruler of the world."
Yep, that'll be me.
And another one here for "iLK."
Oh.
This must be yours then.

Emilio seems to be very comfortable in his new role. I suppose that's a good thing.

Emilio was then called away, probably to deal with something dull and unimportant. I was left in the room with the screens.

As I stood there, watching the world at work; cities bustling, families playing, scientists exploring; sipping my delightful hot chocolate, I couldn't help but think...

It's a shame we're going to blow it all up.

Invasion 101, Day 68

I was wrong to be grumpy. I was wrong to yell. I probably shouldn't have shoved him, nor should I have thrown the cake.

It was neither his fault, nor the cake's.

I was invited to the White House in the USA for some kind of memorial, or anniversary, or celebration or... something.

I can't really remember what it was, but for some reason it warranted cake.

Yip, yip, yip!

I wasn't in the mood for the Dullrat's overexcited jibber jabber, or this photo opportunity.

I was in the mood for cake.

But at least I felt like the cake had been put to good use when the Dullrat stopped bothering me to clean it off his face and shirt.

The feelings of guilt didn't arrive until later.

I'd been thinking about home. Longing for my bedroom. I had thoughts of lying quietly with no one to bother me.

Well I wouldn't mind if TalC was there, and Y-bot, but he's like part of the furniture so of course he'd still be there.

And if Marina was there too that would be OK I suppose. It would be even better if she could bring the Amazon Rainforest with her.

I guess Emilio could come too, and it would be great if Jorge could be there to fix a few things.

And if everyone else is there, it feels mean to leave the Dullrat out. At least he could keep everyone else organised.

But of course, no one from Earth would actually be there.

It would just be me, on my own again.

At least I'd have my first letter by that point.

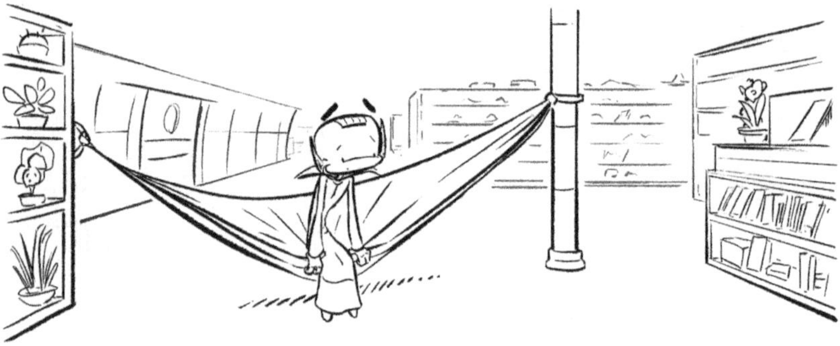

This is what I was thinking when I threw the cake.

Shortly after the photo op, I was sitting in the private study they had set up for me at the White House. I still hadn't perked up.

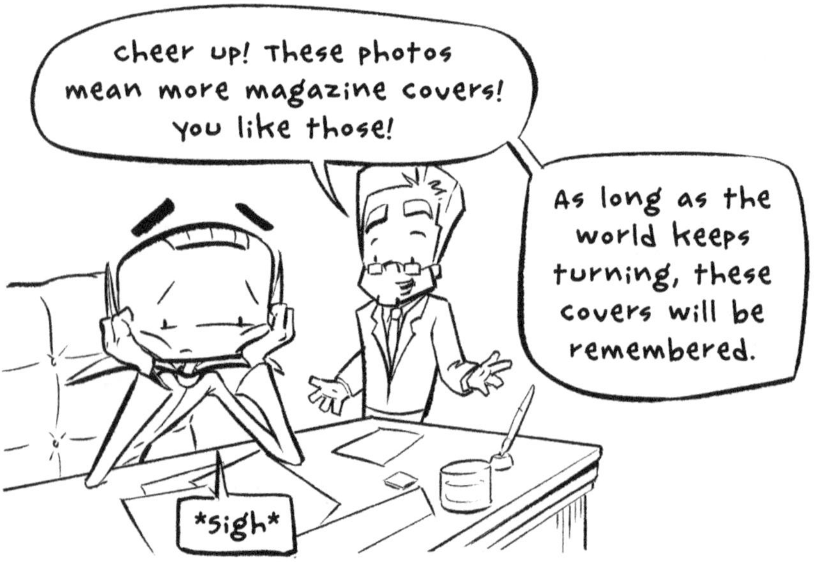
cheer up! These photos mean more magazine covers! you like those!
As long as the world keeps turning, these covers will be remembered.
sigh

I couldn't shake this horrible sense of foreboding.

And then my dad called.

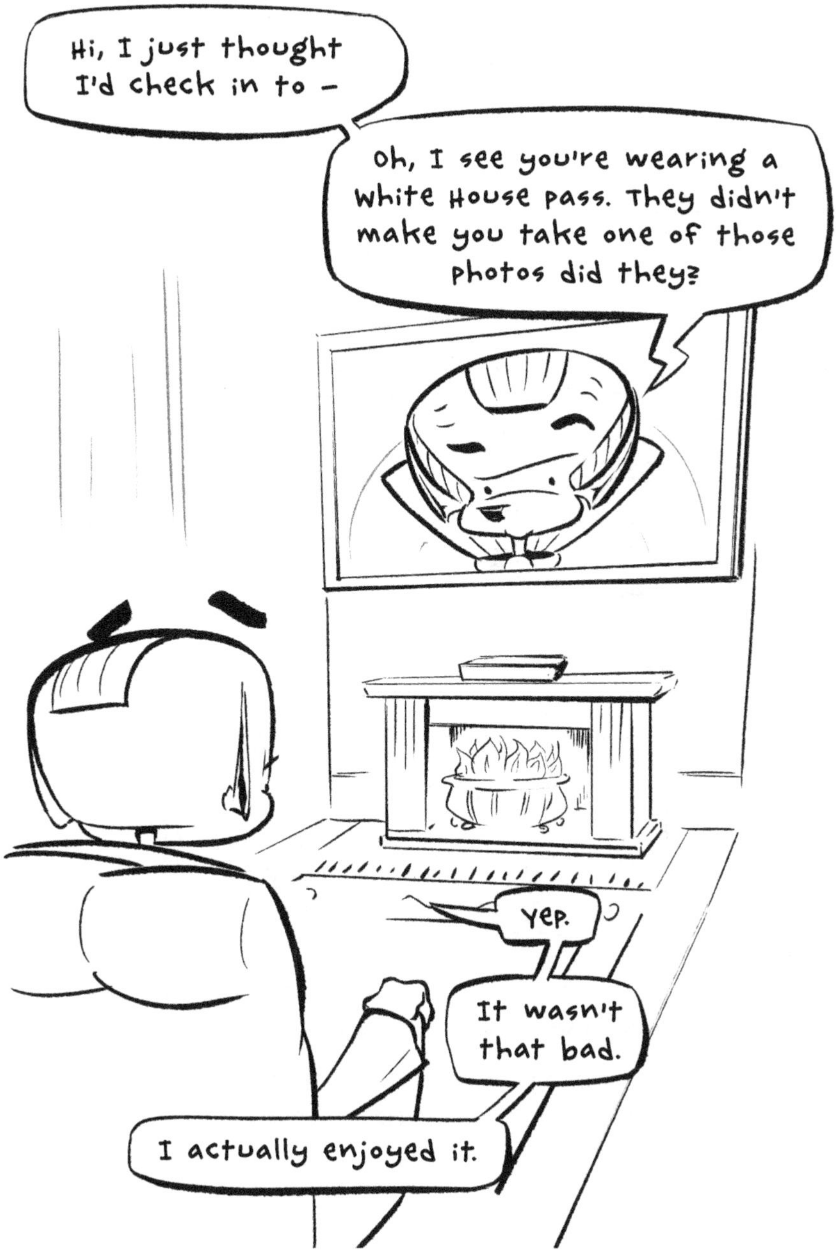

Hi, I just thought I'd check in to -
Oh, I see you're wearing a White House pass. They didn't make you take one of those photos did they?
Yep.
It wasn't that bad.
I actually enjoyed it.

No I didn't.

Dad saw straight through my lie.

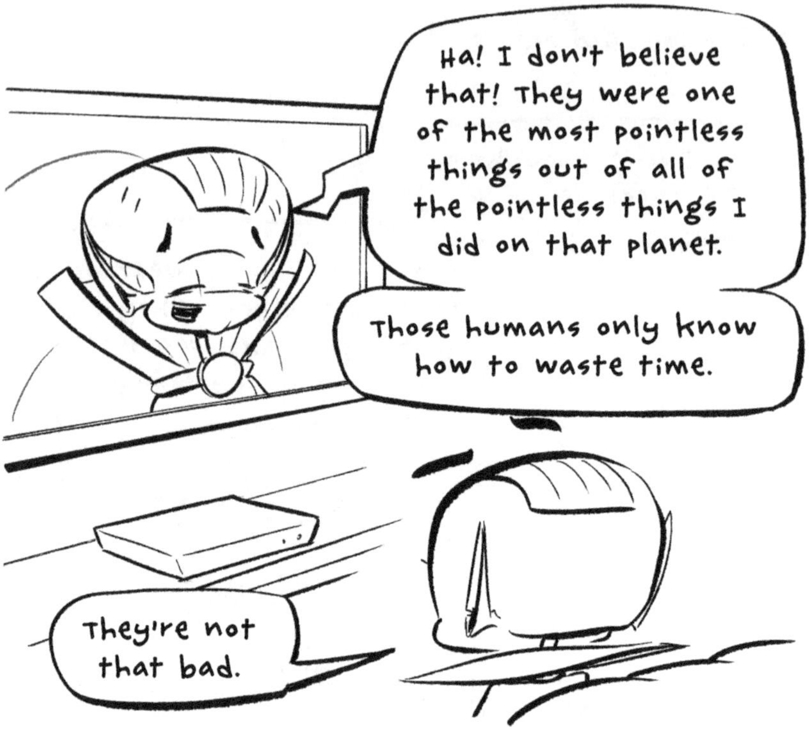
Ha! I don't believe that! They were one of the most pointless things out of all of the pointless things I did on that planet.
Those humans only know how to waste time.
They're not that bad.

That was true.

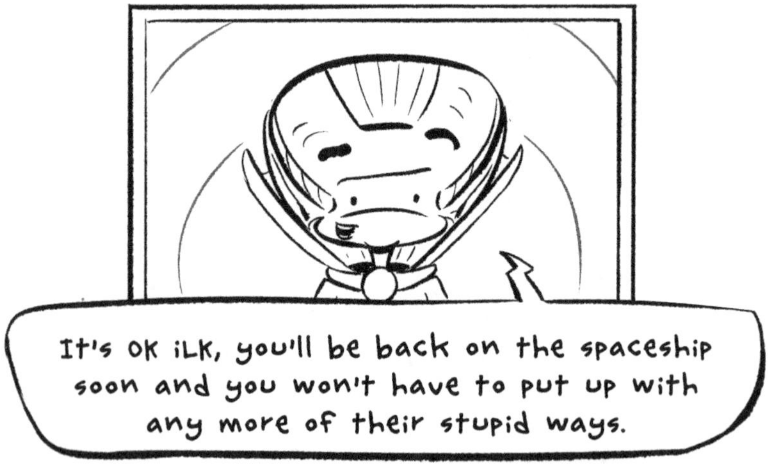
It's OK iLK, you'll be back on the spaceship soon and you won't have to put up with any more of their stupid ways.

Dad was wrong.

They weren't stupid.

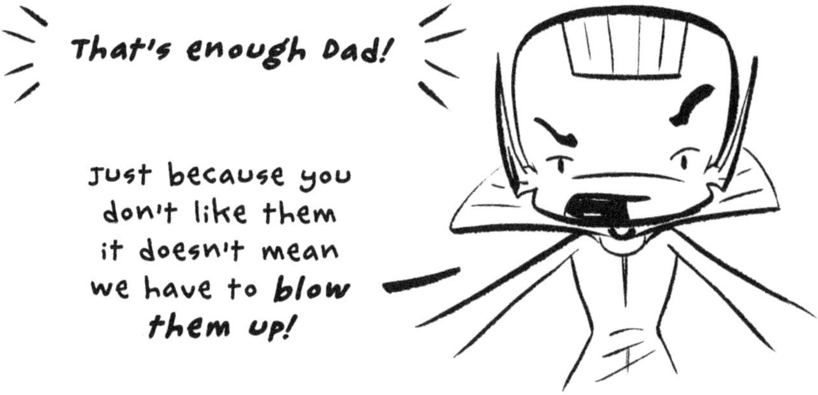
That's enough Dad!
Just because you don't like them it doesn't mean we have to blow them up!

Maybe I shouldn't have said that, although it was another truth.

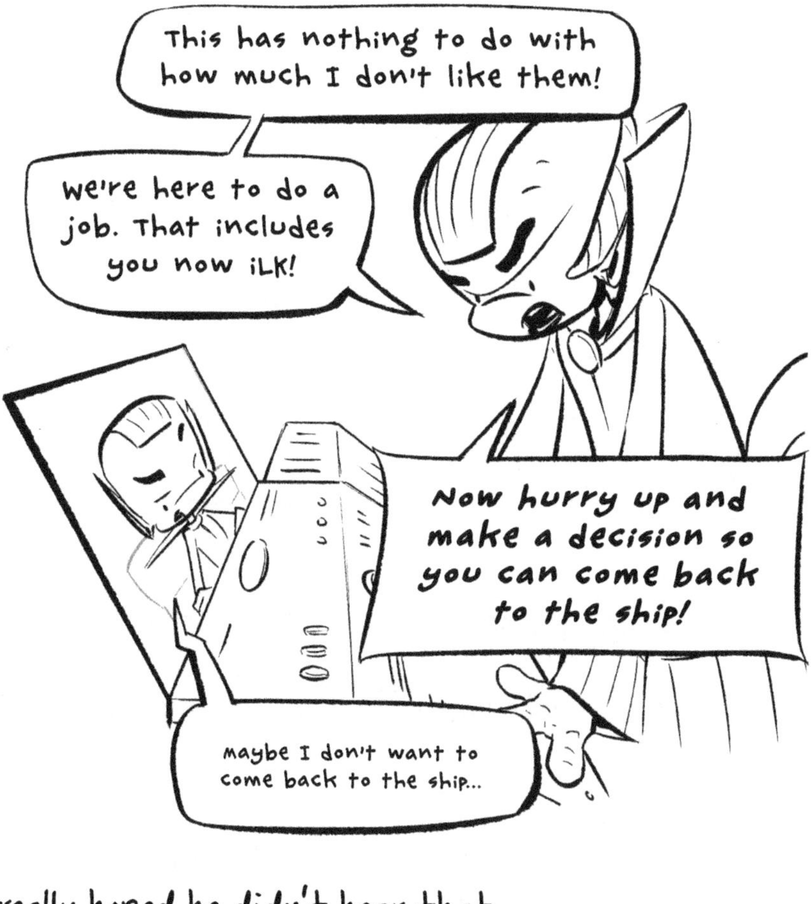
This has nothing to do with how much I don't like them!
We're here to do a job. That includes you now iLK!
Now hurry up and make a decision so you can come back to the ship!
maybe I don't want to come back to the ship...

I really hoped he didn't hear that.

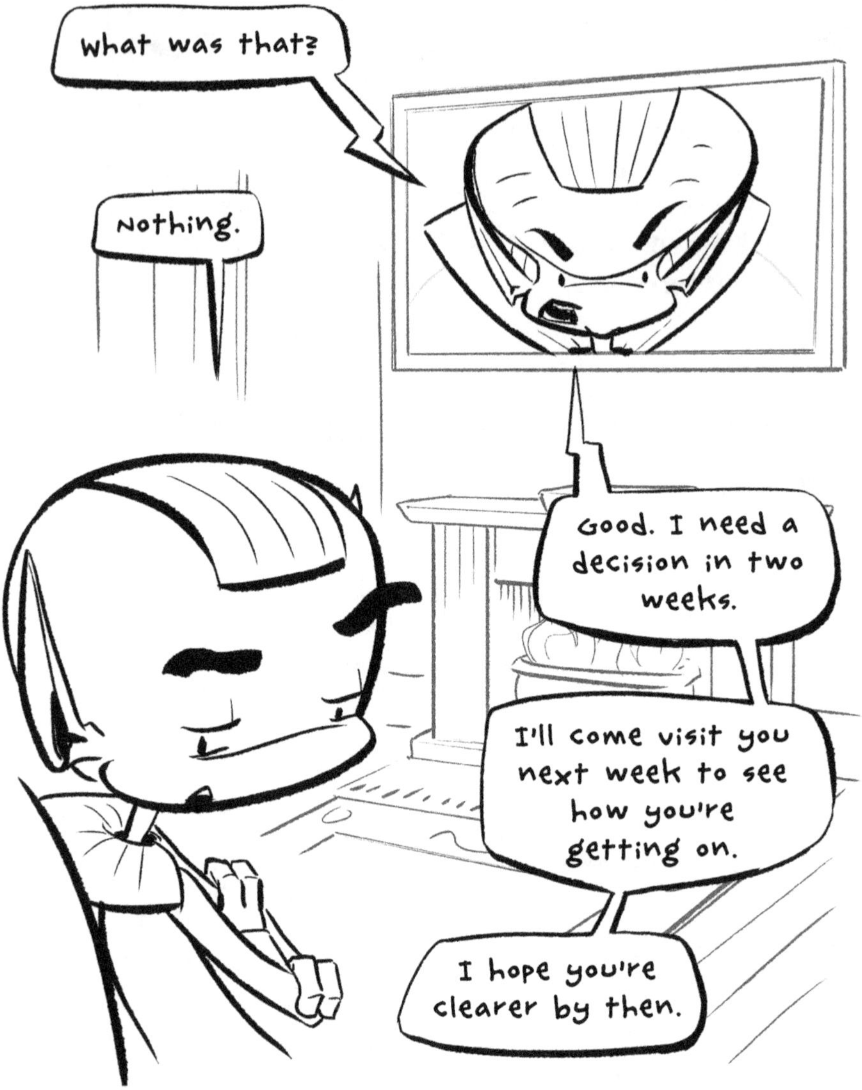
What was that?
Nothing.
Good. I need a decision in two weeks.
I'll come visit you next week to see how you're getting on.
I hope you're clearer by then.

With that I hung up and went back to my friends.

I now know that I can't make the decision he wants me to make.

I have to think of something else. Something that involves zero explosions and no planets being destroyed.

Invasion 101, Day 70

I woke up feeling hopeful. Today was the day I would collect Y-bot. I started to think about all the improvements Jorge and his team might have made to my inquisitive little friend and it put a big smile on my face.

This confused a lot of people.

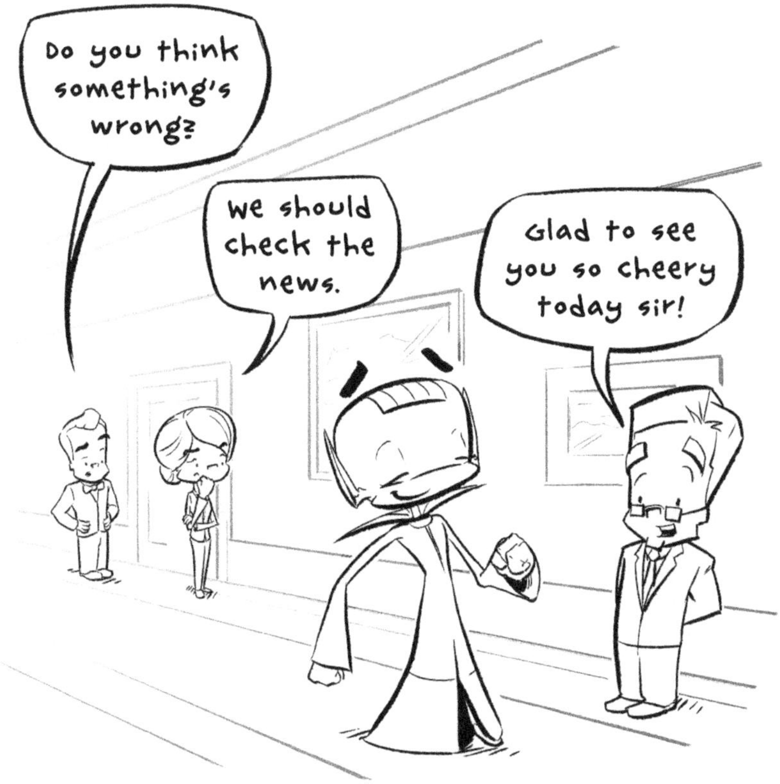

Do you think something's wrong?
We should check the news.
Glad to see you so cheery today sir!

If I could show Dad all of the incredible things that this small group of humans were able to achieve with Y-bot, then he'd realise how much potential there was on Earth. Then he might reconsider his plan to destroy it!

At least, that was the idea. In my head it went something like this...

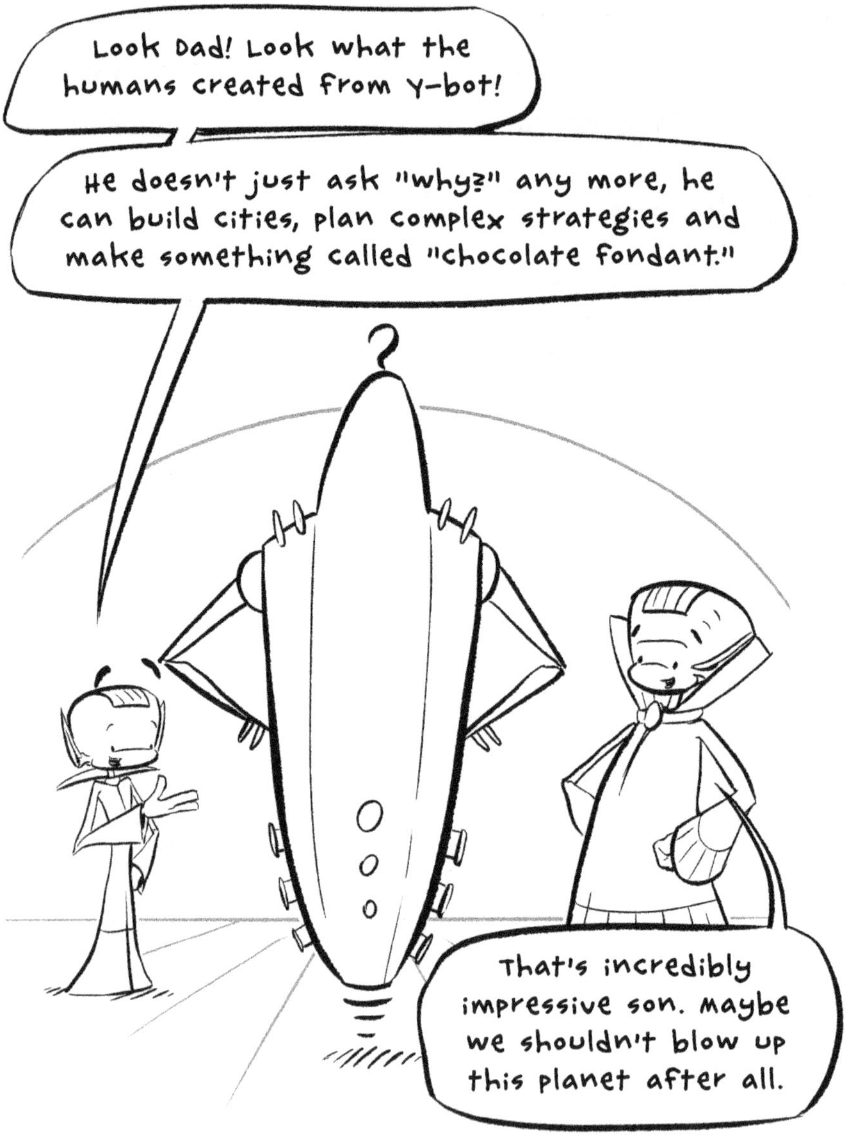
Look Dad! Look what the humans created from Y-bot!
He doesn't just ask "why?" any more, he can build cities, plan complex strategies and make something called "chocolate fondant."
That's incredibly impressive son. Maybe we shouldn't blow up this planet after all.

Of course I had no idea what Y-bot would be when they finished fixing him.

This was just one idea.

Here are some other ideas I had for the new and improved Y-bot...

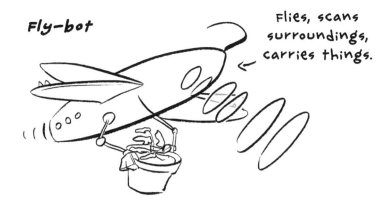

Fly-bot

Flies, scans surroundings, carries things.

Jive-bot

spectacular dancer. That's all he needs.

Tie-bot

Not sure what he does, but he looks cool.

Given how much Jorge had promised to deliver, anything was possible.

Unfortunately my hopes were all dashed when I arrived at his sorry excuse for an engineer's studio.

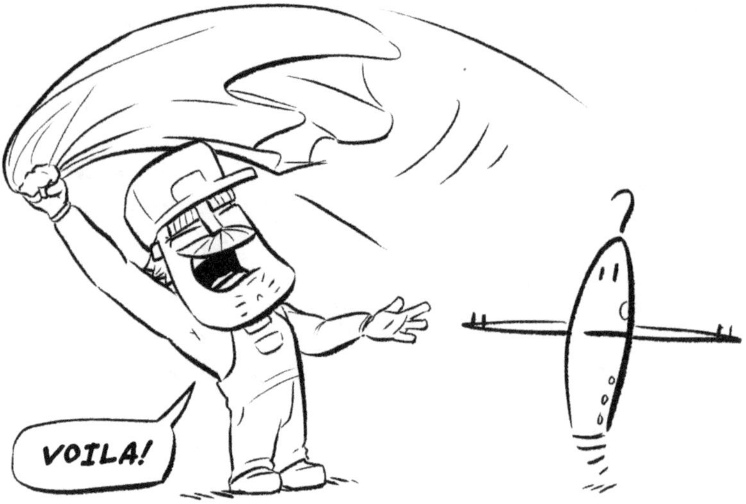
VOILA!

I'd never heard the word "Voila!" before today. Clearly it meant, "Sorry. This a poor excuse for a new and improved robot. We are pathetic and have let you down."

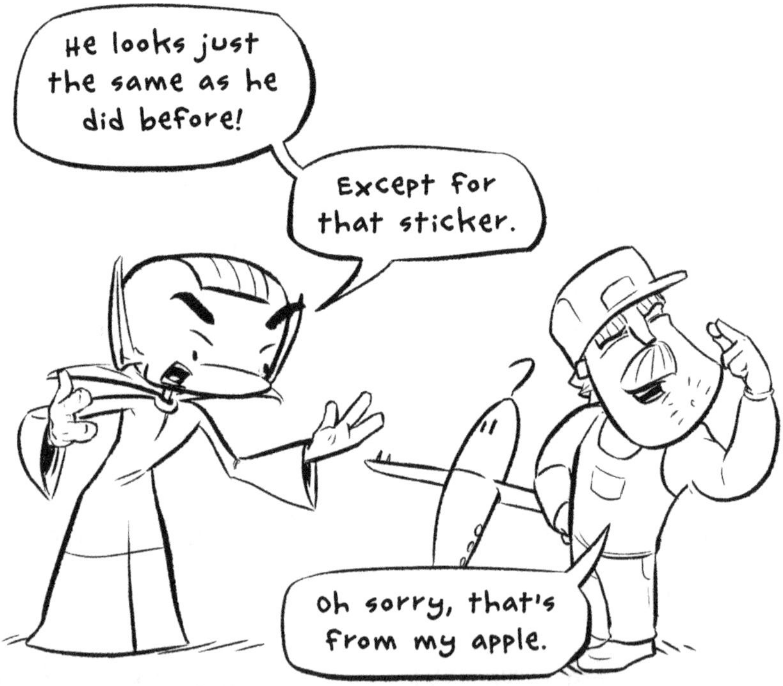
He looks just the same as he did before!
Except for that sticker.
Oh sorry, that's from my apple.

This was a disaster!

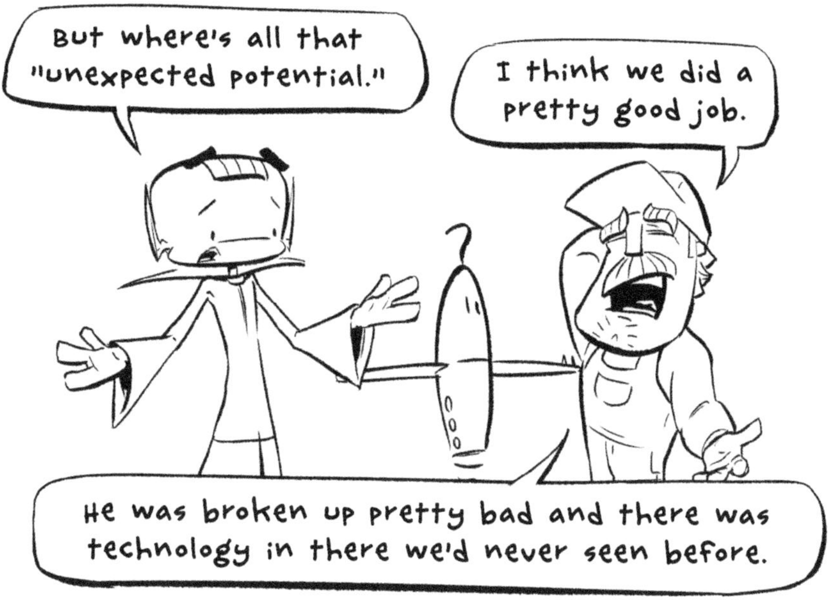
But where's all that "unexpected potential."
I think we did a pretty good job.
He was broken up pretty bad and there was technology in there we'd never seen before.

That wasn't a good enough answer. This will impress Dad less than my sculpture of him as a stone.

It was just a stone.

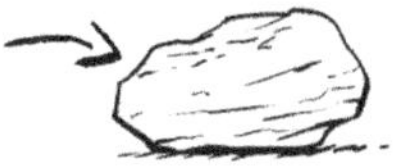

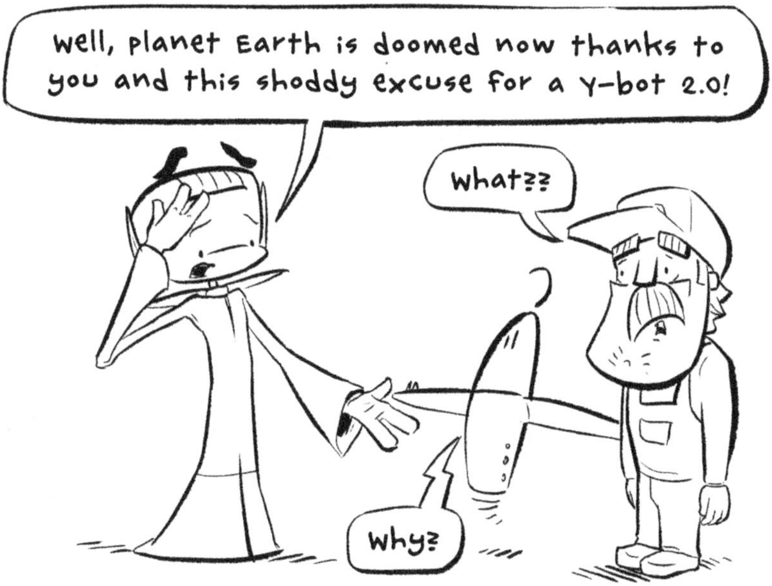
Well, planet Earth is doomed now thanks to you and this shoddy excuse for a Y-bot 2.0!
What??
Why?

At least Y-bot can understand me again.

Invasion 101, Day 75

I started the day thinking about the fact my Dad would be here tomorrow and I had nothing to prove to him that the Earth was worth keeping.

It was a real downer.

I didn't want to talk to a single person.

Talking to Y-bot was OK though, he wasn't a person.

If only they'd turned you into a cool flying robot or the one with the tie. That would have been so much better.

why?

I hadn't really thought about why that would be better. Dad's seen plenty of flying robots before and he doesn't even like ties.

Y-bot is pretty special as he is.

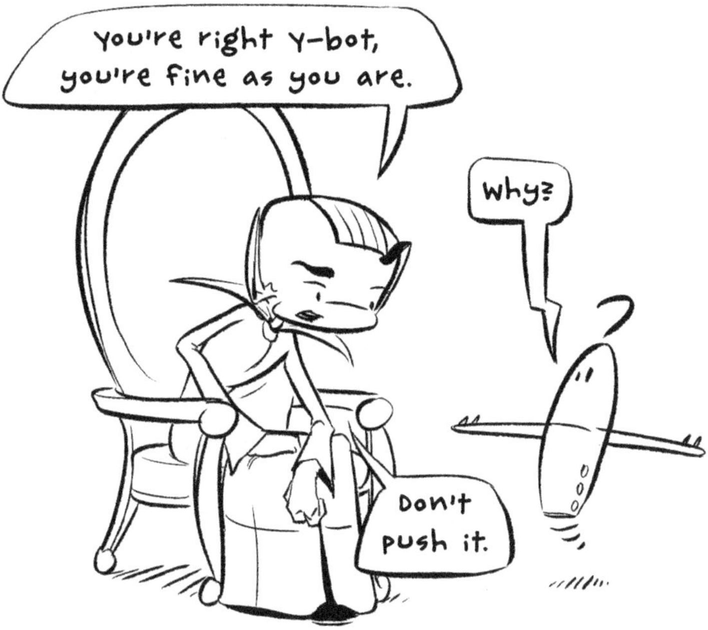
You're right Y-bot,
you're fine as you are.
Why?
Don't
push it.

Unfortunately this meant I was stuck. As long as I had nothing new to show Dad, he would continue with his plan to destroy the planet.

I was completely out of ideas. I felt entirely hopeless.

Nothing could help me now.

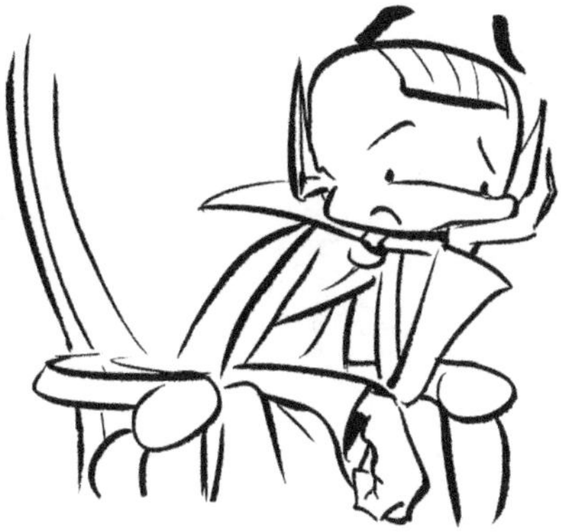

And then Marina called.

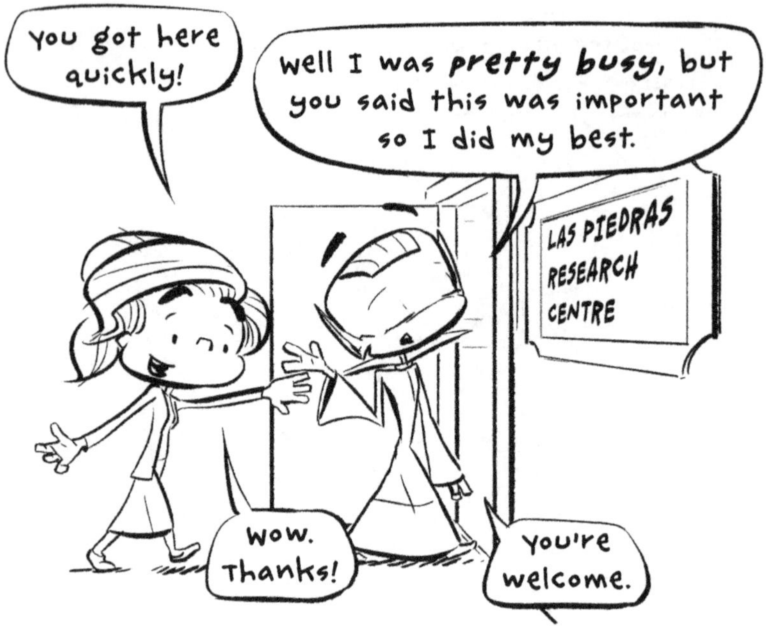
you got here quickly!
well I was pretty busy, but you said this was important so I did my best.
LAS PIEDRAS RESEARCH CENTRE
wow. Thanks!
You're welcome.

She was really excited, which started to make me excited, but then I remembered the last time I got too excited, I was really disappointed, so I tried to stay calm.

Apparently the resulting expression was a little confusing.

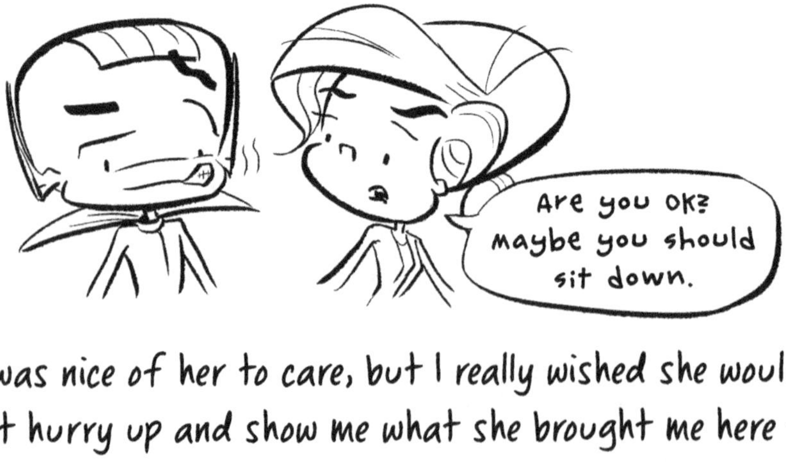
Are you OK? maybe you should sit down.

It was nice of her to care, but I really wished she would just hurry up and show me what she brought me here to show me.

Fortunately I wasn't disappointed.

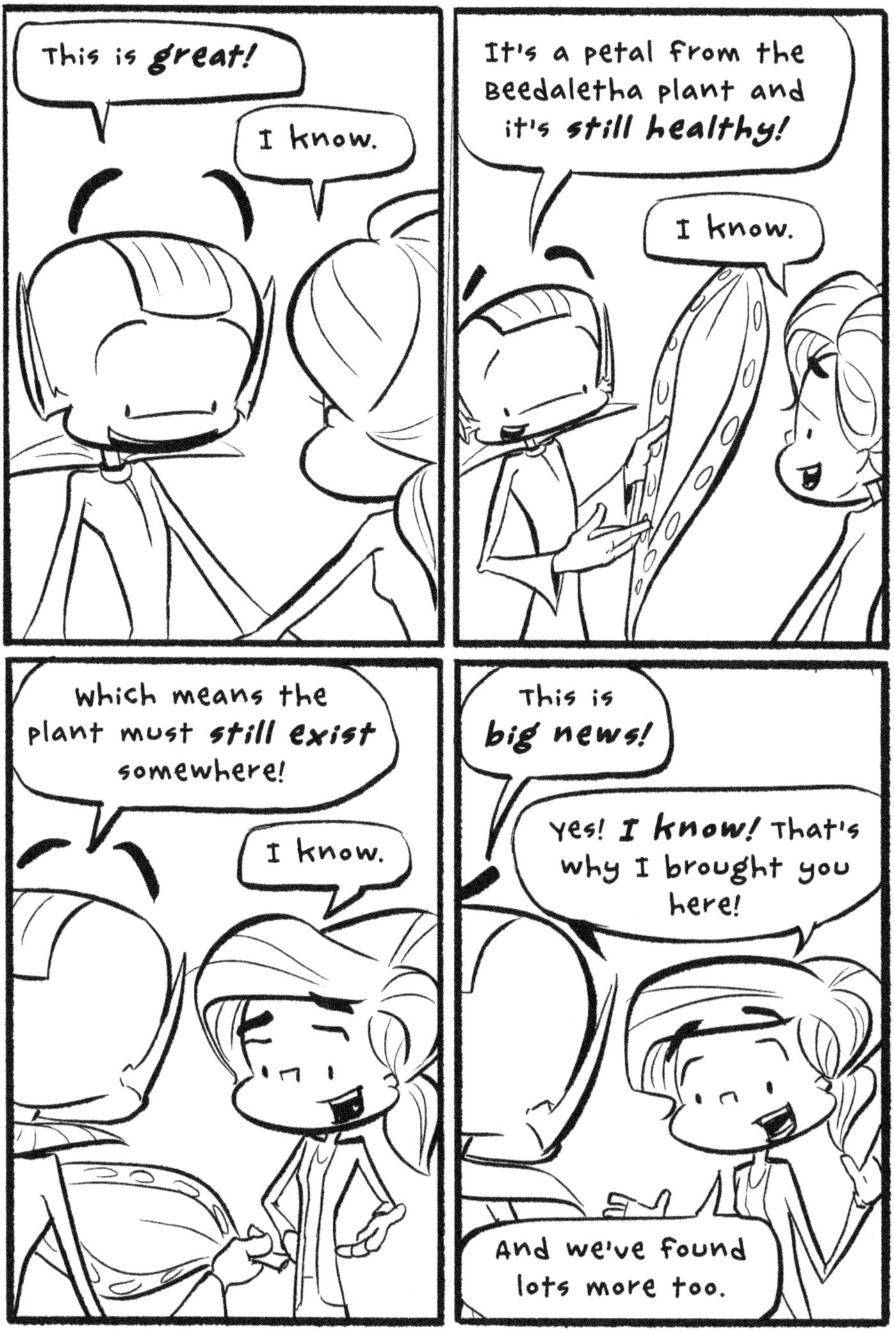

This is **great!**
I know.
It's a petal from the Beedaletha plant and it's **still healthy!**
I know.
Which means the plant must **still exist** somewhere!
I know.
This is **big news!**
Yes! **I know!** That's why I brought you here!
And we've found lots more too.

She found these even without using the Toca-Ray transmitter or the wildlife scanner!

They have simply been going into the jungle and searching using their hands and faces.

I almost didn't believe her, but then I reminded myself that they are very simple creatures that loved touching things...

These petals will help to convince Dad that this planet is not dead yet, but they might not be enough.

I had to know how far away they were from finding the actual plant.

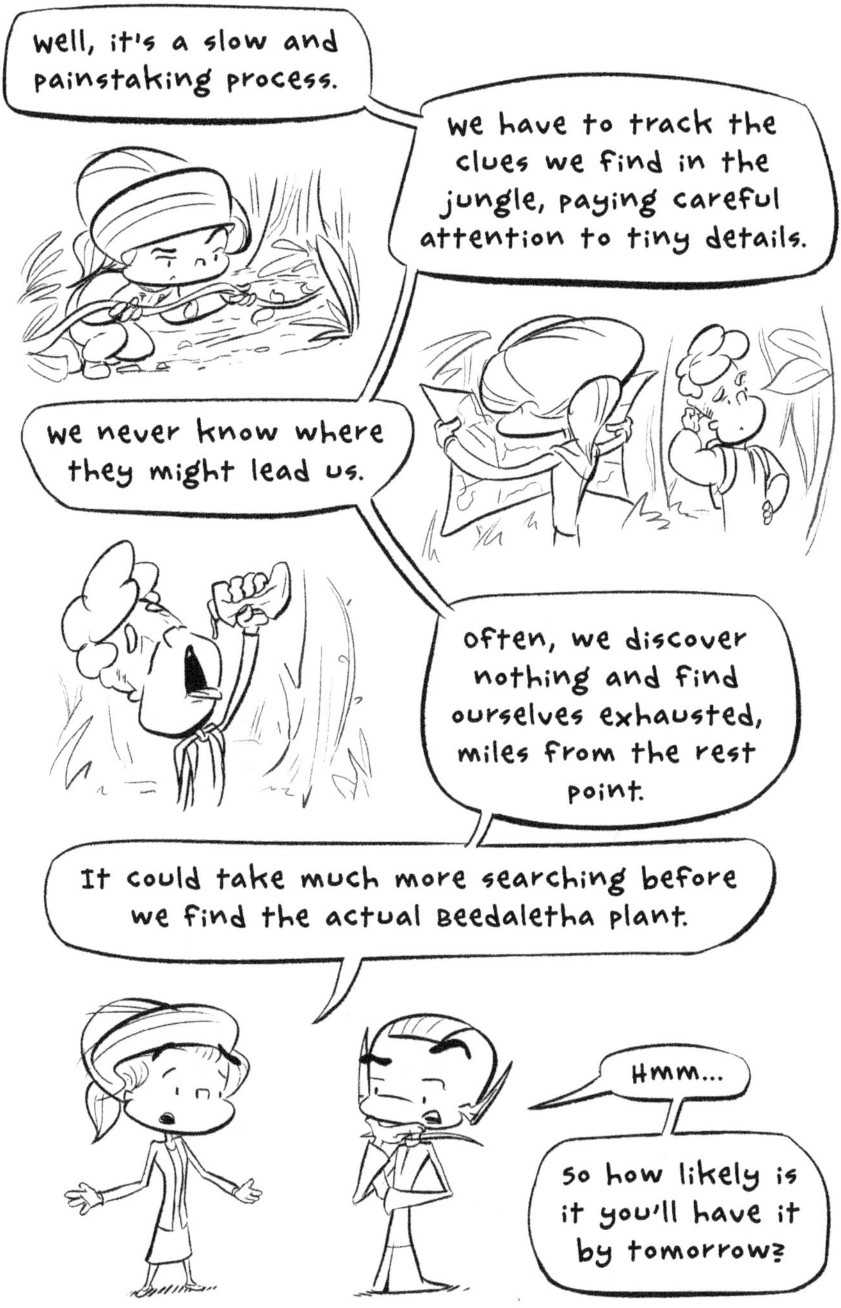
Well, it's a slow and painstaking process.
We have to track the clues we find in the jungle, paying careful attention to tiny details.
We never know where they might lead us.
Often, we discover nothing and find ourselves exhausted, miles from the rest point.
It could take much more searching before we find the actual Beedaletha plant.
Hmm...
So how likely is it you'll have it by tomorrow?

I had to admire her commitment. She's clearly slow and often ineffective, but her commitment is admirable.

Unfortunately, admirable commitment is useless to me.

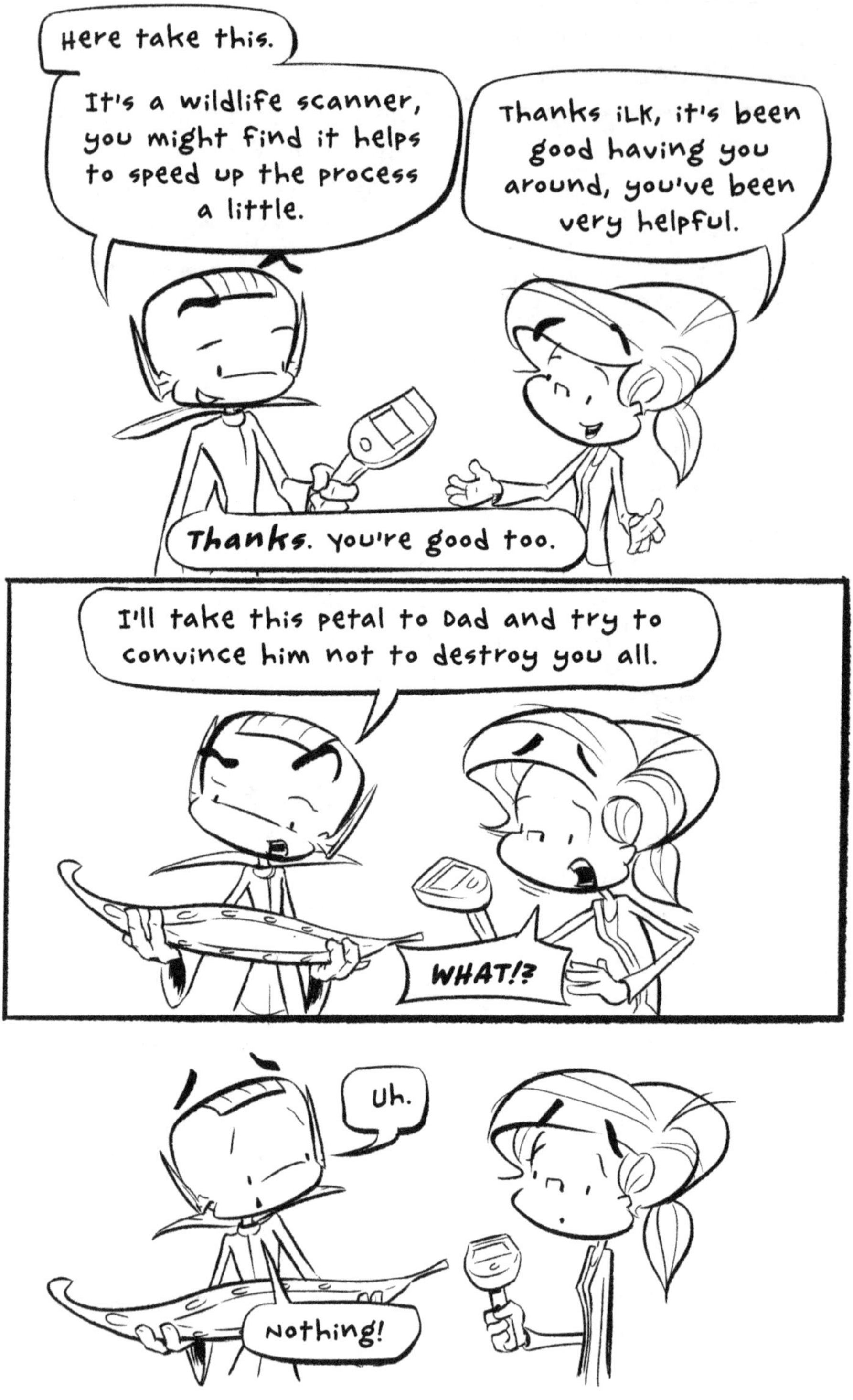
Here take this.
It's a wildlife scanner, you might find it helps to speed up the process a little.
Thanks iLK, it's been good having you around, you've been very helpful.
Thanks. You're good too.
I'll take this petal to Dad and try to convince him not to destroy you all.
WHAT!?
Uh.
Nothing!

Phew, that was close.

Invasion 101, Day 76

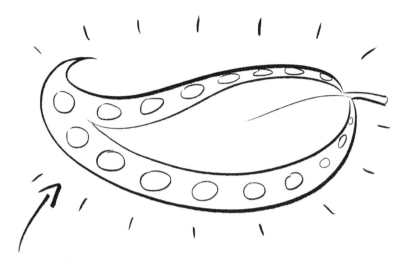

This petal showed a lot of promise. Showing this to Dad could encourage him to continue the search for the Beedaletha plant, before killing this planet too soon.

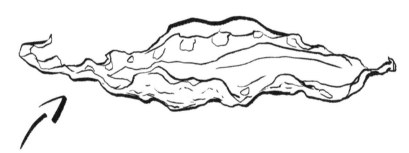

This leaf shows a lot less promise. It's dead and won't convince anyone of anything.

Sadly the latter is how it looks now.

Nevertheless, my objective was still to convince Dad not to go ahead with his plan to blow up the world.

Dad started off friendly.

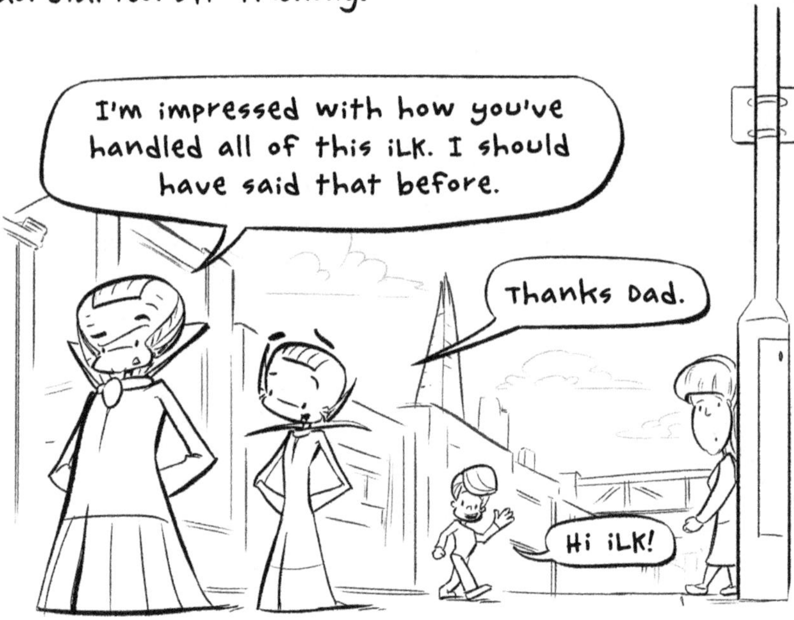

I'm impressed with how you've handled all of this iLK. I should have said that before.
Thanks Dad.
Hi iLK!

I took him to one of my favourite places to eat in London.

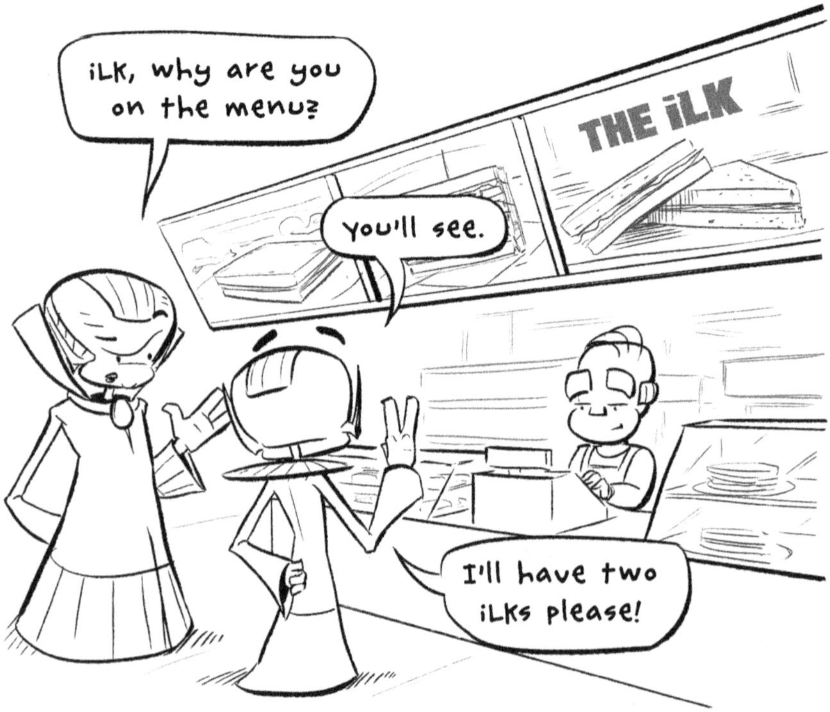

iLK, why are you on the menu?
THE iLK
You'll see.
I'll have two iLKs please!

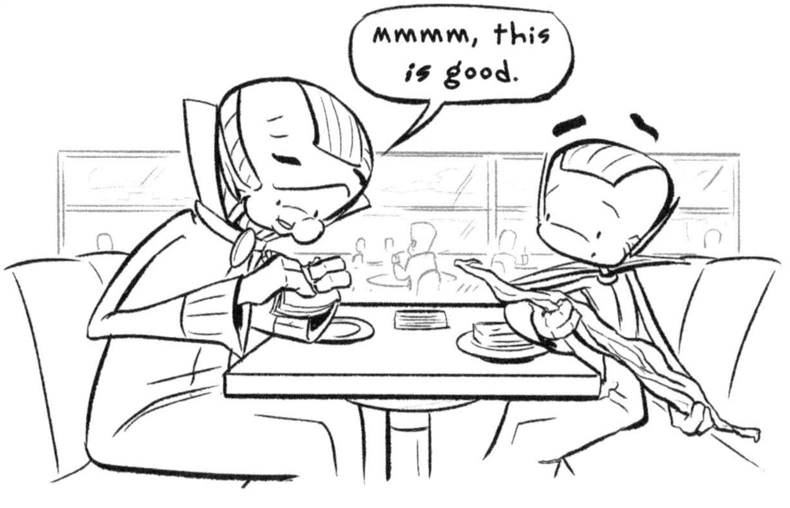
mmmm, this is good.

This was it. My moment; my chance to save the world...

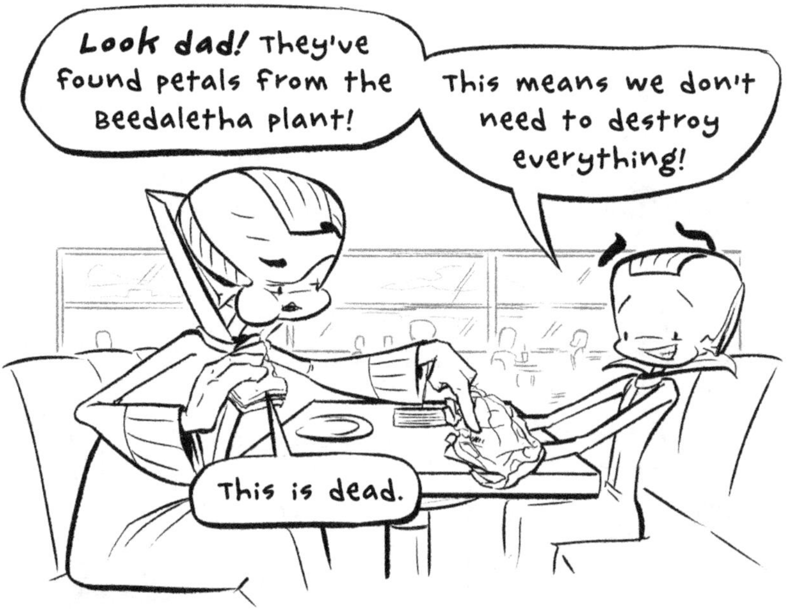
Look dad! They've found petals from the Beedaletha plant!
This means we don't need to destroy everything!
This is dead.

He was right.

It was very dead. It was a long shot and it had failed.

It was downhill from there.

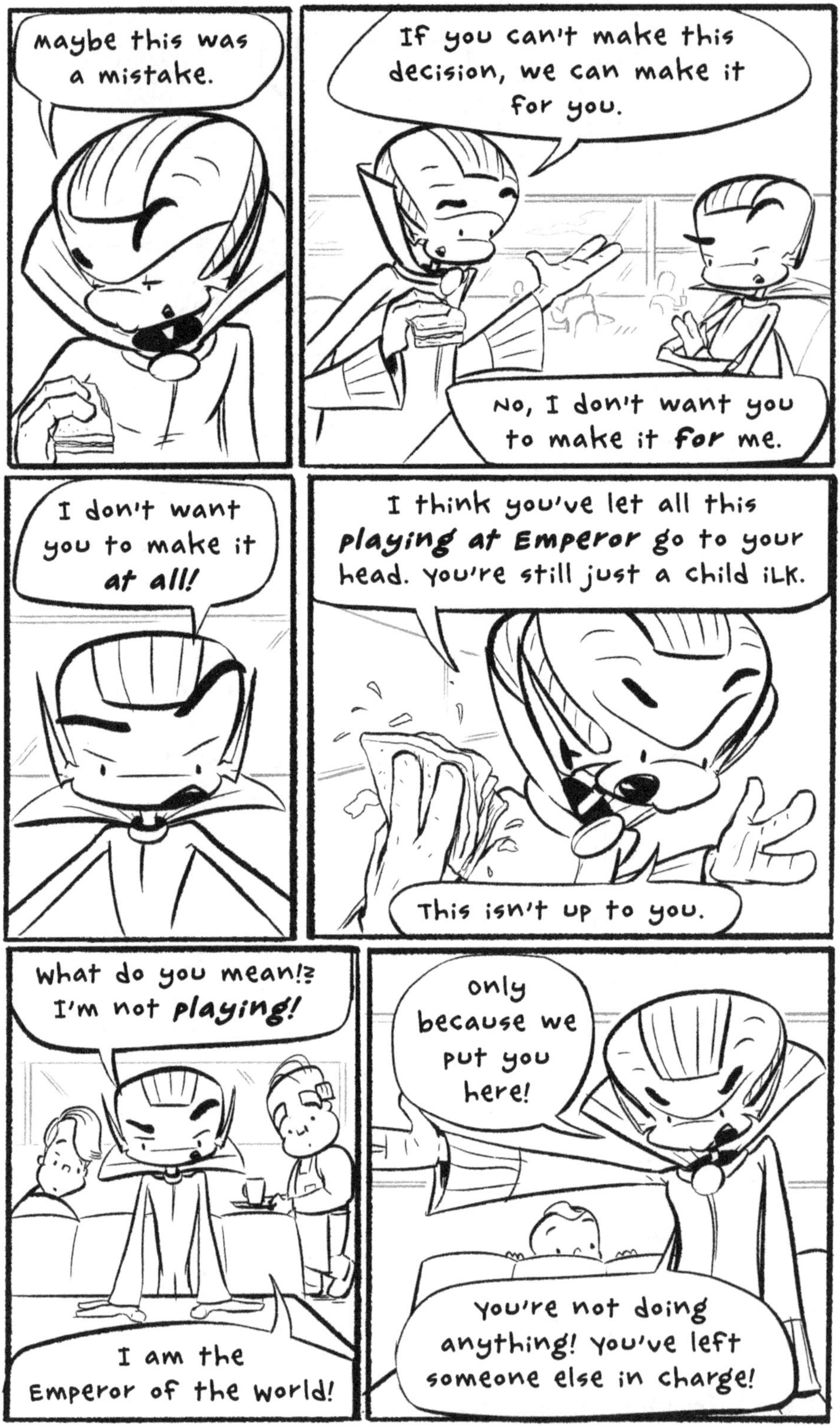
maybe this was a mistake.
If you can't make this decision, we can make it for you.
No, I don't want you to make it **for** me.
I don't want you to make it ***at all!***
I think you've let all this ***playing at Emperor*** go to your head. You're still just a child iLK.
This isn't up to you.
What do you mean!? I'm not ***playing!***
I am the Emperor of the world!
only because we put you here!
You're not doing anything! You've left someone else in charge!

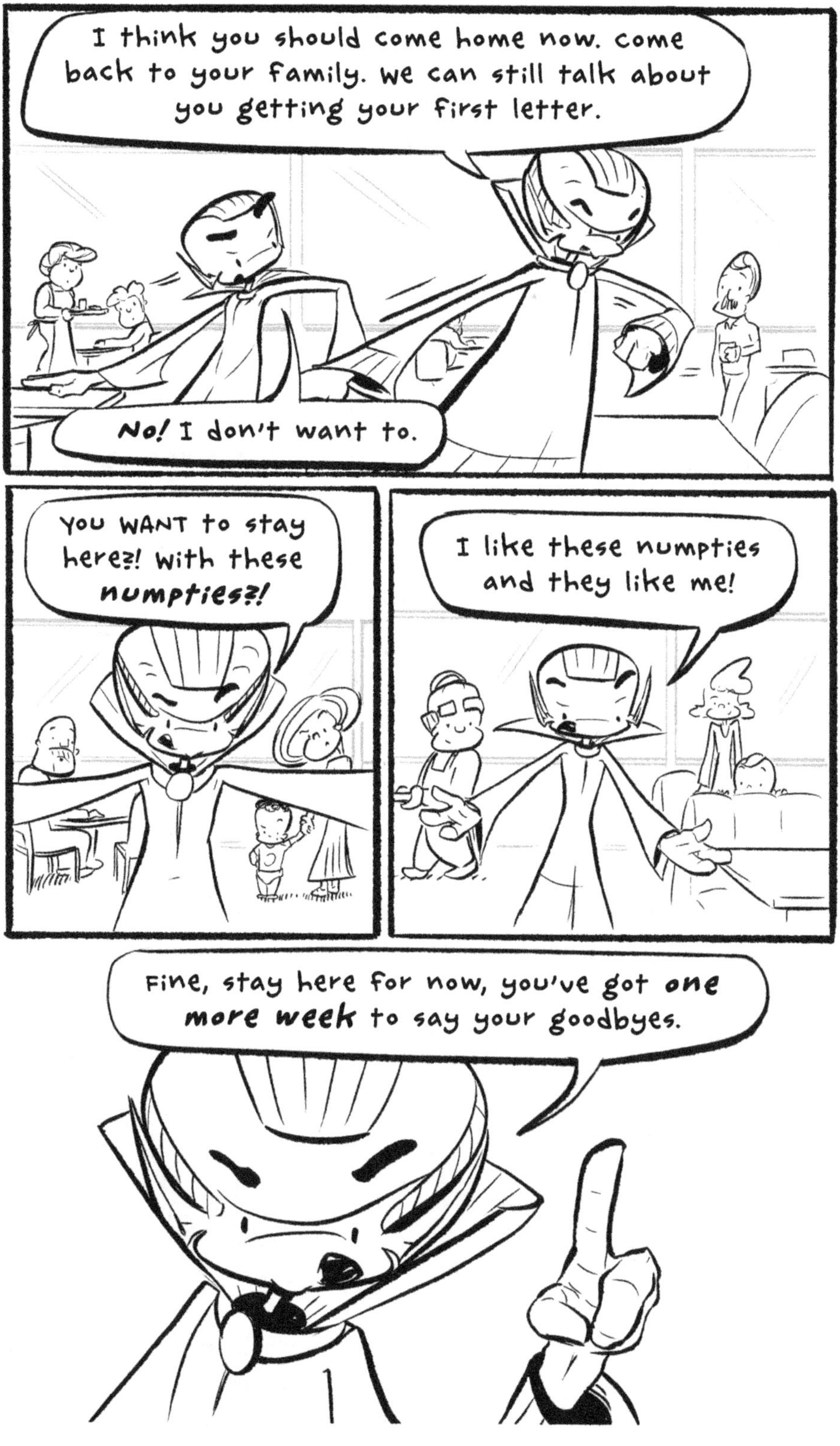
I think you should come home now. come back to your family. we can still talk about you getting your first letter.
No! I don't want to.
You WANT to stay here?! with these numpties?!
I like these numpties and they like me!
Fine, stay here for now, you've got one more week to say your goodbyes.

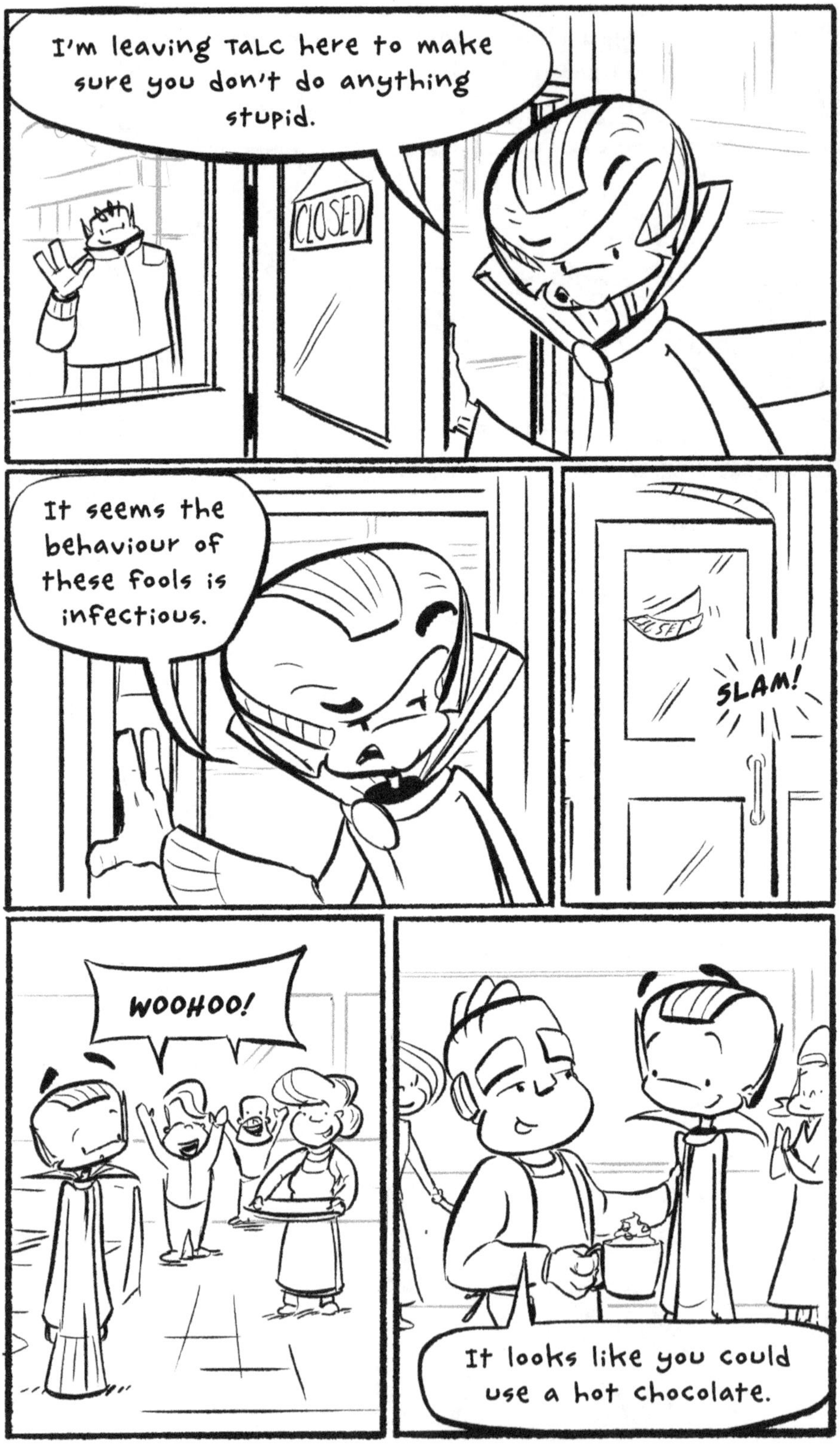
I'm leaving TALC here to make sure you don't do anything stupid.
CLOSED
It seems the behaviour of these fools is infectious.
SLAM!
WOOHOO!
It looks like you could use a hot chocolate.

Invasion 101, Day 79

TalC's been behaving strangely recently.

Dad told him to stay here to keep an eye on me, but he's watching EVERYONE and EVERYTHING.

What's this?

It's a present for iLK.

How can I be sure?

It has a bow on it. Plus it comes with a card.

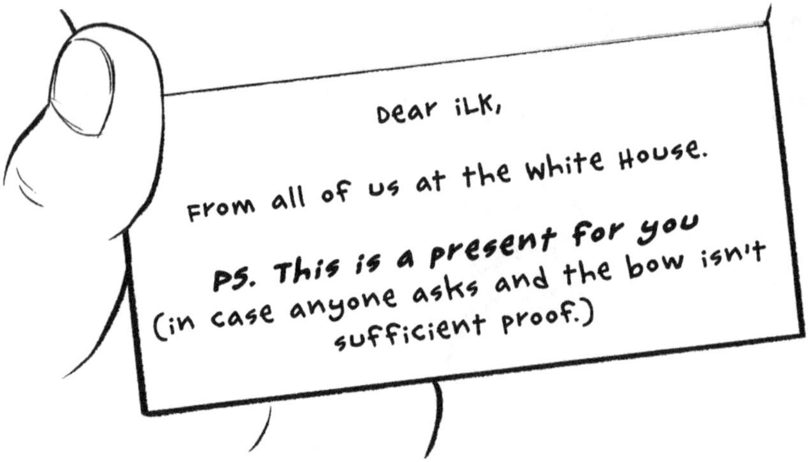
Dear iLK,
From all of us at the White House.
PS. This is a present for you
(in case anyone asks and the bow isn't sufficient proof.)

Once the Dullrat had made it past TaLC, he presented me with the gift.

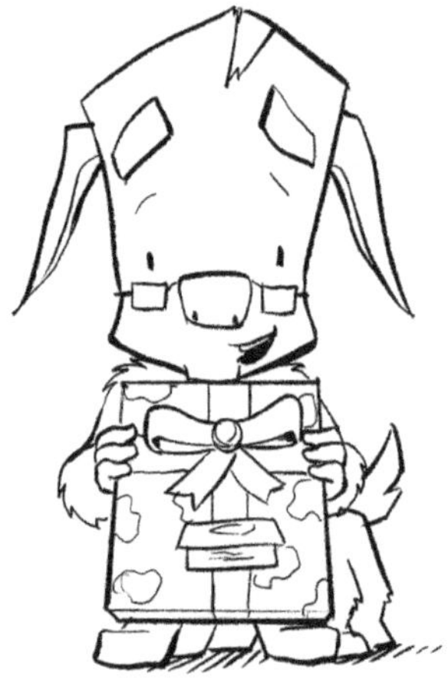

Apparently presents need to be unwrapped before they can be enjoyed. A bit like an orange I suppose, but unlike an orange, humans also need to spend time wrapping them in the first place.

It seems clear to me that if they skipped the initial wrapping stage they could also avoid the unwrapping stage. Maybe I should explain this to them.

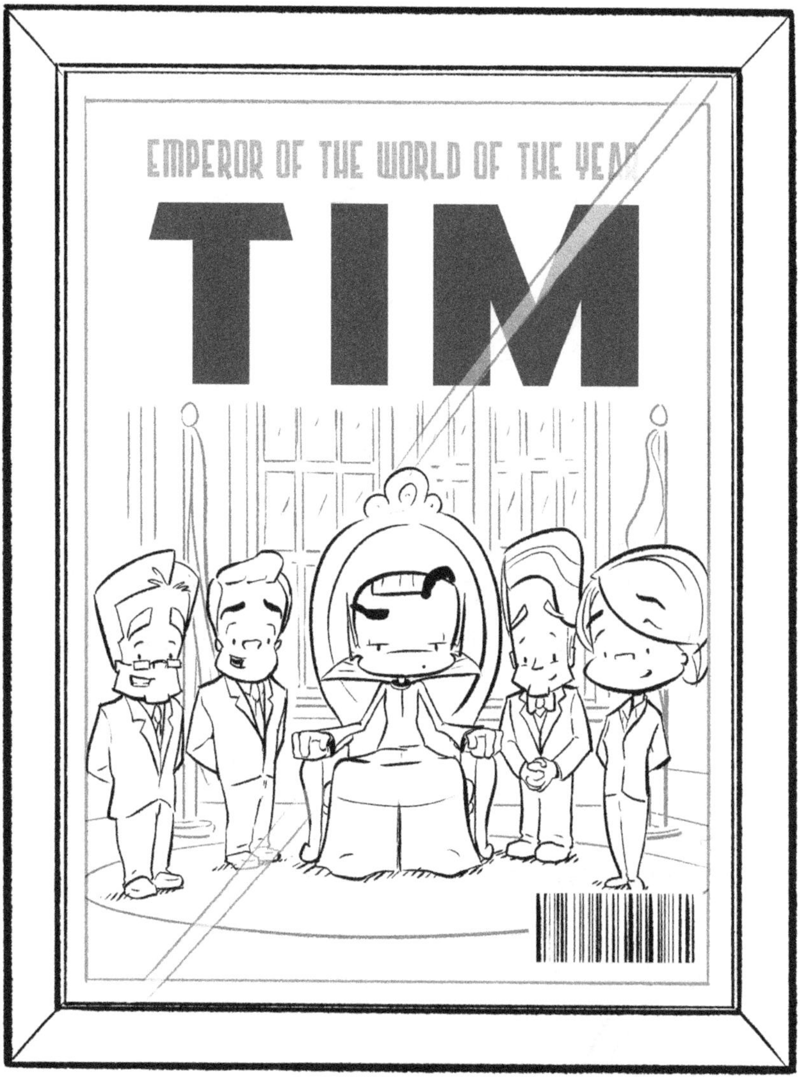
EMPEROR OF THE WORLD OF THE YEAR
TIM

Hidden behind the unnecessary, colourful paper was a framed copy of TIM magazine with our photo on the front.

I had done my best to pose like someone who ruled the world. I was quite proud of the result.

It was a nice picture and it made me think.

me thinking.

Everyone in the spaceship is wrong. They thought there was nothing here, but there is. They just missed it.

Earthlings use tools that we Glubwarks don't, like their hands and their faces.

These thoughts kept me busy for a while.

me still thinking.

They might still be able to find the beedaletha plant, maybe if I help them...

But then TalC interrupted me.

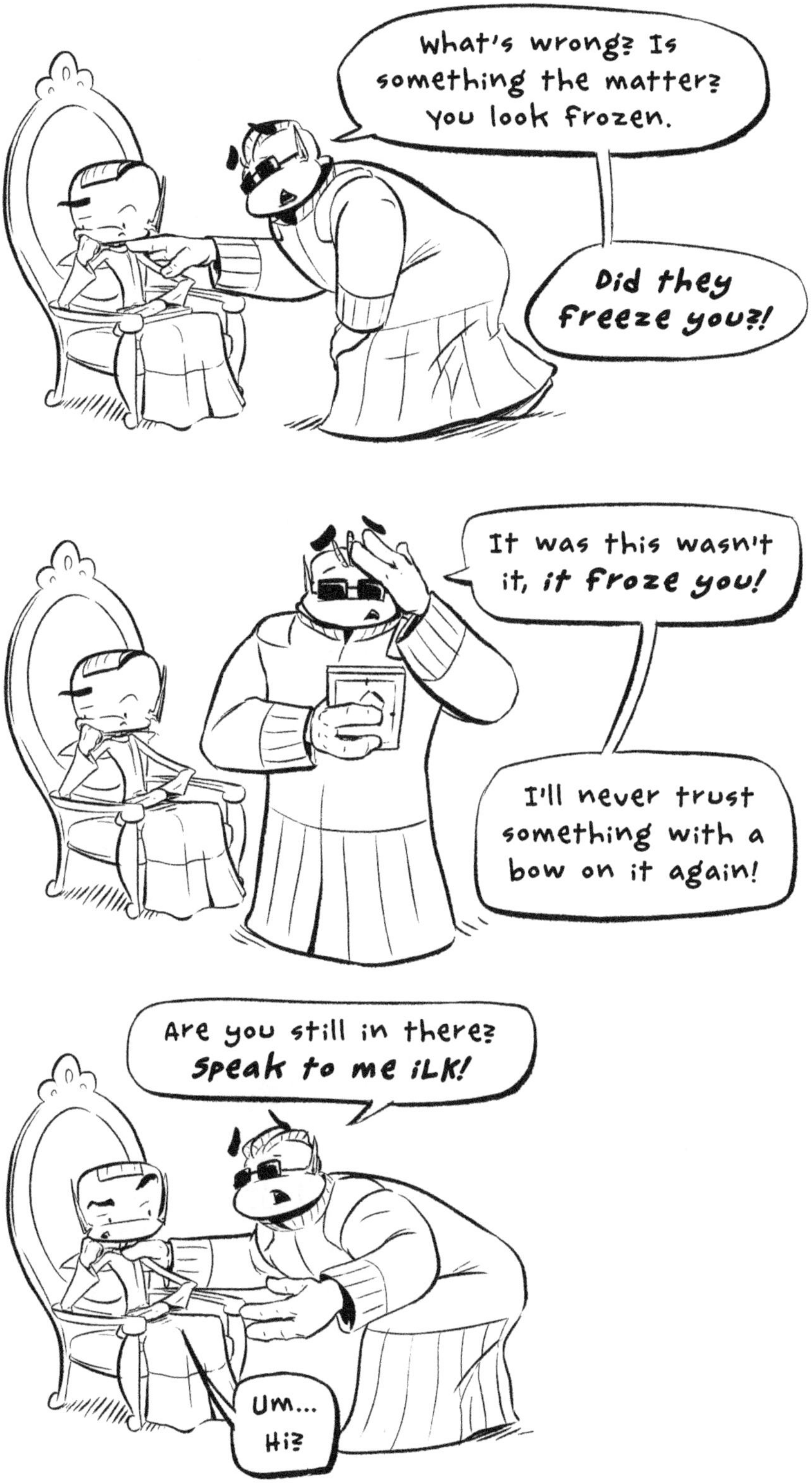
What's wrong? Is something the matter? You look frozen.
Did they freeze you?!
It was this wasn't it, it froze you!
I'll never trust something with a bow on it again!
Are you still in there? Speak to me iLK!
Um... Hi?

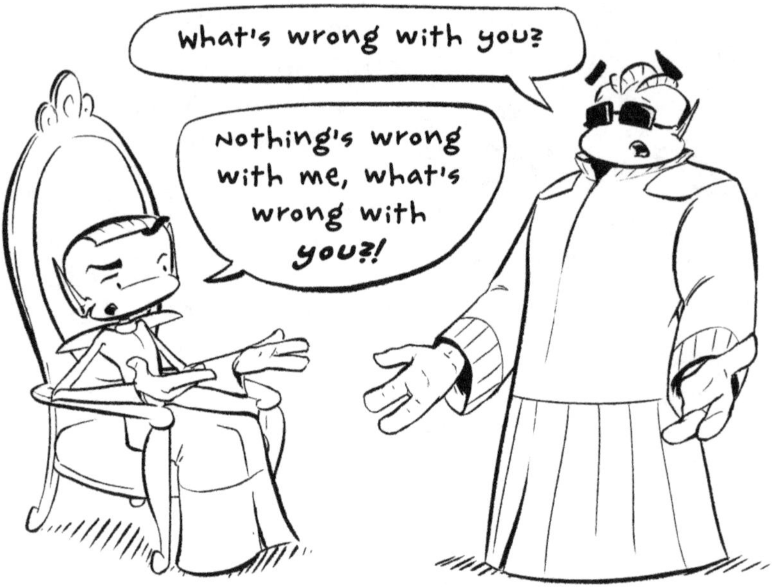
What's wrong with you?
Nothing's wrong with me, what's wrong with you?!

It's definitely safe to say that something was going on with TaLC.

Unfortunately I'm an expert in neither subtlety nor Glubwark psychology, so I decided to just ask him, directly and politely, what the matter was.

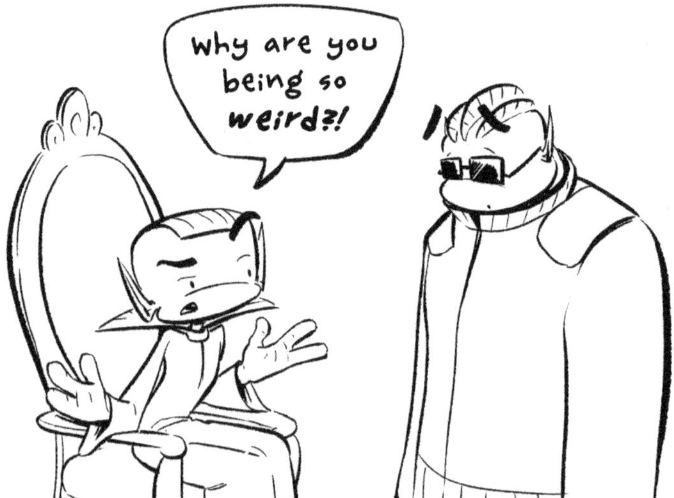
Why are you being so weird?!

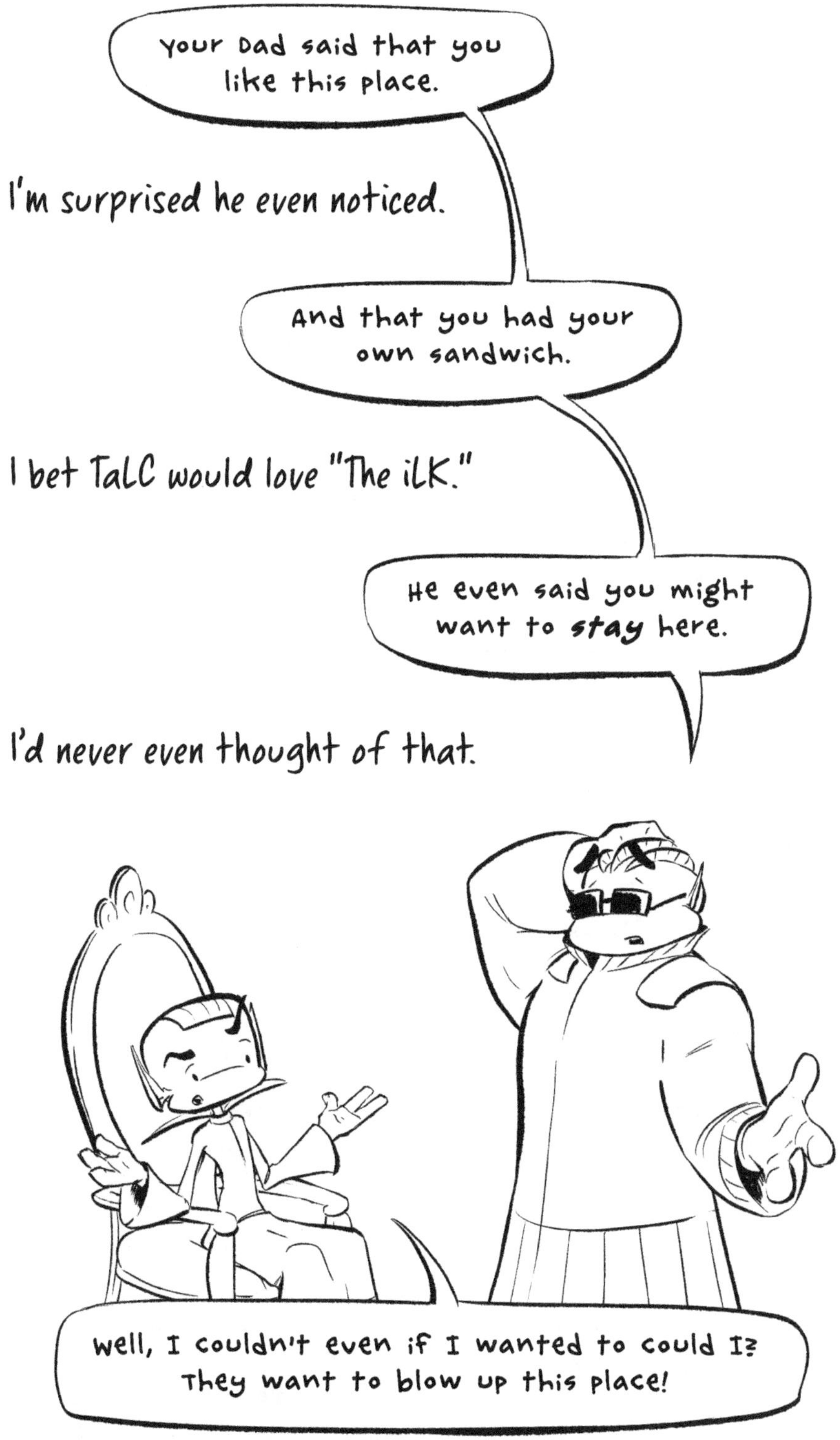
Your Dad said that you like this place.
I'm surprised he even noticed.
And that you had your own sandwich.
I bet TaLC would love "The iLK."
He even said you might want to stay here.
I'd never even thought of that.
Well, I couldn't even if I wanted to could I? They want to blow up this place!

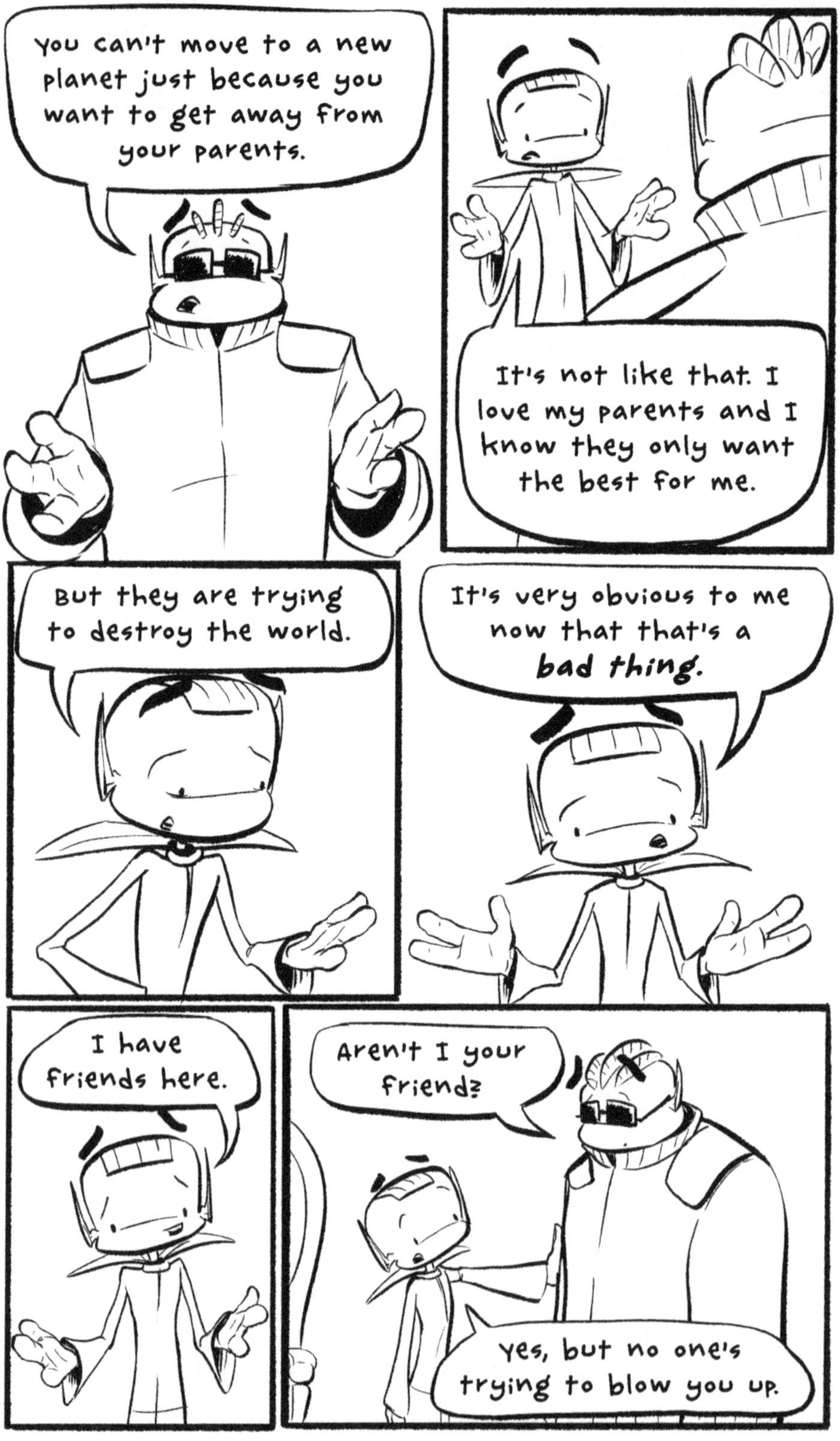
you can't move to a new planet just because you want to get away from your parents.
It's not like that. I love my parents and I know they only want the best for me.
But they are trying to destroy the world.
It's very obvious to me now that that's a ***bad thing.***
I have friends here.
Aren't I your friend?
Yes, but no one's trying to blow you up.

I felt sorry for TalC. He was definitely my best friend on the ship.

However, he had just given me an idea and things were about to get even more complicated.

I was going to miss him, that's for sure.

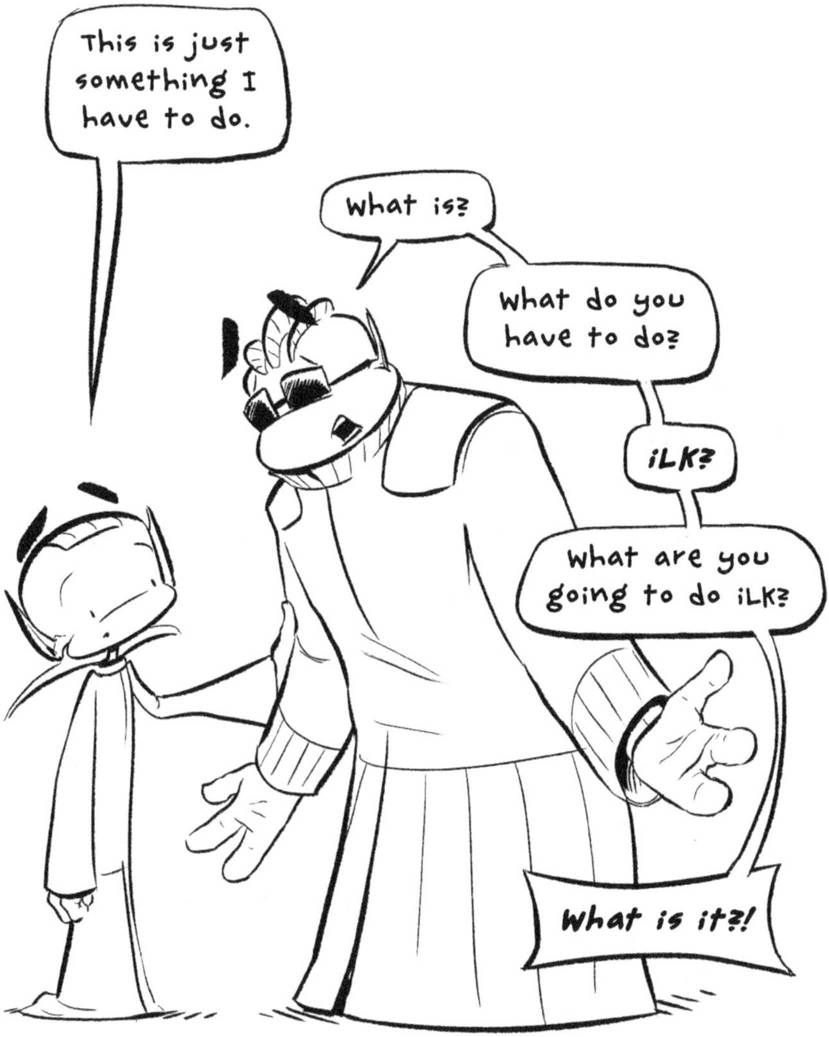
This is just something I have to do.
What is?
What do you have to do?
ILK?
What are you going to do ILK?
What is it?!

Invasion 101, Day 81

How do you tell someone that you're planning to blow up their home with a Fluplipper?

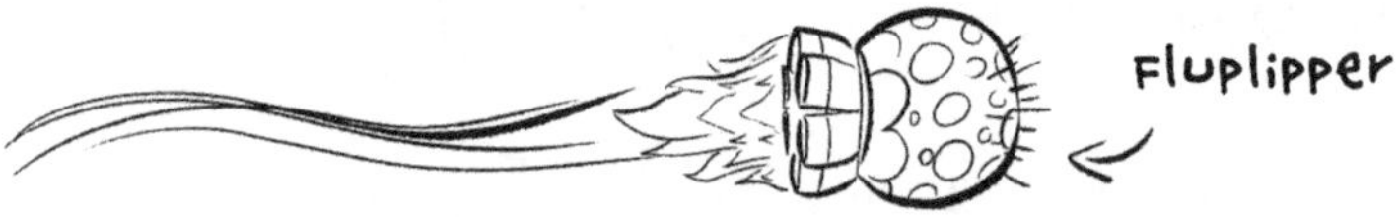
Fluplipper

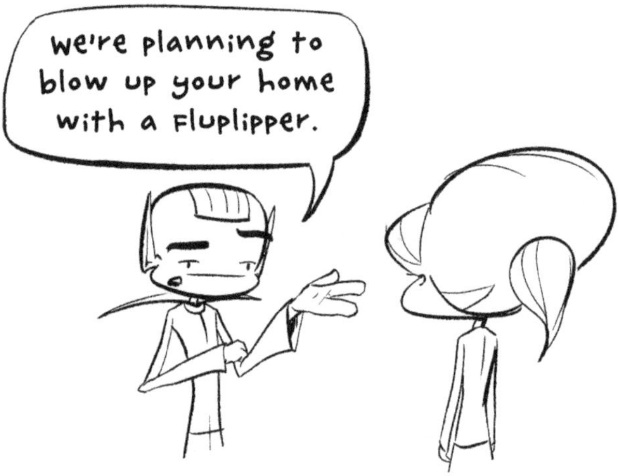
we're planning to blow up your home with a Fluplipper.

I went with the obvious.

It seemed ineffective a first, but after some explanation I think she understood what I was saying.

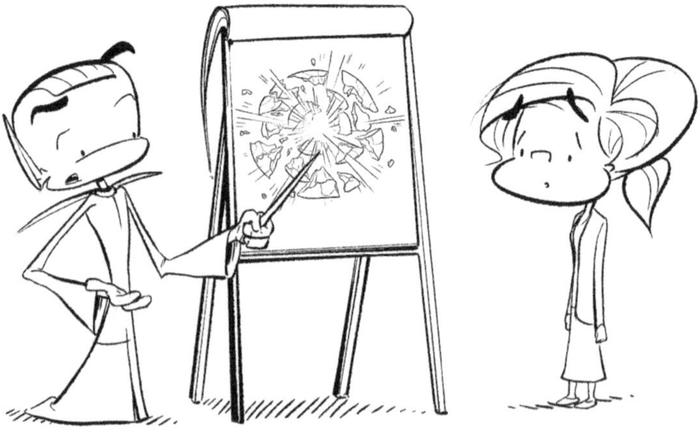

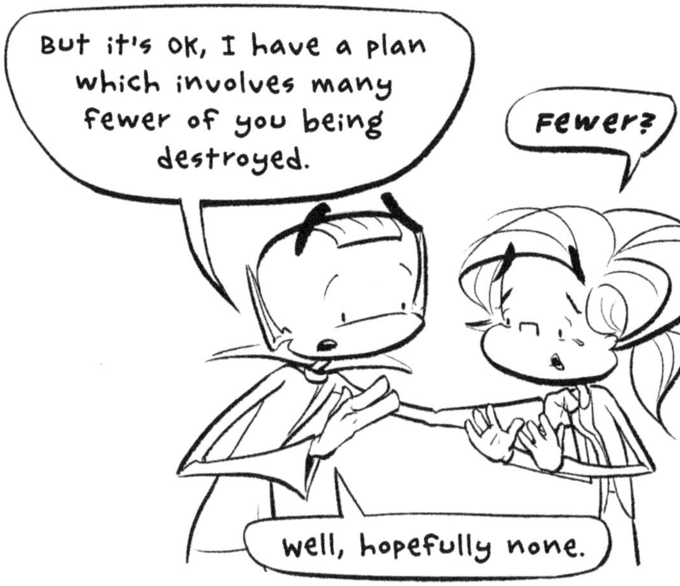
But it's OK, I have a plan which involves many fewer of you being destroyed.
Fewer?
well, hopefully none.

I described to her my plan to stay on Earth.

If I could convince Dad to let me stay here while they put all the humans to work, I could help them look for the Beedaletha plant.

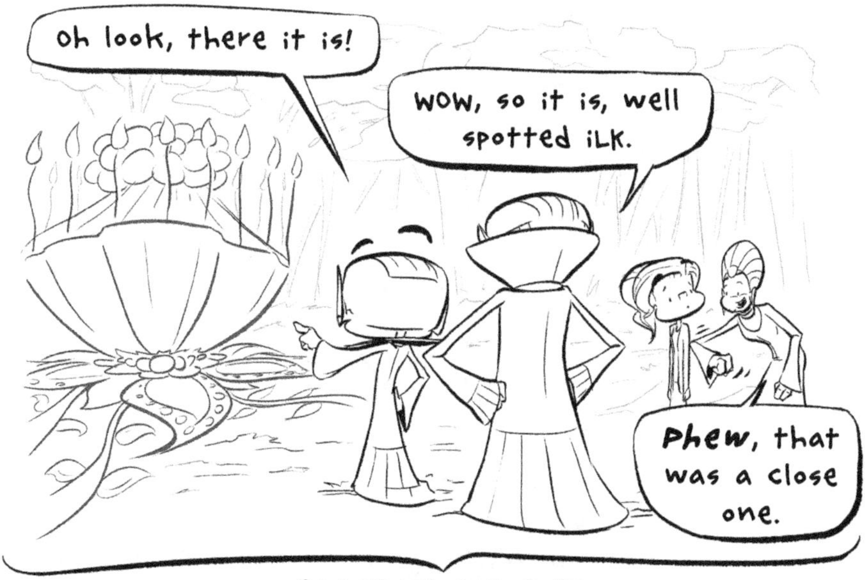
oh look, there it is!
WOW, so it is, well spotted iLK.
Phew, that was a close one.

IMAGINED SCENARIO

With my help this could still become one of the healthiest planets in the system.

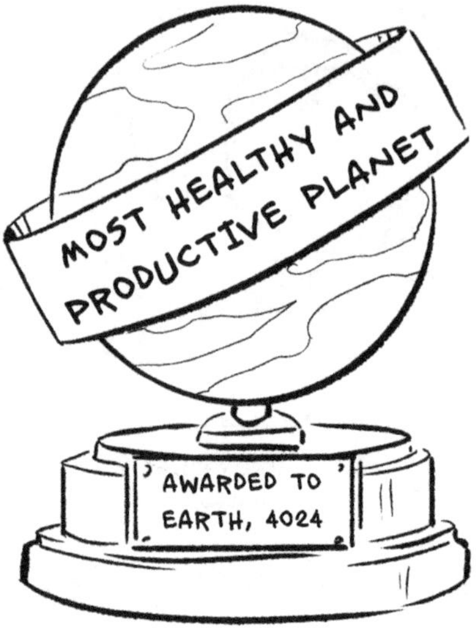
MOST HEALTHY AND PRODUCTIVE PLANET
AWARDED TO EARTH, 4024

Marina wasn't immediately convinced however.

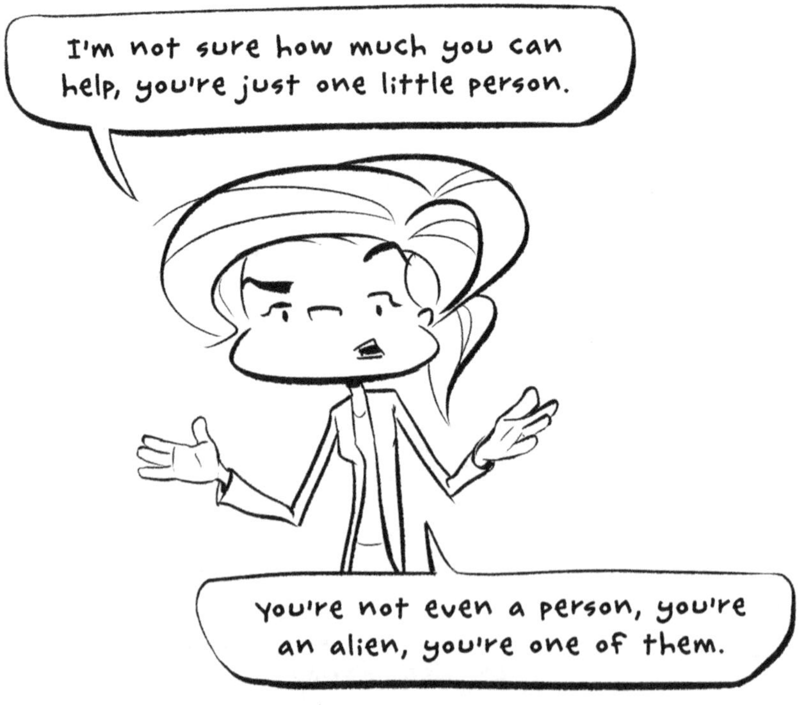
I'm not sure how much you can help, you're just one little person.
you're not even a person, you're an alien, you're one of them.

It didn't feel good when she said that, but that didn't change my decision.

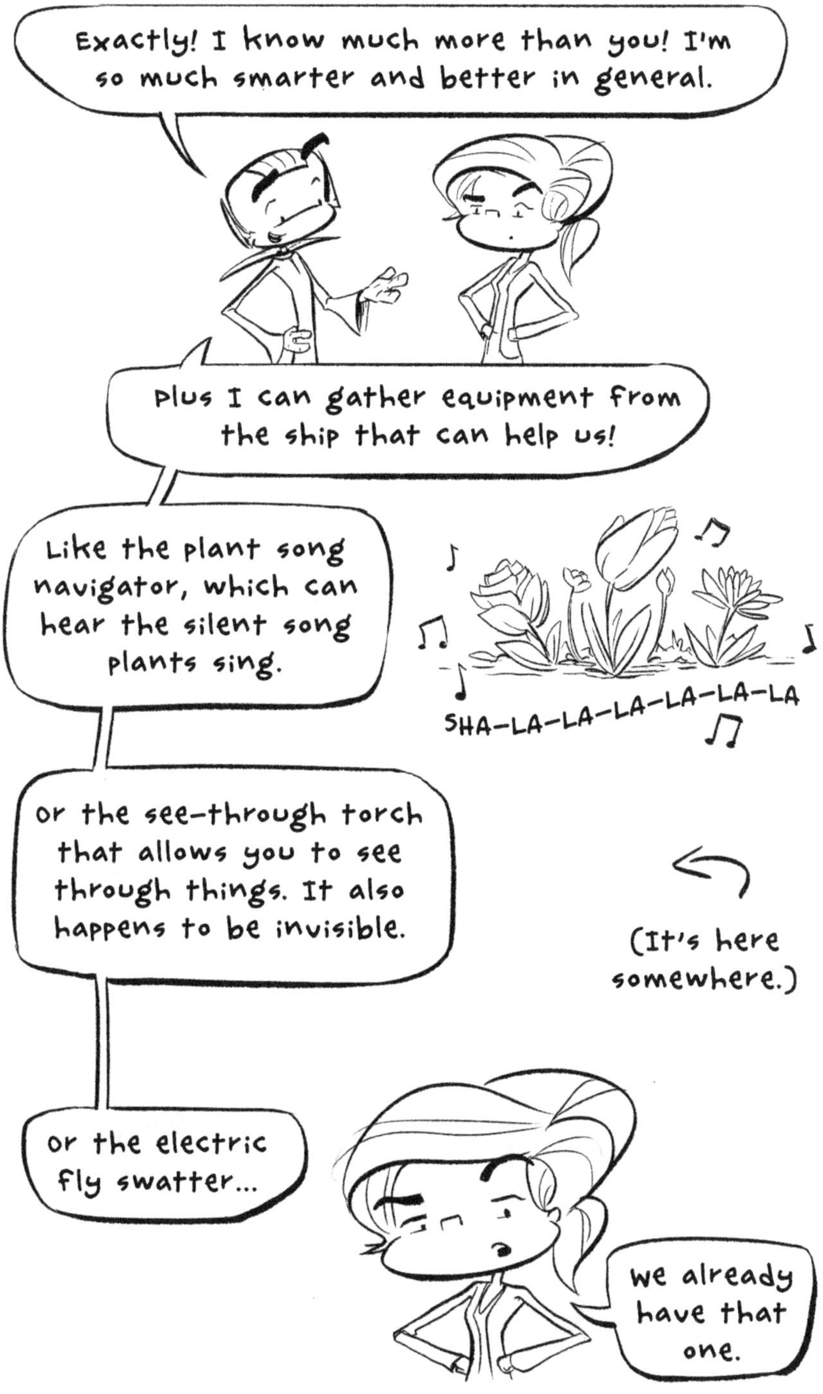
Exactly! I know much more than you! I'm so much smarter and better in general.
Plus I can gather equipment from the ship that can help us!
Like the plant song navigator, which can hear the silent song plants sing.
SHA-LA-LA-LA-LA-LA-LA
or the see-through torch that allows you to see through things. It also happens to be invisible.
(It's here somewhere.)
or the electric fly swatter...
We already have that one.

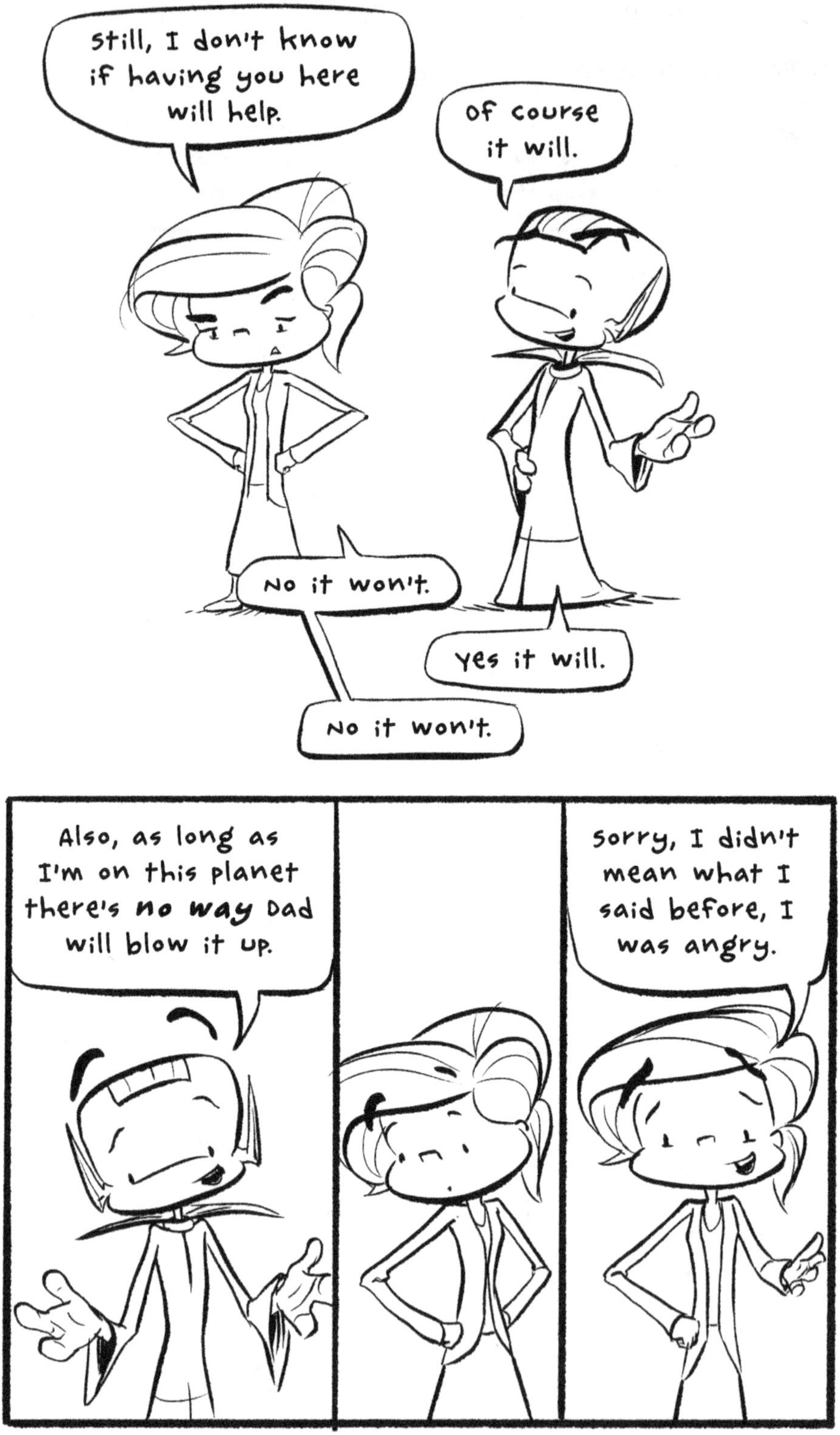
Still, I don't know if having you here will help.
Of course it will.
No it won't.
Yes it will.
No it won't.
Also, as long as I'm on this planet there's **no way** Dad will blow it up.
Sorry, I didn't mean what I said before, I was angry.

There were lots of reasons why I thought Earth might be worth saving. Unfortunately I couldn't think of any of them when Marina asked so I just said this.

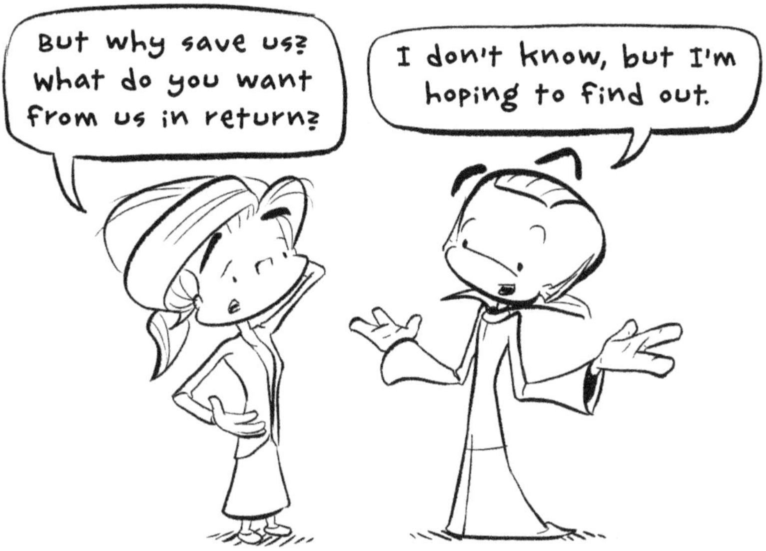
But why save us? What do you want from us in return?
I don't know, but I'm hoping to find out.

Glubwarks don't know everything. I was sure there was more to discover here. Things that could help us, I just couldn't prove it yet.

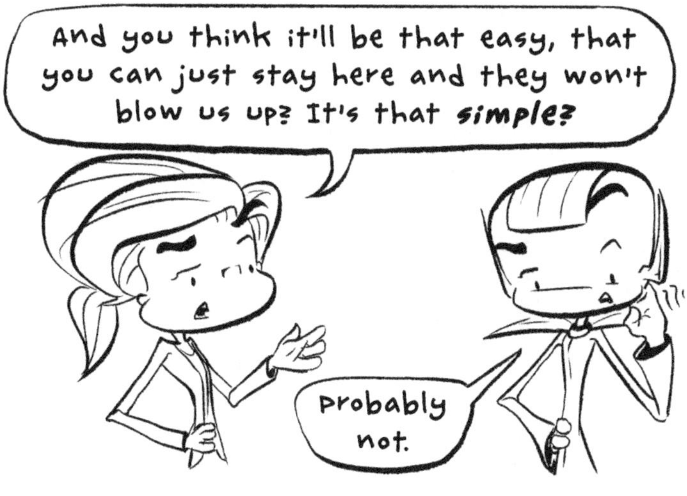
And you think it'll be that easy, that you can just stay here and they won't blow us up? It's that *simple?*
Probably not.

This was in fact going to be very difficult.

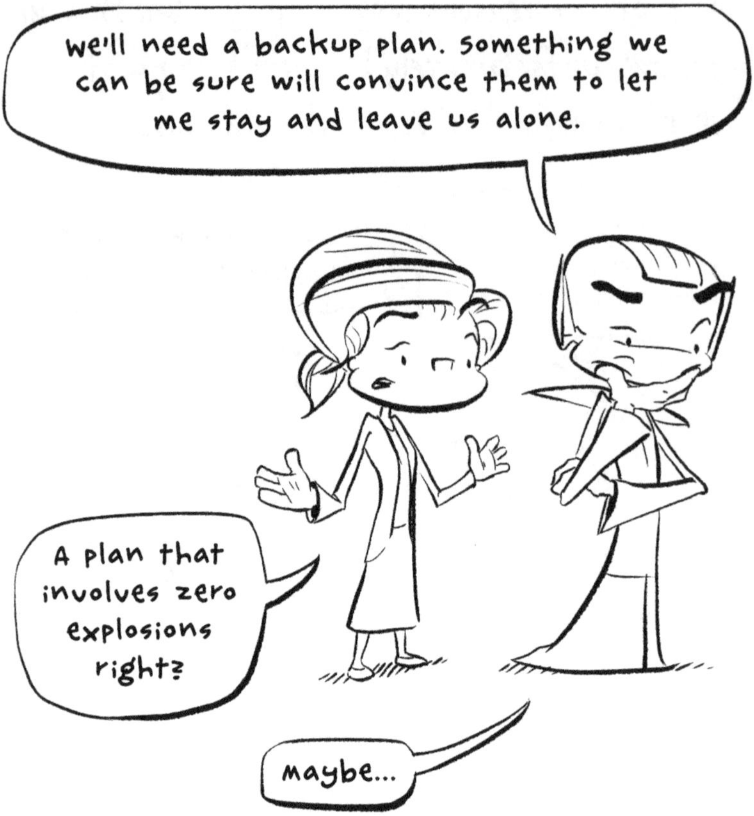
we'll need a backup plan. something we can be sure will convince them to let me stay and leave us alone.
A plan that involves zero explosions right?
maybe...

Maybe it's not about having NOTHING explode...

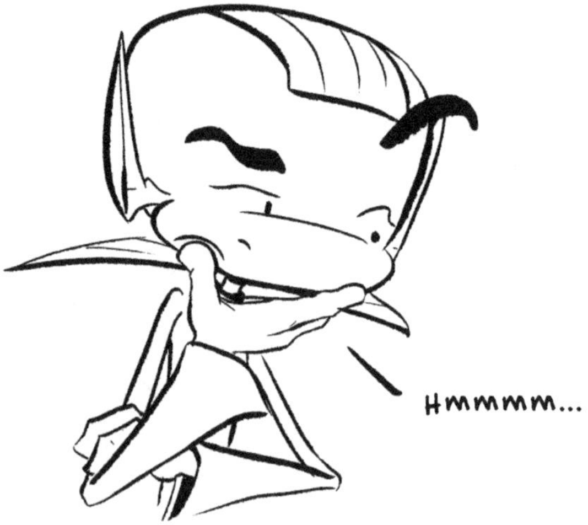
Hmmmm...

Maybe it's about having LOTS OF THINGS explode!

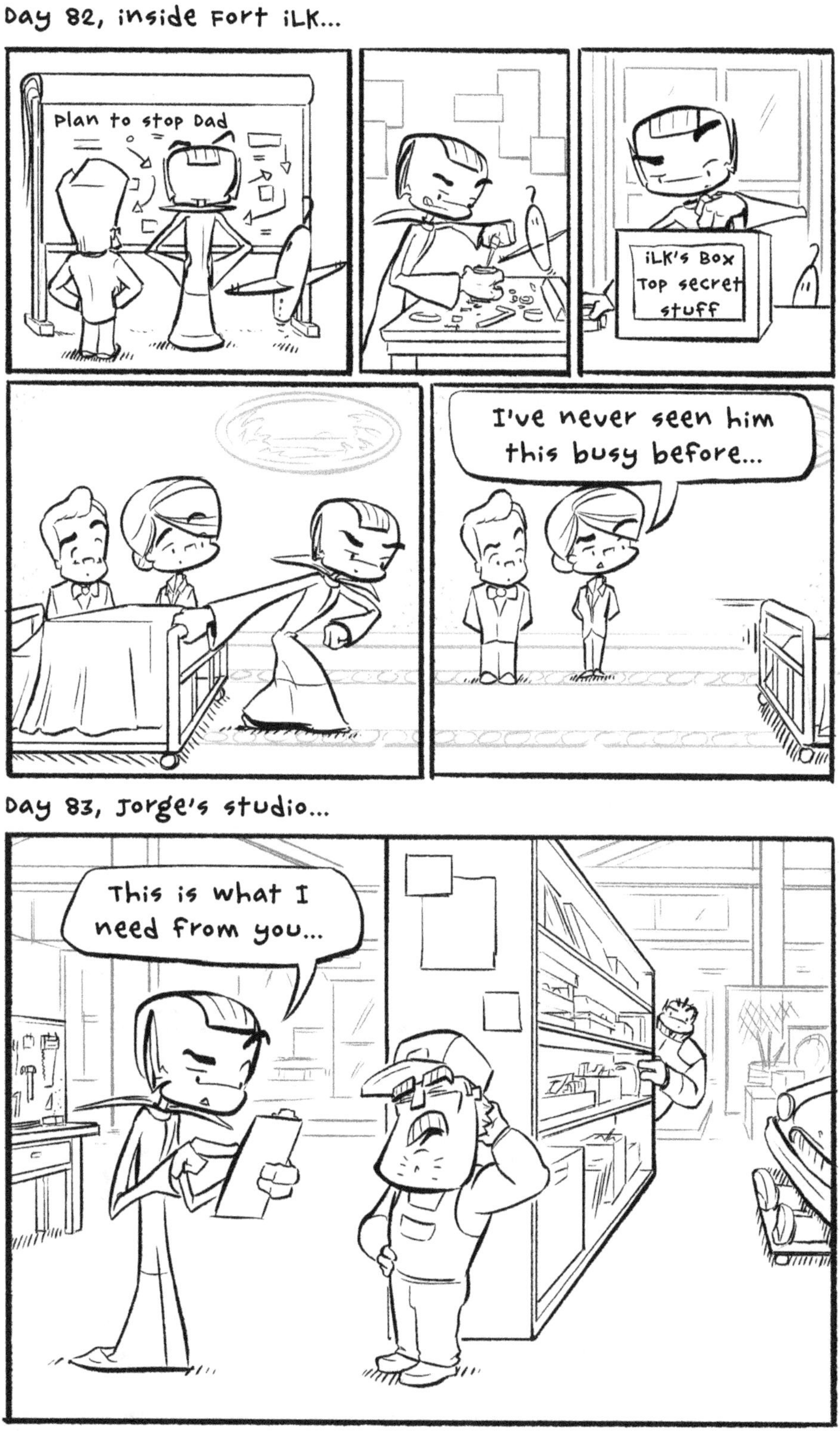
Day 82, inside Fort iLK...
Plan to stop Dad
iLK's Box Top secret stuff
I've never seen him this busy before...
Day 83, Jorge's studio...
This is what I need from you...

Later that day, inside Fort iLK...

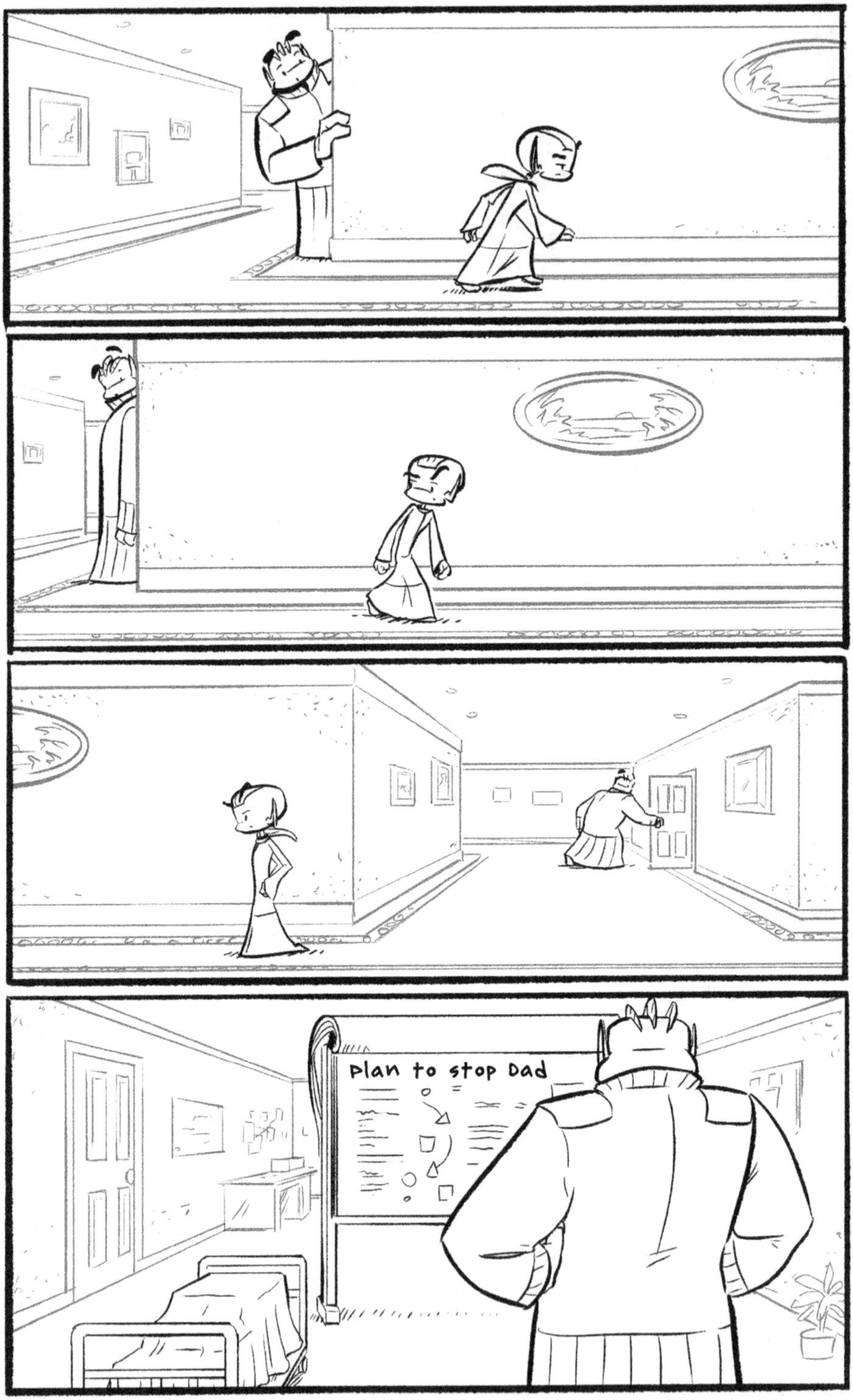
Plan to stop Dad

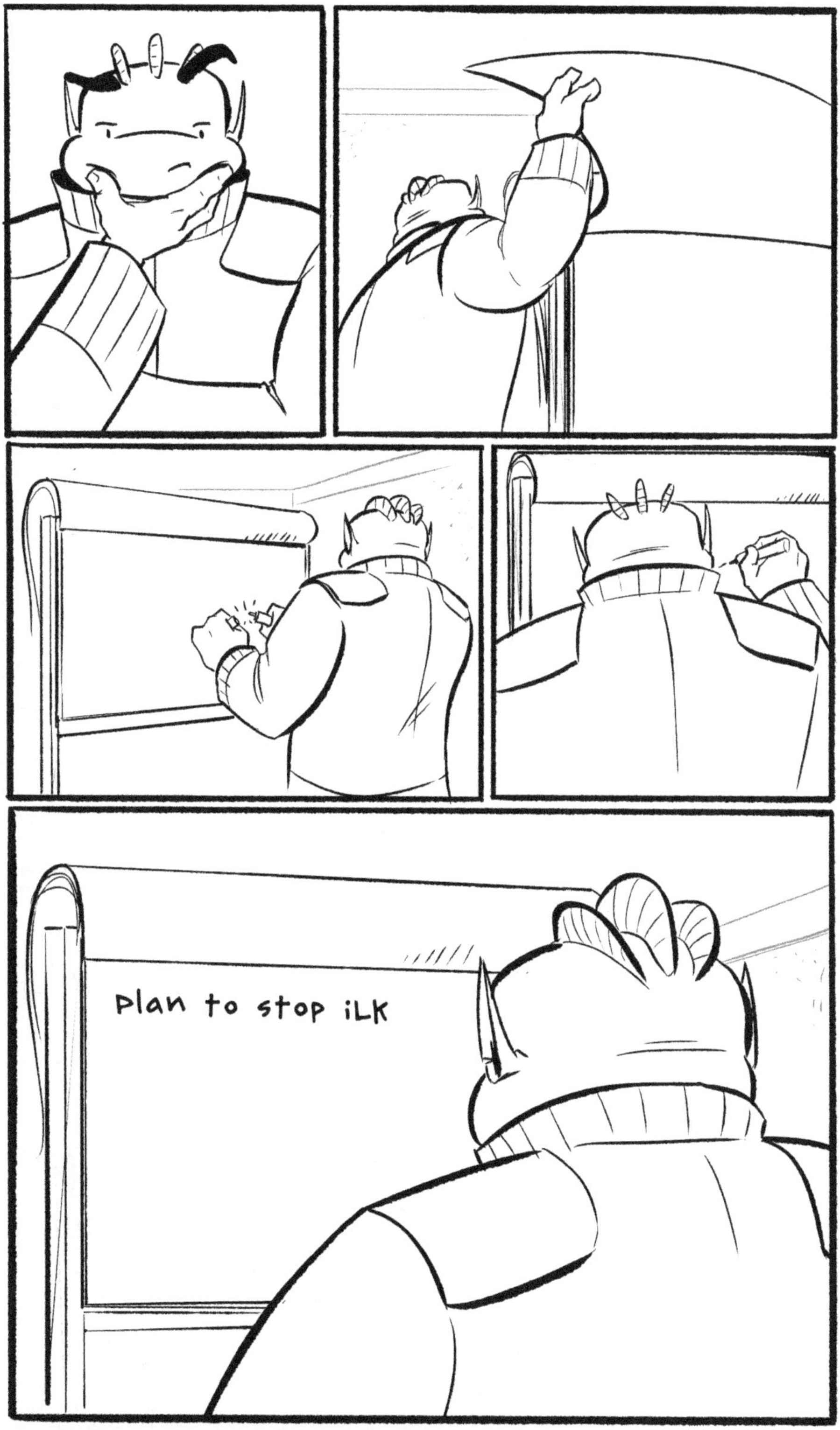
plan to stop iLK

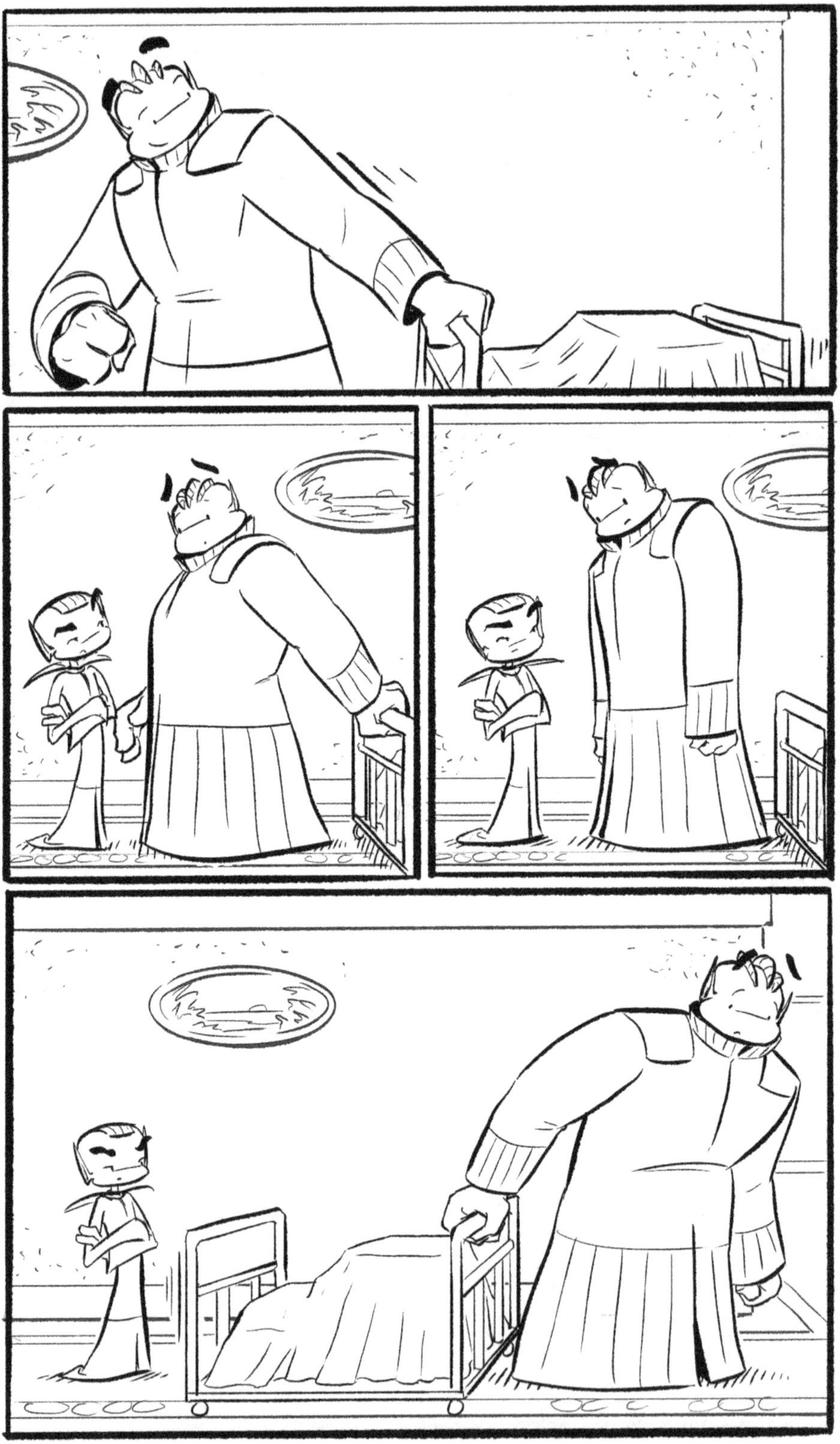

Day 84, inside the Glubwark's ship

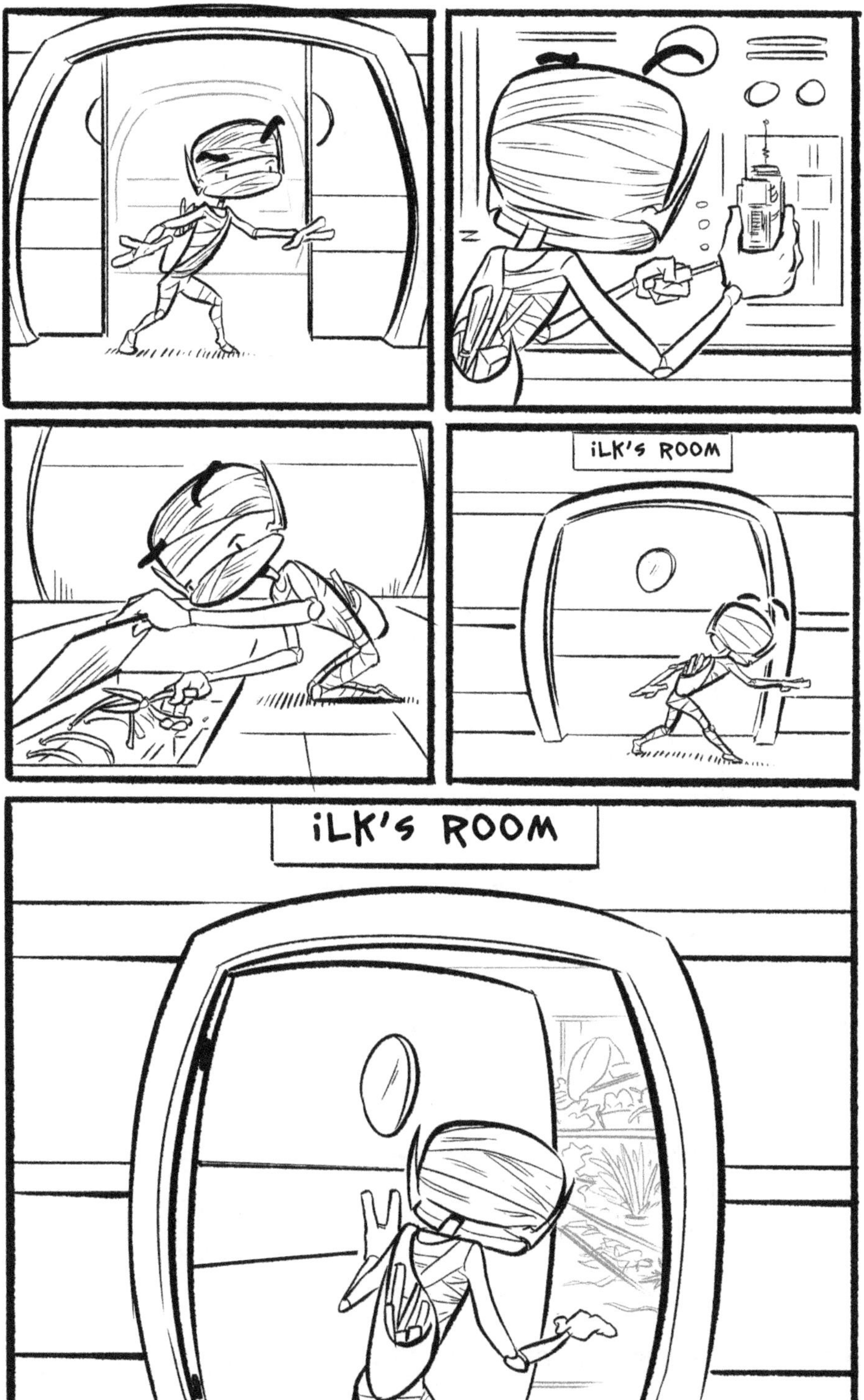
iLK'S ROOM
iLK'S ROOM

Invasion 101, Day 85

Being back in my room again felt weird. TaLC was still taking care of my plants and some of them had grown to nearly three times the size.

iLK's plants:

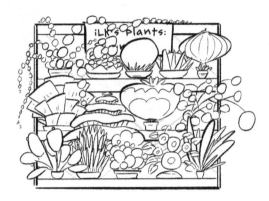

Despite his confidence with my plant collection, TaLC had completely avoided some other areas of my room. He'd been particularly careful to go nowhere near the traps leftover from Fort iLK version 6.0.

Maybe if he'd known none of them were active, he wouldn't have been so cautious.

In hindsight, I should have showed the same caution. However, I saw this and I couldn't help myself.

AQUA GEL
CAUTION:
EXTRA SLIPPERY

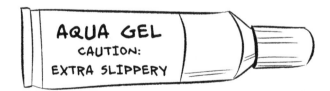

What would someone even use this for if not for setting a trap?

I carefully began to reassemble one of my favourite mechanisms by placing the weighted bed sheet back above the raised pad. I finished by spreading the gel on the floor just beside it.

I stood up and that's when it happened...

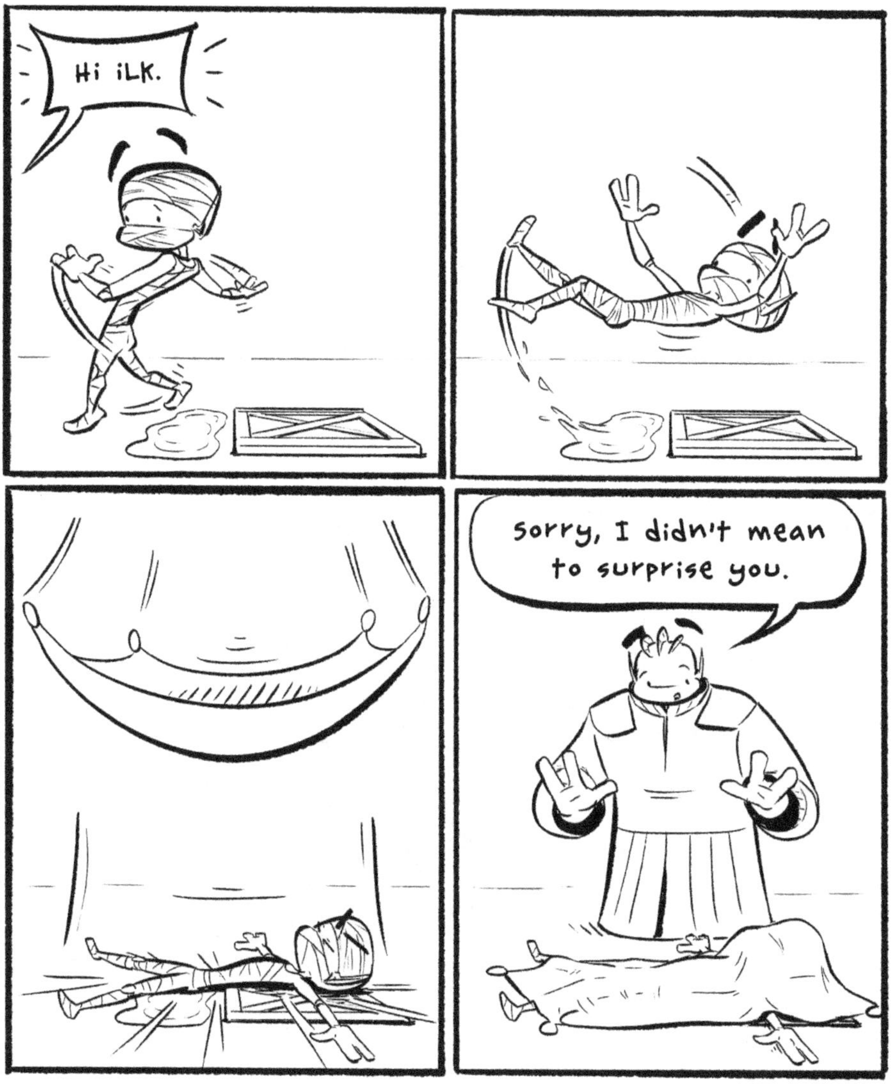
Hi iLK.
Sorry, I didn't mean to surprise you.

Now I understand why TaLC was so careful to avoid my traps. They hurt.

He kindly helped me to get up and remove the bed sheet. Apparently he followed me because he thought I was up to mischief.

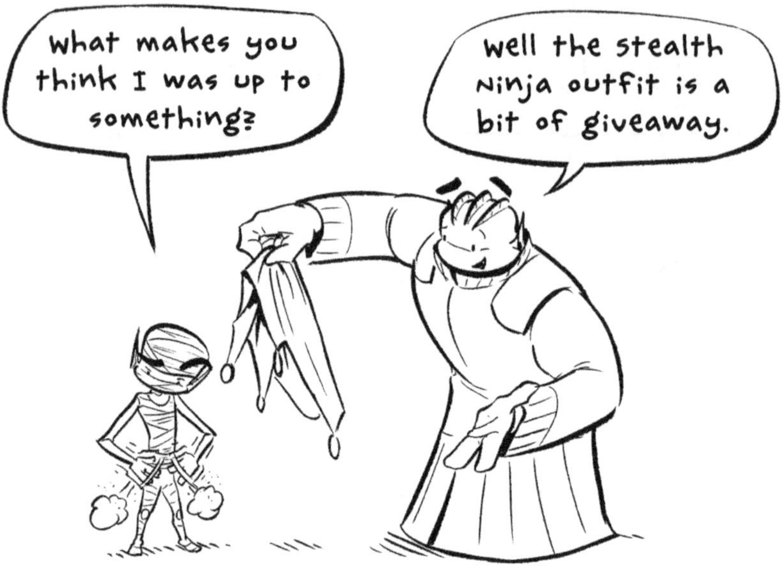
what makes you think I was up to something?
well the stealth Ninja outfit is a bit of giveaway.

It's not just an outfit, it's a state of mind.

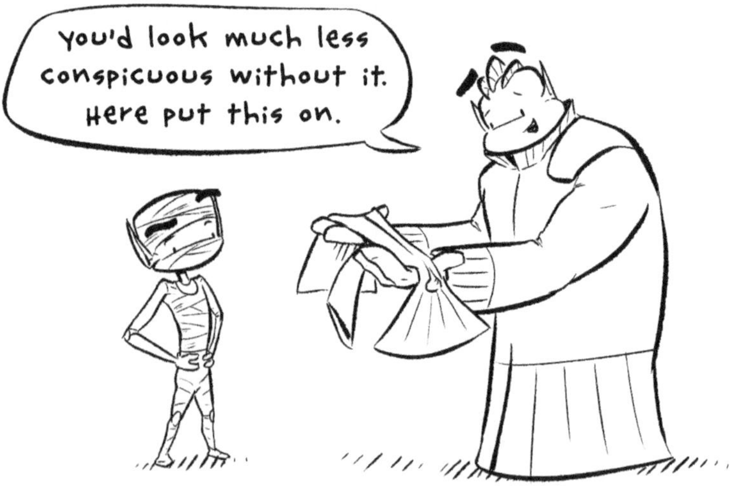
You'd look much less conspicuous without it. Here put this on.

TaLC then explained something to me, which no one had thought to explain before.

I'd assumed we were just lucky that the humans speak the same language as us. Apparently that's not the case.

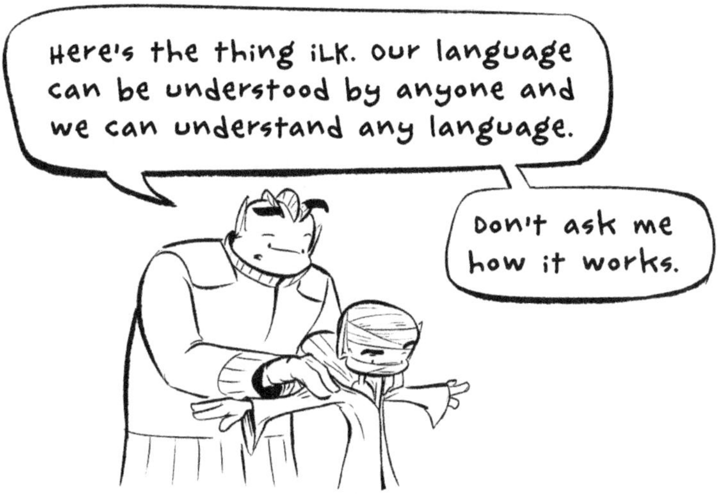
Here's the thing ILK. Our language can be understood by anyone and we can understand any language.
Don't ask me how it works.

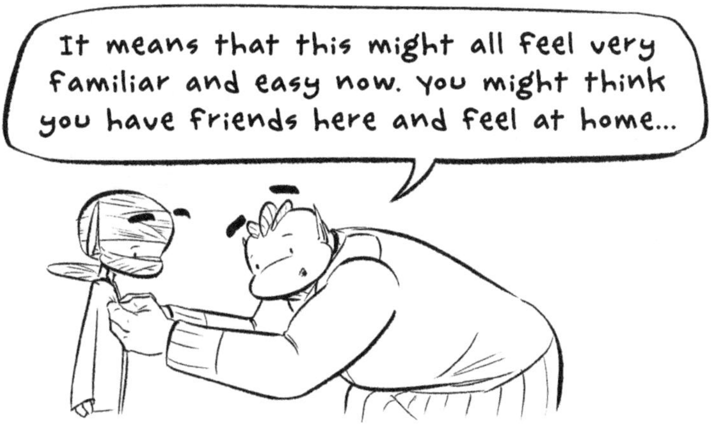
It means that this might all feel very familiar and easy now. You might think you have friends here and feel at home...

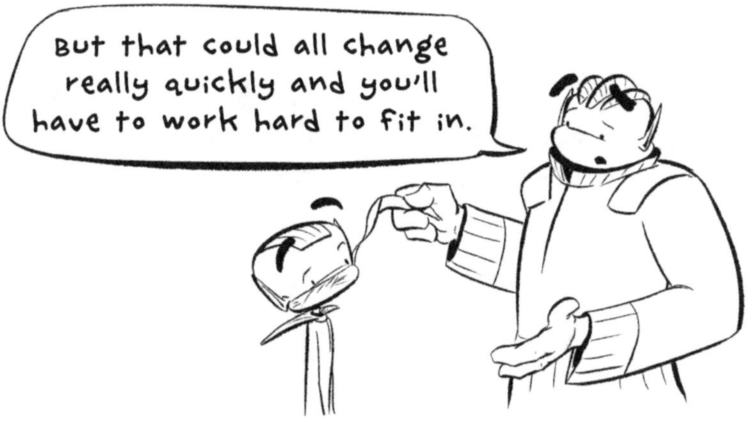
But that could all change really quickly and you'll have to work hard to fit in.

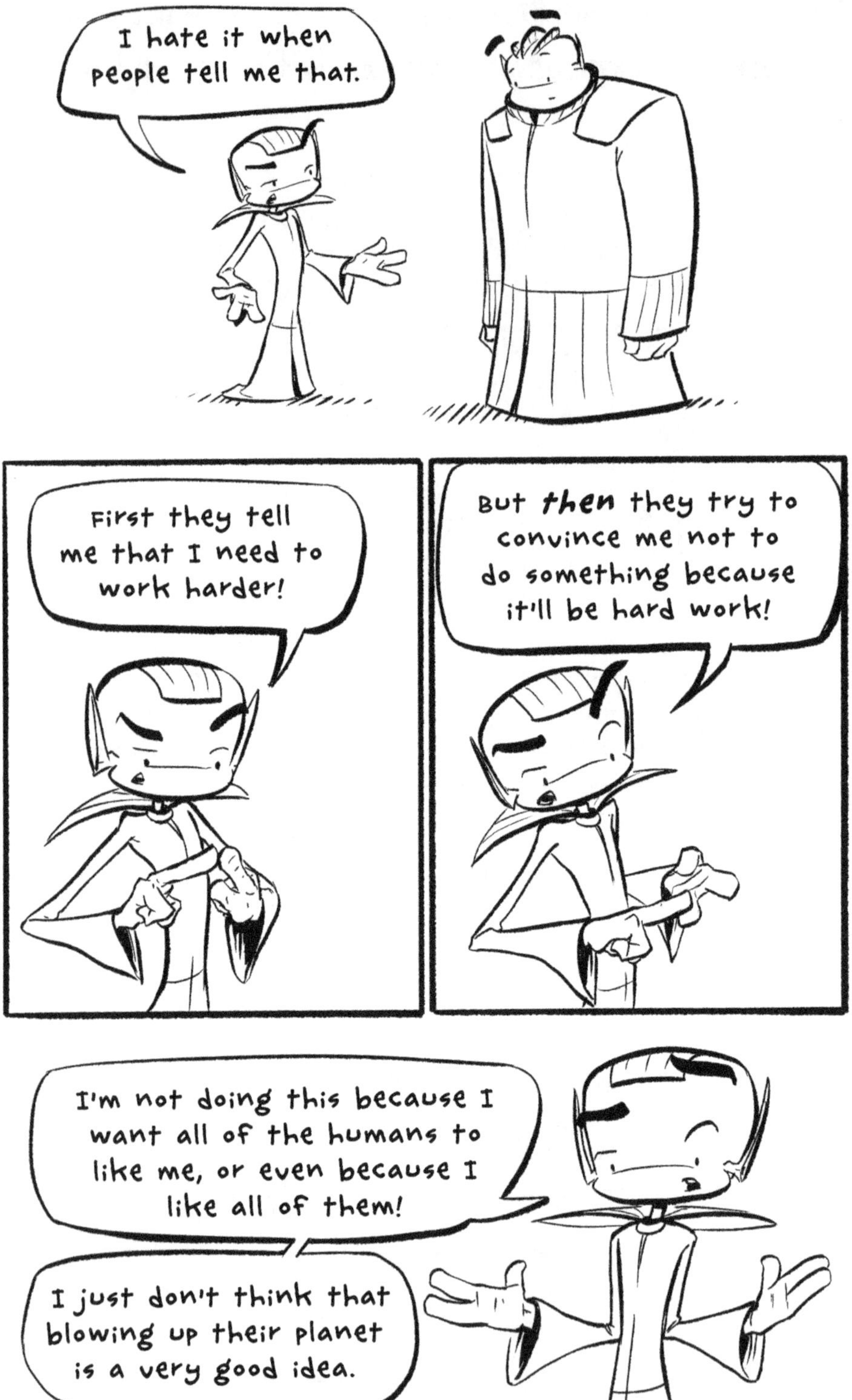
I hate it when people tell me that.
First they tell me that I need to work harder!
But *then* they try to convince me not to do something because it'll be hard work!
I'm not doing this because I want all of the humans to like me, or even because I like all of them!
I just don't think that blowing up their planet is a very good idea.

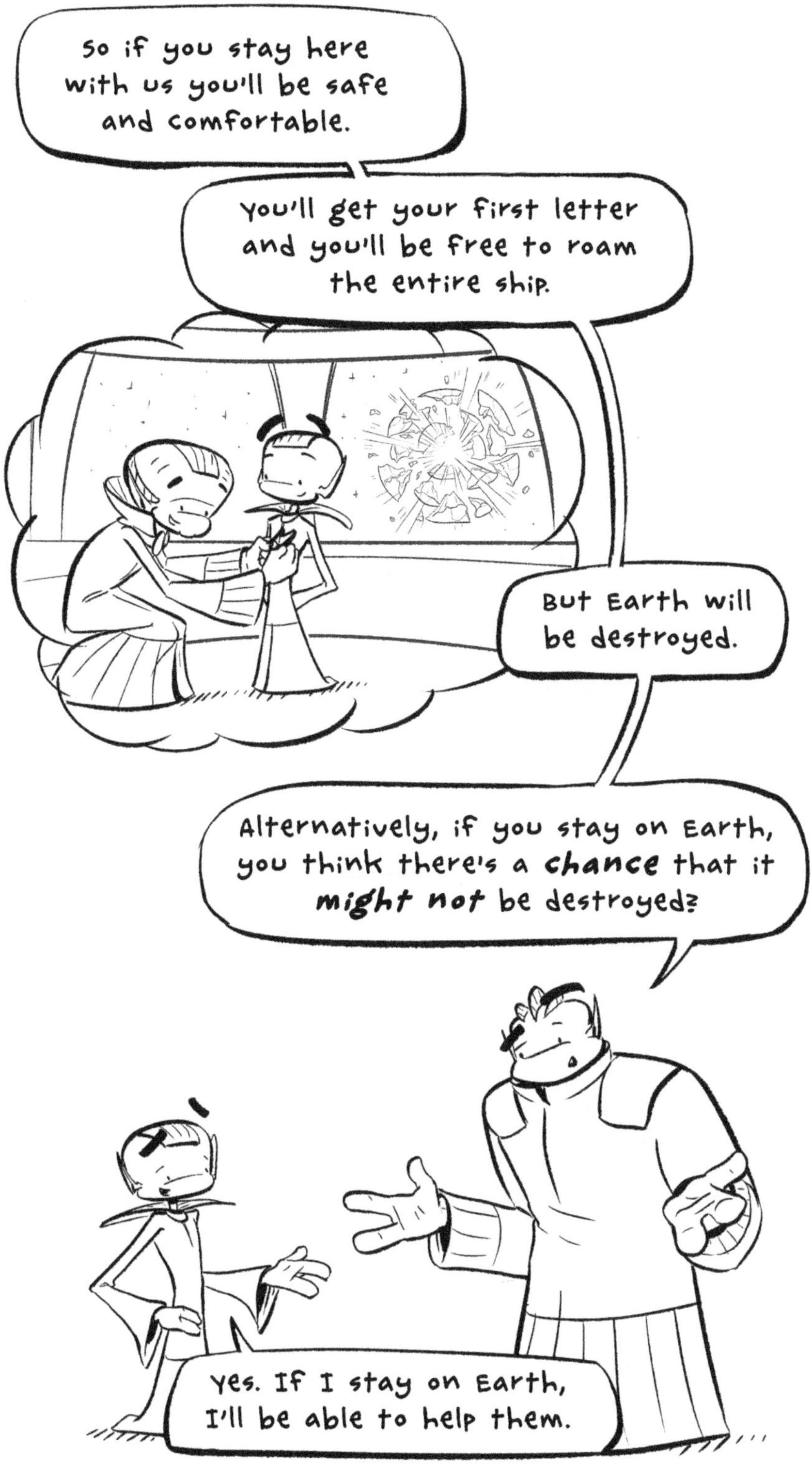
So if you stay here with us you'll be safe and comfortable.
You'll get your first letter and you'll be free to roam the entire ship.
But Earth will be destroyed.
Alternatively, if you stay on Earth, you think there's a **chance** that it ***might not*** be destroyed?
Yes. If I stay on Earth, I'll be able to help them.

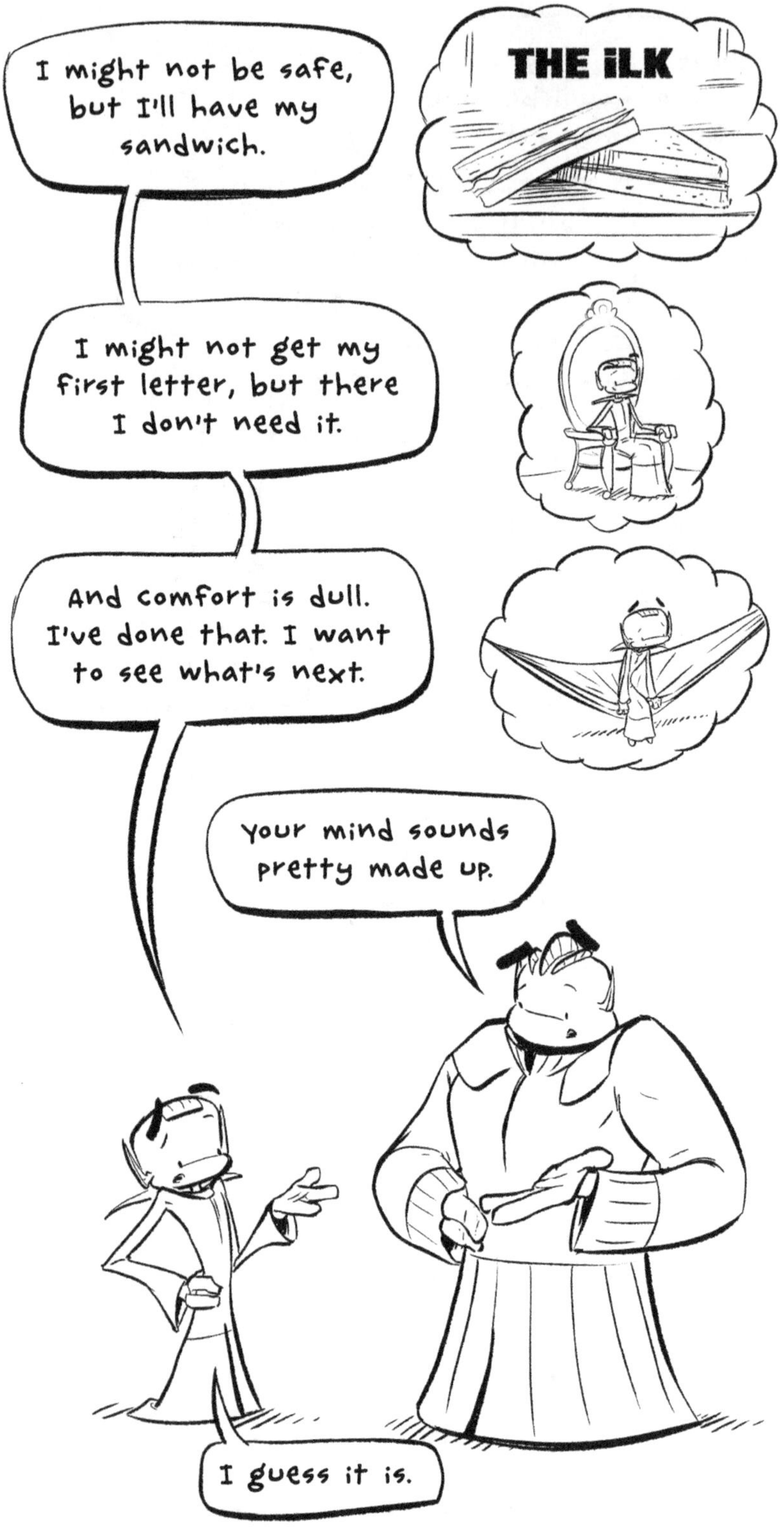

I might not be safe, but I'll have my sandwich.
THE iLK
I might not get my first letter, but there I don't need it.
And comfort is dull. I've done that. I want to see what's next.
Your mind sounds pretty made up.
I guess it is.

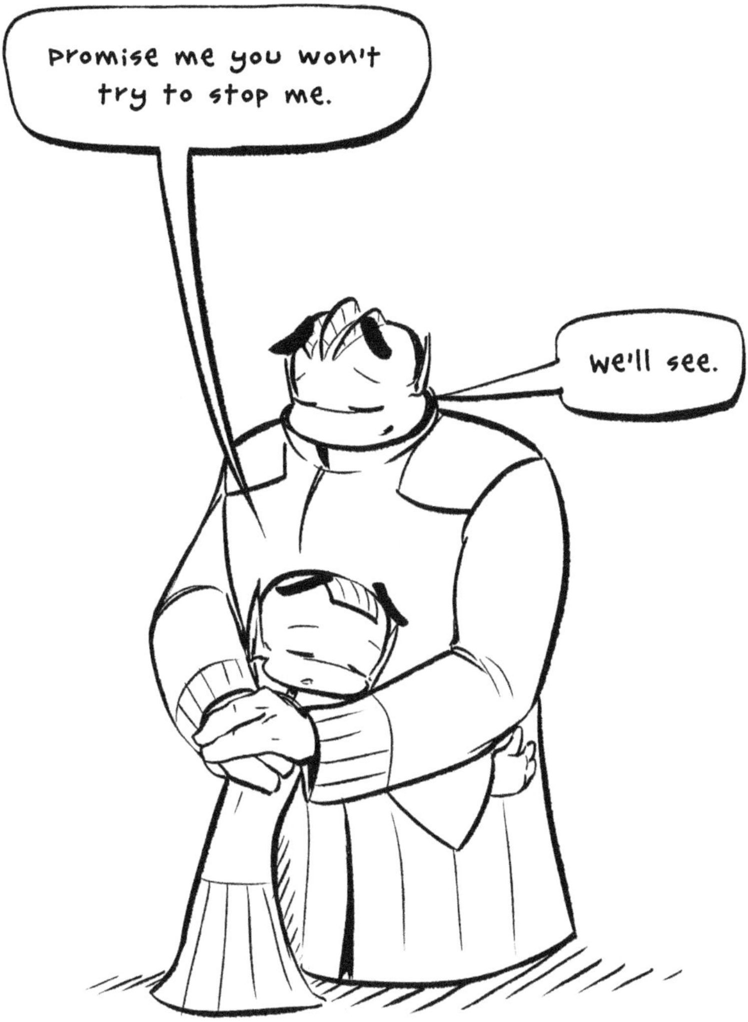
Promise me you won't try to stop me.
We'll see.

Invasion 101, Day 86

This was it. This was the day it all went down.

My recollection of what happened is a little blurry so I might get some facts wrong.

I remember that Dad was happy to see me on the ship again.

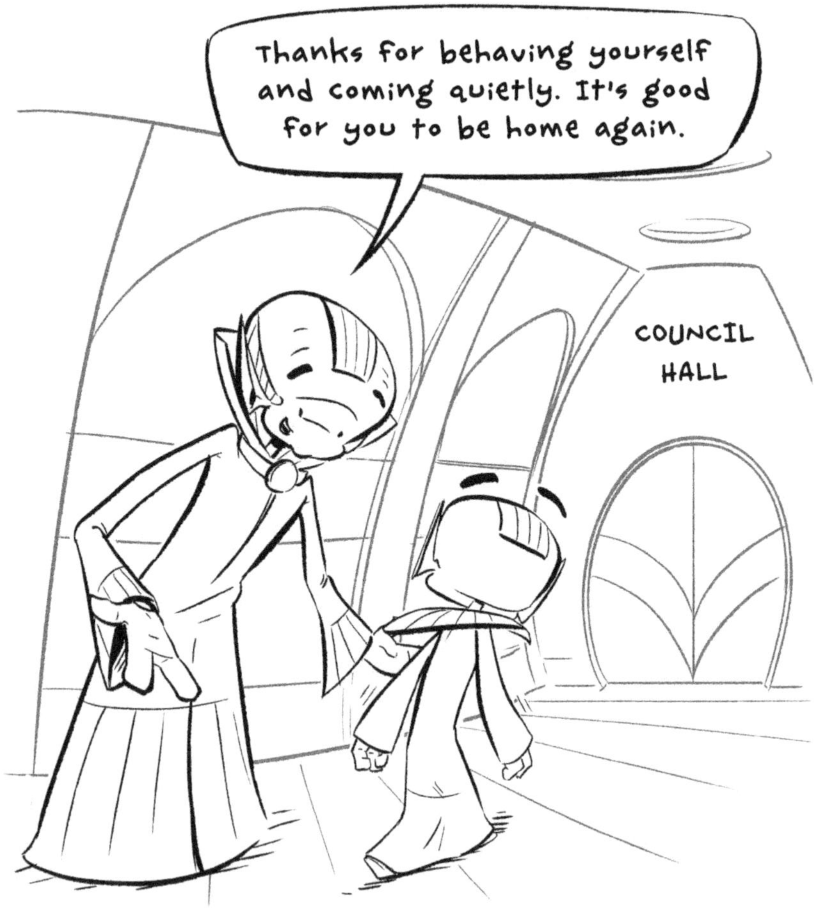
Thanks for behaving yourself and coming quietly. It's good for you to be home again.
COUNCIL HALL

Hmmm... or maybe he was sad.

Or was he angry?

I can't remember which, I was very nervous. I assume Dad could tell, I think he thought the next thing he said would make me relax.

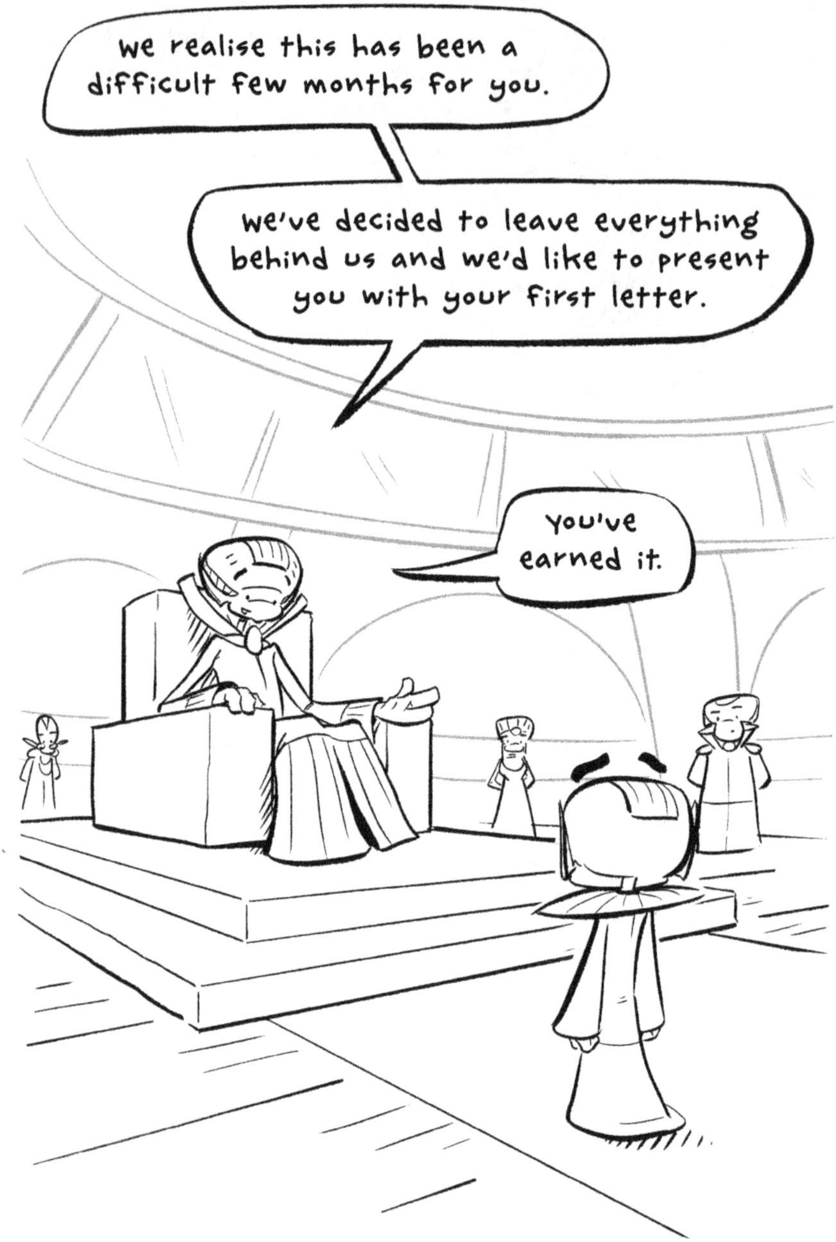
we realise this has been a difficult few months for you.
we've decided to leave everything behind us and we'd like to present you with your first letter.
You've earned it.

This did not relax me.

There was only one thing I wanted to know.

I decided to be direct.

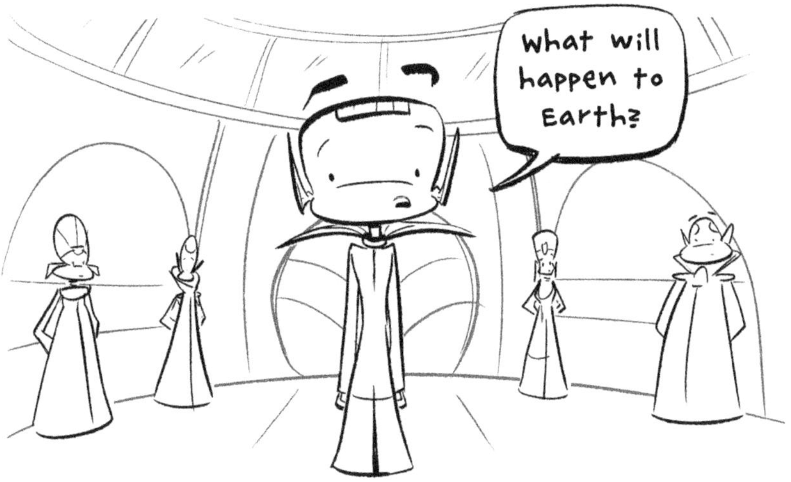
What will happen to Earth?

I shouldn't have been surprised by his response, but for some reason, I was. Those stupid humans had taught me about hope and now it was messing with my expectations.

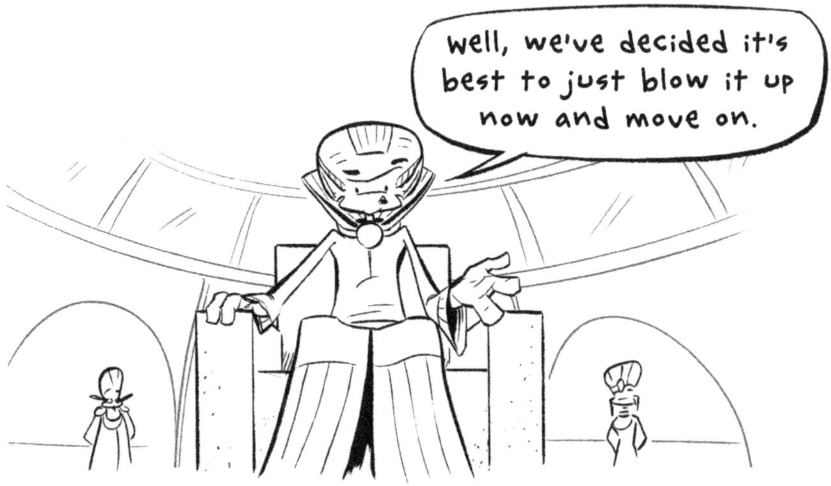
Well, we've decided it's best to just blow it up now and move on.

This was it. I had one final plea before I had to turn to Plan B. I didn't want to turn to Plan B. I didn't like Plan B.

I think it's the name. "B" is my least favourite letter.

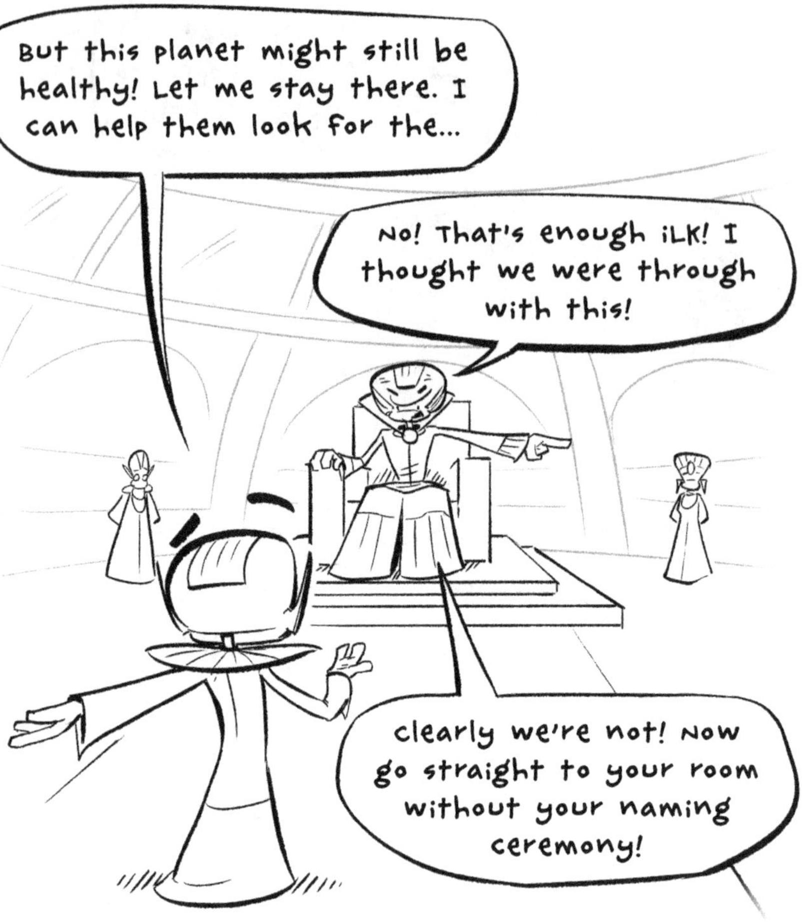
But this planet might still be healthy! Let me stay there. I can help them look for the...
No! That's enough iLK! I thought we were through with this!
Clearly we're not! Now go straight to your room without your naming ceremony!

With that, I pressed a button in my pocket and initiated Plan B.

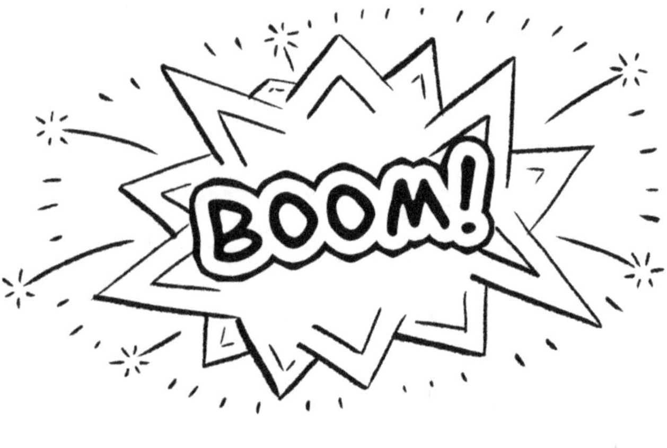
BOOM!

It was a sudden and dramatic change.

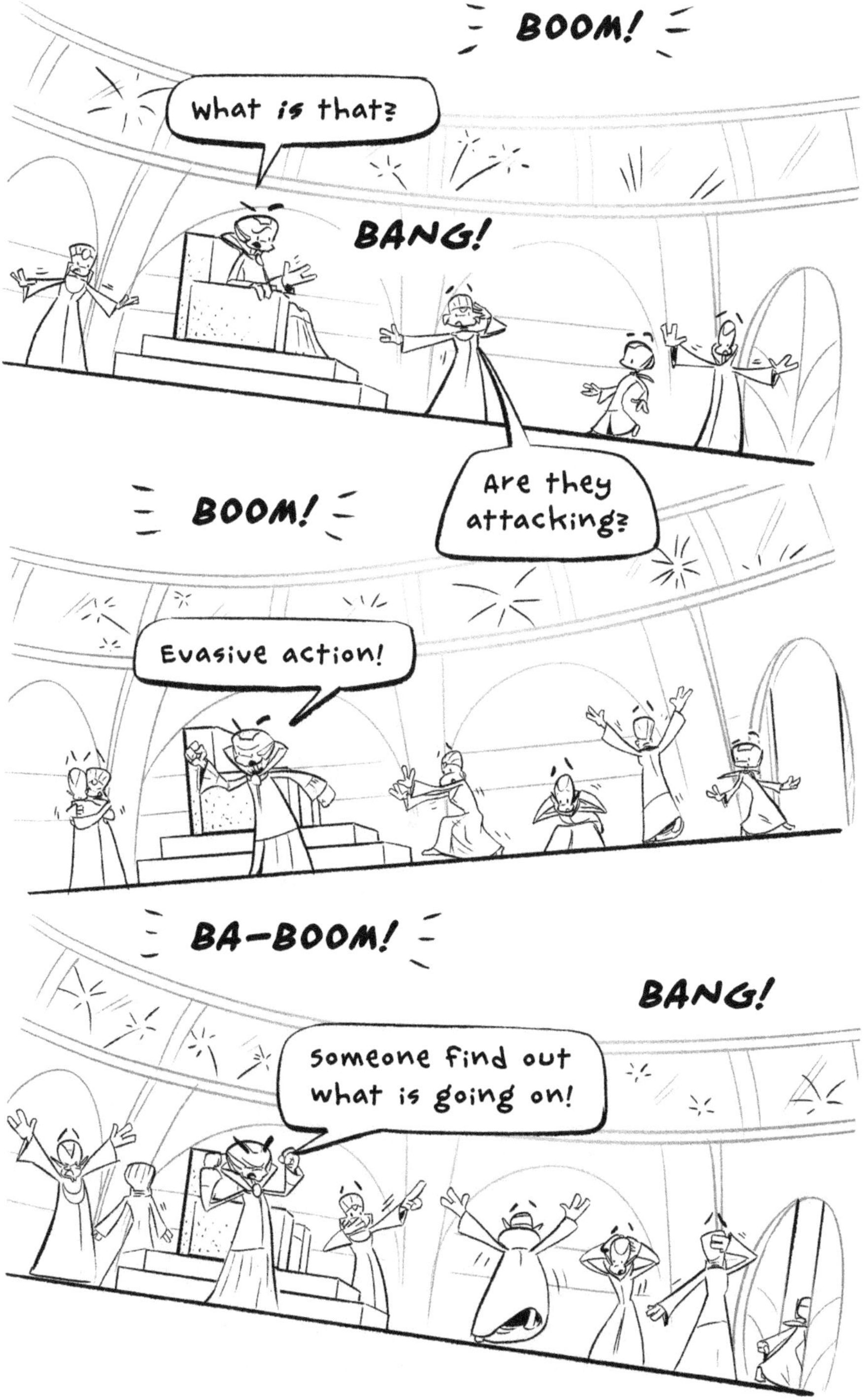
BOOM!
What is that?
BANG!
Are they attacking?
BOOM!
Evasive action!
BA-BOOM!
BANG!
Someone find out what is going on!

If they'd stopped to look at them they were actually very beautiful. They cost a lot of money those fireworks.

I'm not really sure what that means, but it's something I hear people on Earth say a lot.

What happened next went ALMOST entirely as planned.

The order went out for "evasive action" to be taken, as expected.

But thanks to the device I'd attached to the controls, the ship was about go into light speed instead. In a matter of moments it would be be sent light years away from Earth.

once the order is given you'll have only a very short time to escape. you'll have to move quickly.

I must remember to thank Jorge for his excellent work.

I'd also cut the wire to the ship's navigation system so it would take them a long time to find their way back.

Not least because I took this.

INSTRUCTION MANUAL
HOW TO FIX YOUR SHIP'S NAVIGATION SYSTEM

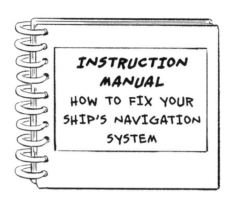

Everyone hurried around, trying to figure out what was going on, unaware that they were about to be transported very, very, very, very, very, very far away.

Meanwhile I rushed to the escape pods where I encountered the one hiccup in my plan.

ESCAPE POD

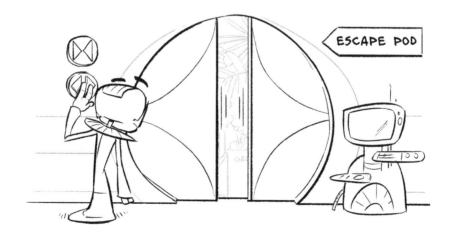

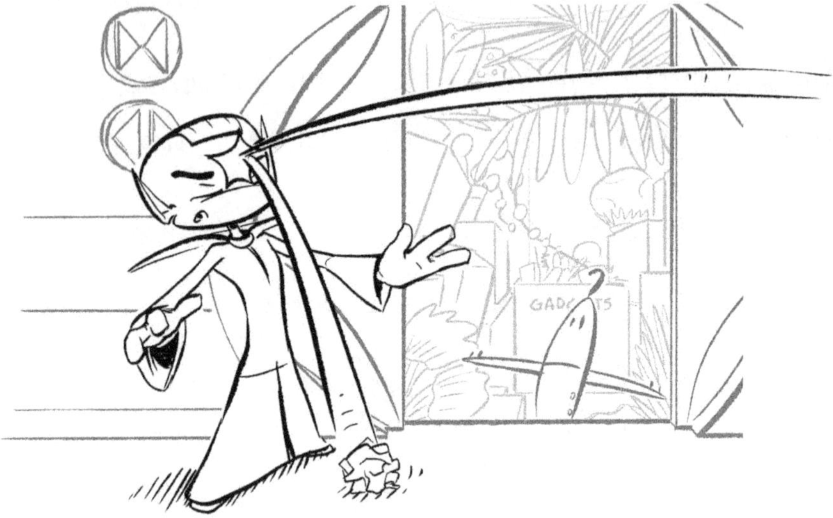

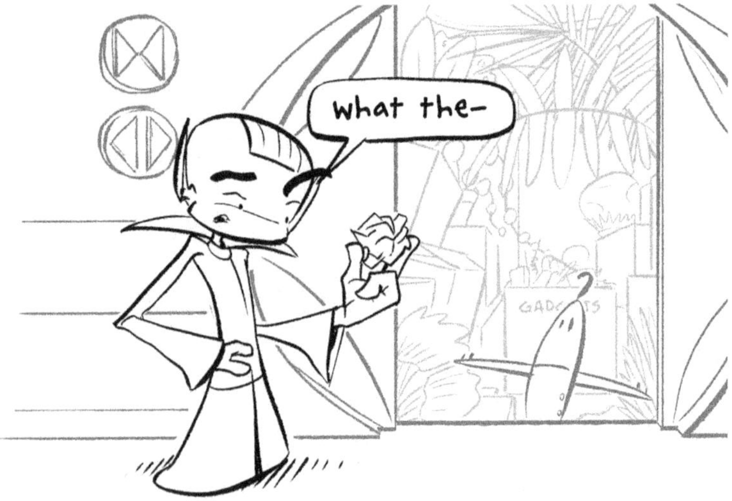
what the-

I had not accounted for flying, balled up pieces of paper.

It was a mild annoyance.

Everything made more sense when I saw where it had come from.

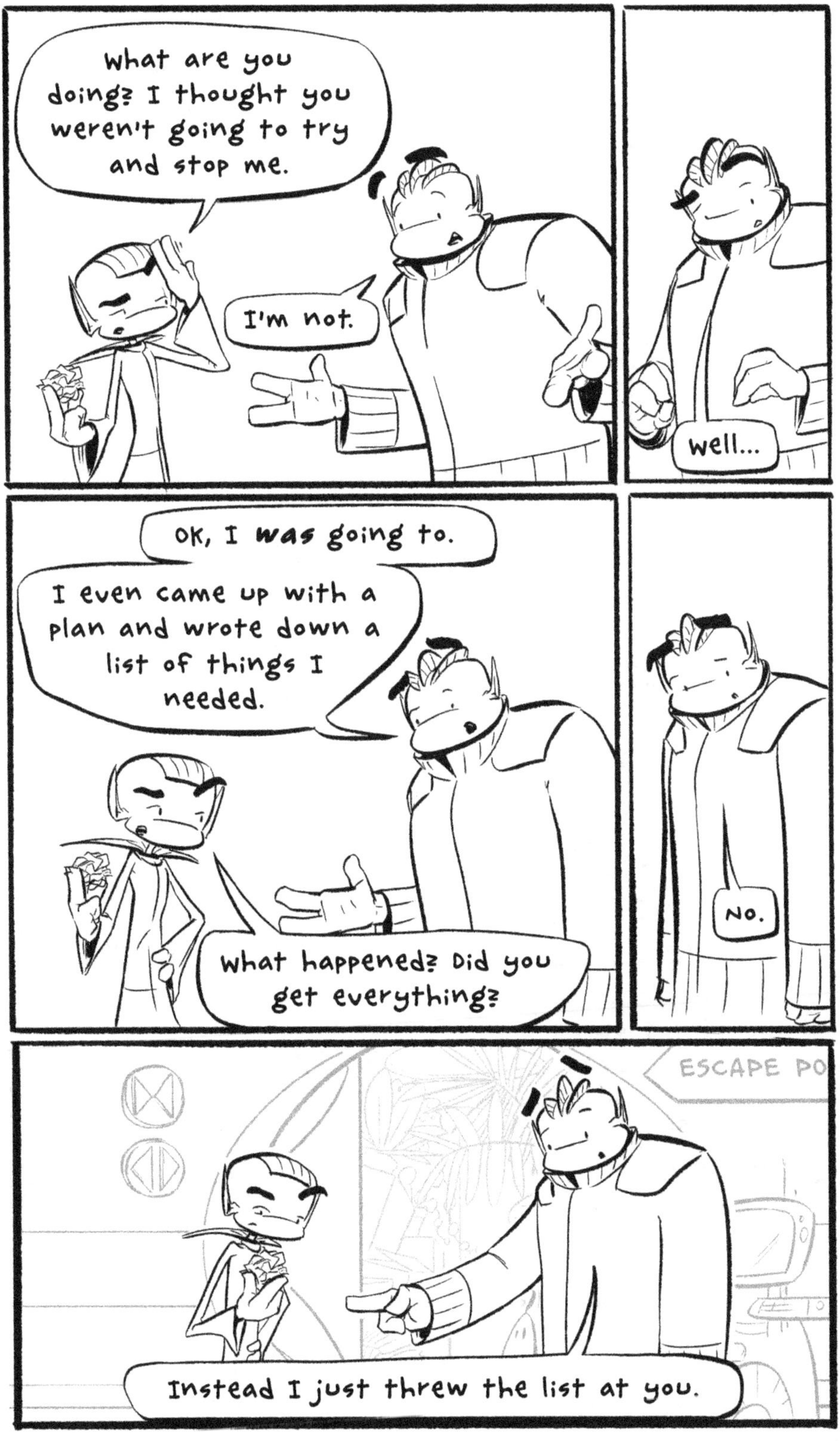
What are you doing? I thought you weren't going to try and stop me.
I'm not.
Well...
OK, I was going to.
I even came up with a plan and wrote down a list of things I needed.
What happened? Did you get everything?
No.
ESCAPE PO
Instead I just threw the list at you.

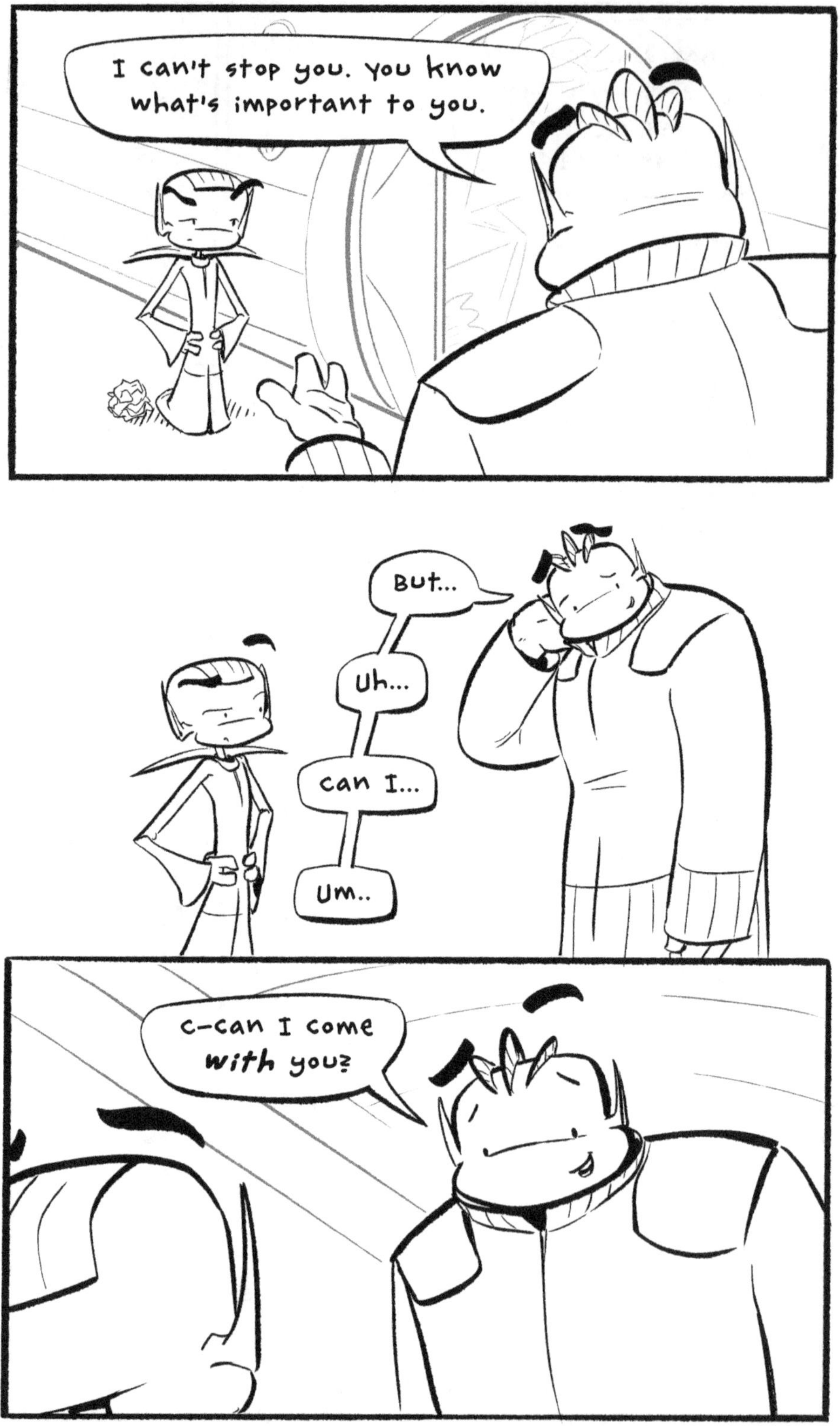
I can't stop you. you know what's important to you.
But...
Uh...
can I...
Um..
c-can I come *with* you?

So we all piled into the escape pod and got ready to disembark.

There was just one thing I had to leave behind.

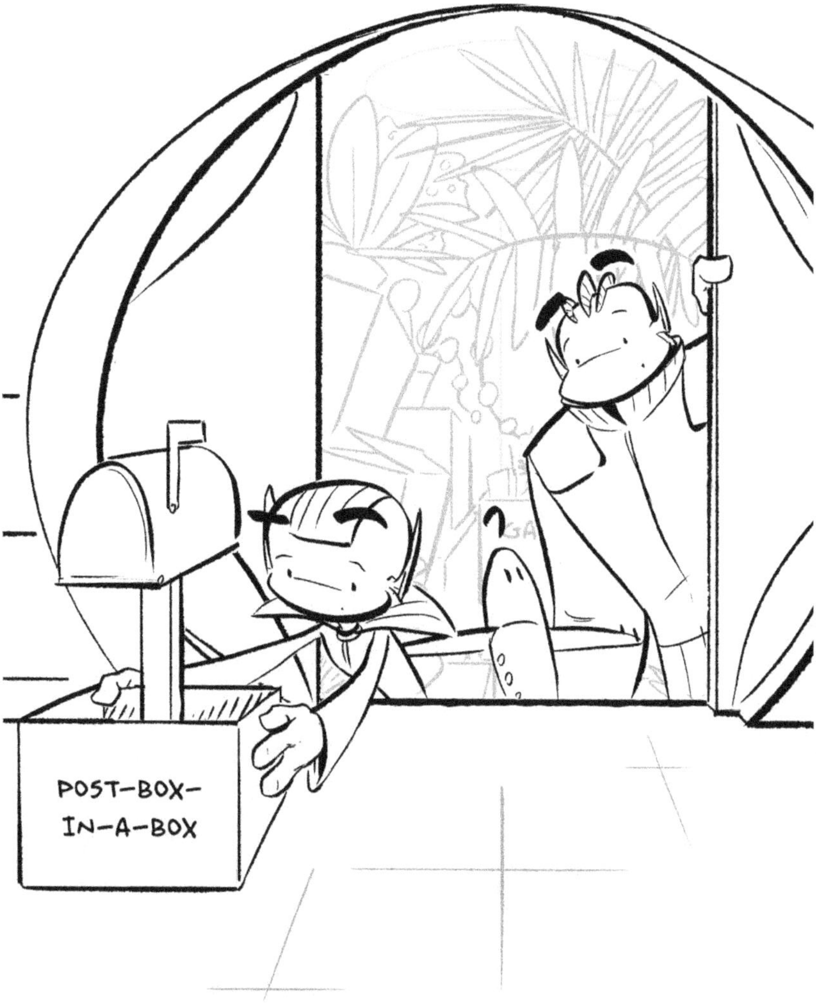
POST-BOX-
IN-A-BOX

They'll figure out what that is for eventually.

The next day, light years away from Earth...

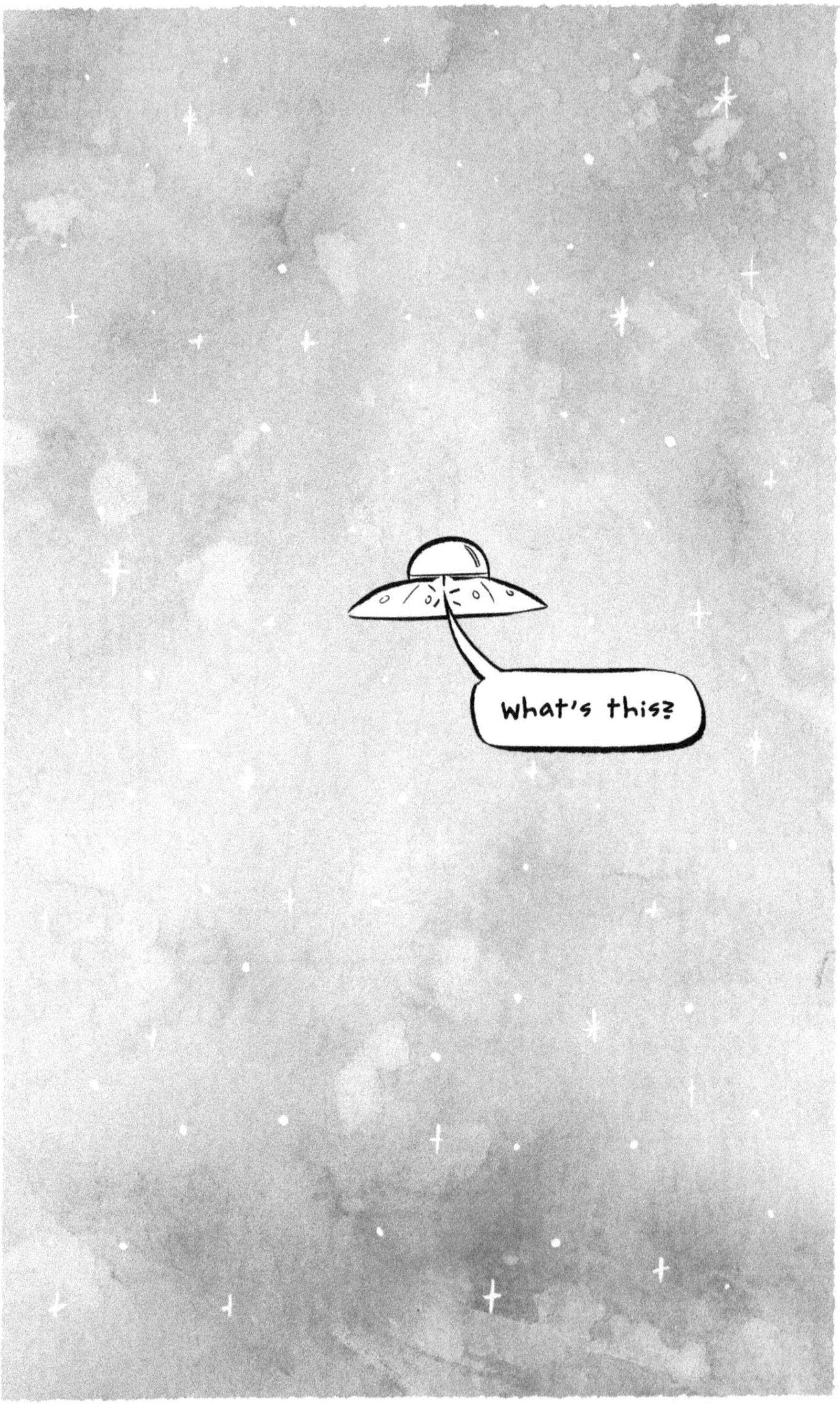
What's this?

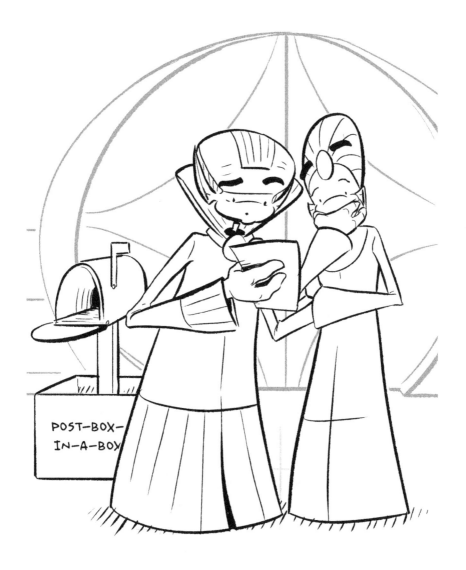

POST-BOX-
IN-A-BOX

Dear Mum and Dad,

I'm sorry for sending you away like that.

Other than the fact you were so set on blowing up this planet, this had nothing to do with you.

I hope you understand why I needed to do this.

Since you've been gone, I've been helping them to look for the Beedaletha plant. I know we're getting closer.

I miss you and I promise to keep in touch.

Lots of love,

Spacekid iLK. 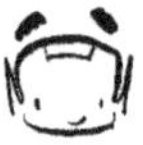

P.S. Seeing as I never received my first letter, I have adopted a name in line with the traditional human naming system.

They decided my FAMILY NAME, was "iLK," which left me without a first name.

There was a vote and the whole world chose a new name for me together.

They've decided my GIVEN NAME will be, "Spacekid."

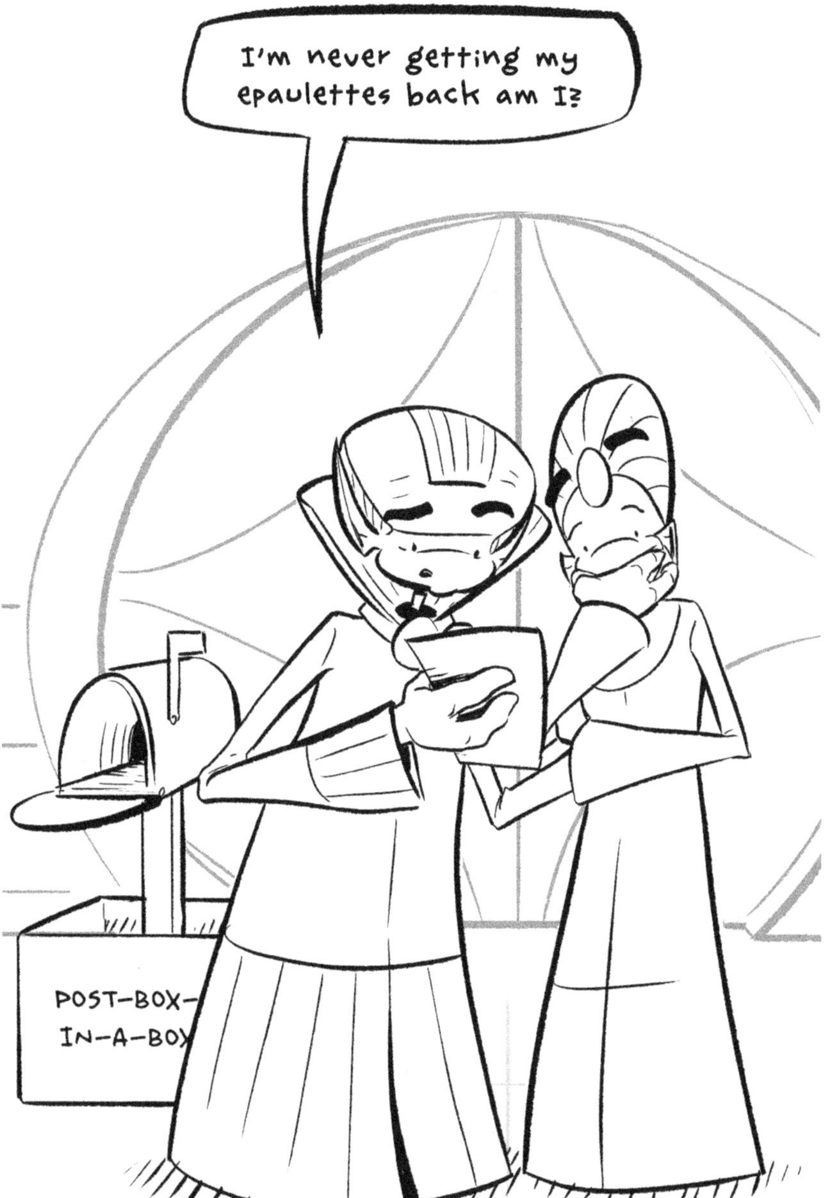
I'm never getting my epaulettes back am I?
POST-BOX-
IN-A-BOX

EPILOGUE

meanwhile, back on Earth...

Stranded, Day 1

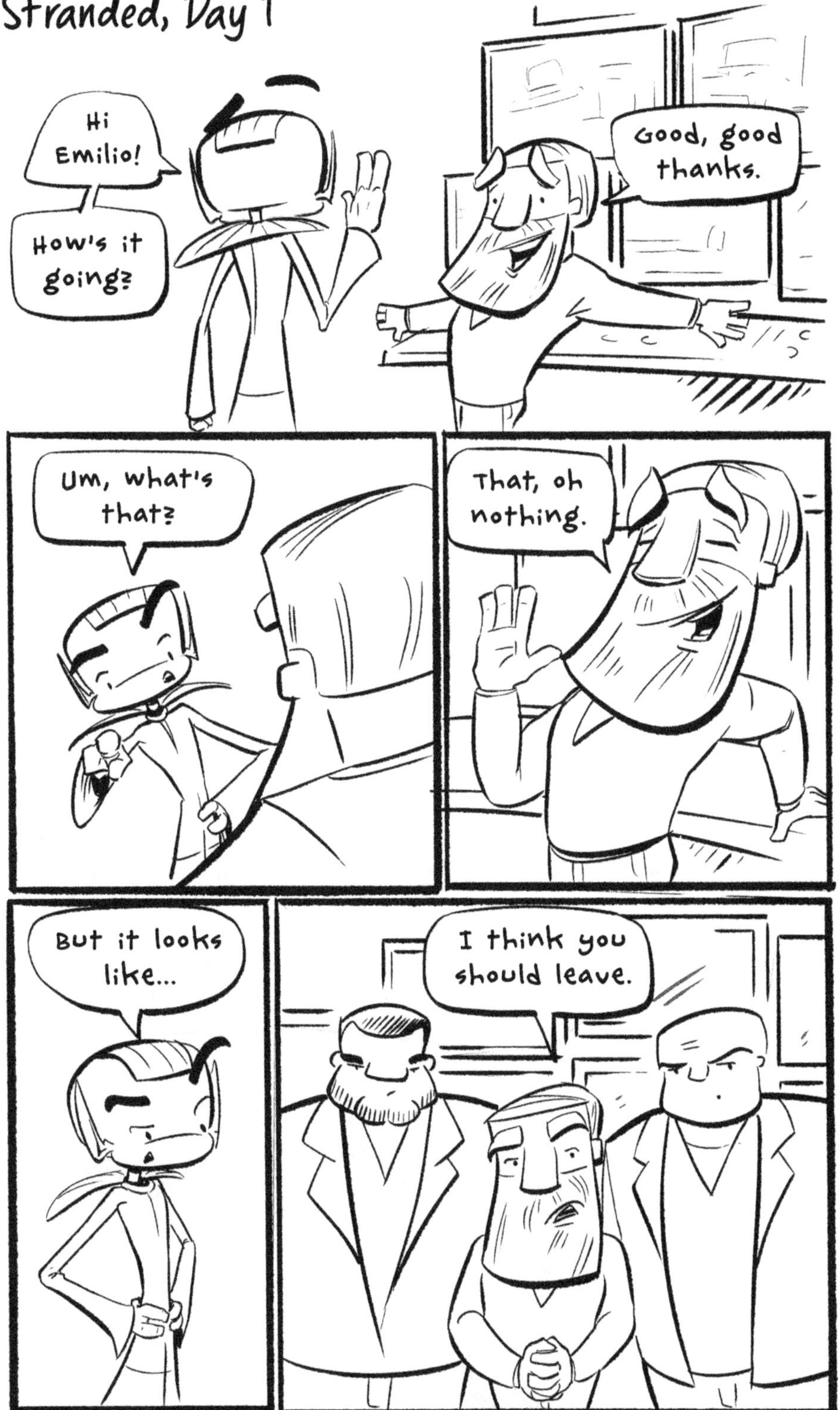
Hi Emilio!
How's it going?
Good, good thanks.
Um, what's that?
That, oh nothing.
But it looks like...
I think you should leave.

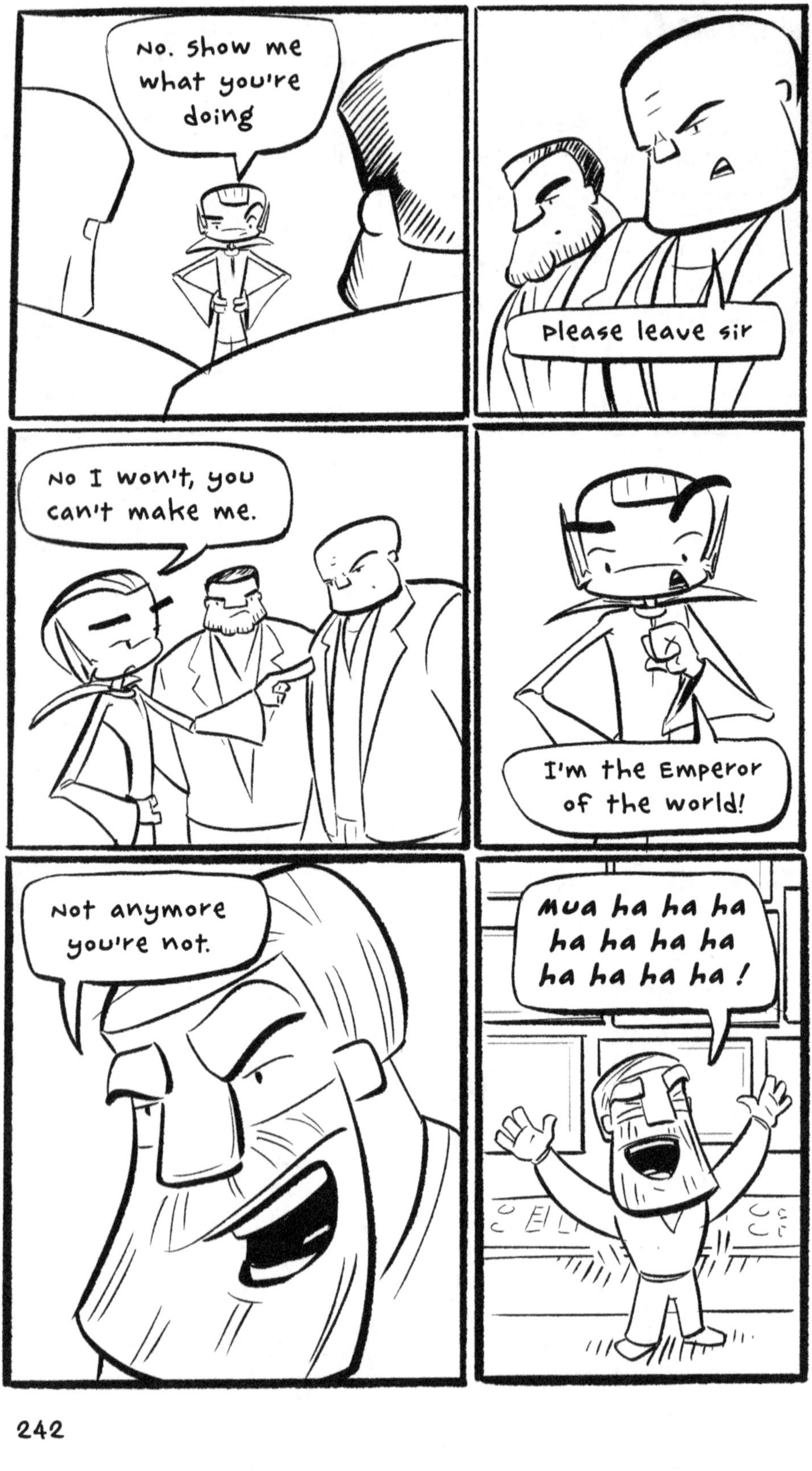
No. Show me what you're doing
Please leave sir
No I won't, you can't make me.
I'm the Emperor of the world!
Not anymore you're not.
mua ha ha ha ha ha ha ha ha ha ha ha !

TO BE CONTINUED...

Acknowledgements

A big thank you to my parents.

I also would not have been able to create this book without the support, advice, words of encouragement and sometimes even spare rooms and sofas of my friends and family.

To all of you, thank you.

About the author

Andrew is a writer and illustrator from London with a passion for sequential art and storytelling.

He studied Film & Video Production, specialising in Screenwriting. After leaving university he started to work as a freelance storyboard artist.

Having finished "Invasion 101," he's now excited to write more stories about iLK and his friends.

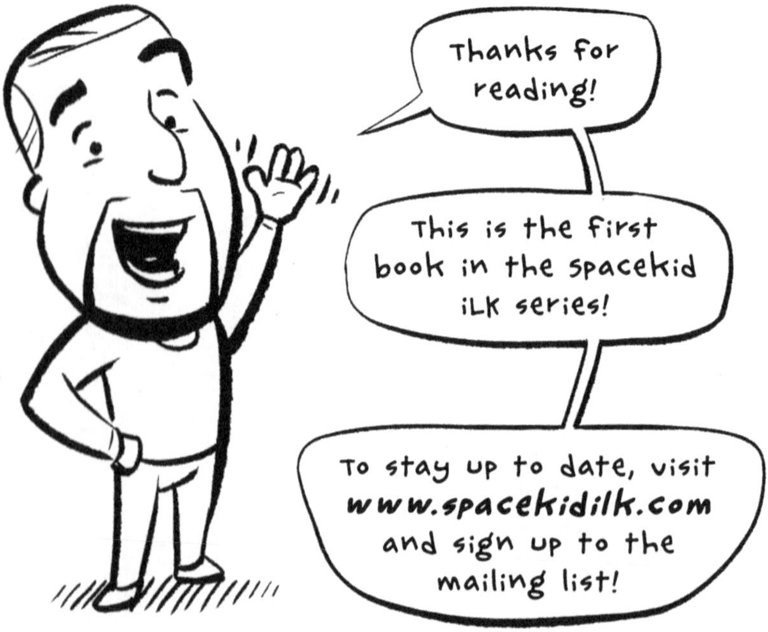
Thanks for reading!
This is the first book in the spacekid iLK series!
To stay up to date, visit www.spacekidilk.com and sign up to the mailing list!